To the Third Generation

Boxed In: Volume 3

Novels in the Boxed In Series

Every novel in the *Boxed In* series is an independent story in its own right and the series can be read in any order. Each novel is told from the viewpoint of the main character who is, in some way, 'boxed in'. Some characters also appear in other novels – which allows the reader to see them in a different light. Across the *Boxed In* novels, interconnecting lives build into a fascinating interplay of human choices and intersecting circumstances.

Slings & Arrows

Outrageous Fortune

To the Third Generation

Soul to Soul

Turn Around Twice

To the Third Generation

Riach Wilson

Parbar Publishing

CHAPTER ONE

Sarah reread the letter from the county court.

So: she was divorced.

How did she feel?

How was she supposed to feel?

She had no idea.

Twelve years ago, when she married Dom, her wedding day had been a blur, but with the benefit of hindsight, she could write a list of her feelings: happy, anxious, relieved, nervous and determined. On her wedding day, though, if anyone had asked her to describe her mixed feelings in one word she would have said; love. She had loved Dom; why else had she married him? Dom had loved her too. He had said so.

She reread the letter and sighed. Of course, what Dom meant by love was not exactly what Sarah, or most other people, meant by love...

Her wedding day, though, had been wonderful. She had been sure that she wanted to marry Dom. The priest who married them had been happy about it and so had the guests; and if her parents had gritted their teeth and if Dom's parents had refused to attend the ceremony, well, that was just some unresolved history between their families.

In a way, the family antagonism had added spice to their courtship. It was almost like being Romeo and Juliet; except that they were both twenty-seven, not teenagers; and they lived in Yelmouth, not Verona; and they got married rather than committing suicide…

In the end, though, their relationship had been a tragedy too and if Romeo and Juliet had died because of a misunderstanding, Sarah and Dom had married because of one; but their wedding day had been wonderful, even if their years of marriage hadn't.

On that day Sarah had been the centre of attention but now, twelve years later, she stood alone by her front door reading a Decree Absolute. Twelve years ago she had worn her bridal gown and never looked more beautiful; now she was wearing a pair of elderly, comfortable jeans, a sweater with holes at the cuffs and battered, fur-lined moccasins.

She studied herself in the mirror that hung on the wall beside her. She was thirty-nine and she looked thin and tired. Her blonde-tinged hair was combed but untidy and she wore no makeup. She looked her age or older. On her wedding day, it had taken her five hours to get ready for marriage but today she had opened a letter and discovered that she had been divorced for nearly a fortnight and didn't even know it. How did she feel? How was she supposed to feel?

She shrugged at her reflection. It was a good thing she was a coper.

She folded the Decree Absolute back into its envelope, pulled off her engagement ring and her wedding ring and dropped them into the envelope too. She wandered through to the study, hauled out the second drawer of her filing cabinet, found the file pocket labelled 'Divorce', filed the envelope at the front and pushed the drawer. It closed with a final-sounding 'thunk'.

Sarah sat down at her desk. So: she was divorced. After twelve years of hope and confusion and self-doubt, she was divorced. She was now the lone parent of two children; she had a lovely home to live in and alimony to support her — that's what she got for marrying, and being divorced by, a barrister.

She also had no job and her whole life ahead of her. What was she supposed to do with it? Dom wanted her to stay at home and look after Minnie and Josh — that's why he had insisted that she remain in their home, even though, technically, he owned half of it. If she did what he wanted, she could live here and he would pay her to be a mother — which was pretty much what he had always wanted anyway. He had never been interested in the realities of their relationship or in the practicalities of family life. He had just wanted photographs of it to show to his colleagues; to pay for an illusion that would impress. He had wanted a wife but had never, really, wanted to be a husband, and now Sarah knew why.

She and Dom had grown up together, gone to the same schools and always been friends. Whereas other boys had been rough, Dom had always been kind and, while other boys seemed to delight in dirt, Dom had always been fastidious about his clothes and his appearance.

Sarah laughed ironically. How could she have been so stupid? How could she not have noticed what, looking back, was so obvious? She had married Dom because she had loved him but he had married her because, when he proposed, she had accepted. How could she not have noticed that he was gay?

'More fool me!' she said aloud. It was hard to know what to feel and there were so many unanswered questions. She checked her watch; she would need to get a move on if she was going to go to the supermarket before she collected the children from school.

She sighed and stood up. It was a good job that she was a coper.

'That's one hundred and forty-two eighty-nine,' said the check-out clerk. She was middle-aged with dyed black hair, grey roots, heavy eye makeup and, by the look of her, a passion for cake.

Sarah packed the last virtuous lettuce into her vegetable bag and checked to see if everything was where it should be. Her trolley was tidy and all of her shopping was packed as she liked it. Nothing would be crushed or spoiled when she transferred her shopping bags into the back of her car. There were even a few extra treats for the children today, too – if Dom expected Minnie and Josh to be excited about his new relationship with Alex, paying for some treats was the least he could do!

She rescued her wallet from her bag, pushed her credit card into the keypad and entered her pin number. She waited for the keypad to tell her to remove her card.

It didn't. It asked her to key in her pin number again.

Sarah smiled at the check-out woman and rolled her eyes. She re-entered her pin number.

The check-out woman stared at the display on her till.

Sarah waited.

The woman cleared her throat. 'I'm sorry, but your card has been declined.'

It felt like a kick in the stomach. How could her card be declined?

She glanced past the till; six other people were waiting. The next customer was an elderly man and he was glaring at her.

Sarah laughed shrilly and apologised. She pulled the card out of the machine, shoved it back in her wallet and grabbed her debit card. She pushed it into the keypad, keyed in her pin number, smiled reassuringly at the check-out woman and said, 'Sorry about this. I don't know what's gone wrong. It's never happened before…'

She was still gabbling when the check-out clerk said resignedly, 'That one's been declined too.'

It was like being kicked in the back of the knees.

She had to get the shopping and she had to collect the children but she had no cash and neither of her cards worked and what was she supposed to do – walk away? With everyone watching? Would the supermarket expect her to put everything back on the shelves? What was she supposed to do? Phone Dom? But he was in court and she couldn't phone his flat because Alex might be there and anyway she had to collect the children and she needed the shopping and she was on her own and she was divorced and she was… she was… she was… a coper?

She tried to smile at the check-out clerk but the woman had her head down.

She felt a strong urge to explain to the man behind her but he was glaring irritably at the floor.

She glanced around; no one was looking at her; everyone was ignoring her.

The kick in the stomach and the kick on the back of her knees joined forces and suddenly she was gasping for air. She staggered and grabbed her trolley for support but it just rolled away from her.

She had just enough time to say, 'I–' before everything went black.

CHAPTER TWO

Sarah's mother, Margaret, eased the seatbelt across her ample chest and tried to catch Sarah's eye in the vanity mirror that was set into the car's sun visor. 'You heard what the doctor said.'

'Yes, Mum,' Sarah answered. She gazed fixedly out of the car's side window. She didn't need meaningful glances from her mother right now.

She caught a flicker of movement out of the corner of her eye as her mother nudged Terry, her father.

He kept his hands on the steering wheel, glanced back towards Sarah and said, 'She's right, you know. You should listen to what the doctor said.'

'Yes, Dad,' Sarah answered, still staring out of the window. It was all very well for them; they had been married to each other for most of their lives. They had married very young, just as their own parents had. They'd had their ups and downs, of course, and didn't they just love to mention that little fact over and over again? Life had been hard for them, as they so often said, because Terry had been away from home so much. In spite of that, they'd kept their marriage together; no divorce for them! Just good old British stamina and now their only daughter was divorced! Oh, the shame! And *yada yada ya*...

From what they *didn't* say, though, they clearly thought that the divorce was all her fault. Apparently, as far as they were concerned, divorce statistics were irrelevant, as was the issue of Dom being gay. This small fact was just a cobweb to be brushed away – a problem so small that it ranked no higher than a disagreement over which TV channel to watch. After all, as Margaret was fond of declaring, the *intimate* side of marriage was just a small part of life. Yeah; right. Tell that to Dom. It was him who had fallen in love with another man, not Sarah!

Oh God! How depressing! She was nearly forty years old and she was sitting in the back of her parent's car like a petulant teenager having imaginary conversations in her head! It was the Smale family as it had always been; father, mother and daughter and no one saying anything of consequence. Why didn't she just say what she thought? Why did her parents still wield such power over her? Her eyes refocused and she caught sight of her reflection in the car window. She could still see the houses and trees beyond the glass, but a translucent version of her face too.

She looked at the back of her mother's head and glanced at her father. They were both in their sixties but they were still fit and active. Margaret had been overweight all her life and now the plumpness of her face disguised her wrinkles as effectively as the dye that camouflaged her grey hair. Terry, by contrast, had always been slim and rangy but now his constant, restive movements were beginning to look arthritic and his swarthy, handsome face was fringed with a shock of white hair. In fact, from behind, age was starting to hang in heavy folds on both of their necks.

Sarah stared determinedly out of the car window, through her own reflection. What would the future hold as her parents aged? Would they expect her to care for them? What if, when they were in their eighties, she, as a sixty year old woman, was still in the back of their car? Still feeling like a child?

'It hasn't been easy for you,' Terry declared as he signalled and turned right. 'What with… the last year.'

Margaret snorted and breathed in loudly.

Terry continued determinedly, 'And you know I've never thought much of Dominic!'

Well hallelujah for understatement! Whatever the root cause of the feud between their families, Sarah was pretty certain that if they'd lived in a less law-abiding country, one dark night before the wedding her father would probably have taken a machete to Dom…

'Still,' Terry concluded. 'Even though I can't say that I'm sorry you're not together any more, now that you've decided not to stick it out, you have the children to think of. So you can't go around having *episodes*. You need to do what the doctor said and get some counselling.'

Margaret heaved her bulk around in her seat and, with a theatrical nod that set her jowls rippling, agreed, 'Counselling.'

Sarah returned her attention to the window. Her ghostly reflection was still there. Maybe the reflection was the truth? Maybe she had come to a point in her life where she was just a ghostly reflection of the woman she might have been? Maybe it was time for her to stop ignoring herself and to do a bit of navel-gazing?

The doctor seemed to think so.

The last few hours were rather hazy but Sarah remembered trying to pay for her shopping in the supermarket and then waking up in hospital. She had been fully clothed and lying on a hard, plastic-covered, raised bed. As she had opened her eyes and turned her head a young nurse had said, 'I'll fetch the Doctor.'

Sarah had sat up and swung her legs off the bed. The curtain around her temporary cubicle had twitched and a young Asian woman had appeared.

'Mrs Price?' she had asked. Her hair was long, lustrous and so black it was almost blue; and she had beautiful skin. Her eyebrows were a little bushy, she had a gold stud in her nose and her accent made her *esses* sound like *zeds*.

Sarah hesitated. She certainly wasn't *Mrs Prize*, but now that she was divorced was she even *Mrs Price*? Should she revert to her maiden name and become *Ms Smale*?

The young doctor consulted her notes and her head seemed to dance from side to side on her neck. 'You've had an episode. You passed out in a supermarket and were brought here in an ambulance. Do you remember any of this?'

Sarah coughed. 'I remember being in the supermarket…'

The doctor consulted her notes again. 'We've checked your stats and there's nothing wrong with you. Have you been under any stress lately? Or crash-dieting? Or anything like that?'

Sarah smiled ruefully. 'I found out that I was divorced today, so I guess you could say I've been under a bit of stress…'

The doctor nodded. 'I see. Well, this is an Accident and Emergency Department, so not the right place for you. We found your documents when you were admitted and as you were already on our system, we called your parents as your next of kin. They are waiting for you in reception.'

Sarah tried to process this information. Were the hospital allowed to do that? Didn't that violate patient confidentiality?

The Doctor said with an air of finality, 'You can go.' She pulled back the curtain and revealed a bleak corridor. She hesitated and then said, 'We are seeing very many people experiencing episodes of stress. Go to your own doctor and arrange for some counselling. It will help you.' She turned and was gone.

Sarah slipped her feet into her shoes and set off down the corridor. There was a sign that helpfully directed her to reception, which was a large room with about fifty plastic chairs in it. They were all bolted to the floor, probably to stop drunks from using them as weapons. About ten people were scattered across the seats; sitting, waiting patiently. Near the door, her parents stood up and waved.

Sarah had smiled back and joined them and now they were driving her home and using the opportunity to lecture her.

From the front seat of the car, Margaret said again, 'Counselling. That's what the doctor said. Counselling.'

'Counselling,' Terry repeated.

'Counselling,' Sarah muttered and her parents glanced at one another with satisfaction.

Well – why not? It couldn't do any harm and she *had* blacked out in the supermarket so maybe she wasn't coping as well as she'd thought? She would go to her doctor tomorrow and get a referral. She'd pick a nice expensive counsellor too; and Dom could pay. Yes, Dom could pay…

Pay…

She felt suddenly anxious. 'Mum?'

'Hmmm?'

'After we pick up the children, could we stop off at the supermarket? Just for a few things. I've mislaid my cards so if you could pay, I'll settle up once I've been to the bank and got some cash.'

'Of course, darling,' Margaret said.

Sarah closed her eyes. Oh God! This really was just like being a teenager again.

CHAPTER THREE

Sarah sat in her car and toyed with her necklace. On either side of her, two rows of redbrick, Victorian, terraced houses stretched away to distant junctions. The front doors of the houses opened directly onto the pavement and most people had net curtains in their windows to give them privacy from passing pedestrians. Some people had painted the stone lintels above their doors and windows black, others had chosen cream and some had gone for bold, primary colours. There was litter in the gutters and, more worryingly, many householders had fitted wrought-iron bars across their windows and lockable, metal gates across their front doors.

It was similar to many of the streets in this part of Yelmouth, but was it safe to leave her car here? It seemed quiet enough – maybe the residents only took precautions at night?

She checked the address. She was definitely in the right place even if the terraced house across the road looked like an unlikely Counselling Centre. On the other hand, what had she expected? A sanatorium set in well-tended, rolling acres?

Well… yes…

She checked her watch and made up her mind. She got out of her car, made sure that it was properly locked and crossed the road. There didn't seem to be a doorbell so she tapped on the door with her knuckles.

A moment later it opened and a young woman with frizzy, blonde hair smiled at her, introduced herself as Jackie and invited her in. She directed Sarah towards an elderly settee. 'You can wait here. Miss Steele will come and find you in a minute.'

Sarah sat down. If Miss Steele was expecting to 'find her', should she hide? Behind the settee perhaps? Was this a new form of counselling? She didn't fancy the idea of crawling around on the floor, though; it didn't look very clean. Or maybe the floral carpet was just old? In fact the whole place looked as though it needed redecorating. The wallpaper was blue and fading, the ceiling was that particular shade of yellow that white paint becomes when it is neglected for a very long time, and the mirror over the unused fireplace was chipped on one edge. Given how much Dom would be paying for these counselling sessions, surely a little could be spent on paint?

Sarah glanced towards the other end of the room. She could hear feet descending the stairs, and a pair of legs, followed by a body and a head, came into view. The woman was short, probably in her thirties, with a decent figure and short, mousy hair. She wore only a hint of makeup and designer glasses with burgundy frames. Her shoes were low-heeled, her trousers were black and she wore a white blouse under a burgundy sweater which was embroidered with subtle, floral highlights.

The woman reached Sarah and held out her hand. 'I'm Dianne Steele. Call me Di.'

Sarah stood up and shook her hand. Did Counsellor Di always co-ordinate her glasses with her sweaters? Sarah followed her up three flights of dingy stairs and by the time they reached the top, she had assured Counsellor Di's backside that she had had no trouble finding the address and had parked outside; agreed that the weather was very nice for the time of year; and that the stairs were, indeed, quite steep.

Counsellor Di unlocked a door and ushered her into an attic room with a sloping roof with a skylight window along one side. At one end there was a small bookcase, at the other a cupboard, in the middle there was a low coffee table with a sorry-looking plant, a notepad and a box of tissues, and the rest of the room was taken up by four easy chairs.

Counsellor Di waved her hand. 'Do sit down.'

Sarah did as she was told and smiled at her counsellor from across the coffee table.

Counsellor Di settled herself into her easy chair and said, 'So. What would you like me to call you?'

Sarah resisted the urge to wisecrack 'A Cab!' and said, 'Sarah.'

Counsellor Di smiled. 'So, Sarah, as you know, these sessions will take place fortnightly. This first session is where we get to know one another. And that's important; getting to know one another. We may decide that it isn't appropriate for me to be your counsellor, in which case we'll chalk this session up to experience and think again.'

Sarah blinked. 'I'm sorry. I'm not sure that–'

Counsellor Di smiled reassuringly. 'We'll have this first session together, but if, at the end of it, you feel that I'm not the right person to counsel you, that's fine; you just say so and we'll try you with someone else.'

'Oh… I… er…'

Counsellor Di continued, 'And if, after this first session I don't feel comfortable, that's fine too; we'll just try you with someone else.'

Sarah found it hard to breathe. Could that happen? Could Counsellor Di find her so unpleasant, so hateful, so appalling, that she could refuse to counsel her?

Counsellor Di went on, 'We need to talk about the fee, too. The Centre needs to cover costs but we never turn anyone away. We therefore operate a sliding scale of fees and ask our clients to pay what they can afford. That way, those who are better off subsidise those who are not.'

Sarah began to breathe more easily. That explained the tatty building and the high fees. She asked, 'What's your top rate?'

Counsellor Di told her.

It didn't seem much, but never mind. Sarah smiled, 'I'll pay that.' Well; Dom would!

Counsellor Di ducked her head. 'That's very generous, thank you.' She picked up the notepad that was on the coffee table and asked, 'So; tell me why you are here?'

Sarah crossed her legs and put her hands in her lap. 'Because, Counsellor Di, I've always been a coper.'

The corner of Counsellor Di's mouth twitched and she said, 'Just call me Di. And you're a coper?'

Sarah nodded. 'I always have been. Right from when I was a little girl.'

Di raised an eyebrow, 'So why are you here?'

Because the doctor said she should come. Because her parents wanted her to come. Because she wanted it to cost Dom a fortune. That's why.

Di waited.

Maybe it was the quiet strangeness of the room. Maybe it was the quiet concern of a stranger. Sarah didn't know, but before she could stop herself, tears began to trickle from her eyes.

Di pushed the box of tissues across the table.

Sarah took one and dabbed at the unwelcome moisture. This was stupid. Why was she here, sitting in a room with someone she didn't know?

Di was still waiting.

Sarah screwed the damp tissue between her fingers and said simply, 'Because I didn't cope. That's why I'm here. In the supermarket. I didn't cope.'

Di's eyebrow twitched.

Sarah made a face. 'I'd gone in to do the weekly shop and when I got to the checkout my cards were declined and I didn't know what to do. Apparently I fainted and when I woke up in hospital the doctor said I'd had a stress-related episode and suggested counselling so here I am.'

Di frowned. 'That must have been terrible for you.'

Sarah nodded. 'It was. It was all to do with my divorce. You see my husband, well, my ex-husband as he is now – that's Dom, short for Dominic – anyway, as well as the divorce settlement, the children and I get to stay in our home and he pays the bills. What I didn't know was that he'd changed the bank account. He insists that he told me, but I don't think he did. So there I was, standing at the checkout with no means of paying! It was terrible!'

Di shifted in her seat. 'Actually, that's not what I meant. I meant the *not being able to cope* bit. Not being able to cope must have been terrible for you.'

Sarah looked at her fingers. She had shredded the tissue.

Di reached under the coffee table, pulled out a blue plastic waste bin and set it down next to Sarah's chair.

Sarah allowed the pieces of tissue to tumble into the bin.

Di consulted her papers and said, 'Before we go any further, can I make a rough family tree, so that I don't have to interrupt you to ask who you mean? There's you, and Dom, and the children. What are their names?'

Sarah said, at intervals, while Counsellor Di wrote names and drew lines, 'Minnie and Josh; my parents are Margaret and Terry Smale; my grandparents on my father's side died when I was little but my mother's parents are still going strong: they are Captain Jack and Mrs Gwen Wenton. On Dom's side, his parents are Sandy and Roy Price and he's never met any of his grandparents and never mentions any of them. I do know that Sandy was Sandy *Grant* before she married, though.'

Di considered her piece of paper; 'There's a few things I'd like to ask but, for now, do you have any brothers or sisters? Does Dom?'

Sarah shook her head, 'No. It's just us. No uncles or aunts either. That's probably a bit unusual, is it?'

Di tapped her notes and then smiled and said, 'When it comes to families, I'm not sure that there *is* a usual. And you're divorced?'

Sarah leaned back in her easy chair, closed her eyes and nodded. 'He left me and the children. Things had never been great between us, but things aren't always great between lots of couples; and there were always reasons. Either he was very busy at work, or the children were demanding – or something. There was always something. Most of the time I thought it must be my fault. He was always so sure of himself and so firm in his opinions and I just, sort of, assumed it must be me.'

Di said quietly, 'And?'

Sarah laughed and the laugh sounded brittle. 'And just less than a year ago he said that he needed to sort his life out and that he was seeing someone. I thought he meant that he was seeing a counsellor, like you.'

Di said, 'But?'

Sarah laughed mirthlessly. 'More fool me! Six months ago he said that we needed to talk, so when the children were in bed he gave me a letter.'

Di's eyebrows shot up. 'A letter?'

'Yes; a letter! That was his idea of talking. He said that I should read it and when I was finished he said we could talk about it if I thought we needed to.'

'And what was in it?'

'Oh – nothing much. Just that he'd always suspected that he was gay and that as he'd grown older he'd realised that he must be and that he'd fallen in love with a man and that he was moving out and that this would be best for everyone and that he was sure that I would be happy for him and that he'd make sure that neither the children or I would be affected financially. And when I'd read it, he asked me if I had any questions.'

Di stared at her, 'And what did you say?'

Sarah grabbed another tissue. The tears were back. 'I asked him not to go.'

Di said softly, 'You *asked* him?'

Sarah dabbed at her eyes and nodded. 'He wouldn't stay, though. He left straight away. His boyfriend, Alex, was waiting outside in Dom's car. I watched them drive away.'

Di waited and then asked, 'And what happened then?'

Sarah tried to remember. 'I drifted around the house for a bit, did some tidying up and then went to bed.' She shrugged. 'I did what I always do; I coped.'

Di picked up her pencil and briefly sucked the end. 'Until the supermarket?'

Sarah shrugged again, 'I guess.'

Di tapped the pencil against her leg. 'Okay. Now I know why you're here. What do you hope to gain from these sessions?'

The words were out before Sarah had time to think: 'I want to make sure that I cope!'

'And?'

'And I kind of want to know how I managed not to notice that the man I married was gay…'

Di smiled a small, resigned, smile. 'All we can do here is help you to peel back some of the layers of your life. Whether you will be able to cope with what you find will be up to you.'

Sarah leaned forward. She needed to check what Di had just said. 'Does that mean you'll counsel me?'

Di laughed easily. 'Okay. Yes, if you're happy with me, I'll counsel you – but don't change the subject!'

Sarah grinned. She was accepted!

Di picked up her notepad. 'Now that I know who your family are; tell me about them.'

Sarah considered this. It was hard to know where to start. 'Well, I know that my mother's parents, Jack and Gwen, knew the Grants, Dom's grandparents. Both families are Yelmouth families and go way back.'

Di checked one of her papers. 'I thought you lived in Upper Fleaking?'

Sarah sat forward. 'Well – I do and I don't. I live in Twisle Drift. Dom was really keen to move there. It's that estate of big new houses on the way to Binderfield, the one that was built at the end of the nineteen-seventies; every house is identical; you know, they all have the same yellow bricks and layout; even the gardens are the same. The developers wanted it to be Upper Fleaking because the houses would be worth more but the Upper Fleaking people wouldn't have it and insisted that it should be classed as Binderfield. In the end the whole estate was reinvented as Twisle Drift and– oh…'

Di was staring at her.

Sarah made a face, 'I don't suppose that's especially relevant?'

Di said, 'No, not really. You were telling me about your family?'

Sarah said, 'Yes, well. As I said, Dom's never met his

grandparents and his parents don't talk about them. My grandfather, Jack, was a Captain in the Royal Navy and my dad, Terry, and Dom's dad, Roy, were friends in the merchant navy. Yelmouth was the home port for all of them but there was some kind of big family fall-out in the nineteen-sixties. I don't know if it was a navy thing or something else, but Dom and I were at school together and later on, when we started spending time together, my dad and his mum were dead set against us being together. The family row almost spilled over onto us, but we just went ahead anyway.'

Di nodded and made an encouraging noise.

Sarah tried to order her thoughts, 'We were twenty-seven when we married. Dom had just finished his pupillage – he's a barrister – and I was in a going-nowhere desk-job and when we started courting and he asked me to marry him, I thought it was my last chance.'

Di said, 'That's quite old-fashioned language: "courting", "last chance"?'

Sarah blinked. 'I suppose it is, but going out with Dom was a bit old-fashioned, really. We went on dates and had a nice time and, apart from the odd kiss, Dom said that he respected me and that sex should wait for marriage.'

Di raised her eyebrows again.

Sarah snorted and shifted in her easy chair. 'Well I know it sounds ridiculous now; now that I know that he's gay, but at the time it was actually quite romantic. I didn't have much experience with boyfriends and when Dom and I started going out I didn't really have much of a yardstick to measure him by so I just, sort of, accepted what he said and, actually, I was grateful that he didn't push me for sex all the time.'

Di suggested, 'It was a relationship you could cope with?'

Sarah said excitedly, 'Exactly!'

The room was suddenly silent and Sarah felt as if she had been kicked in the chest. What had she just said? That she'd accepted Dom's lack of attention because she could cope with it?

Di put her papers and notebook back on the coffee table. 'There's a layer, right there, and next time, we'll start by exploring what it means for you to *cope*. Between now and then, I'd like you to think about the good things about coping and the bad things about it. Make a couple of lists on paper if it helps.'

Sarah felt as if she was swimming through treacle. 'Is that it? Is that the end of the session?'

'For today,' Di confirmed. 'These sessions are one hour for a reason. In that time we get to the heart of something and, between sessions, you have time to reflect and consider. The time between sessions is even more important than the sessions themselves. That's when you do the real work. When we meet, it's just to help you understand where you've got to and point you in the right direction.'

Sarah checked her watch. Good God; the time had flown!

Di stood up. 'You can sort out the finances with Jackie on the way out.'

Sarah stood up too but was that it? No feedback? No encouragement? What about her outrageous emotional outbursts? Her tears and tissue shredding? Was that kind of behaviour acceptable? She said hesitantly, 'I suppose you see lots of people like me.'

Di opened the door and led the way downstairs. 'Everyone's different and we all express ourselves in our own way.'

Sarah nodded; most people were probably just like her: 'Floods of tears and so forth?'

They reached the bottom of the stairs and Di shook her hand in farewell. 'Some people, yes. Others are more like you and keep everything inside.'

CHAPTER FOUR

'I won't,' screamed the small, malignant creature in Sarah's kitchen. It contrasted strangely with her white, shaker-style, fitted cupboards and gleaming, stainless steel appliances – as if the twenty-first century had been visited by an ancient, primeval troglodyte. The creature was less than four feet high, very slim and had sandy hair and a freckled face. It clutched a small overnight case to its chest and it shook with rage. 'I won't!' it screamed again, its face flaring red.

Sarah regarded the enraged creature. It looked a little like Josh but it behaved completely differently.

Minnie set her own overnight bag down on the slate-black floor tiles and shoved her brother gently. 'We have to go. It's Daddy's weekend, and anyway, he's taking us to the zoo.'

The creature hugged its case more tightly to its chest and screamed, 'I won't go! I hate him and I hate everything!'

Sarah could feel her eyes starting to prickle. She took a step forwards.

The creature glared at her and spat, 'And I hate you too!'

She gathered the creature into her arms and said, 'I know, but I love you very much. We all do.'

The tension in the creature's body shuddered away, it dropped its case and Josh was back, weeping uncontrollably into her chest.

'I know,' Sarah soothed over and over again. 'I know.'

What was she supposed to say? That she hated what the divorce had done to their family? That she knew that her children, like so many children, blamed themselves for what had happened? That they wanted one home, not two? That they wanted two parents, not three?

How could she say any of that to a nine year old boy, though? How could she comment on what Dom had done or on his relationship with Alex without turning the children against their father and his new life?

She had to be fair – and that meant keeping quiet. The children would just need to cope…

'I'm sorry Mummy,' Josh mumbled.

'I know,' she said again.

He held her tightly 'I don't really hate you, Mummy. I love you.'

She stroked his hair. 'I love you too.'

His head was still buried in her chest. 'You won't leave too, will you?'

Minnie handed her a piece of kitchen paper and she dabbed at his eyes. She handed the damp paper back to Minnie and squatted down.

Josh held tightly to her hands. His breathing was ragged and he stared at her with terror in his eyes. His lips trembled as he whispered, 'Please don't leave me…'

She held his gaze and squeezed his hands. 'I will never leave you. Never.'

He flung his arms around her neck and wept again.

Sarah caught Minnie's eye.

Minnie rolled her eyes theatrically and pointed towards the kitchen clock.

Sarah said, 'Never mind. If we're late, we're late.'

Rage surged within her. If only Dom could just see this. It not only happened every time the children went to stay with him but at bedtime too; every night. Josh in tears, Minnie trying to console him, his first exhausted sleep and then his waking howls in the early hours of each morning and Sarah's new routine of rousing him, and taking him to the lavatory, then back to bed when he would finally sleep, only to wake up tired and moody the next morning.

For God's sake! He was only nine!

Dom, though, saw what he wanted to see; his happy new life with Alex; his regular phone calls to the children when he politely enquired about how they were getting on at school; his one weekend a month when the children stayed with him and the trips and treats he filled it with.

According to Dom, his decision to embark on a new life had made everyone happy. If only he knew!

There was no point in telling him, though. Even if he listened, he would become the advocate for the correctness of his decision, argue convincingly that black was white and white was black, remind her that he was paying for everything, bow to an invisible judge and waft away in an almost palpable cloud of self-justification.

Sarah stood up. 'He's your daddy, Josh. He loves you and he wants to see you.'

Josh glared at the floor. 'Do I have to go? Why can't Min go on her own?'

'Because he's your daddy too and he loves you and wants to see you.'

Josh kicked his case and then picked it up.

Sarah sighed with relief and collected her car key from the hook where it hung, next to the notice board crowded with school information sheets and some of Josh's art work.

Minnie shifted her case, took Josh's hand and led him out to the car. They piled in and Sarah set off, out of Twisle Drift.

Once they hit the Yelmouth traffic Sarah negotiated a roundabout and said brightly, 'So you're off to the zoo?'

Minnie answered, 'That's what he said when he phoned on Wednesday.'

'Well, that'll be nice,' Sarah affirmed.

Minnie just looked out of the window and Josh said nothing.

Sarah glanced at Minnie in the rear-view mirror. She was shapeless in her anorak but her breasts were beginning to grow and Sarah had explained to her about periods and she knew what to expect. Hopefully, Minnie's first period wouldn't arrive when she was with Dom and Alex.

Sarah glanced at her daughter again. She was going to be pretty, too. She, like Josh, had sandy-blonde hair, but her eyebrows were a shade darker and made an attractive contrast to her hair. She was intelligent, too, and doing well at school.

'I hear there's a white tiger,' Sarah volunteered.

The children said nothing.

'And elephants,' Sarah went on. 'African and Indian!'

Still nothing.

'Have you got your cameras?'

'I've got my phone,' Minnie replied.

End of conversation.

Sarah drove on in silence. She was taking her children to see their daddy and yet it was like… like what? She had no words for it and no imagery to explain it. All that she knew was that her children, like so many children, were experiencing something that no one had any words for – and if there were no words, what was left but behaviour?

Minnie coped by being brave and caring. Josh coped, after a fashion, by behaving badly. He became *the creature* and, in her heart of hearts, Sarah wished that she could become a creature too. It must be wonderful to just rage without any thought for the consequences! She was an adult though, and a mother, so she coped by being motherly.

Sarah nodded. She must add that to her 'coping list'. It was coming along nicely and now it could include: 'motherly'.

She drove along the sea front at Yelmouth and then turned off the promenade into a street with a park on one side and a gently curving, elegant Georgian terrace on the other. She slid the car to a halt towards the middle of the row and turned off the engine. The front door of the house opposite opened and Dom came down the smart, granite steps. He was stylishly dressed in black jeans and a blue shirt. He was growing his hair longer and his thick, blonde curls wafted as he moved while his sharp, petulant features were set in a serious expression.

He reached the car as Sarah got out and stated, 'You're late.'

'My fault,' she said. 'I dropped a dish and had to clear it up.'

Dom tutted, turned away from her and clicked an inner switch. He smiled at the children and said, 'Got your things?'

They held up their overnight bags and Josh glanced gratefully at Sarah.

'Come on then,' Dom cried. 'The fun begins here!'

He bounced back up the steps and Josh trailed after him, head down, shoulders hunched.

'Bye Mum,' Minnie said. She kissed Sarah on the cheek and followed her brother up the steps. At the door she stopped, turned, and called, 'You have a good weekend too!'

She was not yet twelve years old, but in that moment she looked older than Sarah.

CHAPTER FIVE

Sarah sat down at her kitchen table with a plate of fruit cake and raised her eyebrows as the sound of significant swearing drifted down the stairs. She said, 'It's a good thing the children are at school!'

Margaret's nose wrinkled as if she had encountered a noisome smell. She sniffed; 'It's your father's years at sea. I expect he's slipped and banged his head or something.'

'It's kind of him to sort out the shower, though,' Sarah said gamely.

Margaret sniffed again, helped herself to a slice of cake and waved it towards the kitchen ceiling. 'Well he did start out as an engineer, you know, and he still thinks that he can mend anything.'

Sarah grinned. 'Like the famous video recorder?'

Margaret took a bite of cake and muttered, 'Like the famous video recorder.'

Sarah chuckled at the memory. All through her childhood, her dad had prided himself in his ability to mend anything, but then technology had overtaken him and his years of omnicompetence had come to an end. When Sarah was eight he had attempted to improve the performance of their newly purchased video recorder but instead, he had destroyed it.

Margaret finished her slice of cake and rolled her eyes. 'Don't remind me!'

Another flood of swearing cascaded down the stairs.

Sarah said, 'Should we go and find out what's going on?'

Margaret took another slice of cake. 'I shouldn't. Just leave him to it.'

Sarah studied the ceiling; there was no sign of dampness so perhaps the job was going better than the swearing indicated? She said, 'It's very kind of him to help out.' If he managed to fix her overflowing shower tray it would save her calling in a plumber and sending the bill to Dom.

Margaret studied the remaining slices of cake. 'Are you going to have some?'

Sarah said. 'No; you go ahead. Finish it off if you like.'

Margaret exuded offence, 'Oh I couldn't; that would be *greedy*!'

Sarah sighed and decided it would be easiest just to play the game. She pushed the cake across to her mother and said, 'In case you change your mind…'

Margaret fluttered to an invisible audience and simpered, 'Well, if you *insist*.'

Sarah watched as she took the largest remaining slice and bit into it.

Margaret dabbed crumbs away from the corners of her mouth and glanced critically at Sarah. 'Are you eating enough?'

Sarah sighed. 'I'm fine, Mum.'

Margaret swallowed and pursed her lips. 'You look thin to me.'

Sarah decided not to point out that, when they were beside her mother, most people looked thin…

Margaret finished the slice of cake thoughtfully and asked, 'So you've started going to a counsellor?'

Sarah stretched out an invisible hand to catch this fast-ball. 'I have; there's a counselling centre up near the quarry.'

Margaret said in surprise, 'Really? I thought it was all terraces and rented flats up there.'

Sarah sighed. Now she would have to negotiate her way through her mother's snobbery. 'It is, mostly. But that's where the counselling centre is. In fact, maybe that's why it's there? Cheap rents? They don't charge much so there can't be much money in it.'

Margaret sniffed. 'I hope you're not getting cheap advice!'

Sarah avoided her mother's gaze. 'I'm not getting any advice. Counselling's not about getting advice.'

Margaret thought this over. 'Is there any point to it, then?'

Sarah decided that she needed to refer to a higher authority; 'Well, the doctor said I should get some counselling.'

Margaret nodded slowly. 'So she did. Well, just don't tell your father.'

Sarah made an indeterminate face. 'But he already knows. He was there, in the car, when we talked about it.'

Margaret made a noise that signalled that she was talking to an imbecile. 'I don't mean about the counselling; I mean about where the counselling centre is! He'd be most unhappy to hear that you're mixing with the kind of people who live up by the quarry.'

Sarah said nothing; it was easier.

Margaret said thoughtfully, 'Still, I suppose it'll do you some good.'

Sarah said, 'I suppose it will.'

Margaret's eyes flicked to Sarah.

Sarah backed down, 'At least; I hope it will…'

Margaret nodded. She reached for the remaining slice of cake and munched it appreciatively while vague, banging noises drifted down the stairs. She finished the cake and asked, 'And how are the children?'

'They're fine,' Sarah answered.

'Such good children,' Margaret affirmed.

Sarah stayed quiet. She was not about to tell her mother about Josh turning into *the creature*; instead, she pushed her plate and the half-eaten slice of cake that was on it, towards her mother. 'Do you want that? I'm not hungry.'

Margaret dithered briefly and then pounced.

Sarah smiled; with her mother, it was always easy to change the subject – as long as there was food around.

Margaret pushed her empty plate away. 'Mustn't have any more. Wouldn't want to spoil my dinner!'

'No,' Sarah said. 'That would be terrible.'

Margaret glanced sharply at her but was interrupted by footsteps descending the stairs.

Terry appeared in the doorway. He had a long, bent, piece of wire in one hand and, in the other, what looked like a shrunken head. 'There you go; it was just hair blocking the u-bend. You ought to get one of those filter things that you put over the plug hole. That would stop the hair collecting in the pipe and causing problems.'

Sarah stood up, took the hair-ball from him and poured some tea while he scrubbed his hands clean in the kitchen sink.

He dried himself, picked up the mug of tea, wandered towards the kitchen table and asked hopefully, 'Is there any cake?'

Sarah glanced at the empty plate. 'There was…'

'Not enough for three, though,' Margaret said. 'Sorry.'

He shrugged and sat down.

Sarah deposited the hair-ball in the bin and joined her parents.

'How are the children?' Terry asked.

Margaret said, 'They're fine; and Sarah's started the counselling sessions.'

Terry glanced at Sarah out of the corner of his eye. 'Is it helping?'

Margaret said, 'Of course. The doctor said it would!'

Terry nodded. 'And you're coming over on Saturday, with the children?'

Margaret said, 'Of course she is. It's all arranged.'

Terry drank some tea and then said, 'I don't suppose you'll be seeing anything much of the others, now.'

Sarah said, 'The others?'

Terry drank some more tea and said, 'The Prices.'

Margaret snorted, 'Well of course she won't! Not now that Dominic's shown his true colours! Why would she have anything to do with that family any more?'

Sarah tried to stretch out another invisible hand to catch this new fast-ball but she missed it and it dropped away from her.

Margaret continued, 'It's not as if the children need *two* sets of grandparents anyway. And it's not as if the Prices have been important in their lives, is it?'

Terry nodded. 'True.'

Sarah closed her eyes. It was simpler to just say nothing.

Margaret and Terry began to bicker about the state of his trousers and the effect it would have on their car's upholstery.

Sarah let their conversation wash over her. When she closed her eyes, it was easy to imagine that the last twelve years had never happened. It was just like being back, living with them, listening to them sparring with one another and wondering whether she would ever leave home.

Her eyes sprang open. When she had married Dom – had she married him just to escape home?

She sat back; maybe she should talk this idea over with Counsellor Di?

Her parents had resolved the problem of Terry's dirty trousers; he would drive home in his underpants.

Sarah shook her head. There was no point in her saying anything; this might be her kitchen, in her house but, as far as her parents were concerned, she might as well not be here. Maybe she should mention that to her counsellor too.

CHAPTER SIX

Sarah parked her car, turned around and shouted, 'Will you two stop arguing!'

Josh looked aggrieved. 'But Min won't–'

Sarah shouted, 'I'm perfectly well aware that you want Min to hold your dinosaur while you flick it with a rubber band! I *am* here, you know, only four feet in front of you! Now shut up; both of you! And if you behave badly in front of Grandma and Grandpa Price, I'll have your guts for garters when we get home! Now behave!'

Minnie took a breath and Sarah snapped, 'Both of you!' She brushed her hair out of her eyes, got out of the car and breathed deeply to calm herself. Fortunately, the street seemed to be deserted and no one was watching, or listening.

Sarah checked up and down the street again; this was where Dom had grown up and it was almost as familiar to Sarah as her own road. These days, most people had, like Roy and Sandy, bought their houses from the local council and very few were rented any more. The houses were built of rather ugly, municipal-looking red bricks and looked small and mean. The front gardens, although mostly tidy, were narrow and the back gardens were long and thin.

Sarah opened the car door and Minnie and Josh clambered out and followed her up their grandparents' front path in stony silence.

Sarah adjusted her sweater, rang the bell and glared briefly but meaningfully at the children.

The door opened and Grandma Price, Sandy, threw her arms wide. She had always relied on her looks to get her through life, and now that she was a glamorous granny, she used theatricality to compensate for her deficit of youth. 'Come in, come in! There's toast and blancmange in the kitchen!'

Josh and Minnie piled inside and their excited voices disappeared with Sandy down the short, dingy hall. Sarah stepped inside, closed the door and followed.

In the small kitchen, with its outdated wood-effect units and peeling, patterned wallpaper, Sandy caught sight of Sarah. She stopped wobbling a plate with a pink blancmange on it.

Sarah stood in the doorway and smiled.

Sandy handed the plate to Minnie. 'Oh. Are you staying?'

Sarah nodded. 'I thought I might.'

Sandy found a serving spoon and handed it to Josh. 'There's no need. We'll be just fine. I am their *Grandma*, after all.'

Sarah closed her eyes. 'Well, if you're sure?'

'We'll be just fine,' Sandy repeated. 'You go off and do some shopping, or something. You can collect them later, or Roy can drop them home this evening. Whatever's best for you.'

Sarah grimaced. Yeah; right!

Sandy ignored her and said to the children, 'Grandpa's just gone down to the supermarket. We were completely out of chocolate ice cream! Can you believe it?'

The children chorused their disbelief that anyone could run out of chocolate ice cream.

Sarah eyed them suspiciously but they returned her look with one of mutual, seraphic, innocence.

Sandy walked towards her, 'I'll see you out.'

Sarah allowed her mother-in-law, or ex-mother-in-law, or whatever she was now, to escort her to the front door, but before she left she turned and said, 'Sandy, there's something I want you to know.'

Sandy's defences went up a notch, 'Oh yes?'

Sarah said, 'I just want you to know that, even though Dom and I aren't together any more, you're still the childrens' grandparents.'

Sandy seemed poised; ready to move in any direction.

Sarah ploughed on, 'So I'll still bring them to see you. I won't leave it to Dom to bring them on the weekends he has them.'

Sandy's defences seemed to lower slightly.

Sarah said, 'And at Christmas too, and birthdays, and things like that. I'll make sure that you see them.'

Sandy's tone was neutral, 'That's very gracious of you.'

Sarah tried to work out the direction of Sandy's comment; was she being sincere or sarcastic? She gave up. 'I just wanted you to know that you're still their grandparents…'

Sandy made a noise in the back of her throat but her smile seemed genuine. 'Thank you, Sarah.'

Sarah continued, although the conversation was much harder than she'd imagined it would be, 'And Roy's birthday's coming up, isn't it?'

Sandy's defences rose again, but she nodded.

Sarah said, 'So I'll bring them, shall I? It's half-term so they won't be at school. We'll come as a family, shall we? Then I can wish Roy a happy birthday too?'

Sandy hesitated and then said neutrally, 'That would be lovely. He'd like to see them… you… on his birthday.'

Sarah smiled, 'We'll come over in the afternoon then, shall we?'

Sandy paused; 'Come for lunch and then the children can make some things for tea.'

Sarah relaxed, 'Brilliant. When should I collect them today, then?'

Sandy considered this. 'Don't worry. Roy will drive them home this evening. You go off and have some *you* time.' She stepped forwards and as Sarah backed away, Sandy shut the door.

Sarah stared at the green-painted wood just inches from her face. It was surprising how clearly the wood grain showed through the paint.

She turned and walked back to her car. She had the whole afternoon in front of her and, probably, most of the evening. What was she going to do?

She got into her car and started the engine.

Should she, as Sandy suggested, go shopping?

No. There was nothing she needed at the moment, and if she went browsing for clothes or new shoes, Dom might want to know why she had bought them when she already had more than she needed. As he so often pointed out, he might be well paid, but his income came one legal case at a time; if the cases stopped coming, so did his income.

Should she visit her parents?

No; she'd rather go home and clean the toilets with a toothbrush than have a second dose of her parents in as many days.

Should she visit a friend?

Sarah laughed mirthlessly. Everyone she knew would either be at work or busy with their own children. No one would want her hanging around like a bad smell.

What about Yelmouth Museum? That was a thought. She often took the children to the museum, but they had their favourite displays so they usually ended up in the dinosaur hall or looking at the doll's house collection. If she went on her own, she could browse through the ethnic costume hall at her own pace or have a good look at the Egyptian jewellery.

On the other hand, she could visit the Art Gallery. The children never wanted to spend much time there and, when they did, Josh was just an embarrassment; he made a point of finding paintings of nudes and declaring with a silly, rising inflection: 'Oo-oo!'

Sarah smiled and put the car into gear. The Art Gallery, then.

She pulled away and saluted Sandy. By offering to baby-sit the children her ex-mother-in-law had done her a favour and she would now be able to spend time appreciating Yelmouth's art collection.

Something, somewhere, niggled for Sarah's attention, but she ignored it. She had squared things up with Sandy and she would have a similar conversation with Roy. Everything was fine and, this afternoon, she was going to have a good time; she was not about to listen to niggles.

CHAPTER SEVEN

Di studied the sheet of paper and Sarah shifted in her seat. They had been discussing *coping* for half an hour and Sarah had the distinct feeling that her 'homework' – the sheet of paper on which she had listed the good and bad aspects of coping – was, somehow, wrong. Di had not criticised her list, but her questions had hinted at her disapproval.

Di looked up and said, 'So basically, you distinguish between coping and expressing emotion?'

Sarah shifted in her seat again. The attic room seemed identical to her previous visit but today Di was wearing a pale blue sweater and a dark blue skirt. She had good legs too, although they would never grace the cover of Vogue; they were too short. Her glasses were the same burgundy fames, so Sarah's original theory about matching frames and sweaters was wrong.

Di waited.

Sarah hauled her attention back to the question. 'Not exactly. I was talking about bad emotions rather than good ones. Good emotions go together with coping. It's the bad ones that don't.'

Di handed the paper back to Sarah and said, 'We're going to need to think about that. Let me see; why don't we start with a very old analogy? You know that coins have two sides?'

Sarah nodded briefly; this was infantile.

Di said, 'Well think of good emotions as "heads" and bad emotions as "tails". Good and bad emotions are just two sides of the same coin. If you don't want what you call the bad side, you end up with no coin. If you want the good side, you have to accept the bad side. Does that make sense – that coping is about dealing with every kind of emotion rather than just the good kind?'

Sarah said nothing. It was easier than pointing out just why Di was so very wrong.

Di put her elbows on the arms of her easy chair and steepled her fingers. 'Let's leave that for now, though. Tell me a bit more about your marriage in the early days.'

Sarah thought for a moment and then answered, 'Well, in a lot of ways, it was just like courting, except that we were living in the same house. I gave up work and became a housewife and Minnie came along very quickly so I had loads to do. And as Dom worked very long hours he often left for work before I got up and didn't come home until I was ready for bed.'

'Even at weekends?' Di asked.

Sarah nodded. 'Sometimes; no; more than sometimes. He was either busy networking with colleagues or going into chambers to prepare his next case.'

Di frowned. 'And was that okay?'

Sarah nodded; 'As a barrister, he works case by case rather than nine to five.'

Di looked quizzical and said, 'That sounds like a quote?'

Sarah laughed. 'You're right. It is; it's what Dom always says!'

Di folded her hands in her lap and asked gently, 'And do you think he says it to Alex?'

Sarah felt suddenly nauseous but managed to say quietly, 'I doubt it.'

Di waited.

Sarah took a deep breath and continued. 'I kind of knew, deep down, that things weren't right.'

Di suggested, 'You had a feeling?'

Sarah nodded. Yes, that was right; she'd had a feeling that things weren't right between her and Dom even on their first honeymoon night together. 'The thing is, there were always reasons…'

'Reasons?' Di repeated.

Sarah nodded again. 'I wanted him to spend time with me but he was always busy and he said he was doing it for us.'

'Did you believe him?'

'Well yes; no; I don't know. It was a difficult situation and I just coped.'

'You coped,' Di said.

Sarah nodded vehemently. 'Yes; I coped. I'll admit that after a few months I was very unhappy and I mentioned it to Mum but she put things into perspective. You see, she and Dad were often apart. He was in the merchant navy and sailed off all over the world, sometimes for months at a time, and Mum was left on her own to bring me up. And she said that me being married to Dom wasn't much different.'

Di considered this, 'And what about sex?'

Sarah stopped herself from responding 'What about it?' Instead she said, 'Well we did have sex, just not very often. Dom was always tired and then, when I had Minnie, Mum said that I should be grateful; because I could get on with being a mother and not have to put up with Dom in bed any more. Then, of course, I had Josh a couple of years later and life became even busier.'

Di made a note in her notebook. 'And did your mother's advice seem, well, normal to you?'

Sarah shrugged.

Di continued, 'What did your friends say?'

Sarah shrugged again. 'To be honest, I didn't really have any that I could talk to about that sort of thing. I had lots of friends when I was at school – we all went around in a gang. But then, as we grew older, the others started spending more and more time with their boyfriends and then they got married and we just, sort of, lost touch. That's why my friendship with Dom was more important than anything else, I suppose.'

Di made another note in her notebook. 'Can I ask you something?'

Sarah opened her hands. 'Of course.'

'Do you think you coped well with your relationship with Dom?'

Sarah smiled ironically; they were back at *this* topic! 'Yes. I think I did.'

Di continued, 'Until?'

Sarah frowned, 'Until the divorce, I suppose.'

Di made another note. 'And did you love him?'

Sarah laughed, 'I think I did! I certainly tried to!'

Di asked, 'And now – do you still love him or do you hate him?'

Sarah shut her eyes tight and whispered, 'I don't know. I just don't know!'

Di put down her pen and said gently, 'That's not what I'm asking you, Sarah. I'm not asking what you *know*, I'm asking what you *feel*. Do you love him or hate him?'

Sarah found it hard to breathe. It was like being cornered by a monster and she wanted to run and run and run…

Di made a sympathetic face. 'You don't need to answer. That's another layer – right there – and it's what I was talking about earlier; the two sides of the coin of emotion. Love; hate; and so forth. You experience both or neither, and keeping a lid on them is, ultimately impossible. If you try, it'll blow you apart.'

Sarah grabbed at what Di had said and leaned forward in her chair. 'Is that what happened to me in the supermarket? Is that what my *episode* was? Me blowing apart?'

Di sat back in her chair and laughed. 'You are very, very good at that!'

Sarah blinked. 'Good at what?'

Di laughed again. 'You sit there and tell me the most heart-rending things, we begin to lift the lid on your emotions, you change the subject and, whoosh, they're gone.'

Sarah blinked again. Was that a compliment or a criticism?

Di sat forward. 'Please don't be offended. However you've developed that mechanism, it serves you well. The experience you've gone through would destroy many people, but here you are, composed and getting on with life. You are a very remarkable woman!'

Sarah frowned. So it *was* a compliment?

Di cleared her throat. 'Let's leave that for now. Tell me a bit more about your childhood and growing up.'

Sarah considered the question and answered, 'It was very happy.'

Di said, 'And your father was away a lot?'

'Well, yes. In a way, it was like belonging to two different families. When he was away, we did things Mum's way and when he was home, we did things his way.'

'What sort of things?'

'Well, things like food. I mean, we often had beans on toast and things like that when it was just Mum and me, but Dad didn't like that sort of food, so when he was at home we had proper meals with meat and potatoes. We had to eat at the table, too, but when he was away we often had tea on our laps in front of the telly. To be honest, I never really understood why we had to act differently when Dad was around. I mean, Mum was always in charge; she wore the trousers; but when Dad was there she always, sort of, *pushed* him into being the head of the home. When I was older I wondered if she did it as a sort of heavy sarcasm, but I don't think so and, as I say, I've never really understood them.'

Di made another note in her notebook, 'We'll think about their relationship more deeply in another session; but things were more formal when he was around?'

Sarah nodded. 'I had to behave myself too. He was much stricter than Mum.'

Di glanced at her, 'Did he smack you?'

'Oh no, nothing like that. He just disapproved and when he told me off it was worse than being smacked. When Mum lost her temper, she'd slap me and I'd say sorry and things got back to normal really quickly. With Dad, though, when he told me off I felt completely stupid, like I was a lump of dirt. It was horrible; so I behaved.'

'And what did he tell you off for?'

Sarah considered this; 'Well, for making mistakes or for being noisy or for leaving my toys around or for irritating him. Things like that.'

Di put her pencil down, 'In other words; for being a child?'

Sarah opened her mouth but closed it again. Something in her head clicked into a new focus and she was suddenly aware of the reality of her childhood. It wasn't happy, and she had tiptoed through it to avoid her father's anger and her mother's manipulations and she had often been exhausted by the effort of trying to second-guess them and keep in their good books.

Another thought struck her. What about Minnie and Josh? Was she like that with them? Did she tell them off for making mistakes or try to manipulate them? No, she was patient with them. She tried to help them to understand what they had done wrong so that they wouldn't do it again. And what about when they were noisy and untidy and irritating? Did she show her anger? No, she just made it clear that they were behaving inappropriately and waited quietly until they decided to co-operate…

But what was that like from their point of view?

Her hand flew to her mouth and tears began to trickle down her cheeks, 'My God! I must be just like my parents!'

Di waited and then said quietly, 'I doubt it, but you may have learned more from them than you imagine. There's another layer to consider!'

Sarah shut her eyes. 'Am I a bad mother?'

Di asked, 'Do you love your children.'

Sarah's eyes sprang open and she almost shouted, 'Yes!'

Di smiled and shoved the box of tissues towards her. 'Then I doubt that you're a bad mother. You're probably just normal.'

Sarah paused with the tissue halfway to her eyes, 'Normal? How do you mean?'

Di chuckled. 'There you go again. Whoomph: an emotion. Whoosh: gone!'

Sarah gazed at the tissue in her hand. Why was she holding it?

Di said, 'When you were growing up, did you talk about things as a family?'

Sarah considered this. 'Well, we had family conferences,

but those were really Dad explaining what I'd done wrong and telling me what was going to happen, or Mum telling Dad what to say.'

Di asked, 'So if you had a problem at school, who did you tell?'

Sarah scratched her jaw; 'My teacher, I guess.'

Di paused, 'And what if your teacher was the problem?'

Sarah let her hand drop into her lap, 'Well; I just...'

'Coped?' Di offered.

Sarah nodded.

Di sucked her lip and then said quietly, 'It sounds like your childhood was rather lonely.'

Sarah noticed that one of her finger nails was too long. She must file it later.

Di sighed and muttered; 'Whoomph-whoosh. Let's talk about something else. You said that there was this big family secret that no one talked about?'

Sarah shrugged, 'I guess. But doesn't every family have things they don't talk about? I mean, mums and dads don't talk about their sex lives with their children, do they?'

Di shrugged, 'Some do – in an appropriate way. But from what you've already told me, this rift between your family and Dom's family was more like the mad woman locked in the attic that no one talks about.'

Sarah glanced at the wall. Was that what was in the attic room next door? It was always locked but sometimes noises could be heard through the wall. Was it just another counselling room with another counsellor and client, or was there a mad woman locked in there that no one talked about?

Di sighed again. 'Whoomph-whoosh...'

Sarah glanced across the coffee table, bemused.

Di tidied up her papers and put her notepad on top. 'Let's leave it there. Over the next couple of weeks I'd like you to consider two things. First of all, think about whether what you call bad emotions can ever lead to good outcomes. And, secondly, think about how similar you are to your parents, and how different.' She picked up her papers and stood up.

Sarah stood up too. This was clearly the end-of-session routine and as she followed Di downstairs she allowed herself to relax. She wasn't sure that she had always answered Di's questions correctly, but it was only their second session so she had time to improve. The important thing was that Di seemed to be pleased with her.

When they reached the reception area, Sarah held out her hand.

Di smiled and shook it.

Sarah said earnestly, 'Thank you so much. Today's been really useful.'

Di just shook her head, laughed a warm, friendly laugh and said, 'You are amazing!'

CHAPTER EIGHT

Sarah drummed her fingers on her desk and took a sip of peppermint tea.

'What are you doing?' Minnie asked.

Sarah glanced round. Minnie's feet were bare and she had come silently into the study. She was now peering over Sarah's shoulder.

Sarah gestured at her laptop screen. 'I was just thinking about setting up internet access for my bank account.'

Minnie moved closer and Sarah put her arm loosely around her daughter's waist.

'How far have you got?' Minnie asked.

'Just looking at the details,' Sarah replied.

Minnie leant against her. 'Need any help?'

Sarah kissed her shoulder and said, 'No, I'm fine. I haven't decided yet. Anyway, you need to get ready. We're going in a minute.'

Minnie nodded, 'I know but I can't find any clean socks.'

Sarah squeezed her gently, 'And where might they be?'

Minnie perched on the arm of Sarah's office chair. 'They're not in my drawer.'

Sarah prompted, 'So where else might they be?'

Minnie answered, 'There aren't any in the airing cupboard either.'

Sarah said, 'Tried the tumble-dryer?'

Minnie stood up, 'Oh, right.' She left the study noiselessly.

Sarah smiled. Minnie was growing taller and more graceful every week.

She turned her attention back to her laptop. Since Dom had changed their account, she had received no statements or letters from the bank. Registering for online access had seemed sensible but, according to the bank's pop-up boxes, the account was already registered and she just needed to enter her user-name and password. The problem was: she didn't have them. Dom must have already set them up without telling her.

She tried to work out if this was important. She could easily ask Dom for the internet information but – did she need to? She used her new credit and debit cards and there never seemed to be any problems. Did it matter that she never saw the monthly totals and had no idea how much she had to draw on? Was it okay for Dom to know every detail of what she bought? What about when she wanted new underwear or something just for her? Would she have to tell him before she spent the money? Or ask for his permission?

When Dom had finally got around to explaining the new account to her he had assured her that the change was in everyone's best interests. It seemed weird though, not having any control.

'I'm ready,' crowed Josh from the hallway. 'Ready to go and wish Grandpa Price happy birthday!'

Sarah logged off and closed her laptop lid. She'd think about it another time. She called back, 'Well done!'

'Are *you* ready?' Josh challenged.

Sarah stood up and called back, 'Almost.'

'It's just *Min* then,' he shouted, sounding very pleased with himself.

The kitchen door clattered and Minnie said, 'No it isn't. I'm here!'

Sarah reached for her bag and coat, 'Right. Off we go.'

As she locked the front door she noticed a car in next door's driveway. She pressed the button on her key-fob and the locks on her car clicked open. 'You get in; I'm just going to pop next door.'

She ignored the children's protests. 'I won't be a minute.'

She hopped through a gap in the hedge and knocked on the door.

A shadow loomed through the frosted-glass door panel, the door opened, and a man smiled at her enquiringly. They were around the same age, he looked fit and he had an approachable, open air about him. His clothes were understated but looked expensive and somehow at odds with the very ordinary car parked on his driveway. Wouldn't someone who spent money on clothes buy a more expensive car?

The man smiled pleasantly. 'Hello?'

Sarah smiled back, 'Hello, I'm Sarah; Sarah, er, Price. I live next door and I saw your car and I just thought I'd welcome you to Twisle Drift.' She waved her hand to indicate the surrounding, identical houses.

The man smiled, 'Thank you, Sarah, *er*, Price.'

Sarah made a face. 'Sorry. I'm divorced and I still haven't decided whether I'm going to keep my married name. That was the "er".'

The man looked at her.

Oh God! He must think she was telling him that she was available. By way of an explanation she said, 'I was good friends with the previous people who lived here.' Well, she always said hello…

The man was still looking at her.

Oh God! Did he think that she was asking to be good friends with him?

The man smiled and said, 'It was nice to meet you. Thank you for calling.'

Sarah smiled fixedly. In other words: don't bother to call again.

The man began to close the door but then opened it again. 'I'm sorry; I didn't mean to be rude. It's just that I'm in the middle of something right now. Perhaps we could chat another time?'

Sarah smiled uncertainly. Was he coming on to *her*?

He said, 'I'm Neil, by the way. I'll see you around, I'm sure.'

He shut the door and Sarah trailed down his drive and then back up hers. She resisted the urge to hop through the gap in the hedge; next-door-neighbour Neil might be watching.

Sarah considered Roy's dahlias and tried to look interested. A burst of laughter erupted from the tiny kitchen window at the back of the house and rolled up the garden path towards them. Minnie and Josh were helping Grandma Price to make chocolate brownies and they were evidently having a wonderful time. Once the flour had started to fly, though, Grandpa Price, Roy, had suggested that Sarah might like to see his birthday dahlias so here they were, up at the top end of his thin, narrow garden.

The garden was very tidy and the hours that Roy spent in it showed. He had retired last year and Sandy was only a couple of years behind him. It was odd to think of them entering this new phase of their lives as they had always seemed much younger than her own parents. It was even odder to think of them as growing old – especially as Sandy was still slim and attractive and while Roy's belly bulged over his belt he was still energetic and forceful. Even so, no one could mistake him for a young man; his years at sea and outdoor working had taken their toll on his skin and, apart from a few wisps of grey hair, he was now completely bald.

He bent over to examine a plant and his head glinted in the sunlight. He seemed on edge. So far he had shown her his hedges, his vegetable plot, the new coat of brown wood-preserver on his shed and his new watering can. What did he want to talk about?

Roy picked an insect off a leaf and said, 'Are you okay financially?'

So that was what this was about – but which possible answer should she choose? 'We're coping fine.'

He continued, 'I mean, you have what you need for the children?'

Sarah nodded and said cautiously, 'Yes. Dom's been very generous.'

Roy made a noise that might have been a snort or a chuckle.

She said, 'They have everything they need.'

Roy bent down and examined a leaf and then snipped it off with his nails. 'Sandy's been worried. She didn't want to ask so I said I would.'

Sarah made her own indeterminate noise.

Roy straightened up and regarded her. He had the dangerous look in his eyes that signalled that Sarah should be careful. The last time she had seen it was when they had all been on a family holiday in Cornwall and he had found a wheel-clamp on his car. Fortunately, Dom had been on hand to deal with the clamping company and to stop Roy from doing anything stupid.

Sarah smiled her little-girl smile.

Roy relaxed and muttered, 'It's very hard; being the grandparents. You hear about issues with grandchildren all the time.'

Oh – so it wasn't the finances that were really bothering him. Sarah made a sympathetic face; 'Don't worry, Roy – I've already told Sandy that you mustn't worry. You won't lose touch with Minnie and Josh; I'll make sure of it!'

His mouth became an unreadable line and his eyes became unpredictable.

She tried again, 'They're your grandchildren. Whatever happens between me and Dom, they're still you're grandchildren!'

He opened his mouth to speak but then shut it again and turned his attention back to his plants. 'There's a lot that goes on behind closed doors that no one knows about.'

Sarah wrestled with this non sequitur but nodded. It might be nothing to do with their conversation but it was true. In her case, though, it was more a question of what *hadn't* happened behind closed doors, rather than what had…

He spoke again, 'And things are often not what they seem.'

Sarah nodded positively this time. That was true enough, too.

He regarded her again, 'I just need to know, what with Dom being… you know…'

Sarah understood. Poor Roy. He must be anxious that she somehow blamed him for Dom leaving and he must be worried that she would punish him by refusing him access to Minnie and Josh. What a terribly sad thought – and perhaps her conversation with Sandy had been misunderstood too? She rested her hand on his arm and reassured him. 'You mustn't worry. You'll still see them. They're still your grandchildren.'

He shook off her hand, searched her face and then bent over his plants again.

Sarah sighed and turned. Perhaps it would be better if they talked about this some other time? She could join the others in the kitchen and maybe have another chat with Sandy, and reassure *her*.

Behind her, Roy whispered hoarsely, 'But are they?'

Sarah stopped and turned back to her father-in-law, or ex-father-in-law, or whatever he now was. 'I'm sorry?'

Roy refused to look at her and his voice was soft but firm; 'I said, "Are they?"'

Sarah tried to make sense of this. 'Are they what?'

He still refused to look at her but his voice became hard. 'Are they my grandchildren?'

Sarah's legs began to tremble. 'What?'

He stared at her and the dangerous look was back in his eyes. 'You heard. Are they my grandchildren? Josh and Minnie?'

The whole of Sarah's body began to shake.

Roy surveyed his garden.

Sarah crossed her arms and tried to stop the shaking.

He said, 'I was at sea…'

The shaking just got worse.

'So I know about men like Dom!' He turned and faced her. His eyes had lost their dangerous edge and he looked anguished. He screwed up his features, blinked hard, and blurted out, 'Sarah – are they his?'

All of the breath left her lungs and her ears whistled.

He stepped towards her, grabbed her arms and shook her. 'I have to know. Are they his?'

She could feel and smell his breath and his spit was on her nose. She wrenched away from him; 'Of course they're his! What do you think I am? Do you think I was unfaithful? Do you?'

She turned and ran back towards the house.

Behind her Roy shouted, 'I had to know; I had to know!'

His words cut off as she plunged into the kitchen.

Minnie had a spoon in her hand and Josh was about to flick brownie mix at his Grandma. The smiles froze on their faces.

'Are you all right, Mum,' Minnie asked.

'No,' Sarah said. 'We're going home.'

She glanced quickly at Sandy and muttered, 'Sorry.'

Sandy glared through the kitchen window at Roy who was standing alone on the garden path.

'Sorry,' Sarah muttered again. She rounded up the children's things and together they clattered out of the house. As she started the car she could hear Sandy, on the other side of the house, in the back garden, shouting at Roy. She switched on the radio and turned up the volume.

'Mummy,' Josh said from the back seat.

Sarah managed to say, 'What is it, darling?'

He scratched his head. 'If you're not very well, wouldn't it be better to stay at Grandma and Grandpa's house 'til you feel better?'

Minnie hissed, 'Shut up, Josh.'

CHAPTER NINE

The Head Teacher's office was small and stuffy but opening the window would make the noise unbearable; just beyond the glass, children ran around the school playground, screaming and shouting, and the din was incredible. Sarah tried to ignore the racket and concentrate.

Next to her, Josh slouched in a chair, kicking his feet. It was definitely Josh, not *the creature*, so that was something to be thankful for, but he looked like a truculent teenager and exuded boredom. His shoes were scuffed, his school uniform was a mess, his shirt-tail was visible and his eye was swollen.

Mrs Hopkins, the Head Teacher, repeated firmly, 'We don't tolerate fighting in school.' She was a plump woman with significantly permed white hair and, when she nodded, her jowls wobbled and her pearls rattled. She was, in many ways, very similar to Margaret.

'Of course not,' Sarah agreed.

The Head leaned forwards and her pink-framed spectacles slid towards the end of her nose. She peered over the top of them at Josh. 'And it isn't acceptable for little boys to take matters into their own hands.'

Sarah nodded in agreement.

Mrs Hopkins sat back in her chair, pushed her spectacles back into place and considered the papers on her desk. 'Joshua still hasn't explained what happened but I intend to get to the bottom of this. The other boys say that he hit Ryan for no reason and, if Joshua refuses to speak, I shall have no option but to suspend him.'

Mrs Hopkins turned her attention to Sarah. 'As you know, because of his recent behaviour, Joshua is already on "amber". I've been making allowances due to your, um, family situation, but fighting escalates him to "red". The school discipline procedure is very clear.'

She turned back to Josh. 'I don't think that you appreciate how serious this is, young man. If you are suspended, the suspension will go on your school record and follow you when you leave here and move up to high school. It is a very, very bad thing!'

Josh stopped kicking his feet and flicked an uncertain glance at Sarah.

Mrs Hopkins disguised a smile and continued, 'Now, Joshua, I am offering you this one opportunity to explain yourself and I am only doing it because Ryan is two years older than you. I have some things to attend to, so I am going to leave you here, with your mummy. While I'm gone, you must tell her what happened. When I get back, we'll decide what to do.'

Mrs Hopkins left the room leaving a faint trail of perfume behind her.

Sarah said gently, 'Oh Josh!'

He stayed where he was but his cheeks reddened and his lips quivered.

'Come on,' Sarah said, opening her arms.

He hurled himself out of his chair and into her embrace and his small body rippled with his sobs. He clutched at her and shoved against her as if he was trying to climb inside her.

She held him tight, waited for his inner storm to subside and gazed around the room. The walls were covered with pictures, all signed with the name of the artist and the class to which they belonged. Painted clay models of monsters sat dusty on the window sill and a mobile of fish made from foil-covered cardboard danced on a cord that hung from the ceiling.

Sarah tried to ease the pain that gnawed at her from inside her stomach. If only life was as simple as these pictures and models!

'I see,' Mrs Hopkins said.

Sarah waited. She had told the Head everything that Josh had haltingly, and then in a rush, told her. Now it was up to Mrs Hopkins to pronounce judgement.

The Head Teacher addressed Josh directly. 'Now then, Joshua.'

He stared at her as if his life depended on what she was about to say. His studied boredom had gone and he now sat, hunched over, as if his innards would spill out if he unfolded his arms. His eyes were red-rimmed and his hair was a tangled mess. He glanced at Sarah for reassurance.

She smiled seriously, nodded and said, 'He has something to tell you, Mrs Hopkins.'

His voice cracked as he spoke and new tears spilled from his eyes. 'I'm sorry, Mrs Hopkins. I'm really, really sorry.'

Mrs Hopkins cleared her throat. 'I can see that, Joshua, but I need you to promise that there'll be no more fighting in school.'

Josh nodded vigorously.

Mrs Hopkins continued, 'And, you must apologise to Ryan too.'

Josh shot a horrified glance at Sarah.

She nodded.

Josh swallowed and sat up straight.

Mrs Hopkins said, 'I'm waiting.'

Josh licked his lips, glanced quickly at Sarah and said, 'I promise. I'll say sorry to Ryan and I won't ever fight in school again. Ever. I promise.'

Mrs Hopkins clucked her approval. 'Then I shall make a note on your file and you will stay on amber. If you behave well, you will go back to green – but remember, you are only one step away from red, and you know what that means?'

Josh nodded even more vigorously.

Mrs Hopkins closed the file. 'Good. Now, off you go, back to your class. I just want a little chat with your mummy.'

Josh jumped off his chair, hesitated, kissed Sarah on the cheek and rushed from the room.

'I'm sorry,' Sarah began.

Mrs Hopkins raised a hand and the flesh of her upper arm swayed majestically. 'No need. Ryan shouldn't have said what he said, so we'll think of the incident as six of one and half a dozen of the other.'

Sarah said, 'That's very generous; it was Josh who swung the first punch. I'm very grateful to you for being so understanding.'

Mrs Hopkins smiled thinly. 'Well, to be honest, I'm a bit old-fashioned about these sort of things. I know that all the new rules say that I shouldn't make any exceptions but, to be honest, Ryan can be a bit of a bully and, to be completely honest, I hope he's learnt a lesson too. If a boy as small as Joshua thumps him, maybe he'll think twice before he picks on anyone else!'

Sarah stared.

Mrs Hopkins laughed. 'I expect I'm a dinosaur so it's probably just as well that I'm retiring next term. The new head can do everything by the book – and we shall see if things are better or worse as a result!'

Sarah mumbled a vague agreement.

'Anyway,' Mrs Hopkins continued, 'I wanted a little chat with you because, as you know, I'm well aware of your family situation. It was very wrong of Ryan to call Joshua a "poof" and given the circumstances of Dominic's departure, I'm not surprised that Joshua lashed out.'

Sarah gaped. She had informed the school of her divorce, but had not shared any of the details. How did the Head know about Dom being gay? Who had told her? Josh?

Mrs Hopkins sat back in her chair. 'It must be a difficult time for all of you. Counselling can be a very good thing, you know.'

It was like being kicked in the chest. She knew about that too? How? Not even the children knew about Counsellor Di!

Mrs Hopkins nodded wisely. 'It's not easy to access – especially for a young boy like Joshua – but we might be able to sort something out through the school Educational Welfare Officer. If you are happy to give your permission, we might be able to connect Joshua up with a Children's Counsellor, and although it wouldn't be a magic bullet to make everything better, he may find it helpful to talk to someone outside of the, um, situation.'

Sarah blinked with relief; Mrs Hopkins was talking about Josh!

Then she went cold. When Mrs Hopkins said 'outside of the situation' she meant outside of *Sarah*!

Mrs Hopkins nodded again. 'Have a think about it and let me know what you decide.'

It was probably best if Sarah didn't share what she thought; and yet… and yet… she was receiving counselling and it was probably helping – so why not Josh?

She made up her mind. 'No, I appreciate the offer. If it's possible, I'd like to go ahead.'

Mrs Hopkins sat forward and smiled. 'Very good. Really – very, very good. I'll have a word with the Educational Welfare Officer and we'll see what we can come up with.'

Sarah prepared to leave. She needed time to think about what counselling for Josh might mean. The big question was – should she tell Dom?

'And how are you?' Mrs Hopkins enquired kindly.

Sarah paused. The Head clearly wanted to talk. She forced herself back into her chair and smiled wryly. 'I've been better.'

'I'm sure,' agreed the Head. 'Dominic leaving must have been… must be…'

Sarah nodded vaguely. Did Mrs Hopkins want to gossip?

The Head continued, 'Especially when you think of poor Alexandra.'

Sarah was taken aback. Who was Alexandra?

Mrs Hopkins smiled warmly and lowered her voice to a confidential tone. 'As you know, Alexandra and I grew up together. We were very close when we were young and it's been really nice having Minnie and Joshua here at school. A bit like having surrogate grandchildren around and I've been glad to keep an eye on them.'

'Thank you, Mrs Hopkins,' Sarah said faintly as the pieces tumbled into place. She never thought of her ex-mother-in-law as Alexandra – only as Sandy – and this friendship with the Head Teacher was news to her. Were they still in touch? Was it Sandy who had told her about Dom?

'Marsha,' Mrs Hopkins said.

Marsha? Who was Marsha, and why had she told Mrs Hopkins about Dom?

'Call me Marsha,' the Head said.

Sarah managed to smile. 'Oh; right. Thank you, Marsha.'

'Don't mention it. We do need to help Joshua to control his temper, though. I suppose that, in this respect, he's actually quite similar to Roy.'

She was probably right. Maybe Josh had inherited his quick temper from his grandpa? 'Well, I suppose genes will out!'

Marsha gave her an odd look. 'I suppose so.'

A redolent silence descended between them.

Marsha coughed softly. 'Don't you worry; your secret is safe with me.'

Sarah breathed a sigh of relief. However Marsha Hopkins had found out about Dom, at least she was going to keep quiet about it. The fewer people who knew, the better; it would keep Minnie and Josh safe from deliberately hurtful, childish taunts. 'I can't tell you how grateful I am.'

Marsha's eyes lost focus. 'I was there, you know, when they married.'

Sarah nodded. Perhaps, next time she visited her ex-parents-in-law, she would ask Sandy to point Marsha out in the wedding album? She would, no doubt, have dark hair and a slim, willowy figure.

Marsha continued, 'It was a lovely wedding. Very theatrical of course, but then you'd expect that. Alexandra wore this wonderful, high-waisted, yellow, Regency-style dress − it was really fashionable − and all of the groom's friends were dressed as Regency Gentlemen. It was a real sixties wedding, and of course a lot of them were actors. It was almost like being in a costume drama!'

Sarah nodded with more confidence; now she understood. Marsha was coming up to retirement and her memory was failing her. She must be mixing up Sandy and Roy's wedding with some other couple's wedding. Sarah was familiar with the wedding photographs and, while Marsha's description of Sandy's wedding dress was accurate enough, Roy and his friends had all been in seamen's uniform.

Marsha said, 'I was so glad when Sandy met Roy.'

Sarah nodded sympathetically.

Marsha sighed. 'It was the best thing for her; it was a godsend!'

Sarah smiled, 'And they've been very happy together.'

Marsha grunted. 'Well, I wouldn't go quite that far. What I meant was, it helped Alexandra to get over Gerald.'

Sarah frowned. Poor Marsha. 'Gerald?'

Marsha sighed. 'He was such a handsome man. I wasn't remotely surprised when Alexandra eloped with him. I was lucky to be invited to the wedding – and it was lucky for her too, really…'

Sarah felt her brain grind to a halt. What?

Marsha's voice sank even lower. 'It meant that very few people round here even knew about her marriage, so after… well; you know… she was able to come back here and start again with Roy as if nothing had happened.'

Sarah tried to whip her brain into action but it seemed to be just sitting in her head.

Marsha fell silent.

Sarah's brain began to move sluggishly: a marriage she knew nothing about? Was it true? And, if it was – was this the big family secret that no one talked about? But why? Divorce might have been a big disgrace in the nineteen-sixties, but it was hardly worthy of comment these days; and why would it cause a rift between her family and Dom's, even in the sixties?

Marsha sighed and primped her hair. 'Anyway, I just wanted you to know that your secret is safe with me. I've never mentioned Gerald to anyone in Yelmouth and I won't breathe a word about Dominic either.'

Sarah smiled noncommittally. 'Thank you, Marsha. I appreciate it.'

Marsha waved her hand. 'Don't mention it. As I said, having Minnie and Joshua in the school has been like having family. Anything I can do to help, just you let me know!'

Sarah stood up, shook Marsha's hand and made her way quickly out of the school. She needed to go somewhere quiet and time to work out if there was any truth in what Marsha Hopkins had just told her. If Sandy had indeed been married to a man called Gerald, she needed to find out more – but who could she ask? Sandy? Roy? No. Her own parents? Definitely not. Her grandparents? Maybe…

CHAPTER TEN

'He's a poor old soul!' declared Nanna Gwen. She was, as always, smartly dressed; today, she had clothed her diminutive but still sprightly body in a long, beige, tweed skirt that reached to her shins, a closely knitted brown, polo-neck sweater, over which she wore a heavy gold pendant with a large, green stone in it, and what looked like a dull green riding jacket. Her hair was tucked up in a tight bun at the back of her head and her makeup was, as ever, present, if carelessly applied.

Nanna Gwen smiled, revealing ivory teeth with a smear of lipstick and repeated, 'A poor old soul!'

Sarah smiled appreciatively. She loved her grandparents and Nanna Gwen was right: her grandfather was getting worse.

They were sitting in a small patch of her grandparents' large, overgrown garden behind their house up on Yelmouth Headland. If the garden had been tidy, they would have had a wonderful view of the sea but only a few feet of lawn had been recently mown and Nanna Gwen had hauled some ancient, folding, metal and fabric garden chairs out of an outhouse and set them up in the sunshine. It was like sitting in a forest clearing.

Sarah moved cautiously on her chair and it groaned and threatened to collapse to one side.

Next to her, Poppa Jack sat on another chair with a plaid blanket tucked around his legs. He had been losing weight recently and now his skin hung in folds from his jaw and his eyes moved continually as his fingers drummed restlessly along the edge of his blanket.

'A poor old soul, aren't you?' Nanna Gwen elaborated.

Poppa Jack chuckled and a trickle of saliva ran from the corner of his mouth.

Nanna Gwen tutted and sprang out of her chair, tissue in hand.

She wiped his chin and ruffled his hair. 'I said – you're a poor old soul, aren't you?'

Poppa Jack chuckled again, reached for her hand and kissed it.

Nanna Gwen smoothed his hair and said softly, 'Silly old sod!' She then tucked the blanket more firmly around the old man's legs and pulled her chair nearer so that she could reach him without getting up.

Sarah sighed; how much longer would her grandmother be able to care for Poppa Jack? He was eighty-seven next birthday and she was eighty-four and, although she was as fit and active as her hip allowed, it would only take a fall and a break of that hip to change everything. They were living on a knife edge; coping, but for how long? The answer to that question was probably very simple – for as long as they could.

In a way, Nanna Gwen had been born out of time. She had lived through the Second World War and had made a significant mark on the world; but if she had been born a hundred years previously, she would probably have been an empire builder and a formidable memsahib!

Poppa Jack had used his own years to advantage too. Born in the early nineteen-twenties, he had joined the Royal Navy at the end of the nineteen-thirties and, during the second war, distinguished himself and been promoted to the rank of Captain. After the war he had been given two more commands and had ended his career as Captain of an aircraft carrier. Since his retirement both he and Nanna Gwen had thrown their energies into the Church up the road in Binderfield and various Yelmouth maritime charities.

Ten years ago, Poppa Jack had received an OBE from the Queen and the Freedom of Yelmouth in recognition of his contribution to the city. Now his brain was shrinking inside his skull and he was becoming increasingly vacant.

Sarah rubbed her eyes as if they were itchy.

'Pollen?' Nanna Gwen enquired.

Sarah nodded.

'I didn't know that you suffered from hay fever,' Nanna Gwen asserted. 'If I'd known, I wouldn't have bothered to mow the lawn. Still it's good to be outside and The Captain enjoys a bit of an airing!'

Poppa Jack chuckled again.

Sarah smiled. Nanna Gwen often called Poppa Jack 'The Captain' now. It was a name he still connected with.

Nanna Gwen peered more deeply into Sarah's face and said gently; 'You know, Dear, you really should get your hair done and wear some makeup.'

Sarah smiled and said patiently, 'Why?'

Nanna Gwen flapped her hands, 'Oh; don't get me wrong; you're a beautiful girl but a beautiful girl is like a painting!'

Sarah smiled again; so, Nanna Gwen wanted to spar, did she? 'Surely only a girl wearing makeup, a *painted* girl, is like a painting?'

Nanna Gwen crowed with delight, 'Ah; no. That's where you're mistaken!'

Sarah waited.

Nanna Gwen leaned towards her and dropped her voice confidentially, 'You see: a painting might be beautiful but it looks much better in a frame. Think of your hair as your frame and makeup as the gilding.' She patted Sarah's arm; 'You're a beautiful girl but if you paid a bit more attention to your hair and wore a bit of makeup, you'd be gorgeous!'

Sarah said nothing, allowing her grandmother to win.

Nanna Gwen continued, 'And then you might meet a really nice man!'

Sarah gaped. 'Meet a man? Nanna! I'm only just divorced!'

Nanna Gwen looked unconvinced, 'Well, if you want to talk technicalities, yes — but being married to, what people of my generation would call a "queer" husband, you must have been on your own for a long time now, mustn't you? And let me tell you, the years skip along all too fast! You sort out your hair and slap on a bit of rouge and there'll be a man waiting just around the next corner; you mark my words!'

Sarah tried to cudgel her brain into action but it just sat in her head.

'Right,' Nanna Gwen said in a tone that declared that the conversation was over. She slapped her knees and sprang to her feet. 'Tea.'

Sarah moved in her chair and it creaked alarmingly.

Nanna Gwen commanded, 'No, no. You stay here and keep The Captain amused. I can manage the tea on my own!' She set off up the overgrown path, dipping to the left as she walked. She still stoutly refused to even consider a hip replacement.

Sarah watched as she disappeared inside the elegant house which she and The Captain had made their home for fifty years. Up here, on The Headland, the houses were all individual Victorian mansions set in their own acres of land. When Margaret had grown up here, they had all been private houses but now two were hotels and one was a care home for the elderly. The rest had been either divided into luxury apartments or renovated for the benefit of wealthy families. In the entire Headland area, only Nanna Gwen and Poppa Jack's house remained unrestored, and they frequently received letters from property developers enquiring if the house might be for sale.

Sarah squinted at the upper floors. A few roof tiles were missing, but there was no sign of rain coming through into the bedrooms below – yet; but how long was it since Nanna Gwen had been up there? Since she and Poppa Jack had relocated their bedroom into the downstairs dining room they had no need to climb any stairs. Sarah decided that she would have a quick look around up there later just to make sure that the house was still weather tight.

She understood why Nanna Gwen resisted moving. This was her home and this was where her memories were located but, more importantly, moving would mean sorting through, and clearing out, the antiques that crowded every room.

Sarah shook her head; Di was right; she was changing the subject – even in the privacy of her own head, she was avoiding what she knew she must do. She reached across to her grandfather and held his hand.

Poppa Jack chuckled amiably.

She glanced back towards the house and then squeezed his hand. What she was about to do might be questionable but it was the best plan that she could come up with. 'I was talking to Marsha yesterday. Do you remember Marsha?'

Poppa Jack's restless eyes connected with hers for a moment and his eyes twinkled. 'Marsha? Lovely girl!'

Sarah said, 'Well I–'

'Would have courted her myself if I'd been younger! A corker, Marsha, a corker!' His eyes wandered away again, to the house, to the trees and to his lap. He picked at his blanket in surprise.

Sarah stroked his cheek and turned his face so that he was looking at her. 'And Marsha was talking about Gerald. Gerald and Alexandra…'

His eyes locked on hers and his mouth moved.

She said, 'You remember Gerald?'

Poppa Jack said under his breath, 'That bugger…'

'Who?' Sarah asked. 'Gerald?'

His eyes lost focus and began to roam again.

'Do you remember Gerald?' Sarah asked, attempting to catch his eye.

He chuckled and fiddled with his blanket again.

'Here we are,' Nanna Gwen called. She made her way down the garden path, carrying a loaded tray, walking carefully and dipping all the way. 'Be a dear and lug the table out of the old coal-shed would you?'

Sarah eased herself out of her groaning chair, went to the coal-shed, found a battered fold-away table and brought it back. It was filthy.

'Not to worry,' pronounced Nanna Gwen. 'Everything's on the tray and, anyway, you eat a peck of dirt before you die! It's not going to do us any harm!'

She plonked the tray on the table and handed out plates. 'Cake?'

Sarah considered the dry-looking Battenberg. How long had it been sitting in the kitchen cupboard? 'Not for me thanks, Nanna. Just tea.'

Nanna Gwen paused and regarded Sarah critically. 'Not slimming are you?'

Sarah lowered her eyes. 'Just a few pounds.'

Nanna Gwen made a dismissive noise. 'Ridiculous. If anything you need to put weight on. Why do you young people have such an obsession with being thin?'

What was Sarah supposed to say? That she wasn't really on a diet? That she just didn't like the look of that cake?

Nanna Gwen poured the tea and continued, 'When I was your age, no one was on a diet.' She paused and glanced expectantly at Sarah.

Sarah smiled and prepared to duel. 'I thought that, when you were my age, food was still rationed? So when you were my age, dieting would have been irrelevant, wouldn't it?'

Nanna Gwen licked her lips, relishing the challenge. 'Not when I was your age, no. I was twenty-eight when rationing ended, so when I was *your* age we had bananas and everything else. Had done for more than ten years.' She cocked an eyebrow and waited.

Sarah said, 'There still wasn't much choice in the shops, though, was there?'

Nanna Gwen said, 'Oh yes there was. There wasn't much money, I concede that, so that was one difference between then and now, but it wasn't the main one.'

Sarah smiled. She should have known better than to cross swords with her grandmother. 'What *was* the main difference then, Nanna?'

Nanna Gwen finished pouring the tea and passed her a delicate, antique, porcelain cup and saucer. 'The main difference was that we had to go to different shops for different items.

To the baker for bread; to the grocer for vegetables; to the butcher for meat and so forth.'

Sarah took a sip of tea. 'How was that so different?'

Nanna Gwen handed a thick mug, half filled with tea, to Poppa Jack. He cradled it in both hands and sipped.

Nanna Gwen cut a slice of cake and put it on Poppa Jack's plate, 'For a start, it meant that we walked a lot more than you do, and because none of us had refrigerators, we shopped every day – so we walked a heck of a lot more than you do; and we carried the bags instead of sticking them in a car.'

Sarah nodded. That would, indeed, make a difference to everyone's fitness levels.

Nanna Gwen cut a slice of cake for herself, took a bite, made a face, dunked it in her tea and took a second bite. 'But the main difference is that we were served; by shop assistants.'

Sarah frowned. 'I don't see that as much of a difference.'

Nanna Gwen smiled easily. 'Think about it. When you go shopping today, you go to the supermarket and you dump everything you want in your trolley. Then, when you get to the check-out, the goods go through and you pay for them.'

Sarah frowned again. 'So?'

Nanna Gwen held up her finger as if to command silence, 'So; we were served by shop assistants and we queued to be served. We told the shop assistant what we wanted, they fetched it for us, and everyone heard. We all knew one another.'

Sarah said, 'I still don't see–'

Nanna Gwen continued, 'If someone asked for ten bars of chocolate, the shop assistant, or someone in the queue, would have asked, "Oh. Are your grandchildren visiting?" or something like that. If you'd said, "No; they're all for me," as soon as you left the shop everyone would have gossiped about what a pig you were, and the next day, when you went in for something else, the shop assistant would have made some sarcastic comment and everyone would have tittered. These days, you can buy stupid food and no one holds you to account!'

Sarah nodded, 'I'm sure you're right.'

Nanna Gwen nodded back. She looked very pleased. She dunked Poppa Jack's cake for him and offered it to him. 'So what were you two chatting about while I was making the tea?'

Sarah said, 'Oh, nothing mu–'

Cake flew everywhere as Poppa Jack spoke. 'That bugger, Gerald Bailey!'

'Who?' Nanna Gwen asked faintly.

Poppa Jack chuckled and sipped from his mug.

Nanna Gwen looked uneasy and glanced guiltily at Sarah.

Sarah shrugged and made a face.

Nanna Gwen relaxed and ruffled Poppa Jack's hair. 'Poor old soul! What goes on in that head of yours, eh? What goes on?'

Poppa Jack chuckled and pushed some cake crumbs around his blanket.

Sarah said nothing. She still wasn't sure about asking Poppa Jack about Gerald; it felt like taking advantage of his condition but she was glad that she had. There was still a lot that she didn't know, but Poppa Jack knew a man called Gerald and he didn't seem to like him very much. That, in itself, meant little. Gerald could have been anyone – a sailor in one of his crews, an old acquaintance, anyone.

What *did* mean something, though, was the way that Nanna Gwen had reacted to the name and the way she had glanced at Sarah. That brief glance had spoken volumes: she knew Gerald and didn't want Sarah to hear the name. In all probability, Marsha Hopkins' memory was fine; Sandy had been married twice and now, thanks to Poppa Jack, Sarah had a full name: Gerald Bailey.

The real question, though, was: how had Gerald Bailey managed to divide two families so completely?

CHAPTER ELEVEN

'Just hold that open a bit wider, would you?' Margaret asked.

Minnie dutifully pulled the neck of the green plastic sack open to its fullest extent.

'That's better,' Margaret grunted. She turned her attention to Sarah; 'Now shove it all in there.'

Sarah collected up handfuls of dead plants and old flower heads and deposited them in the bag.

'That's right,' Margaret said. She sat back on her shooting-stick. 'Keep going and we'll get the garden tidy in no time!'

Sarah glanced at her mother; they'd get it tidy even more quickly if she actually helped and didn't just give orders! She filled the green sack and Minnie tied up the top.

'That's another one,' Margaret said with satisfaction. 'Take it round to the front and we'll be almost ready for another trip to the tip!'

Minnie hefted the sack.

Sarah asked, 'Can you manage?'

Minnie nodded, 'It's quite light. I'll do this one.' She set off, round the corner of her grandparents' house, kicking the bag as if it was a ball on a string.

'She's a good girl,' Margaret declared.

Sarah pulled out a tissue and blew her nose. Was that a criticism? Was it a way of saying that Sarah wasn't? She glanced down the garden; Josh was helping his grandpa set a new fence post in concrete; clearly, in Terry's view, fencing was man's work while shifting rubbish was a task for women…

Margaret's shooting-stick creaked as she settled herself more comfortably. 'It's good to do things as a family.'

Sarah sighed; that was as near to thanks as her mother was likely to get.

Margaret continued, 'We always used to do the gardening as a family when you were little; when Terry was on leave.'

Sarah nodded; they did. At least, she and her dad did what Margaret told them to do… her mother, of course, was always struggling with something medical that precluded her from doing any actual work!

Margaret nodded significantly, 'Family is *very* important!'

Sarah nodded; it was. She glanced around the familiar garden and back towards the plain, semi-detached house where she had lived for so many years. There were memories everywhere, but now, as Counsellor Di had helped her to see, they were not as happy as she had thought they were. It was hard to remember the truth and she was sure that her parents loved her but, somehow, they were not able to relate to her as an adult.

She stared at the house; it was much smaller than the house of her memories and, in reality, it was nothing like as imposing as her own house in Twisle Drift, let alone Nanna and Poppa's house up on The Headland. How did Margaret feel about that? Moving from such grandeur to a very ordinary road where bow-fronted windows and a garage at the side of the house were once regarded as an achievement by those on the social rise? It probably explained why she demeaned the Prices even though their house was not much smaller than hers. This house was in a better street, though, and had been built for owner-occupiers. It must gall Margaret that some of the neighbouring houses were now private rentals.

Minnie came back around the house and Sarah said, 'You're right; family *is* important. That's why I've told Sandy and Roy that they're still the childrens' grandparents too.'

Margaret glared sourly but pointed to the roll of green garden sacks, 'Just tear off another one and open it up.'

Minnie did as she was told and Sarah filled it up with the last of the debris. Minnie trailed off with it, towards the front of the house.

Margaret lowered her voice. 'It won't come to any good, you know.'

Sarah pushed some stray hair away from her nose. 'What won't?'

'Mixing with those Prices,' Margaret answered.

Sarah sighed.

Margaret continued, 'You won't get anything from them, you know.'

Sarah picked up the roll of green bags. 'I don't *want* anything from them. All I want is for them not to lose touch with their grandchildren.'

Margaret grunted, stood up and collapsed the seat of the shooting-stick. 'You're too soft, you know. Too soft.'

Sarah watched as her dad and Josh held a spirit level against the new post and adjusted it. She took a deep breath and said quietly, 'You've never liked them, have you?'

Margaret went very still and said heavily, 'I beg your pardon?'

Sarah faced her. 'Mum, I'm not a little girl any more. You've never liked them, have you?'

Margaret considered her and then, using her shooting-stick as a support, leant on it. 'To be honest; no, I haven't.'

Sarah frowned, 'But why? You were friends with Sandy when you were young, weren't you?'

Minnie came back around the house and Margaret said, 'Go and help Grandpa and Josh with the fence, would you? Your mummy and I will take the bags to the tip.'

Sarah blinked in surprise, 'We will?'

Margaret was already striding away from her. 'Come on.'

Sarah followed her mother to the front of the house, loaded up the car with the bags of garden waste and set off for the tip.

Margaret shifted in the passenger seat and demanded, 'Now then, what's all this about?'

Sarah concentrated on the road rather than on her mother; what was the best way to navigate this conversation? She said hesitantly, 'The thing is; now that Dom and I have split up, I've discovered that I'm pretty hazy about the family history and Poppa Jack said something that didn't make much sense.'

Margaret became very still. 'Oh?'

Sarah nodded and changed gear. 'I mean, I know that Dad and Roy were best mates when they were at sea, and the way Poppa Jack talked about them, it just seemed really weird that they never see each other now…'

Margaret sighed heavily, 'These things happen. People fall out. And anyway, you shouldn't set much store by what Poppa Jack says; he gets all sorts of ideas, these days.'

Sarah pulled up at a junction. 'But even if you ignore what Poppa Jack says, I always got the impression that you and Sandy were good friends; once…'

Margaret said in surprise, 'Really?'

Sarah nodded.

Margaret cleared her throat, 'I don't know why. We never knew each other at all. I only met her when she got her claws into Roy. I knew him, of course, through Terry.'

Sarah glanced at her mother but she was looking out of the side window.

Margaret's breath fogged the glass as she said, 'I don't know anything much about her and, to be honest, I don't want to. Even Terry saw sense and ditched Roy.'

Sarah frowned. Had her dad 'ditched' his best friend because Margaret had told him to? She pulled into the tip entrance and stopped beside the garden-waste bin.

Margaret sighed heavily. 'If you must know, your father and Roy fell out over a matter of the heart!'

Sarah stared at her mother who turned her head and dropped her eyes demurely.

Sarah's eyes widened. 'Over you?'

Margaret simpered, 'I *was* something of a beauty, you know!'

Sarah blew out her cheeks. Good God! 'Let me just get rid of this rubbish.' She got out of the car and emptied the plastic sacks into the garden-waste bin. When she'd finished, she shoved the empty sacks in the boot, got back into the car and they returned to her parents' house in silence.

As she negotiated the route, Sarah put the pieces together in her head. Had Roy married Sandy after being rejected by Margaret? Was he on the rebound? That would explain their stormy marriage. It also explained why her dad and Roy had fallen out; and why neither family were exactly over the moon when she and Dom began seeing each other. It was also entirely possible that none of them, apart from Sandy, knew anything about Gerald Bailey…

They arrived back at Margaret's house and Sarah smiled at her mother. 'Thank you for telling me.'

Margaret smiled tentatively, 'Well. Perhaps it was time that you knew?'

Sarah smiled back. 'It's just a pity that there's still bad blood between you; after all these years.'

Margaret's smile hardened. 'You be careful of that Roy Price. He was a bad boy and he's a bad man. Sandy Price is just as bad as him, too. You be careful!'

Sarah avoided her mother's gaze and got out of the car.

Margaret used the shooting-stick for support as she heaved herself out of the other side. 'You mark my words,' she said across the car roof.

'What words would those be?' Terry asked lightly as he appeared around the side of the house.

Sarah said, 'Mum's been telling me about how you and Roy were rivals in love!'

Terry came to an abrupt halt, as if he'd walked into a brick wall.

Sarah smiled, 'But it was you who married the girl, not him.'

He glanced quickly at Margaret and she held his gaze steadily.

He glanced furtively at Sarah, then smiled and nodded.

Margaret set off towards the back garden, 'Let's get some tea, and I think I've got some chocolate wafers for the children somewhere.'

Something in those looks and glances was nudging at Sarah but she ignored it, joined her father and squeezed his hand. 'I'm sorry about you and Roy.'

Terry looked quickly away.

She squeezed his hand again. 'You know; over Mum.'

He gradually relaxed. 'These things happen. People fall out.'

Sarah felt suddenly so uncertain that she almost stumbled. Her father had just parroted the same phrases that her mother had used and his cautious reaction, together with his probable collusion with Margaret, told its own story. There was something big he wasn't telling her!

'Are you all right?' Terry asked.

Sarah forced herself to be normal. 'Just a trip – there must be an uneven flagstone.'

Her father stopped and examined the path. 'I can't see one…'

Sarah said, 'Must be my ankle, then; after driving to the tip. Probably a touch of cramp.'

He straightened up and offered her his arm. 'Let's get you into the kitchen then. We can put some hot water in a bowl and you can sit with your foot in it.'

Sarah took his arm gratefully and let him support her as she hobbled unnecessarily towards the back of his house. If she pretended to be smitten with cramp, it would disguise the thoughts that were racing around in her head. She needed time to think.

Her mother had, apparently, revealed to her that Terry and Roy had both fallen in love with her, and that it had been this love that had ended their friendship. Her unspoken communications with her father, though, had revealed something else and his actions had spoken more eloquently than his wife's words. Sarah had absolutely no doubt that her mother's supposed revelation was nothing more than a pack of lies.

Whichever way Sarah looked at it, she couldn't see that it was Margaret who had been the cause of the animosity between her dad and Roy; it was much more likely to have been Sandy, and if that was true, then it probably had something to do with Gerald Bailey too. No; whatever her mother had said, Gerald Bailey was at the heart of whatever had happened and Sarah was going to find out what.

CHAPTER TWELVE

Sarah waited while Di formulated her next question. The attic room seemed very familiar now and she felt completely relaxed. This week they had been talking about the domestic chores that filled her days.

Di said, 'Given that you've dedicated your life to domesticity, you don't talk much about it.'

Sarah said in surprise, 'I have today!'

Di smiled. 'Only because I asked you – and only because I kept on asking every time you changed the subject.'

Sarah shrugged. 'Well it's not as if cooking and cleaning are exactly interesting is it?'

Di laughed. 'I suppose not – but, as I say, you've devoted yourself to your family.'

Sarah sat up. 'Well, that's the point, isn't it? It's Josh and Minnie who matter, so I do it for them.'

'And for Dom?' Di asked.

Sarah shrugged again, 'Of course.'

'And now that he's gone?' Di persisted.

Sarah scratched her ear. The session had been very dull. What was interesting about washing clothes and scrubbing sinks?

Di sat forward. 'And now that he's gone, do you still feel the same?'

Sarah shifted impatiently. 'It's not a question of how I feel, it's about what needs doing. The house needs cleaning; the children need looking after; end of story.'

Di said, 'And yet, there are many couples who share those tasks, and many women who have their own careers as well as doing their share at home.'

There were also couples who divided up the tasks with one partner earning the money and the other looking after the home.

Sarah grunted.

Di leaned even further forward. 'What?'

Sarah sighed. 'I was about to quote Dom.'

Di sat back in her chair. 'And?'

Sarah smiled, 'And I'll need to think about that.'

Di ducked her head. 'Don't forget to work out how you feel!'

Sarah laughed, 'No, Miss!'

Di bristled.

Sarah said quickly, 'Oh, I'm sorry – I just meant that this was a bit like being back at school; you know, when the teacher tells you what to do?'

Di's shoulders eased and her invisible feathers seemed to smooth back into place.

Sarah made a mental note not to mention her counsellor's marital status again.

Di said, 'And now that things are different for you?'

'Now that I'm, er, a lone parent?' Sarah offered. That was close, she had almost said *single* parent...

Di nodded, 'Maybe this is an aspect of your life that you could think about?'

Sarah nodded in agreement to pacify Di. In reality though, how could she make any changes? It wasn't as if she'd had a career before she met Dom. She'd had jobs but Dom's work had been a vocation and, now that he was paying the bills for the children, would he pull the financial plug if she got a job? And, when it came right down to it, did she want one?

Di asked, 'Did you discuss any of this five years ago?'

Sarah shook her head. Five years ago Dom had announced that he was unhappy so Sarah had suggested Marriage Counselling. 'No. After an exploratory session our counsellor said that, because Dom was so busy with work, and because I was so busy with the children, what we needed to do was to reconnect sexually.'

Di made a note, 'You mean sex therapy?'

Sarah nodded.

Di asked, 'And what did Dom say to that?'

Sarah smiled wryly. 'At the time he agreed, but once we got home he cancelled the sessions and bought a book. We did it ourselves.'

'Did what?' Di asked.

Sarah could feel her cheeks and neck beginning to glow, 'Oh, you know. No sex at all for two weeks – we just went on dates and chatted. Then we held hands for a week, then we kissed, then we massaged each other in turns with scented oils – and so on and so forth until the final consummation two months later.'

'And was it?' Di asked.

'Was it what?' Sarah countered.

'A consummation?'

Tears began to arrive so Sarah said quickly, 'Actually, it was. It was wonderful.'

Di said, 'For how long?'

Sarah laughed ironically, 'Just that once!'

'And then?' Di asked gently.

Sarah took a deep breath, 'And then nothing. After two months, we had that one, wonderful night and I had such hope; and then nothing. If anything, I saw Dom even less than before.'

'And how did that make you feel?'

Sarah slumped back in her chair. 'I didn't know what to feel.'

Di ducked her head. 'And what did you *think*?'

Sarah gazed at the coffee table. 'I thought it was my fault.'

Di said, 'And what did you do?'

Sarah sighed. 'I coped.'

'By cooking and cleaning and making excuses for him?'

Sarah nodded, 'I guess.'

Di said, 'I'd like to meet Dom...'

Sarah sat up horrified.

Di held up her hand, 'I don't mean that I ever will or that I want to make an appointment! I was just thinking out loud.'

Sarah sat back with relief.

Di consulted her notes. 'So; we've talked about the middle years of your marriage and how you related as a couple.'

Sarah relaxed into her chair.

Di said, 'You know, I really think that it would be beneficial if you invested a bit of thought in the future and what you want out of life.'

Sarah said nothing.

Di continued, 'I know that most of us never really get what we want and just muddle through but it may help you to focus.'

Had Di just described herself? Did she just muddle through life without a plan?

Di said, 'Or you could think about Minnie; if she grows up and marries someone and then devotes herself to her home, will you feel that she's spent her life well?'

Sarah sat up. That was a good question and one she needed time to think about.

Di looked at her watch. 'We have a few minutes to spare – is there anything else you want to talk about?'

Sarah cleared her throat. 'Actually, there is.'

Di smiled encouragingly.

Sarah said, 'You know I told you about the big bust-up between my family and Dom's family?'

Di nodded.

Sarah said. 'Well I may have made some progress. I think that Dom's mother was married to someone before she married his dad. No one's ever said anything about it, which makes me suspect that it may be the reason for the fall-out.'

Di considered this. 'It's possible; but it could be equally possible that the first marriage was the result of the fall-out rather than the cause of it, or nothing to do with it at all.'

Sarah nodded slowly. There were, indeed, many possibilities.

Di asked, 'Have you talked to your parents about it?'

Sarah shook her head. 'I tried.'

Di raised her eyebrows.

Sarah said defensively, 'I know. Some families talk about everything, but mine doesn't. Dom's doesn't either.'

Di sighed, 'Which is, kind of, why you're here, isn't it? Your tendency to have conversations in your head instead of out loud? *As if* you've talked, when, in reality, you haven't said anything?'

Sarah felt as if she'd been kicked in the chest. Di was right – how had she never seen it before? It was through not talking that she and Dom had married. It was through not talking that she had accepted his views about their relationship. It was through not talking that she had failed to notice his sexuality and it was through not talking that she had accepted the divorce settlement and the life she now lived.

The truth hit her, hard. If Dom was the master of not talking then she was the mistress, and she had learned not to talk from her parents, just as he had learned from his.

Di leaned forward curiously. 'What?'

Sarah said, 'This family thing. I've just realised how important it is.'

Di laughed, 'There you go again! Whoomph-woosh with your emotions!'

Sarah made a face. 'Yes, well. This family thing, though. I can't ask anyone, so how do I find out more about Dom's mother's first husband?'

Di said, 'If you think it's important, do what everyone else does. Go to the library and browse through the marriage records, see what you can find reported in the local paper and see if there's anything online.'

Sarah said, '*But*? It sounds like there's a "but" in there?'

Di laughed easily. 'But you may find that digging up the past is a false trail. The issue for *you* is not really about what happened to other people; it's about what's happened to *you*. If you go off chasing your family history it may just become an elaborate way of changing the subject – and as we both know, you are very, very good at that. My advice is that you leave the past alone and concentrate on the here and now. It may be more painful but it's what you have to do. Think of it as this session's "layer" to explore: the here and now!'

Sarah nodded meekly. 'I'm sure you're right.'

Di collected her papers together. It was the signal that the session was over.

Sarah followed her counsellor downstairs, said her farewells and left the terraced house. As she sat in her car, ready to drive home, she considered the week ahead. Di had given her good advice but good advice wasn't the same as correct advice. Di's advice might be good, but it was also completely wrong. Tomorrow she would visit the library.

CHAPTER THIRTEEN

Sarah trundled her empty wheelie bin back up the drive and shoved it onto the flagstone area where it would sit until the next rubbish collection in a fortnight's time.

'Hello,' said Neil from next door.

Sarah startled and glared at the fence that continued where the front hedge ended. She could just see his eyes above the wooden panel.

'Sorry,' he said. 'Did I make you jump?'

Sarah grinned, 'A bit. I was miles away!'

He shifted his position and his eyes disappeared. A plastic bag rustled and the contents chinked and rattled. His voice said, 'Have I missed the bin men?'

She answered, 'For household rubbish, yes. They only come once a fortnight. Next week it's paper, cans and plastic. You should have a leaflet?'

Neil's eyes reappeared above the fence. 'I probably have—' There was a soft ripping sound followed by a clatter. His head disappeared and she was treated to some gentle but heartfelt swearing.

Sarah grinned and called through the fence, 'Would you like to see my leaflet? I can rustle up some coffee if you're not too busy?'

She could hear the sounds of cans and bottles being picked up.

His eyes reappeared. 'Thanks, I could do with a break. Give me a few minutes to clear up and I'll be round.'

His head disappeared again and she left to the sound of him muttering and cans clattering.

A few minutes later her doorbell rang and she scurried down the hall.

Neil grinned and handed her a small posy of flowers. 'Hello. I thought you might like these.'

'Thank you.' She ushered him into the kitchen. Flowers? Was that thoughtful or pushy and inappropriate?

He sat down at her kitchen table. 'I found them up at the top of the garden where no one sees them. I've put some on my desk and I thought that you might like a few.'

Sarah relaxed. Appropriate. 'Thank you.'

She handed him a sheet of laminated paper. 'Here's the information about the bins.'

He took it and grinned, 'And they say romance is dead!'

Sarah said nothing. He had nice teeth and kind eyes but why was he talking about romance? She busied herself by finding a small vase and arranging the posy as she watched him out of the corner of her eye; he read the leaflet, pulled out his phone and tapped the screen.

'There,' he said. 'I've logged onto the website. I'll download the leaflet myself later.' He put the laminated sheet down on the table. It slid to the edge and stopped.

Sarah poured two mugs of coffee, handed him one and sat down across from him.

He took an appreciative sip and looked around the kitchen. 'Have you lived here long?'

Sarah said, 'Nearly eleven years. We had the kitchen and bathroom replaced a couple of years ago but we moved in just after we were married.'

There was an awkward pause before he said, 'And now you're not…'

Sarah exhaled loudly. 'I've been divorced for a couple of months now…'

He nodded and sipped his coffee. 'You mentioned it, when we first met, so I thought it must be fairly recent.'

Sarah blinked. 'Really? What made you think that?'

He smiled kindly. 'Well, divorce is a kind of bereavement, isn't it? And when you're first bereaved it's hard to know how much to say. New territory and all that.'

Sarah considered this. 'I guess.'

He nodded again. 'A close friend of mine was divorced after fifteen years of marriage. It was very much like bereavement.'

Sarah sipped her coffee. A close friend. Would that be a close female friend? The sort who visited at weekends?

He stared into his mug. 'Yes, it was terrible for him. Just like a bereavement.'

Sarah considered him across the top of her own mug. He was well groomed, he looked as if he visited the gym regularly and his clothes were beautifully tailored. A bit like Dom. Was his divorced male friend the sort of male friend who was more than just a friend?

He put his mug down on the table. 'Do you like it here?'

Sarah shrugged. 'It's okay.'

He pulled the handle of his mug and it spun slowly on the table. 'But?'

Sarah laughed. 'But it was Dom, that's my ex-husband, who wanted to live here, not me. I mean, don't get me wrong, it's a nice enough place to live but some of the neighbours can be a bit, well, pleased with themselves, if you know what I mean.'

Neil smiled. 'Twisle Drift – an address to aspire to?'

Sarah winced, 'Sorry – you've just moved in…'

He waved his hand dismissively. 'Actually I'm just renting while I look around the area. Will you stay? Now that your divorce has come through?'

Sarah put her own mug down and sat back. 'You're very direct, aren't you? But yes, I'll stay. I have the children to think of.'

He smiled. 'They're great kids. I was chatting to them the other day over the fence. Minnie seems very bright and Josh is really funny!'

A shard of ice materialised in Sarah's gut. She knew nothing about her new neighbour. He looked respectable but why had he been talking to her children behind her back? He lived in a big house all on his own. Did he plan to invite her children in for shared secrets?

He swirled the coffee in his cup. 'My daughter wasn't much older than Minnie when she died.'

Sarah felt her brain go limp.

He swirled his coffee again. 'My wife was driving and they were both killed.'

The shard of ice turned into a hot ball of shame. 'I'm so sorry; I had no idea.'

He looked up and smiled. 'It was five years ago now so I've been putting my energies into work.'

Sarah seized the opportunity to talk about something else. 'What do you do?'

'I work for *Calvi*,' he said.

Something buzzed in her head.

He smiled. 'I'll let you have some samples if you like. I always have a few knocking around.'

The buzz in her head clicked. No wonder he looked familiar. 'Your surname isn't, by any chance, Godley, is it?'

He ducked his head and grinned. 'It is.'

She blew out her cheeks, 'I'd hardly call owning and running one of the biggest cosmetic corporations in Europe "working for"!'

He made a face. 'You'd be surprised…' He finished his coffee and checked his watch. 'In fact, there's a case in point. I'm afraid I have to get back to work. Well look, thank you for the coffee.'

She stood up with him and walked him to the front door.

He said, 'Thanks for the info about the bins, and thanks for the chat.'

She opened the door. Now that she knew who he was, she wasn't sure what to say.

He hovered on the doorstep. 'So, what are you up to for the rest of the day?'

Was he going to ask to see her later? Was he interested in her? They had certainly had an unusually intimate conversation. 'I'm going to the library. I want to find out a bit more about my family tree.'

He smiled. 'Sounds fun. Hope you find a pirate!'

She smiled back, 'I probably will!'

He waved and walked away.

She shut the door. Of course he wasn't interested in her; he was probably just being neighbourly.

The librarian put her hands on either side of the screen and said, in an accent Sarah couldn't identify, 'It's an old microfiche system, I'm afraid. You twist this to scroll left and right, and this to scroll up and down.' She demonstrated the controls. 'Now you try.'

Sarah grasped the two knobs. She twisted and information blurred past on the screen.

The librarian said, 'You need to be gentle. We're gradually getting everything onto the computers but the local papers are still on microfiche. If you get stuck, just come and find me.'

The librarian walked away and Sarah reran the woman's accent in her head. Was she Scandinavian? She shrugged and looked around her. Yelmouth library had been purpose built in the eighteen-fifties. From outside it looked more like a cathedral than a civic building and, inside, the illusion continued as high, vaulted spaces and large, arched windows encouraged hushed reverence. Sarah was sitting at one of four tables, each of which had a different machine on it, in a comparatively small room adjoining the palatial reference section while, around her, shelves with some very large books, legers and files lined the walls. She twisted the controls in front of her cautiously, quickly found what she was looking for and began to read. She began with the first edition of the local Yelmouth newspaper for January nineteen sixty-six.

She had already searched online and found a marriage certificate for Alexandra Celia Grant and Gerald Osmond Bailey. They were married in North London on February the eleventh, nineteen sixty-seven and the certificate noted Sandy's occupation as a 'dancer', which was news to Sarah, and Gerald's as an 'actor'. That tied in with Marsha Hopkins' description of the wedding as 'theatrical' so Sandy had probably met Gerald when he performed at Yelmouth Hippodrome some time during the previous year. It also tied in with her theory that Roy and Terry had fallen out over Sandy, not Margaret. If Terry had loved Sandy, but she had run off with Gerald in nineteen sixty-seven, and Terry had married Margaret on the rebound in nineteen sixty-eight, then Terry may have had very negative feelings about his best friend being free to marry Sandy when her marriage to Gerald collapsed.

She twiddled the knobs and started to skim-read January through to February. In early March a picture caught her eye. Poppa Jack and Nanna Gwen smiled out of the newspaper photograph. He was dressed in full uniform and she was wearing a duster coat. They looked like film stars and they must have been about the same age that Sarah was now, or maybe a little older. The article was about Poppa Jack's new commission and the aircraft carrier he would command.

Sarah smiled. She must ask the librarian if it was possible to get printed copies.

She twiddled the knobs and March came and went but there was nothing of interest. Then April, May, June and July. The newspaper recorded births, deaths, marriages, church bazaars, children's activities and various plays and musicals at the Hippodrome Theatre. There was no mention at all of Gerald Bailey, though.

She soldiered on through August and September but by the time she was half way through October she was having serious doubts. What if Counsellor Di was right? Maybe this *was* a wild goose chase? Should she put her energy into the present, not the past?

She started to skim-read her way through November and then stopped and leaned forward. There it was. The *Pentonville Players* had wowed audiences at the Hippodrome with their interpretation of Macbeth during the Shakespeare Festival. The review was very flattering but it was the photo that captured Sarah's attention; it was of a young man, dressed in a doublet and posing with a dagger held evocatively before his eyes. The caption read: 'Gerald Bailey – a magnificent Macbeth'.

Sarah sat back and stared at the screen; so that was Gerald Bailey. He was real, he was heartbreakingly handsome and Sandy had fallen in love with him. He was evidently a respectable and well thought of Shakespearean actor, though, so why had she eloped with him? Why had they not simply married?

Perhaps there was a clue in the name: 'Pentonville Players'? Did they come from that area of London or were they connected with the prison? If Gerald and the others were ex-convicts, then Sandy's parents might be against the marriage and that would explain why they eloped. The date of the marriage had to be significant too. The wedding had taken place one week after Sandy's twenty-first birthday, the first week in which she could marry without her parents' consent. She had married Gerald as soon as it was legally possible and, as seemed likely, only three months after meeting him.

Perhaps Marsha's use of the word 'elope' was just romantic? Perhaps they had simply married in the face of opposition from her family as soon as Sandy had come of age? Maybe it was just a case of marrying where Gerald lived rather than of 'eloping'?

Sarah considered the facts. Sandy and Gerald had fallen in love. There had probably been some family opposition. They had married anyway. It was hardly earth-shattering and it wasn't so very different to her own story. She and Dom had fallen in love – well, she had fallen in love with Dom – and their families had opposed the relationship. They had married anyway and the marriage had ended in divorce. The two stories were almost identical.

Sarah tapped her teeth with her finger nail. There was a proverb about that, wasn't there? Something about the sins of the parents falling on the children?

She checked her watch and startled. She had been so engrossed in her search that she had lost track of time. She needed to get a move on if she was going to collect Josh and Minnie from school.

She gathered up her things, walked through to the large, high ceilinged reception area, thanked the librarian and hurried out into the car park.

Counsellor Di was right. There was nothing in the past that was any different to the present. She knew that now. It was just the same story all over again. She would concentrate on the present and try and work out how she felt about Dom.

She had almost reached her car when a new thought hit her with such force that she almost dropped her bag. Actually, no; her marriage to Dom was nothing like Sandy's marriage to Gerald. Her marriage to Dom had been public knowledge, but no one talked about Sandy and Gerald. The silence meant something and the look on Nanna Gwen's face when Poppa Jack had mentioned Gerald's name confirmed just how important that silence was.

Counsellor Di was right when she said that while some families talked about things that mattered, her family didn't, but she was wrong when she said that the past was unimportant. When something mattered so much that absolutely no one in her family talked about it – it mattered. It really, really mattered.

So what had happened?

Why was Sandy's marriage to Gerald such a big secret?

Sarah was going to find out!

CHAPTER FOURTEEN

Sandy's makeup was, as always, both subtle and immaculate. Should Sarah ask her for some tips? Nanna Gwen seemed to think that makeup was important; maybe Sandy could help?

Sandy turned away and shot a meaningful glance through her small kitchen window.

Sarah sighed inside; this wasn't the best time to talk about makeup, was it? Or to ask Sandy about her career as a dancer! As soon as Sarah had arrived, Roy had remembered that he had some important task to complete in his garden. He was now marching about out there with a wheelbarrow.

Sandy said, 'I'm sorry about Roy. Sometimes he only opens his mouth to change feet!'

Sarah shrugged. 'I know. I'm used to it.'

Sandy sighed, sat down, and pushed a plate of large cookies, embedded with three types of chocolate, across the table. 'Help yourself. You look like you need a bit of feeding up.'

Sarah took one and nibbled it politely before laying it down on her plate. She would palm it into her bag when Sandy wasn't looking and share it with Josh and Minnie later.

Sandy bit into a cookie and said, 'So Josh is in the school play?'

Sarah smiled. 'Yes. They're doing The Wizard of Oz, and his teacher thinks that he will make a good Tin Man.'

Sandy ate some more cookie. 'I should think he'll be the star of the show!'

Sarah mumbled in vague agreement. 'It'll be a good thing for him; he's been finding school quite hard since Dom left.'

Sandy put down her cookie. She looked as if she had indigestion.

Sarah watched Sandy and said, 'Mrs Hopkins has been very kind to him.'

Sandy wiped her mouth with her handkerchief. 'Who?'

Sarah continued to watch her as she answered, 'Josh's Head teacher; Marsha Hopkins.'

'Oh,' Sandy said disinterestedly. 'Do we have to make the costume?'

'What?' Sarah said.

Sandy grinned. 'Keep up! The costume; for the Tin Man! Do we have to make it?'

Sarah considered her cookie. 'No. The school will do all that. All we have to do is help him to learn his lines and then go to the performance and applaud in the right places.'

Sandy reached for the remains of her cookie. 'Dom always played the lead, you know. In his school plays.'

Sarah smiled. 'I know.'

'He was always fantastic. Star of the show!'

Sarah said again, 'I know.'

Sandy glanced at her. 'Oh – has he told you?'

Sarah frowned. 'Not exactly. I was there?'

Sandy's eyebrows shot up in surprise. 'Were you?'

'Of course I was,' Sarah said firmly. 'I was at school with Dom!'

Sandy laughed briefly. 'So you were. Were you in the plays too?'

Sarah smiled wryly. 'Sometimes. Third milkmaid from the left – that sort of thing.'

'How nice,' muttered Sandy wistfully. 'And now Josh is treading the boards too...'

'It's only the school play,' Sarah offered.

Sandy ignored her and stared out of the window. 'So like his father...'

'I suppose so.' Sarah slipped the cookie into her bag.

Sandy glanced sideways at her and then asked casually, 'What did Roy say, anyway? The last time you were here?'

Sarah picked up a crumb with her finger and nibbled it. 'Hasn't he said?'

Sandy flustered and finished her cookie. 'Well of course! I just wondered what you made of it?'

So. He hadn't said anything.

Sandy continued, 'What one person says isn't always what another person hears…'

Sarah smiled. 'He was just worried that he might not see so much of the children – now that Dom and I are divorced.'

Sandy nodded thoughtfully. 'He's been quite anxious.'

Silence descended and Sarah let it lie.

Sandy nodded again. 'The thing is, Sarah, it's not an easy situation. I mean, from my point of view, Dom's my son. Whatever he does; he'll always be my son. I understand why Roy's so anxious.'

Something nudged Sarah's brain but it was elusive so she ignored it. 'Me too, but he doesn't need to be.'

Sandy made a face. 'He's also a bit of an idiot, but everything will sort itself out; it always does.'

Was that true? Was that really true?

'Anyway, it's nice of you to call in and apologise,' Sandy said. 'I appreciate it.'

Sarah kept her face blank and nibbled another crumb. 'Actually, there's something I wanted to ask you.'

Sandy reached for another cookie. 'Oh yes?'

'About divorce,' Sarah said.

Sandy's hand wavered. 'Oh yes?'

'And remarriage,' Sarah said.

Sandy withdrew her hand without taking the cookie. 'It's a bit early for you to be thinking that way, isn't it?'

Sarah shook her head. 'Not me. I don't suppose anyone would want me even if I was interested. I was just wondering about you, and your family. Now that we're, sort of, not related any more, I realise that I don't know much about your side of the family. Is there any history of divorce and remarriage?'

Sandy shook her head firmly. 'Not that I know of.'

Sarah leaned her elbows on the table. 'You'd tell me if there was, wouldn't you?'

Sandy glanced sharply at her. 'That's rather offensive. What are you getting at, exactly?'

Sarah avoided her gaze. 'It was just something someone said.'

'Who – and what did they say?' Sandy demanded.

Sarah said, 'It doesn't matter who, but they said that you were divorced and that when you remarried, you married Roy.'

The atmosphere in the kitchen hardened to an unpleasant edge.

Sandy cleared her throat. 'Well! I don't know who's been spreading malicious tittle-tattle but let me tell you: I have never been divorced! Never!'

Sarah met her ex-mother-in-law's eye.

Sandy said icily, 'And if that's the sort of thing you said to Roy, I'm not surprised that he lost his temper with you! You need to sort yourself out, young lady!'

Sarah dropped her eyes. She wasn't a young lady; she was thirty-nine – but right now she might as well be a toddler. 'Sorry Sandy. I just needed to ask.'

Sandy's tone warmed slightly. 'Apology accepted, but you need to think about what you say before you say it! I know you've been through a lot, but so have we. A few manners wouldn't go amiss, you know.'

Sarah mumbled, 'Sorry.'

Sandy's tone warmed again. 'Let's forget it! All in the past! Let's leave it where it belongs! Now, tell me about Josh and this school play.'

Sarah did as she was asked but her mind was elsewhere. She had listened carefully to Sandy's denial of a previous marriage, and her words, and indignation, had carried the ring of truth.

Sarah had also watched Sandy's eyes, and they had lied.

'That doesn't sound very good,' Terry insisted from the comfort of his favourite armchair. His tone made it very clear that this was *his* sitting room in *his* house and therefore *his* domain.

Sarah regretted mentioning Josh's recent brush with the school discipline policy. She should have waited until her parents visited her at Twisle Drift but she continued determinedly, 'He's just upset about his daddy leaving and moving in with someone else. It makes him behave badly. He doesn't even know why he's doing it.'

Terry snorted. 'Two separate things, if you ask me. Two separate things!'

Sarah asked, baffled, 'What are?'

'What your husband has done and the way Josh is behaving,' he asserted. 'Two completely different things!'

Sarah sighed, 'Dad, I don't think I quite–'

'Look,' Terry interrupted. 'Dom's buggered off with this man. Literally. Well let me tell you, back in *my* day, we would have sorted that out!'

'I'm not sure that I–' Sarah tried.

Her father warmed to his theme, 'You lot today! You let anyone ride rough-shod all over you! Well let me tell you–'

'Terrence!' Margaret commanded, lowering her knitting. 'For goodness sake!'

Terry looked startled, opened his mouth and then closed it firmly.

Margaret glared at him. 'I should think so too! We don't need to hear your theories about how wonderful life was in the old days and how terrible it is now, thank you very much!'

Terry twisted in his chair. 'Well, all right, but we *can* talk about Josh, *can* we?'

'Of course,' Margaret asserted.

Terry said, 'Discipline. That's what he needs. Discipline!'

Sarah said nothing; but her father was wrong. Josh didn't need discipline; he needed love – and lots of it.

Terry continued, 'Of course if you'd started earlier, it'd be much easier now!'

Sarah stared defiantly. There was no point saying anything.

Her father folded his arms. 'Take you, for instance. As soon as you could walk and talk, if you did or said something wrong, we simply put you out of the room!'

Sarah said quietly, 'I didn't know that.'

'Worked a treat!' Terry laughed. 'Oh, to start with you kicked up a real hullabaloo, but you soon got the message! Kick up a stink and stay on your own or behave yourself and stay with us! You soon worked out which side of the door you wanted to be on, I can tell you!'

'I don't remember that.' Sarah said.

'Well you wouldn't,' Margaret said studying the wool on her needles. 'You were too young. You did remember, though.'

Sarah frowned, 'I don't think I did.'

Margaret laughed, 'Of course you did, because after being put out of the room a few times you were always a good girl. Right through childhood, you always did as you were told. We only had to raise our voices, or, at most, explain the "error of your ways" and you fell into line straight away!'

Terry chuckled. 'You should have done that with Josh! Too late now, of course, but discipline's the thing! It helped you.'

Sarah wasn't sure that it had. She would need to talk this over with Counsellor Di, but it probably explained why she found it so very hard to stand up to her parents, or anyone else, even now.

Another thought struck her. Maybe it was time she argued back?

She would need to think about that…

CHAPTER FIFTEEN

Today Counsellor Di was wearing an orange cardigan that clashed with her burgundy spectacles.

She waved the papers in her hand and said vaguely, 'I'm still not sure why you did this.'

Sarah shifted in her chair. 'I watched the documentary and it got me thinking, so I went onto the website and took the test.'

'About the kind of brain you have?' Di said.

Sarah nodded.

Di made a face, 'It's not exactly scientific though, is it?'

Sarah answered, 'Well, it was a BBC documentary and professor what's-his-name from Cambridge is running the tests so it must have some credibility.'

Di said, 'What I meant was: it's not the test that matters, or the result; it's the interpretation of the result that has scientific worth. That's why most online tests are just a kind of entertainment for those who like completing them…'

Sarah shrugged, 'Well I don't go taking tests all the time. I just saw the documentary and was interested and that's why I brought the test result for you to look at, so that you could interpret it!'

Di held up a hand. 'Okay. Point taken. Let me think.'

Sarah waited.

'Okay,' Di said again. 'It's widely accepted that the human brain can be male, female or a mixture of the two and that this has nothing to do with the gender of the individual concerned.'

Sarah nodded. That was what the documentary had said.

Di continued, 'And your test result indicates that your brain is male. How do you feel about that?'

'I don't know what to feel,' Sarah answered honestly.

Di shuffled through the papers in her hand. 'Which is, possibly, what someone with a male brain *would* say, I suppose!'

Sarah made a sour face. What did that mean?

Di said, 'As you know, having a male brain doesn't make a woman masculine, any more than a female brain makes a man feminine. This test doesn't reveal anything about femininity or masculinity; it just describes how you think.'

'Like a man,' Sarah said quietly.

'No,' insisted Di. 'Not like a man; like a woman – but in a male way. For you, it's part of the reason why *thinking* is the primary way in which you interact with the world. For you, feelings come second.'

'But I love my children,' Sarah objected.

'Of course you do!' Di said quickly. 'It's not about feeling or not feeling it's just about how you connect with the world.'

Sarah considered this, 'I'm not convinced. Men are aggressive and argue all the time. I back down from arguments so surely my brain is female?'

Di tossed the papers onto the coffee table in disgust. 'That's exactly what I mean about online tests. It's all in the interpretation and this may turn out to be not very helpful. Let's try looking at it from another perspective. You control your feelings without thinking about it, don't you? We've talked about that, haven't we?'

Sarah nodded.

Di continued, 'And you tackle problems logically.'

Sarah shrugged. How else?

Di suggested, 'And, right now, you are second-guessing my train of thought and working out where it might lead, aren't you?'

Sarah flicked her eyes to her counsellor. How did she know?

Di smiled. 'Which is what someone with a male brain might do.'

Sarah frowned. 'What would someone with a female brain do?'

Di laughed, 'It depends. If it was a woman, she might, possibly, burst into tears or storm out.'

Sarah asked, 'What if it was a man – with a female brain?'

Di cocked her head on one side, 'Probably shout and threaten? Maybe break something?'

Sarah sat up, 'But I don't want to do any of those things. I just want to understand.'

Di nodded sympathetically. 'I know; but people aren't simple; we are all very, very complicated.'

Sarah nodded back. No one could argue with that!

Di said, 'And it's not just about your brain, it's about your upbringing and all kinds of other factors including your own choices.'

Sarah thought this over.

Di continued, 'For example: we know, now, that your parents put you out of the room when you were a toddler; and even though you can't remember it happening, it had an enormous impact on you. It may also explain why you, when you were a teenager, didn't argue with your parents.'

Sarah rubbed her jaw. 'Are you saying I should have?'

Di shrugged, 'No, yes; maybe. What I *am* saying is that you had a choice. There must have been lots of occasions when you thought about arguing back but decided not to?'

Sarah nodded. 'I can see that. I remember, when I was fifteen, I borrowed these boots from a friend. They came up to my knees and had high heels and I wore them home. As soon as my dad saw them he went ballistic and I remember standing there with him shouting at me that no daughter of his was going to dress like a slut and thinking, "I don't look like a slut!" and I was all ready to stand my ground and defend the boots.'

Di asked, 'Why didn't you?'

Sarah laughed, 'Because they hurt and I nearly twisted my ankle on the way home so I didn't think they were worth fighting over. I thought that, if I won the argument, I'd have to wear the wretched things and all I really wanted to do was take them off!'

Di asked, 'So what did you say?'

Sarah shrugged, 'Nothing. I couldn't see the point. I let Dad shout himself quiet and then just took them off.'

Di said. 'That may be what it means for you to have a male brain. You go for logic first and then deal with your feelings later.'

'Is that wrong?' Sarah asked.

Di shook her head. 'Absolutely not; it's just the way you are.

What is *not* helpful, though, is that you tend to have the conversation in your head instead of with the person in front of you, and leave your feelings until later – and then ignore them. For example, what did you feel when your dad was shouting at you and how did you give vent to your feelings later?'

Sarah tried to remember. 'I don't think I really felt anything. Just relief when he stopped shouting and I could take the boots off.'

Di said, 'In other words; you coped?'

Sarah grinned and shrugged. 'It worked though, didn't it?'

Di made a face, 'Well it did and it didn't. You've described an emotional confrontation with your father at a time in your life when you were establishing your own identity; yes?'

'I suppose so,' Sarah said. 'But that sounds like a bit of a grandiose description; it was only a row over a pair of boots.'

Di said, 'But that's the point, Sarah. For most people, it *would* have been a row, but for you it wasn't. Your father shouted at you and you said nothing back; you just imagined various conversations and outcomes in your head. That's not a row. That's you *not* dealing with your emotions and, as I've already said, that's not helpful.'

'But why is it so bad?' Sarah asked belligerently.

'I didn't say it was bad,' Di answered patiently. 'I said it was unhelpful.'

'Okay,' Sarah countered. 'So why is it unhelpful?'

'Because it leads you to do things before you've figured out how you feel about them.'

Sarah waited and then said, 'You mean like marrying Dom?'

Di nodded, 'Like marrying Dom.'

Sarah was astonished, 'So not arguing over a pair of boots led to me marrying Dom?'

Di rolled her eyes. 'Not directly, *no*; but indirectly, *yes*. How you deal with other people, and how you deal with your feelings on an everyday basis, builds a pattern of behaviour that determines how you deal with the major things in life.

The incident with the boots was probably one of a multitude of incidents that informed your behaviour when you met and married Dom.'

Sarah could feel her eyes stinging. 'But if I hadn't married Dom, I wouldn't have Josh and Minnie!'

Di passed the box of tissues. 'As I said, people are complicated.'

Sarah patted her eyes and blew her nose.

Di tidied the papers on the table into a neat pile. The session must be drawing to a close.

Sarah sat up. 'Can I ask you something?'

Di paused and allowed the papers to sit where they were.

Sarah said. 'This test – that shows that I have a male brain?'

Di nodded.

Sarah gestured to her torso with both hands, 'I'm not exactly curvaceous, am I?'

Di frowned. 'I'm not sure that I know what you're getting at.'

Sarah took a deep breath. 'If I look a bit like a man and think like a man, do you think that's why Dom married me?'

Di sat back in her chair. 'Is that why you took the test? Because you think Dom thought you were masculine?'

Sarah avoided Di's gaze. 'I didn't know what I think.'

Di said gently, 'You are logical, thoughtful, and a very remarkable person but you are not, in any way, masculine. Most women would kill to be as slim as you and most men must find you attractive.'

Sarah could feel her neck growing very warm. Her cheeks were probably glowing as well. She said, 'They don't.'

Di remained silent.

Sarah stared at the tissue in her hands. 'That's why it was so special when Dom started courting me. Now that I know what I'm like, though, I think that, maybe, he wanted to be married to a woman who was like a man and he thought he could cope with being married to me…' The tissue became a blur and before she could stop herself, grinding, gut-wrenching sobs doubled her over.

The storm passed quickly and she stuttered, 'I'm so sorry. I didn't mean to–'

'I know,' Di said quietly. Her voice sounded shaky.

Sarah glanced at her counsellor. Her eyes looked shiny.

Di cleared her throat. 'You see? Having a male brain doesn't diminish your feelings; it's just a question of learning to access them.'

Sarah grabbed a handful of tissues and mopped up the slime on her hands. 'If accessing my feelings is anything like just now, I'm not sure that I want to do it.'

Di leaned forwards. 'But that's what we've talked about, over and over again. The two sides of the same coin. If you can't access the painful feelings, you cut yourself off from the wonderful feelings too. The pain in you that's just come out is the flip side of the love in you.'

Sarah dropped the wad of damp tissues into the blue bin. 'I don't know that I can cope with it, though.'

Di sighed. 'It's not about coping. It's about *being*.'

Sarah resisted the urge to say, 'young grasshopper'.

Di considered her and said quietly, 'Whoomph-woosh again?'

Sarah frowned.

Di sighed; 'A lot has happened to you, in your life. Oh, nothing that would make the newspapers, I know, but even so, a lot. I think it might be helpful if, between now and next session, you reflect on the choices you make. Think of it as another layer to explore: the choices you make.'

Sarah grinned. She felt weak, but more herself. She quipped; 'You mean like: I might choose to become a blubbering wreck or choose to lose my temper or choose to throw a wobbly?'

She waited for Di to laugh but her counsellor looked straight at her and said, so seriously that it took Sarah completely by surprise, 'Yes.'

CHAPTER SIXTEEN

Dom's hair was even longer. If he kept growing it he wouldn't need a wig in court, he could just perm and powder it!

'Glad to see you're in a good mood,' he said.

Sarah allowed her smile to remain as she helped the children retrieve their bags from the back of the car. She hugged Minnie and kissed Josh. 'Have a lovely weekend!'

Minnie nodded and said, 'You too!'

Josh said nothing and followed his sister up the majestic steps into Dom's building.

'You can come in too,' Dom said, hovering.

Sarah kept her smile in place but allowed it to deteriorate slightly.

'For a coffee and a chat,' he offered.

He obviously wanted to talk about something but that would mean going inside his flat; sitting down; with the children there; as if they were still a family; but his flat was where he and Alex shared their lives. How could she pretend to be part of that? The easy option was to say nothing, lock the car, follow him inside, and do what he wanted – but maybe Di was right? Maybe she had a choice? If nothing else she had to, at least, say something out loud! 'Actually, I have other plans.'

Dom seemed flustered, 'Oh, sorry, I didn't... well of course...' His words faded into silence but he stayed where he was.

Sarah opened the car door, fought a brief inner battle and lost, 'What did you want to talk about?'

He shrugged. 'Nothing that can't wait. I just wondered whether you might find it helpful to have a monthly allowance, that's all...'

What did he mean? A monthly allowance? What was that about? She wasn't a child to be given an allowance! The inside of her car was suddenly very appealing. If she could just get in and close the door she would be safe.

She stayed where she was. She had to choose what to do.

Dom relaxed a little, 'I just thought that, as we still have the joint account, it might help if we created a notional sum of money each month just for you.'

Sarah forced herself to look at him and say, 'Like pocket money?'

He relaxed even more and rested his hand on the top of the open car door. 'Exactly!'

She took a deep breath and pushed the car door shut.

He jerked his hand away.

She faced him. It was now or never. 'I think the best thing is for you to write me a letter explaining what you want to do and why. Now, I'm sorry, but I have to go. Okay?'

His mouth fell open.

She opened the car door again, climbed in, started the engine and drove away without ever looking back. She did glance in her rear-view mirror though; Dom was standing where she had left him, staring after her. She turned the corner, found a quiet place at the side of the road, pulled in, stopped, and burst into tears.

Time passed in a blur of rage, elation, fear, guilt and excitement. What had she done? What would Dom do? Was this what speaking her mind felt like? No wonder she had always avoided it – and yet… and yet… the look of shock on Dom's face made it kind of worthwhile!

She was just blowing her nose into her already soaking tissue when someone knocked on the glass beside her ear. Her head nearly hit the car roof.

She glanced sideways. A man on a bicycle motioned with his hand. He wanted her to lower her window. She pressed a button and as the window slid gracefully down she mopped up the remainder of her tears.

The man leant his elbows on the handlebars of his bike so that his head was at the same level as hers. He had red, curly hair, ginger stubble, and he was probably a few years younger than she was. His cycling gear showed that he was slim and the thigh muscle next to her was well developed.

Sarah said, 'I'm sorry – is there a problem? Have I parked in a cycle lane or something?'

The man smiled apologetically, 'Oh no; nothing like that. It's just that I rode past a couple of minutes ago, going the other way, and I noticed that you were upset, so I turned around and came back to see if you're all right?'

Sarah stared.

The man began to retreat, 'Oh look; I don't want to intrude; I just thought that you might be in trouble…'

Sarah blinked away the last of her tears, 'I; no; I'm fine; I…'

He grinned shyly. 'I've probably made a fool of myself but you just looked so upset! Look, I'm going down to the harbour. There's a shelter just along from the marina, up where The Headland starts. If you want some company, I'll be there. Come and find me.'

He pushed on his pedal and went off down the street.

Sarah watched him go. What was that all about? Why had he stopped? Why would he ask if she was all right? What did he want?

Something Counsellor Di had said scratched at the back of her mind. Something about men…

Sarah shrugged and started the car. She pulled out carefully and turned onto the main road that would take her back to Twisle Drift. She had the whole weekend ahead of her; what was she going to do with it? Go home? Clean the house? Watch DVDs and drink wine? Basically, she was going to fill the time until she could collect Minnie and Josh and life could go back to normal…

What was it that Minnie always said? *You too.* You have a good weekend too.

Sarah made a face. It sounded like a pretty crap weekend!

What else was she going to do, though?

Meet a man on a bike who had knocked on her window?

She grabbed her chest. What was that sensation about? Panic? Excitement? Why would she be excited about chatting to a ginger cyclist?

Sarah slowed the car and turned left.

Was this another of those choices Di had talked about? Well, she certainly had a choice; she could drive home and ignore the cyclist or she could go up to The Headland and find him. She knew exactly where he would be; the shelter was near her grandparents' house and, as a child, she had sat in it many, many times.

She reversed her car into a side street, turned around and headed back towards the harbour.

'Hello,' Sarah said.

The cyclist stood up. He looked pleased. 'Hello. I didn't think you'd come.'

Sarah grinned. 'Neither did I.' She sat down on the bench which, this season, had been painted green, and the cyclist sat down next to her. The bench was fixed inside the glass panelled shelter and it was quite cosy. The glass took the edge off the wind and the view was spectacular. Several dinghies were tacking across the harbour entrance and a large yacht was sailing off towards the horizon.

'I love it here,' the man beside her said wistfully.

Sarah folded her hands in her lap and said nothing. It was probably best not to point out any of the graffiti that, years ago, she had carved into the bench with Poppa Jack's borrowed pocket-knife.

He pointed down towards the piers where boats were moored. 'That's mine down there. The blue one with the white cabin; next to the red one with the wooden decking.'

Sarah nodded. What did you say when a cyclist pointed out his boat? Oh good? That's nice? Well done? What?

He said, 'I go sailing most weekends.'

Sarah suggested, 'When you're not cycling?'

He laughed and bounced his hand on his bike's saddle, 'This is just to keep fit, really. Yachting's for pleasure.'

Sarah smoothed a crease from her coat, 'Not in my family!'

He looked at her quizzically.

'My grandfather was in the navy and my father was a seaman too.'

He said, 'Oh?'

Sarah relaxed against the hard, familiar, wooden bench and folded her arms. 'So for them, the sea was a job. When they weren't working they never went near it.'

He nodded. 'I can understand that. It's quite different for me though.'

Sarah grinned, 'Oh?'

He laughed easily. 'Yeah; I'm a software designer so for me the sea is a complete break.'

Sarah gazed at the sea beyond the harbour. She could understand its allure and she could also see that her own life was a bit, well, samey. Should she take up yachting? Keep the family tradition alive?

He gestured towards his boat, managing this time to brush his arm against hers. 'I could take you out sometime, if you'd like?'

Sarah nodded slowly. 'Actually, that might be nice.'

She stood up and he stood up with her.

He looked disappointed; 'Are you going so soon?'

She nodded. This was another choice time, wasn't it – say something or say nothing... She made a decision: 'I just came to explain. I was upset – back there – because I'm divorced and I've just had a row with my ex-husband. He has the children this weekend. It was kind of you to stop but I'm fine.'

He smiled, 'I'm Ewan; and you are?'

Sarah flustered, 'Oh; sorry; Sarah. I'm Sarah.'

His smile deepened. 'Well Sarah, it's nice to meet you. Do you have a phone number?'

She paused. Why would he want her number?

He waited and leaned casually against his bike.

Of course – so that he could invite her to go sailing some time! She opened her bag, scribbled her mobile number on a piece of paper, handed it to him and said, 'Thank you.'

He took the piece of paper, folded it into his pocket and looked at her quizzically, 'Er… you're welcome?'

She vacillated. She'd missed something, hadn't she?

He said, 'I'll call you.'

'Thank you,' she said again.

He leant forward and kissed her on the cheek.

She took a step back; she'd definitely missed something. She turned and walked away before her face matched the colour of his hair.

'Thank you for the tea,' Sarah said. It was strange to be sitting in Neil's house – it was identical to hers and yet oddly and utterly *other*.

'You're welcome,' Neil answered. 'I was just about to make some when I noticed you arriving home without the children.'

Sarah closed her eyes and relaxed. 'It's their weekend with Dom. I dropped them off and then did a bit of shopping.'

Neil nodded and asked, 'How's it going?'

'How's what going?'

'The dropping them off for the weekend with Dom?'

Her eyes flicked open.

He said, 'Sorry; is that rude?'

She closed her eyes again. 'No; it's fine. It just takes a lot of getting used to.'

'The dropping them off for the weekend?'

She nodded.

'What will you do?' he asked.

She opened her eyes and sipped her tea. 'Pick them up on Sunday afternoon.'

He frowned into his cup. 'I meant between now and then…'

Sarah shrugged. 'I have plenty to get on with.'

'To fill the time?' he suggested.

She eyed him narrowly, 'Are you sure you work in cosmetics?'

He looked puzzled. 'Why?'

'Because you sound exactly like a friend of mine who's a counsellor!'

He laughed. 'Sorry. I was just remembering what it was like when I lost Mel and Naomi – my wife and daughter. I tried to fill every hour with work…'

Sarah relaxed. 'It must have been awful…'

He made a face, 'Tell you what; I won't impersonate a counsellor if you don't!'

She grinned. 'It's a deal!'

She sipped some tea and he savoured his.

It was a pleasant room but his furniture was a bit utilitarian and not very comfortable. Against the wall by the French door – which gave a pleasant view out into his well-tended garden – stood an old upright piano which looked polished and loved. It might be a family heirloom or it could just have been left in the house by the previous neighbours…

'Do you play?' Sarah asked.

Neil smiled. 'I do. Not as well as I'd like; but I enjoy it.'

She snapped her fingers. 'Do you play most evenings at about nine o'clock?'

Neil nodded, 'That's when I practice.'

Sarah whistled. 'You play pretty well, then. I thought it was a CD!'

He laughed. 'You're very kind but no one would ever ask me to record, and anyway, my real love is for church organs.'

She regarded him with surprise; 'Really?'

He made a face; 'It's not *that* unusual is it?'

Sarah said quickly, 'No, of course not. Do you ever, er, perform?'

He shrugged; 'I used to, but these days I just don't have the time. I've been helping a friend out at Binderfield church though – playing for weddings and funerals, that sort of thing, and it's been very enjoyable.'

Sarah nodded, unable to think of anything else to say.

He looked at her seriously, 'I hope my practice sessions haven't been disturbing you?'

'Oh no! Not at all! I only hear you from the kitchen when the window's open and I'm pottering around getting the children's sandwiches ready for the morning.' She sipped her tea and tried to work out whether she had just complimented or insulted him.

He sipped his tea too.

'How's the house hunting going?' she asked.

'Nothing much on the market,' he said. 'But I've got someone on it and I'm sure something suitable will come up sooner or later.'

She took another sip of tea. It was nice of him to ask her in and it was nice of him to sympathise with her and it was even nicer of him to stop! She sighed. This was better than mopping the kitchen floor.

A thought scratched at the back of her mind again. It was the same thought that had scratched at her earlier but she still couldn't work out what it was.

'Are you okay?' he asked.

She made a face. 'Yes; fine. I was just thinking about something that, er, a friend said.'

He smiled, 'Oh yes? What's that?'

Sarah made another face. What was it Di had said? 'Er; I can't remember…'

He nodded as if she had said something infinitely wise.

She chuckled and he joined in.

After a companionable silence he finished his tea and set his cup down on a small side table. 'Actually, I'm glad of a chance to talk.'

Sarah considered the small shreds of tea leaf in the bottom of her cup. So was she. He was such a nice man and she was lucky to have him as her neighbour.

He said, 'I know it's early days, but things must be very tough for you.'

She swirled the dregs in her cup.

He continued, 'So I wondered if you might want to think about something new?'

She stopped swirling the remains of her tea. What was he talking about?

He waved his hand to indicate the room. 'I'm on my own here and as you're just next door I wondered if you might like to pop round a couple of times a week?'

The words that had been scratching away in the back of her mind crashed into her brain like his piano down a flight of stairs. Di had said that she was attractive to men. At the time, Sarah had dismissed her comment as ridiculous but was this what she meant? Did Neil find her attractive? And, if he did, what did he mean by suggesting that she should 'pop round a couple of times a week'? Was he suggesting an affair?

Another thought landed in a lump. Was that why Ewan had knocked on her window? Because he found her attractive?

She shook her head. She must be imagining it. Men never paid attention to her; they never had – or had they? Memory after memory of conversation after conversation slammed into her head. So many casual conversations with so many men who had approached her with a tentative smile.

Good God! Di was right and Nanna Gwen was wrong; even without makeup men *did* find her attractive – and she had never noticed! She shook her head ruefully. This must be what Di meant about ignoring feelings; her heart had probably recognised that men were interested in her but her head never had!

Neil sighed, 'Never mind. I just thought I'd ask.'

Sarah flustered, 'Oh, no; sorry. I haven't said no! I was just thinking about something else!'

He smiled encouragingly.

She smiled back; she needed to find her feelings; what did she feel about Neil? He was such a nice man and he was *flirting* with her! Could she imagine having sex with him? Well yes, she could, and, in fact, it was an exciting thought! Something inside her leapt into life. That was a feeling, wasn't it? A very positive feeling!

She became aware that he was still talking, so she hauled her attention away from the feeling that was now leaping around in a really distracting way and said, 'Sorry – you were saying?'

He said, 'I was just saying; here I am on my own and the company takes up so much of my time that I really don't have the energy to look after this place.'

She nodded. He was often away all day and sometimes overnight and, even when he was at home, he always seemed to be working.

He continued, 'So I just thought that, if you wanted an excuse to get out of your own house for a bit, you might do some cleaning and sorting for me.'

The feeling inside her stopped leaping. 'Pardon?'

He smiled, 'It would only need to be an hour or two if that's what you wanted, and I'd pay you a good rate of course. I was just thinking about how, when I was first bereaved, it was work that kept me going so I wondered if a little job would help you and as I don't have the time to keep this place tidy you'd be helping me too!'

The feeling inside her died. He was offering her a job! How could she have been so stupid as to think that he was flirting with her? Or Ewan, come to that! They were just nice men who wanted to help; that was all.

Neil said, 'Well don't say yes or no right now. Think it over.'

Sarah nodded. 'I will. In fact I've got a lot to think over; so, thank you for the tea and for the company but I ought to go home now.'

She stood up and Neil escorted her to the door.

'Thank you again,' she said.

He smiled, 'Don't mention it; and you're sure that my piano practice doesn't disturb you?'

'Of course not. It's lovely to hear someone play properly!'

He opened the door. 'And think about what I said. If you want that job it's yours. It's not much, but I'd be very grateful if you said yes.'

She stepped through the door. 'Thank you. I'll think about it.'

She was glad to walk away, down his drive; she didn't want him to see her face burning with shame. What a fool she had nearly made of herself! Choosing to think about her feelings wasn't nearly as simple as Di had made it sound.

She walked up her drive and let herself into her own house with relief. She looked in the mirror by her front door – her face wasn't as pink as she'd expected but her neck was glowing beautifully.

She walked into the sitting room and dropped onto the sofa. What a day! And so much to think about too! Happily, neither Neil or Ewan could see her thoughts – they were, mercifully, a secret.

She mulled over her conversation with Neil. Actually, it was a kind offer and she might well take him up on it. She wouldn't tell Dom, or the children, or anyone else about it either. She would organise things so that she could clean for Neil when the children were at school and she would ask to be paid in cash.

She smiled – it was a choice she could make. She could cope with that!

She smiled more broadly – and Dom could stuff his offer of an allowance too! She would be earning her own money! She laughed aloud but stopped. The house was very quiet and her laughter seemed out of place.

She went through into the kitchen and as she began to tidy up she went back over her conversations with Ewan and Neil. Di was wrong; they were just being friendly, that's all, just as men had been friendly to her all of her life.

It was a relief, really. Getting through life was complicated enough without having to second-guess other people's motives. It also put her back in control – if she ever wanted to attract a man she could put on makeup as Nanna Gwen suggested.

She finished scrubbing the sink, pulled off her rubber gloves and smiled ruefully. As if she had been persuaded to think that men found her attractive! Well; it proved one thing – Di wasn't right about everything!

Another thought hit her: if Di was wrong about this, she could be wrong about other things too…

Sarah made herself some cheese on toast and scattered some chopped tomato, a splash of Worcestershire sauce and a scattering of fresh basil onto the bubbling crust. She fetched a knife and fork and was about to cut a slice when her phone chimed. It was a text from an unknown number; it was probably some company offering to consolidate all her debts into one. She ignored it and ate her meal.

When she had washed up, she drifted through to the sitting room and switched on the television. Her phone chimed again; it was a text from Josh and it said: *I love you, mummy.*

She texted back: *I love you too xxx.*

She considered the unknown text and opened it. It read: *Hello Sarah it's Ewan. Tomorrow lunch time? About twelve? By my boat?*

What a nice man. He was going to take her sailing.

She texted back: *Lovely*, and added his number to her phone's 'friends' folder.

She settled down to watch the TV. Perhaps her weekend wasn't going to be complete crap after all?

CHAPTER SEVENTEEN

When Sarah woke up she was pleased to find a surprisingly sunny Saturday waiting for her but, even so, she decided to take no chances. Once Ewan's boat was out of the harbour, the water might be choppy and the wind might be cold, so she would need to dress appropriately.

Towards the end of the morning she changed into sensible underwear along with a nice warm tee-shirt, jeans, a sweater and a fleece. She found some thick socks and an old pair of moon-boots in the bottom of her wardrobe, rescued a woolly hat with a floppy bobble from Minnie's cupboard and completed her ensemble with an old, orange kagool that Dom had left behind.

She parked her car on the edge of The Headland and walked down to the harbour, swishing with every step. One or two pedestrians stared at her as she walked past but she greeted them with a loud: 'Good Morning,' and they quickly looked away. Now that she was approaching Ewan's boat though, her legs were growing heavier with every step.

She had noticed, from a distance, that his sail was still furled; folded against the mast and strapped inside its protective cover. Perhaps that would be their first task? To remove the cover and unfurl the sails?

Now that she was closer though, she could see Ewan standing beside his boat, waiting for her. He was dressed in newly pressed trousers, brown, polished shoes, a shirt and tie and a casual jacket. He looked very smart and he didn't look as if he was about to go sailing…

She reached him with a final swish.

He smiled, kissed her quickly on the cheek and said tentatively, 'Hello.'

She made a face and looked at his boat. 'I've missed something, haven't I?'

He shuffled his feet. 'Um; possibly?'

She glanced at his face; he looked very uncertain.

They both spoke together and stopped.

He put his hands in his jacket pockets. 'Did you think we were going sailing?'

Sarah sighed and nodded.

He laughed and said, 'Oh; good; that's a relief!'

'Pardon?'

He adjusted the hood of her elderly kagool, 'If you normally wore clothes like this for a lunch date, I'd be worried!'

She laughed uncertainly. 'Is that what you thought we'd be doing?'

He jerked his head across the marina, 'I thought we might go to the yacht club.' He pulled off his tie, 'Never mind; we can go there another time. I know a place over the other side of Yelmouth. Let's go there.'

Sarah flapped her kagool. 'Can I take this off?'

He smiled and offered her his arm. 'You can take off anything you like.'

His joke wasn't very funny; was she supposed to laugh? She took his arm; it meant that she could walk beside him and he wouldn't see her face.

'We can go in my car,' he offered, 'if that's okay with you?'

They reached the end of the jetty. Sarah unhooked her arm and said firmly. 'I'll go and get my car and follow you.'

His cheeks coloured. 'Oh; all right.'

'Which is yours?' she asked.

The colour in his cheeks deepened but he smiled; 'I'll show you.'

He offered his arm again and she took it. They walked towards the marina car park and Ewan pointed out various boats of interest – at least, boats of interest to him…

Sarah left him beside his black Audi and walked back along the headland towards her own car. She needed time to think things over.

They weren't going sailing and she could see how the mix-up had occurred but they were going out for lunch and she wasn't dressed for the occasion. Did that matter? It was just lunch with a friend – or was it? Ewan might be dressed for a date or he might always dress smartly; how was she to know? Until today she had only seen him dressed in his cycling gear so she had no point of reference. Was it lunch or something else? The only way to find out was to go with him.

She reached her car and hauled off the woolly hat, the kagool, the fleece and the moon-boots. She pulled on her driving shoes; they would do even if the thick socks made them rather tight. There, now she was dressed normally, if scruffily, in jeans and a sweater.

She headed down towards the marina, spotted Ewan's Audi already waiting, slowed as she approached him and flashed her lights. He raised his hand in acknowledgement and drove ahead, leading her through Yelmouth to an area which the Victorians, with their British Empire view of geography, had nick-named "Palestine", because the streets had names such as: Bethlehem Terrace and Jordan Road. He pulled into a pub car park and stopped between a battered van and some motorcycles.

'Here we are,' he said as she climbed out of her car. He looked very pleased and offered his arm again.

Sarah allowed him to escort her into the pub which was made up of various small rooms. As they searched for an empty table, no one paid them any attention. It was quite full but surprisingly quiet. Eventually, in a small conservatory overlooking a bramble patch, they found somewhere to sit down.

Ewan settled Sarah into her seat and said, 'I'll go and get us a drink; what would you like? Here have a look at the menu.'

He went off to get the drinks and she investigated the card he had handed her. It looked interesting and not at all what she might have expected in a pub like this.

He came back and handed her a large glass of white wine.

'I *am* driving, you know,' she said.

He grinned, 'And eating!'

She sipped her wine; it was delicious.

His grin widened, 'That's a Ruettes Sancerre. Good vintage too!'

She wafted the menu. 'What is this place?'

He lowered his voice and leaned across the table, 'Best food in Yelmouth.'

She raised her eyebrows, 'Says who?'

He leaned closer, 'Oh, you won't find it in any of the guides. The landlord-cum-chef, Lonny, isn't interested in all that. He just makes fantastic food and keeps a spectacular cellar!'

She frowned; it didn't seem very likely. A tatty old pub filled with very ordinary people – the best food in Yelmouth? She caught a glimpse of her reflection in the grubby window – ah well, at least she was dressed to blend in…

He smiled, 'No, honestly. Anyway, you'll see! What would you like?'

Sarah considered the menu card. 'I'll just have a starter, thanks. I'll go for the goat's cheese salad.'

Ewan nodded and went through to the bar.

When he returned she asked, 'So how do you know about this place?'

'I worked with Lonny's brother for a while. Then he, um, got into some trouble and Lonny got implicated too. After, um, a while away, he started up here on his own; it was easier than working for someone else.'

Sarah sucked her cheek; Ewan had evidently just given her a highly edited version of events. What kind of trouble had Lonny's brother got into and where had he gone 'for a while'? She could imagine…

A man with an enormous belly arrived by their table and put down two plates of food. He grunted: 'Enjoy,' and waddled away.

Sarah asked, 'Lonny?'

Ewan sniffed his soup reverentially and nodded.

Sarah took a tentative forkful of her salad and then stared at Ewan.

'Good?' he asked.

'Wonderful,' she answered.

They ate in silence. Now she understood why the pub was so quiet.

After a second starter of 'queenies mornay' and a dessert called: 'chocolate six ways' she and Ewan were back outside in the car park.

He made a face, 'Maybe this was a bad idea.'

'No, no,' she reassured him. 'It was fabulous. Best meal I've had for ages!'

He laughed. 'That's not what I meant. If we'd gone to the yacht club, the food is so ordinary that we would have chatted and got to know each other. I should have known better than to bring you here!'

Sarah frowned. This was another decision moment, wasn't it?

He stepped closer. 'Can we go out again; soon?'

She peered up at him. 'And get to know each other?'

He smiled and leaned towards her.

She put a hand on his chest. 'Can I just ask you something?'

He made a face and stepped back from her. 'I'm not married and I don't have any children. I was in a long term relationship but my partner met someone else and I've been single for more than a year…'

She made an apologetic face, 'Actually, that wasn't what I was going to ask you.'

He looked startled. 'Oh. What *were* you going to ask me?'

She took a deep breath. 'Do you think I'm attractive?'

Ewan exploded with laughter.

Sarah could feel her cheeks beginning to burn. Of course he didn't! She turned towards her car but he reached his arm around her waist, drew her to him and kissed her softly.

She felt as if she might fall backwards and clung to him.

He finished the kiss, pulled away from her and asked gently, 'Does that answer your question?'

She leaned against her car; it seemed nice and solid; and nodded.

He smiled. 'And I can call you again?'

She nodded again, climbed into her car and waved. She needed space to think. She negotiated her way around the parked motorcycles and once she was out in the road she blew out her cheeks. She had so much to think about. If Ewan liked her, did that mean that her life had just become more straightforward or more complicated? She had no idea but one thing was clear and another thing was highly irritating.

The thing that was clear was that if she was going to be friends, or more, with Ewan, she was going to have to explain it to Minnie and Josh. The thing that was highly irritating was that Nanna Gwen was wrong and Di, evidently, was right about men finding her attractive… and what did that mean? That Di was right about everything else too?

She reached the end of the street, pulled out onto a roundabout and was hurled sideways as a car slammed into her.

CHAPTER EIGHTEEN

'But I'm pretty sure I'm all right,' Sarah protested.

The paramedic, who had introduced himself as Chris, pushed her gently down onto the ambulance gurney. 'We'll just get you to hospital and check you over.'

Sarah pulled at the collar around her neck.

'You just stop fretting,' Chris said kindly. 'Everything will get sorted out.'

Beyond the thin wall of the ambulance Sarah could hear the fat middle-aged man who had driven into her; he was still shouting. At least he wasn't shouting at her any more. He had called her every name he could think of and accused her of pulling out in front of him. If it hadn't been for the kind man who had stopped to help her, the fat man would probably have hit her. He had still been heaping abuse on her when the police arrived.

She said, 'I don't think it was my fault…' her voice sounded very small.

Chris finished hooking up a machine that went 'bip' and said, 'There's no need to worry about any of that. It'll all get sorted out. That's what insurance companies are for. You've received a severe sideways blow, so we need to make sure that there's no trauma to your neck.'

Sarah wiggled her fingers and moved her feet. 'I'm pretty sure I'm all right…'

Chris smiled patiently and ignored her.

A new male voice said something outside and the fat man stopped shouting. The new voice rumbled for a while and the fat man started complaining. The voice said something else and the fat man's voice took on a whining tone which receded into the distance.

The ambulance rocked and the kind man who had helped her blocked out the light. He was very tall and looked like he might be a rugby player. His nose had a ridge where it had been broken but his teeth looked real and his nails suggested office work. He wore his light brown hair slightly over his ears and collar and, as he moved, a faint trail of aftershave hung in the air. 'How is she doing?' he asked the paramedic.

Chris answered tartly, 'We're about to set off, Sir.'

The kind man said, 'I'll follow.' The ambulance rocked as he got out and light briefly flooded back inside before Chris slammed the doors and called to the driver, 'Okay Bob.'

They set off beneath a wail of sirens.

Chris sat down. 'Is there someone we can call?'

Sarah considered this, 'No need. Not yet. If I'm not all right, I'll call my parents.'

Chris raised one eyebrow but said nothing.

Sarah stared at the roof. The ambulance was swaying from side to side and she was beginning to feel sick. Maybe going sailing with Ewan was a bad idea?

'So; Mrs Price,' said the same young Asian doctor who had spoken to Sarah on her last visit to the Accident and Emergency Department of Yelmouth Hospital. Once again 'Price' had become 'Prize'. 'It seems that you have been lucky.'

Sarah regarded the young woman; she didn't appear to remember their previous meeting and Sarah wasn't about to remind her.

The young doctor continued, 'You have no skeletal damage. You will be uncomfortable for a few days because of the bruising but that will subside. When you are ready, you may go.'

The young woman went off in search of her next patient and Sarah waved vaguely at her back. She tried turning her head but it hurt and she wasn't sure if the neck brace made things better or worse.

'Knock knock,' said a male voice.

She turned stiffly. It was the kind man who had stopped to help her. She smiled but her chin and her cheeks rubbed on the brace.

'Are you okay?' he asked.

She tapped the brace, 'Apart from this, I think I'm fine.'

He smiled sympathetically. 'It's best to keep it on. When people take them off it can take ages to heal. It's better to wear that for a week than take it off and have problems for months.'

Sarah moved slightly, 'I'd nod if I could. Are you a doctor?'

The man snorted. 'No. I'm a policeman. I'm DCI Driffield.'

He extended his hand and she shook it. 'Well thank you, er, Mr Driffield.'

He smiled, 'Henry. Call me Henry.'

'Isn't that a bit informal?' she asked.

He squeezed her hand. 'Probably; but I won't tell if you won't!'

Sarah retrieved her hand. 'Sorry – but if you're with the police, why didn't you mention it to the fat man who ran into me?'

DCI Driffield might be a policeman but when he grinned he looked like a rogue. 'I'm kind of off duty. It's better if I'm not involved but I saw what happened so I decided to stop and make sure everything calmed down until the duty officers arrived.'

Sarah said, 'Well, er, mission accomplished – or whatever you say.'

He saluted casually. 'No problem. So are you okay?'

She moved her head. 'I guess so. I have to wear this and go to my own doctor for a check-up next week.'

'In that case – you'll be fine. They slap those on everyone who has a wreck. If they were remotely worried, they'd ask you to come back here. So wear it like they say and you'll be fine. Are you okay to get home or would you like a lift?'

Sarah blinked. 'Oh I couldn't impose on you. You've been very kind as it is!'

He laughed and offered her his arm. 'Don't be ridiculous; I couldn't leave a damsel in distress now, could I?'

Sarah took a deep breath. 'Look, it's very kind of you but I don't know that I want you to take me home…'

His face became serious. 'Quite right too. I'm a strange man; you shouldn't trust me. Here–' He reached into an inside pocket, pulled out a small black wallet and flipped it open. The warrant card and photo confirmed that he was Detective Chief Inspector Henry Driffield.

Sarah could feel her cheeks starting to glow, 'Oh look; I didn't mean to insult you…'

He held up his hand; it looked very large. 'Not at all. Let's just go along to the hospital café and I'll explain what's going to happen.'

That sounded ominous. Sarah got off the bed and fell in step beside him.

The café was populated by various people with their arms and legs in casts talking to, presumably, friends and relatives with no discernible injuries.

'There you go,' he said cheerfully. 'You'll fit right in!'

Sarah sat down at a plastic-coated table and waited.

DCI Driffield arrived with a pot of tea and two cups.

Sarah prepared herself; he was going to tell her that the police were going to prosecute her for dangerous driving.

He took a large gulp of scalding tea, seemingly oblivious to the heat, and said, 'Right. You'll hear all this when the duty officers contact you but you might as well hear it from me; it'll put your mind at rest. I was following the driver who hit you and I noticed that he was driving erratically. I was just wondering whether to pull him over when he ploughed into you. He was driving too fast, he was texting on his phone and, I suspect, once he's given a blood sample, he'll show positive for drunk-driving. I think that's why he was so aggressive – hoping to shift the blame onto you.'

Sarah said, 'But he said it was my fault. That I pulled out in front of him…'

DCI Driffield gulped some more tea and refilled his cup. 'Well, technically, you did. It doesn't matter though; his speed and blood-alcohol count will make it all his fault. When the duty boys ask you for your version of events just tell the truth; and keep it simple – don't go into long explanations and don't hypothesise.

Just say what happened and you'll be fine. You shouldn't even lose your no-claims bonus.'

Sarah eyed him over the brim of her cup. 'Are you really off duty?'

His eyes flicked to hers, 'Why?'

She put her cup down, 'You're not under cover or anything and following fatty as part of a case?'

He put his cup down and sat back in his chair.

She waited.

He grinned his roguish grin. 'You know what?'

'What?'

He held her gaze. 'I like *you!*'

She dropped her eyes and stared at her cup. 'Oh.'

He reached over and patted her hand. 'Don't be embarrassed.'

She looked at his face; his expression was serious.

He said quietly, 'I didn't mention to the man who drove into you that I'm a policeman and it's probably best if he doesn't know but I really am off duty; kind of…'

'Ah,' she said.

He smiled. 'I'm glad I stopped, though.'

He took her hand in his; it felt very warm. 'You've had a shock, so right now you'll be all over the place. I'll give you my card. Give me a call in a couple of days and I'll get back to you.'

He withdrew his hand and passed a small business card to her. It contained his name and rank and included a mobile number.

She looked from the card to his face. 'Don't you use walkie-talkies or something?'

He laughed. 'The beat-boys and CID use airwaves. These days, most of the time, the rest of us just use mobiles. Don't worry; if you phone me on that number you won't get switchboard. You'll get me. Now; can I give you a lift home?'

Sarah smiled gratefully. 'Thank you, but no. I'll call a taxi.'

He nodded and stood up and smiled. 'Will you call me?'

She moved her head.

He grinned again, 'Was that a nod or a shake?'

Sarah chuckled, 'A nod.'

His grin broadened and echoed in his eyes, 'I'll look forward to it.'

'Thank you, Mr Driffield.'

His eyes softened; 'Henry.'

She watched as he walked away. He was taller than Dom and, just like her ex-husband, he exuded confidence, but there was something different about Henry Driffield. He had something that Dom did not possess, and the word that came to mind was: 'power'.

She considered the card he had given her, tucked it away in her bag and finished her tea. Everyone said that trouble came in threes – but since her divorce, it seemed that nice men came in threes; Neil, Ewan and now Henry. Perhaps Di was completely right about men being attracted to her? Perhaps all three of them were showing interest in different ways?

Would that be a problem? If it was, it sounded like an interesting sort of problem to have, and she laughed aloud. Several other people in the café looked at her.

'It's the pills,' she said. 'Sorry.'

They all looked sympathetic and turned away.

She collected her things and stood up and something inside her soared. If Di was right about men finding her attractive, maybe Dom was right too? Maybe his leaving would turn out to be, as he had so strongly asserted, for the best?

On the other hand, if she was going to consider a new relationship, at some point she would have to run the gauntlet of her parents' disapproval...

CHAPTER NINETEEN

'Lean forwards,' Margaret commanded.

Sarah closed her eyes. This was like being a child again. Her parents' sitting room had hardly changed in thirty years; only the extra pottery ornaments spread across every available surface marked the journey through time. The walls had been redecorated with the same old colours and even the sofa on which Sarah sat with her feet up was the same sofa that she had curled up on as a child.

She opened her eyes. Her mother was relishing this; in her view, the car accident had put Sarah right back where she should be – dependent on her parents.

'Go on; lean forwards,' Margaret insisted.

Sarah did as she was bidden and her mother plumped the sofa cushions behind her and arranged them to her satisfaction.

'There,' Margaret said. 'That's better.'

Sarah leaned back against the cushions and said, 'You really don't need to fuss, Mum. Apart from my neck I'm fine and, to be honest, I think my neck is perfectly alright too.'

Margaret subsided into an easy chair and said, 'If you didn't need it, the hospital wouldn't have put it on; would they?'

Sarah eased her neck brace and closed her eyes again. She had to admit that she was very comfortable and, now that she had relaxed, perhaps a little snooze would do her good… She opened her eyes again. This was what Counsellor Di was talking about, wasn't it? Her mother saying something ridiculous and her saying nothing about it. This was a moment when she could choose to say something, wasn't it? When she could have a conversation out loud instead of in her head? She took a deep breath and said firmly, 'Yes they would.'

Margaret frowned.

Sarah swung her legs off the sofa and sat upright. 'We live in a litigious culture, Mum. The hospitals want to avoid being sued so of course they put neck braces on people for no reason!'

Margaret's frown deepened. 'That's the sort of thing Dominic would say, isn't it?'

Sarah caught her breath; her mother was right. She was just parroting Dom; just as she always did. Her eye rested upon a particularly garish ornament – a duck with a basket tucked under one wing and an umbrella over its shoulder. Dom had given it to Margaret as a present – was that what had prompted her to quote him?

Sarah tore her attention away from the hideous ornament. She was changing the subject, wasn't she? Di had talked about that too. She mustn't get distracted from actually talking! 'It doesn't matter what Dom says. It's what I'm saying now that matters!'

Margaret smiled and stood up. 'I'm sure it is. Let's have some tea, shall we?'

Sarah watched in stunned silence as her mother left the room.

How was she supposed to converse with someone, let alone argue with them, when they just walked away? The way Di described it, if Sarah stood up for herself, everything would be better, but how was she supposed to do that if her mother just wouldn't argue back?

Sarah eased her neck brace again. Arguing was obviously more complicated than Counsellor Di seemed to think it was. It had worked with Dom, though, and the thought of him standing on the pavement outside his flat like a fish out of water made Sarah chuckle.

Actually, standing up to Dom hadn't been funny and her emotional outburst afterwards had shown just how stressful it had been.

'Here we are,' Margaret said, holding a tray and standing on one foot while attempting to close the door with the other. She looked uncannily like one of the ballet-dancing hippos in Fantasia. Before Sarah could stop herself she let out a shout of laughter.

Margaret smiled, crossed the room and put the tray on a small table. 'There; you see? Coming home has done you good!'

Sarah made a decision: her mother's similarity to a ballet-dancing hippo was *not* a topic worth arguing about.

Terry came into the room with an expectant smile. 'Is that tea?'

Margaret retreated from the room saying, 'I'll get another cup.'

'And a plate,' called Terry. He sat down, adjusted his shirt and asked solicitously, 'So; how *are* you?'

'I'm fine,' Sarah said. 'I don't think I really need this brace.'

Terry nodded in agreement. 'Lot of namby-pamby nonsense! Half the time they only put these things on because they're frightened you're going to sue them!'

'That's what I just told Mum,' Sarah agreed.

Margaret returned with another plate, saucer and cup. 'What did you tell me?'

Sarah said, 'About me not needing this neck brace.'

Margaret poured the tea and said patiently, 'Now we've been through this. The hospital know what they're doing, don't they Terry?'

Terry nodded and avoided Sarah's eye.

Sarah frowned. This was even more complicated than before. Could she have a proxy argument, on behalf of her father? But if she did, what if he denied what he'd just said? In fact how was anybody expected to have a decent argument if no one stuck to the rules? Ah: there was a thought. What *were* the rules of arguments? Did they exist or did everyone just make them up as they went along? She must ask Di…

Margaret handed her a plate with a slice of chocolate cake on it. 'Penny for your thoughts?'

Sarah balanced the plate on her knees. Here was her opportunity. She could choose to ask anything she liked! Why did Terry allow Margaret to boss him around? Why had they been so strict with her as a child? Did they love her and what, exactly, did they mean by love? Why had Terry always been so anti-Dom? Had they known Gerald Bailey? How would they feel if she, like Sandy, met another man?

There were so many questions and this was her chance!

Margaret handed a slice of cake to Terry and glanced over her shoulder, 'Hmmm?

Sarah stared at her cake. How could she possibly ask any of those things?

Terry bit into his cake and said jovially, 'What's up? Cat got your tongue?'

Sarah blinked hard; she could choose to speak or chicken out. She cleared her throat; 'Actually, there was something I wanted to talk about.'

Margaret and Roy exchanged glances. Margaret took a deliberate sip of tea and Roy put his cake down.

Sarah nodded. 'I was talking to Sandy and we had a misunderstanding.'

Margaret clinked her teacup back into its saucer. 'Well you would, wouldn't you?'

Sarah met her gaze. 'About remarriage.'

Margaret became very still.

The silence seemed to sing in Sarah's ears but she ignored it. She looked at Terry, swallowed hard and said, 'It was all a misunderstanding but she thought I was talking about me.'

Terry glanced at her and then studied his cake. 'What about you?'

It felt as if an invisible barrier was enveloping her, pushing against her, suffocating her. Even though her voice seemed desperately small and quiet she managed to say, 'It was just a hypothetical question, but what if I met someone else? What if I married again?'

The atmosphere changed and Sarah held onto the settee arm to stop herself falling forwards.

Margaret looked genuinely surprised. 'Why would you want to?'

Because, with someone else, it might be a proper marriage; that's why. Because Sandy remarried. Because she might fall in love... Sarah shrugged, her voice gathering strength, 'I'm not saying I will. I just wondered what you thought about it?'

Terry asked, 'Have you met someone? A man?'

What did that mean? Was he asking her if she was a lesbian? 'No; it's just a hypothetical question.'

Margaret flumped around in her chair. 'I should think you're better off just looking after those wonderful children.'

Oh: bravo. Heap it on with a trowel, why don't you? 'I plan to, but maybe, if I met someone else who would be a good father for the kids, it would be good for them too?'

Margaret considered this. 'Well it's your life and you've already amply demonstrated that you're not interested in our advice!'

That would mean her marriage to Dom…

Margaret continued, 'But in my opinion, and I'm sorry to say this, people who get divorced are just showing that marriage is not for them.'

Sarah gaped. Surely her mother couldn't, possibly, believe that?

Terry nodded in agreement; 'Dead right.'

Margaret gestured with her plate and crumbs dropped onto the floral carpet. '*We* understand, completely, that the idea of another man seems like a solution. What *you* need to understand is that another man will just bring more problems.'

Sarah glanced at her father. Was he just another problem in Margaret's life?

Margaret continued; 'If I were you, I'd stay as you are and put your energies into the children.'

Sarah glanced at her mother; that was, rather the point, wasn't it? Margaret *wasn't* her and Sarah needed to make her own decisions. 'I'll think about it.'

Margaret sniffed. 'You make sure that you do.'

Sarah nodded. She would also think about why the powerful silence that had appeared when she had mentioned the subject of remarriage had disappeared when it became obvious that the conversation was about her. Unless there was *another* remarriage that she knew nothing about, that silent barricade must refer in some way to Gerald Bailey.

She regarded her parents.

Margaret and Terry ignored her and ate their cake in silence.

As Sarah had suspected, there was no point asking them about the past. As far as they were concerned, as long as she was a good little girl they could all eat cake and talk about nothing and everything would be fine. The moment she did what Di said, though – the moment she entered into anything that resembled an adult conversation – the barricades went up and that was that!

She closed her eyes and leaned back against the sofa cushions. No; there was no point asking them about the past and if she were to consider a new relationship, it would clearly be without their blessing.

She would need to choose her future carefully. Would a step-father be good, or bad, for Josh and Minnie? Josh in particular was still finding life without Dom very, very difficult. Would a step-father make life better or worse for him?

CHAPTER TWENTY

Sarah looked around Mrs Hopkins' office with a sense of deja vu but her neck-brace reminded her that this was a different occasion – even if the reason for the meeting was the same…

Mrs Hopkins regarded Josh over the top of her glasses. 'I explained before, Joshua, that fighting is not acceptable!'

Josh fidgeted in his seat.

Sarah turned her body towards Josh so that she could look at him. 'What is it, Josh?'

He shot a glance at her, fixed his attention on his Head Teacher and protested, 'I didn't break my promise!'

Mrs Hopkins face became a mask of shocked indignation, 'But you were fighting! Ryan! Again!'

Josh shot another glance in Sarah's direction before saying, 'But not in school. I promised I wouldn't fight in school and I didn't. We weren't in school!'

Mrs Hopkins said, 'But it was in school *time*. Lunch time is school time.'

Josh fidgeted in his seat again.

Sarah eased her neck brace with her finger and said gently, 'What is it, Josh?'

He stared at his knees but said quite clearly, 'No one said anything about school time. Before. Just school and I didn't fight him in school! We were down by the chip shop; at lunch time!'

Sarah turned uncomfortably to Mrs Hopkins, 'He has a point.'

Mrs Hopkins' mouth was a thin line. She regarded Josh and shut the file on her desk. 'Let me make myself quite clear this time, Joshua. If you fight Ryan, or anyone else, during a school day, wherever you are and whatever the time is, you will go from amber to red and you will be suspended. Is that quite clear?'

Josh's face worked but he nodded vigorously and said, 'I can't fight ever.'

Mrs Hopkins said, 'What you do on Saturday or Sunday is up to you. If you become a thug like so many others before you, that's up to you. If you break your mother's heart and become a bitter disappointment to your father; that's up to you too. But on school days; no fighting. Is that clear?'

He nodded meekly. 'Yes, Mrs Hopkins.'

She said, 'Then go back to your class and I never want to see you in my office again!'

He scurried out, pausing only to glance exultantly at Sarah.

'Thank you, Mrs Hopkins,' Sarah said, disguising her smile.

The Head Teacher took off her glasses and rubbed her eyes. 'Marsha – and don't thank me; Joshua has escaped by the skin of his own something or other! He's a right little back room lawyer, isn't he? Takes after his father, I suppose, in that respect anyway...'

Sarah blinked. She had never considered it before but what if Josh took after Dom in other respects too?

Marsha replaced her glasses and chuckled. 'Quite clever really!'

Sarah made a face, 'I'm not sure that I approve, though.'

Marsha chuckled again. 'Well, that's for you to decide. You can punish him for fighting Ryan if you like but I'd be tempted to let them work out their differences themselves. From what I hear, it was pretty much a stalemate – which is quite a feat for a boy as small as Joshua. If I know Ryan, and I think I do, he'll either avoid Joshua or try to make friends. It reminds me a bit of your father and Roy.'

'Really?' Sarah said. Had they known one another before their merchant navy days?

'Oh yes,' Marsha said dismissively. 'Of course, they were older than Josh when they first bumped into one another. They must have been, what, sixteen or so?'

Sarah nodded and grunted encouragingly. If she pretended that she already knew, perhaps Marsha would tell her more?

'But they were always at each other's throats until they realised that they liked each other! Still, that's men for you, isn't it? And boys! Same behaviour; just a different size, eh?'

Sarah nodded in agreement, 'How true!'

Marsha continued, 'Mind you, things were much more violent back then. Most school boys got into fights, then they grew up and became Mods or Rockers and the fighting got really serious. Oh yes, punch-ups were common then!'

'I suppose so,' Sarah agreed. Was Marsha talking about Terry and Roy?

Marsha removed her glasses again and polished them. 'People look back on the sixties and only remember the hippies and flower power, but there was a lot of violence. Oh yes; a lot of violence.'

Sarah said encouragingly, 'It's different now, though.'

Marsha paused. 'Very. Well, Joshua is just lucky that I'm still his Head. When I leave at the end of this term he'll have to buck his ideas up.'

Sarah moved her upper body in a parody of a bow, 'I'll make sure he does.'

Marsha replaced her glasses and smiled. 'It'll be for the best in the long run. People remember the past with rose-tinted glasses but, as you well know, it was a very different world…'

Sarah made an indeterminate noise. What would Marsha tell her?

Marsha asked, 'Are Terry and Roy still best buddies?'

Sarah grunted. 'No; not for a long time.'

'Pity,' Marsha said. 'But, then again, these things happen.'

Sarah waited.

The Head Teacher sighed wistfully. 'Ah well…'

Sarah tried to remain utterly still.

The Head roused herself. 'Yes; but we can make sure that things are different for Joshua, can't we?'

Sarah eased her neck brace.

Marsha's thin smile returned and she fixed her eyes on the file on her desk. 'At least we can do our best for the children!'

Sarah sighed; the conversation was moving on and she had learned nothing. 'We can – and thank you for looking after Josh.'

Marsha shrugged, 'Well you know I can't take sides, even if I wanted to, but it's been a pleasure to have him in the school.'

'Mostly?' Sarah suggested.

Marsha laughed. 'Oh; don't you worry. Compared to some, Joshua has been a delight.'

Sarah asked, 'Will Ryan's parents complain?'

Marsha shrugged, 'I don't suppose Ryan will even tell his mother. If he did, she'd probably just slap him for being a sissy – you know, for being beaten up by a smaller boy.'

'Is his home so bad?' Sarah asked.

Marsha looked her in the eye, 'It's not great, but his mother loves him and there are some children who don't even have that.'

Sarah looked down.

Marsha continued, 'No; don't you worry about Ryan, and don't worry about Joshua either. Take my advice and let them sort their differences out in their own way. No – everything will be just fine; you'll see.'

Sarah eased her neck brace again.

Marsha said sympathetically, 'That must be very uncomfortable.'

Sarah smiled ruefully. 'It's starting to rub but I take it off at night and I'm expecting to get the all clear in a few days.'

Marsha asked, 'And you weren't hurt, apart from your neck?'

'I was very lucky,' Sarah said.

'And is your insurance company being fair?'

Sarah raised her hands, 'Oh yes, it's all very straightforward. They've provided me with a temporary car and I've already had a letter confirming that it wasn't my fault. I should get a cheque in the post soon so that I can buy another car.'

Marsha grunted, 'And will you sue?'

Sarah stared, 'How do you mean?'

Marsha said, 'For the whiplash. Will you sue?'

Sarah frowned, 'Do you know, it never even occurred to me!'

Marsha laughed mirthlessly. 'It will. Take it from me, you are going to get texts and phone calls and emails by the bucket load from companies offering to sue on your behalf!'

Sarah made a face. 'How will they know?'

Marsha shrugged, 'No idea; but they will!'

Sarah smiled ruefully again.

Marsha's attention returned to the file on her desk. Clearly, the conversation was over.

This was another of those moments that Di had talked about; Sarah was beginning to recognise them. She could say nothing or have a conversation; she had a choice. She cleared her throat and said, 'Well, I ought to make a move. Thank you again, Marsha, for looking after Josh, but before I go can I just ask you about my dad and Roy?'

Marsha's thin smile reappeared. 'Mmm?'

Sarah said, 'I just wondered about their friendship? In the early days?'

Marsha blinked and stood up. 'I don't suppose I can tell you anything you don't already know.'

Sarah stood up too and said, 'It's just interesting to hear about things from a different point of view.'

Marsha walked to the door of her office, 'It wouldn't be appropriate to gossip about the old days. You should ask them.'

Sarah smiled. 'Of course. Thank you again.'

She said goodbye and left the office.

When she reached the school gate she stopped and mulled over the little that Marsha Hopkins had told her. It was an open window into a past that she knew nothing about and, more importantly, it was a window that Marsha had shut as soon as Sarah had asked for more detail.

There was both friendship and violence in the past that Marsha didn't want to talk about. It concerned Sarah's father and her ex-father-in-law and Marsha assumed that Sarah knew all about it. Well, thanks to Marsha, Sarah had already found out about Gerald Bailey; maybe there was something else that she should know? Maybe it was time for her to make another visit to the library?

CHAPTER TWENTY ONE

'Back again?' asked the librarian in her mysterious accent. 'What a coincidence!'

Sarah frowned. A coincidence? Why?

The librarian looked past her, smiled and beckoned.

Another woman, with a book in her hand, arrived at the reception desk. She was a little older than Sarah and she had dark hair, a mischievous smile, and she was wearing a smart business suit. She was also wearing a rather grimy surgical collar.

'What happened to you?' the woman asked pleasantly.

Sarah smiled; 'Car crash; someone ran into the side of my car. You?'

The woman grimaced; 'Shoved down some stairs!' She fingered her collar and said, 'Wretched, isn't it?'

Sarah smiled again. 'I'd nod if I could!'

The woman chuckled. 'When does yours come off?'

'In a couple of days, I hope. You?'

The woman pantomimed luxuriating in an imaginary bath; 'Tomorrow!'

Sarah chuckled, 'Well; all the best!'

'You too!' The woman gave her book to the librarian and then, when it was returned, said, 'See you later.'

The librarian said: 'Bye Bella,' and turned to Sarah. 'What can we do for you today?'

'Same as before. But I'd like to look through the local papers from nineteen-sixty through to nineteen-seventy this time.'

The librarian slid out from behind her desk. She had dark hair, darker than her friend with the surgical collar, but she had blue eyes and the contrast was striking. She was similar in height and size to Sarah, although her breasts were larger, and she was wearing a pencil skirt with a smart white blouse and a pendant that enhanced her cleavage and heels that emphasised her hips.

The librarian said, 'No problem – they're all on the microfiche you were using before. I'll load up the viewer for you.'

Sarah followed her through the reference section and through double-doors into the room she had visited before. The librarian was undoubtedly an attractive woman – should Sarah dress a little more like her? She waited while her guide opened a cabinet by the wall and found what she was looking for; then followed her to the viewer.

The librarian fiddled about behind the machine and then pressed a button. The screen came to life. 'There you are,' she said. 'You're at the beginning of nineteen-sixty and you can scroll on to any year you want.'

Sarah sat down sideways and then eased herself around so that she could see the screen. 'Thank you.'

The librarian patted her shoulder. 'You're welcome. If you get stuck, come and find me. I'm Ruth, by the way.'

Sarah said, 'I'm Sarah. Excuse me for not turning round.'

Ruth patted her shoulder again and said, 'Don't you worry. What a coincidence; you and Bella both turning up with neck braces! It's almost spooky!'

Sarah could hear the librarian's heels as they clicked across the floor away from her and back through the double-doors. Maybe she *should* think about the kind of clothes she wore.

She considered the screen and cautiously twiddled a knob. She had decided to start at the beginning of nineteen-sixty because that was when Terry had turned sixteen. She would work her way forwards from there but there was no point going much beyond nineteen sixty-eight because that was when Terry and Margaret had married. If Terry and Roy had been wild young men, they would be in the papers before domesticity tamed them…

She turned the controls and began to skim-read. Apart from a small piece in nineteen sixty-one about Roy winning a race at a community sports day, there was nothing of personal interest, but the local news revealed the past to be a different world, as Marsha

Hopkins had said it was. Violence seemed to be everywhere and it was evidently much more common in the so-called 'swinging sixties' than it was now.

She paused to read a report from nineteen sixty-four about a fight that had begun in a dock-side pub and then spilled out into the surrounding streets. Eventually the police had arrived and, by today's standards, they had brought the riot to an end with brutal force. She finished the article; could she imagine Henry Driffield behaving like those long gone policemen? She shifted slightly in her seat; she had only met him once – but yes, she could... Perhaps it would be better if she didn't call him?

She reached the end of nineteen sixty-five and looked quickly through nineteen sixty-six. She was already familiar with the news stories from her previous visit and she only paused to look more closely at some articles that previously had been of no interest. During the summer, there had, over several weeks, been a running battle between youths from different areas of Yelmouth. Palestine, the enclave of streets near the docks, was mentioned more than once and racism, or 'racialism' as it was called in the paper, was cited as the prime motivation in that area. Clearly the black families who lived in Palestine had had a very tough time. At one point the Royal Marines had intervened and, later on, the army had been drafted in to sort things out. The other fighting, though, seemed to be driven by different gangs of white boys and there was a small allusion to 'the brave men of the merchant navy' who had cleared a rowdy crowd of troublemakers out of a church dance.

Sarah sucked her pencil. Had Marsha Hopkins been at that dance? Had Terry or Roy been involved? Was that what Marsha had been thinking of when she had talked about the violence of the sixties?

She found Gerald Bailey's photograph and re-read the article from November, nineteen sixty-seven, about him playing Macbeth. He was certainly a very handsome man and, by the sound of it, a very talented actor. It was strange that she had never heard of him but maybe he was a stage-actor who had never made it into television or movies? Perhaps he was still treading the boards in pantomimes and summer shows? Or, maybe the review was just hot air; maybe he was actually a lousy actor who had left the profession and now ran a shop in Pentonville?

She started to look through nineteen sixty-eight. In June, there was a photo of Poppa Jack standing on the dock with his aircraft carrier behind him. Apparently, they were back for a brief refit after a tour of duty in the Indian Ocean; his ship had been a 'British presence' during some kind of local negotiations. That must have been a nice few months for Poppa Jack; swanning around the Indian Ocean with nothing much to do apart from training exercises! She also found a picture of her parents' wedding in July, with both Terry and Margaret looking impossibly young, but there was nothing else of personal interest.

She reached the end of nineteen sixty-eight. The gang violence of the previous year seemed to have blown over but street robberies were common. Interestingly, these incidents were not referred to as 'muggings' – that term must have come into common use later on; perhaps in the seventies?

She started on nineteen sixty-nine. The story was much the same as the previous years; people went to school, grew up, got married and sent their own children to school. Along the way, the factories, offices and shops in which they worked opened and closed, they celebrated on high days and holidays and they entertained, or were entertained by, each other.

She reached a report of Easter celebrations and paused. Was it worth going on? The newspaper stories had confirmed Marsha's assertion that fighting was common in the sixties but there was no mention of her dad or of Roy. Presumably they were just part of the background rumble; everyone seemed to use their fists to sort out arguments – even the women. Was that what her dad had meant when he had said that, back then, families had sorted out their own problems? Was that what had happened between her family and Dom's? Had Margaret and Sandy scratched each other's eyes out?

Sarah rubbed her own eyes; she couldn't imagine them squaring up to one another but, then again, the sixties were evidently quite different to today so maybe it was possible?

She sucked her pencil and considered the blank piece of paper on the desk beside her. She had found nothing worth noting down; maybe this was just one big waste of time? She hesitated and then reached for the controls; she might as well look through the rest of the file. There probably wouldn't be anything to find, but at least she'd know.

She scrolled quickly through the summer news reports and glanced at her watch; it was nearly lunch time. She settled herself for the remainder of her trawl and, with the feeling of finally reaching the downhill stretch, scrolled through the autumn months.

There was nothing – until she reached the front page headline for Friday the twenty-fourth of October nineteen sixty-nine. She twisted the controls delicately until the photograph filled the screen. It was Gerald Bailey. He was dressed in a suit and tie, and he seemed to be holding an award. It was definitely Gerald Bailey but the headline proclaimed: 'Tragic Loss'.

She read the article – but it wasn't an article; it was an obituary. It listed his acting credits, waxed lyrically about his successes and proclaimed what a great loss he was to England's acting fraternity. It also recounted how he had died and, as she read it, Sarah felt sick. Gerald had lived a large life, but his death had been small and mean. On Saturday the eighteenth of October he had finished a performance of King Lear at a theatre in Shoreditch and taken the underground home. He had got off at Angel, walked through the streets and, in an alleyway within sight of his flat, thugs had set upon him and robbed him. He had been beaten and kicked in the head; and that was it – he had died alone in that alleyway. He was only thirty-one. The article concluded with a few desultory sentences about there being no witnesses and the police having no leads to follow.

Sarah sat back and stared at the screen. What a terrible, pointless, horrible thing to happen. No wonder Sandy never spoke of it, or about Gerald either; and, of course, this explained why Sandy had so vehemently denied that she had been divorced. She hadn't; she had been widowed – and in the most terrible of ways.

According to the article, or obituary, or whatever it was, Gerald had been poised on the cusp of fame and fortune and Sandy must have been looking forward to a completely different life – with money and a big house and everything that a famous husband could provide. Then, in one pointless attack, it was over; Gerald was gone and so was her future! Sandy must have then moved back to Yelmouth and married Roy; ordinary, Merchant Seaman, Roy.

Of course she didn't talk about Gerald! How could Roy ever compare with him? No wonder everyone kept quiet about her first marriage to such a handsome, successful and talented man! To even mention him would be to suggest that Roy was a failure.

Sarah reached for the power switch and turned the viewer off. She stuffed the blank piece of paper back into her bag, collected her things and walked towards the double-doors.

When she reached the reception desk, the librarian, Ruth, smiled a friendly smile. 'You were a long time; is your neck all right?'

Sarah eased her neck brace. 'It's fine. It just rubs a bit.'

Ruth smiled sympathetically. 'And did you find what you were looking for?'

'Yes,' Sarah lied.

She turned away before Ruth could ask her any more questions. She had found out what had happened; but now that she had, she wished that she hadn't. Perhaps Di was right; perhaps she should have left the past exactly where it was – in the past.

CHAPTER TWENTY TWO

'So you've had what we can euphemistically call an "interesting time"?' Di asked.

Sarah fingered her neck brace and mumbled in agreement. She had been completely honest with her Counsellor about her inability to argue, but it seemed increasingly unlikely that Di would be able to suggest any kind of solution.

'Maybe we should recap?' Di suggested.

Sarah nodded as best she could. 'I was just thinking that myself.'

Di smiled and perused the papers in her lap. 'Okay; we know that you can be a very contained person and we know that the roots of this go back into your childhood. We also know that this has led you to be what we are calling a *compartmentalised* person. Something that happens in one area of your life doesn't necessarily connect with the other areas of your life.'

Sarah made a sour face; that pretty much summed her up, but it was old news.

Di smiled at her, 'We also know that being a contained and compartmentalised person is sometimes a very good thing. It enables you to live through very difficult situations. So it's just a description of who you are, not a value judgement!'

Sarah smiled. Even if her counsellor could offer no solutions, at least she understood herself much better now.

Di considered her notes again. 'It also means that you are very objective about conflict.'

Sarah suggested, 'Which is not so good?'

Di caught and held her gaze. 'In many ways, being objective about conflict is very good indeed.'

'But?'

Di laughed, 'The "but" is that, generally, whenever you experience a strong emotion, instead of facing it, you immediately hop into a different compartment – and have the conversation you should be having out loud silently in your head.'

Sarah rubbed the fabric of her trouser legs. She had a mountain of ironing to do at home. How could she bring this counselling session to a swift conclusion without offending Di?

Di persisted, 'In a way, it's a very useful strategy, but the downside is that your feelings about what's happening can get lost between the compartments.'

Sarah noticed mud on her shoe. The childrens' shoes needed a good polish too; but it was probably best not to check the time on her watch, though.

Di muttered, 'Maybe the concept of *compartments* doesn't help? Would it be better to think in terms of *chapters?*'

Sarah looked up. If they talked about that for a while, maybe Di would be happier?

Di continued enthusiastically, 'If the story of your life was a book, it would probably involve countless plot-lines where the only connection was you – and the chapters would probably be individual entities in their own right, too.'

Sarah grunted noncommittally; a book about *her?* How dull *that* would be!

Di shrugged, 'Okay; maybe books and chapters is a bad analogy; let's go back to thinking in terms of inner compartments! You know what you think, but you find it hard to figure out what you feel because your feelings tend to get lost between the different compartments of your life.'

Sarah caught sight of her watch; half an hour left before the end of the session. She would have to walk out or play along; she sighed and tried to concentrate: 'Which is why you say I have to choose what I feel?'

Di said, 'Not exactly. Think of conflict as a way of creating a new compartment. When conflict arises, instead of changing compartments, you could choose to face it head on; like you have been doing.'

Sarah eased her neck brace. If she was staying, she might as well be honest: 'But it doesn't seem to make any difference! When I try to do what you say, it all goes wrong! Take my parents as an example; they just want to avoid arguments at all costs!'

Di laughed, 'And does that description sound familiar? At all?'

Sarah could feel her neck growing warm. 'Yes; well...'

Di continued kindly, 'As we've already established, everyone has feelings and no one likes conflict. How other people deal with conflict is beyond your control but how *you* deal with it isn't. What we need to think about is how you can connect what you feel with the right "inner compartment".'

Sarah could think of nothing to say but Di clearly expected an answer; 'I know that's all true, but it doesn't exactly help...'

Di sat back in her chair. 'All right; what are you feeling right now?'

Sarah considered the question; it was, in its way, quite an interesting question. 'Not much at all.'

Di said, 'I expect that's because you are currently in your "counselling compartment". I expect you've created it during these sessions and I expect you have silent conversations in your head instead of with me. I don't suppose your "counselling compartment" connects with your home compartment, your Dom compartment or any other compartment.'

Sarah eased her collar; her neck had grown even warmer.

Di asked, 'Am I right?'

Sarah took a risk; 'Yes. Probably.'

Di said, 'And how do you feel about that?'

Sarah stared at the coffee table, 'It's embarrassing...'

Di leaned forwards. 'And did you notice what you just said?'

Sarah frowned, 'No; what?'

Di said, 'You said: "It's embarrassing," not: "I'm embarrassed". You are still in your counselling compartment so that you can be objective about this conversation and, in your mind, you are probably exploring other compartments of your life to avoid the feelings you are experiencing right now!'

Sarah's frown deepened. 'And is that a good, or a bad thing?'

Di chuckled, 'Neither; it's just *a thing*. But think about it – you have personal feelings about this session with me but where are they? Which compartment are they in?'

Sarah said, 'I'm not sure…'

Di smiled sympathetically. 'Neither am I.'

Sarah raised her hands helplessly.

Di continued gently, 'Sarah, I'm not sure that you *have* a compartment for your feelings to go into; I think that's why it's so hard for you to find them.'

Sarah choked as shame rose within her and, for a few brief moments, consumed her, but then she recognised the feeling. It felt identical to her experience of shame when she had thought that Neil might have an unhealthy interest in children, and then discovered that his wife and daughter had been killed in a car crash!

Di said softly, 'You see? That feeling comes with a whoomph from somewhere inside you; but then, whoosh, you hop into a different compartment, become objective, and it's gone! But gone where? If we do nothing else in these sessions, maybe we can help you to create a new compartment; somewhere for those feelings to whoosh into; somewhere you can find them?'

Sarah nodded absently. 'There's something else we need to talk about too. I know you said that I shouldn't go digging up the past but I did it anyway and I found out that Sandy's first husband was killed by muggers and now I understand why no one talks about him…'

Di stared at her.

Sarah stopped talking and said, 'What?'

Di said, 'There you go again!'

Sarah blinked hard, 'I'm sorry but I don't understand. I was just telling you a bit more about my family history.'

Di said, 'Exactly. I was talking about helping you to create a compartment for your feelings and then off you go, changing the subject and hopping into a completely different compartment!

You are now talking about something that happened before you were even born!'

Sarah opened her mouth but shut it again. Di was right.

Her counsellor said firmly, 'It's your conflict strategy and it's second nature to you, but I'm not the enemy here – your inner strategy is!'

Sarah said nothing; there didn't seem much point. If she said anything, Di would probably only accuse her of changing compartments!

An unusual silence sat between them and Sarah resisted the urge to check her watch.

Di blew out her cheeks and said, 'Okay. I'm going to try something. Now this is a bit of an experiment but I'm going to try it anyway. Sit back, close your eyes and relax.'

Sarah did as she was told; it would keep Di happy.

'Now,' Di said. 'I want you to find a quiet place inside and say softly, "I am Sarah".'

Sarah decided that she might as well. She relaxed and found a quiet, inner place. It was quite dark but it seemed safe.

'Now,' Di continued. 'Remember this place. It can be your "Sarah compartment".'

Sarah imagined a sign, like a house sign, with 'Sarah' written on it, and hung it in the space. It seemed odd that, although there wasn't anything to hang it on, the sign stayed where it was.

Di said, 'Now. Let's put something into this new compartment. Just now, when we talked about your compartments, you were embarrassed. See if you can find that embarrassment and then channel it into this new place.'

Sarah poked at her memory of a few minutes ago. The shame that she had felt slopped around in the back of her head so she imagined it as a spring of rancid water seeping up around her sign.

Di said, 'And you were probably irritated with me. Allow your irritation to settle next to your embarrassment.'

Sarah watched as some thick ooze joined the rancid water. That was surprising – where had the ooze come from?

Di said, 'And think of a recent point of conflict. Let your feelings about that settle into this new compartment.'

Sarah remembered Dom's suggestion that she should have an allowance. What did she feel about that? Her breathing quickened and her cheeks began to burn; hopping mad – that's how she felt! She herded her anger into the putrid broth around her sign; at first the fetid water hissed but then it caught fire and burned with a foul odour.

Di said, 'Now let's even things up. Sarah, you are an intelligent, remarkable person. Put that in your new compartment.'

Sarah breathed in and allowed the words to drift down into the dark, burning pond around the sign. Nothing changed, but the scene looked a little lighter.

Di said, 'And you are objective about conflict, which is a great strength.'

Again, Sarah allowed the words to drift onto the water around her sign like leaves falling from a tree. Some burned away, but others settled and began to smother the flames.

Di said, 'And now, think about some good things that have happened recently.'

Sarah remembered Neil's kindness. It was like a beautiful flower growing beside the foul pond. There was Henry's kindness too, but his was more like a tall, strong tree. And Ewan's kiss, but that was like fire. It was a good fire though, not like the fire of her anger…

Di said, 'Now, open your eyes.'

Sarah opened them reluctantly. The attic room looked small and gloomy. 'Was that hypnotism?'

Di snorted, 'No, and don't change the subject! How do you feel?'

Sarah said, 'I'm not sure…'

Di said, 'Okay, now think about the compartment you just created and try again: how do you feel?'

Sarah allowed herself to connect with the place she had just left. It was much larger than she had imagined and there was room for a lot more feelings… It was more like a forest glade than a pond and, presumably, every time she put a new feeling into it, the forest, or whatever it was to become, would grow?

Di snapped her fingers several times. 'Stop thinking about it! How do you feel?'

Sarah smiled slowly; she felt at peace. She allowed the feeling to drift down into the forest glade and it became a mist across the water. 'I feel very peaceful.'

Di made a fist as if she was catching a fly and hissed, 'Yes!' She then cleared her throat and said, 'Sorry!'

Sarah grinned.

Di said, 'Now; every time your feelings emerge, or something happens, or you choose to face conflict head on, think of that place inside you called "Sarah" and put your feelings in there. And, whenever someone says something nice to you, or does something nice for you, put how you feel in there. It doesn't matter if the feelings are good or bad, just put them in there. Does that make sense to you?'

'Yes. Complete sense,' Sarah said quietly. She allowed her love for Josh and Minnie to ripple down into her misty forest glade. The scene turned from twilight to noon.

Di blew out her cheeks, 'Well that's a relief 'cos it wouldn't to a lot of people…'

Sarah said, 'Does that make me—'

'It makes you *Sarah*,' Di interrupted.

Sarah closed her eyes. That sounded like a compliment so she let the words settle and a bee buzzed in a daisy.

Di said, 'Good. Now let's talk about Josh.'

Sarah opened her eyes and looked quizzically at her counsellor.

Di said, 'By the sound of it he lives in one big compartment where every area of his life connects with every other area.'

Sarah frowned, 'What makes you say that?'

Di said, 'Well, take home and school as an example. Josh doesn't keep them separate. His father leaves home and his behaviour at school deteriorates. The divorce comes through and he picks a fight he can't possibly win. You have an accident and he fights again.'

Sarah stared at the skylight in the sloping roof. Clouds were scudding overhead.

Di said, 'You wouldn't do that. When you were his age you kept home in your "home compartment" and school in your "school compartment" but Josh is different. He doesn't have compartments; for him, everything is mixed up together.'

Sarah took a deep breath, 'So do I need to help him to create different compartments?'

Di rubbed her face, 'No. He's not you; he's Josh. If you want to help him, he just needs to be able to express how he feels.'

Sarah leapt to his defence, 'But he already does; all the time. Every day at bedtime and whenever he goes to Dom's for the weekend!'

Di said, 'And now you are in your Josh compartment. Okay – how do you feel about bedtime and weekends?'

Tears were back in Sarah's eyes and she grabbed a tissue.

Di said gently, 'I know; it hurts! Now put your feelings about this into your new compartment and let's talk about Josh; about how he feels and about how his feelings are spilling over at school.'

Sarah's mouth trembled as something huge and painful rose within her. She closed her eyes and tipped it towards her forest glade. It crashed into the water like rubble off a builder's truck. She choked out; 'I try; I really, really try…'

Di said, 'I know; but Josh needs help.'

Sarah shut her eyes tight. The school had let her down; there would be no counselling for Josh; if he was going to be helped it would be Sarah who would help him. She allowed her anger and disappointment to settle into her forest glade; it was like burning, poisonous pollution.

She shut her eyes more tightly as something new rose within her.

Di said gently, 'What?

Sarah forced her eyes open and stared at her counsellor. 'I'm frightened…'

Di waited.

Sarah's face collapsed into a distorted, silent howl.

Di whispered with infinite gentleness, 'Of what?'

Sarah screwed her eyes shut as if to blot out the agony, 'Of Dom!'

Di whispered, 'Of Dom?'

Desperately, Sarah deflected her fear into her forest glade; it brooded like a dark cloud over the waters but the paralysing terror subsided. Now that she had admitted it, and now that she had a place to locate it, it seemed almost possible to discuss it. 'Minnie says Josh behaves himself when he's with Dom; he's just slow and truculent.'

Di asked quietly, 'And what do you think is really going on?'

A new agony ripped through Sarah but she managed to choke out, 'I love him so much and it hurts so much and he's only a little boy!'

Di waited.

Sarah allowed her love and helplessness to sink into the glade.

Di said, 'And you are a really good mother; you love your children and you want the absolute best for them.'

Sarah blew her nose. 'But I'm not! If I was…'

Di waited.

Sarah said nothing.

Di suggested, 'If you were, Dom wouldn't have left?'

Sarah twisted the tissue in her hands and said hopelessly, 'It's not true; is it?'

Di said, 'No. It was nothing to do with you; why he left was nothing to do with you.'

Sarah smiled wryly; except that it *was* her fault because she had married Dom in the first place. Then again, if she hadn't, she wouldn't have Josh or Minnie, so then it wouldn't have mattered if Dom had left or stayed. She rubbed her forehead; this was more complicated than working out if the chicken or the egg came first…

Di said gently, 'Have you finished?'

Sarah raised her eyebrows in surprise. 'Finished what?'

Di smiled, 'Have you finished thinking about something in another compartment? Something that isn't relevant to Josh?'

Sarah laughed hesitantly, 'Sorry?'

Di shrugged, 'Like I said; it's second nature to you. You're not going to change in a few minutes!'

Sarah sighed, 'I guess not.'

Di grunted. 'So; let's think; how can you help Josh?'

Sarah looked her counsellor in the eye, 'By choosing to?'

Di smiled. 'Go on.'

Sarah continued, 'By choosing conflict with my family?'

Di nodded and said, 'And?'

Sarah grimaced, 'And with Dom?'

Di nodded emphatically. 'But it may be best, at first, to react when things come your way rather than to go looking for trouble?'

Sarah nodded thoughtfully, 'To get used to it?'

Di smiled and asked, 'However it feels?'

Sarah smiled back. 'However it feels!'

Di began to tidy her papers and Sarah reached for her bag; the session was over and she was exhausted. Should she mention that to Di? Probably best not to; the session was over.

Di stood up and headed for the door.

Sarah followed her. And what about the other things that she had, somehow, not gotten around to mentioning – like Ewan?

Di began to descend the stairs.

Sarah went down after her. Should she mention Ewan?

Downstairs, in the tired reception space, Di opened the front door. 'See you next session, then.'

Sarah smiled and left. Too late now; maybe next time?

She crossed the road and climbed into the car her insurance company had provided until they decided who should pay for a new one. She reached for the ignition key but stopped and sat where she was. She felt, somehow, different, and it wasn't because this was a different car...

She caught sight of herself in the rear-view mirror and said, 'Do you hear that? I *feel* different! Me!' She began to chuckle and then to laugh and, as laughter consumed her and her sides began to ache, the laughter bounced around her inner forest glade like heavy, glorious bubbles.

Her reflection laughed back.

Sarah grinned; 'Maybe Di's right. Maybe this inner glade thing will really help me. And who knows, maybe this will finally let me find out just what happened in the past!'

CHAPTER TWENTY THREE

'You should have brought the children,' Sandy chided as she sashayed around her small kitchen; every movement graceful.

'Were you ever a dancer?' Sarah asked; her heart beating wildly in spite of her innocent expression.

Sandy stopped by her large, upright freezer in mid-pirouette. 'What an extraordinary question!'

Sarah gestured, 'It's just that you're always so graceful. I wondered if you ever went to ballet school?'

Sandy smiled, 'No. I went to dance classes when I was little. Doesn't every little girl?'

'I didn't,' Sarah said.

Sandy opened the freezer door, 'I expect you were busy climbing trees.'

Sarah allowed the low blow to slide into her forest pond. If she could just stay connected to her inner glade and say things out loud instead of in her head, she might finally get somewhere! She said, 'No; it was just that, with Dad being away so much, it was too difficult for Mum to organise lessons for me.'

Sandy peered over the top of the open freezer door. 'I'm sure it was.'

Sarah looked her in the eye, 'But you never pursued it? Dance, that is?'

Sandy's head disappeared behind the freezer door and the sound of rustling competed with her voice. 'No. I suppose I grew out of it.' She emerged from the freezer and shut the door.

'More interested in boyfriends?' Sarah suggested.

Sandy shrugged, 'Not really. My parents were quite strict and, in those days, we had to do what our parents said.'

Sarah nodded. That would explain the elope. 'How about Roy? Did he have lots of girlfriends?'

Sandy shook her head and studied the label on the frozen

chicken in her hands. 'No, not really. He had girls who were friends but nothing serious.'

So he hadn't been in love with Margaret, then? Or had it been love from afar?

Sandy poked at the chicken label. 'You know, I should have got this out yesterday and let it defrost overnight. Still I'm sure it'll defrost in the microwave.'

'Why don't you have it tomorrow?' Sarah suggested. 'It can defrost tonight.'

Sandy looked at her as if she was mad. 'Today's Thursday.'

Sarah nodded. That was true.

Sandy opened the microwave and shoved the chicken-shaped boulder inside. 'We have chicken on Thursday and then chicken pie with the leftovers on Saturday.'

Sarah made a face at her coffee mug. She had forgotten Sandy's unchanging two-week menu.

The microwave light went on and the machine began to hum. Through the glass door, the chicken began to revolve at a stately pace.

Sandy sat down with her coffee and said, 'You should have brought the children, you know.'

'It's a school day,' Sarah said.

'Oh is it? I thought it was half-term or something.'

'No. That's in two weeks' time.'

Sandy sipped her coffee. 'Well you must bring them over then! We'll make chocolate crispy-cakes!'

Sarah smiled, 'I will.'

Sandy's bonhomie slipped as she glanced sideways at Sarah. 'It was nice of you to pop in.'

In other words: Why are you here?

Sarah counted the fruit in the fruit bowl. 'As I said before; I think it's important to keep in touch.'

Sandy grunted.

Clearly it was important for Sandy to keep in touch with the children but not with Sarah.

She tried again, 'Can I ask you a question?'

Sandy's mouth became a thin line, 'It's always questions with you, isn't it? Questions, questions, questions!'

Was that a yes or a no? Sarah decided that it was a yes. 'Last time we talked, we had a misunderstanding about remarriage.'

Sandy tapped her coffee mug with a finger nail. 'That's not a question.'

'No,' Sarah conceded. 'But this is: if I met someone, another man, what would you think of me getting married again?'

'Have you met someone?' Sandy asked quickly.

'No,' Sarah lied. 'I was just asking.'

Sandy pursed her lips. 'I should say it's too early to even think about such a thing. That's what I think. It's never a good idea to hop from one bed straight into another, if you know what I mean?'

So – not like Dom, then, who was now sharing a bed with Alex? And not like Sandy, who had rolled off Gerald's death bed and into Roy's?

Sarah's cheeks grew hot and she tried to guide her shame into her forest glade.

Sandy clucked sympathetically. 'You think men are the answer, but they aren't you know.'

Sarah blinked. Wasn't that almost exactly what her mother had said? 'Is that a quote?'

Sandy blinked back, 'I don't think so; why?'

Sarah shook her head, 'It's just that someone else said more or less the same thing to me the other day.'

Sandy smiled, 'There you are, then. It must be true! No; if I were you, you'd do well to wait until the children are much older. Five years, maybe? Something like that?'

There it was again: almost the same. Were Sandy and Margaret actually still in touch?

'How's the neck, by the way?' Sandy asked.

Sarah fingered her neck brace; 'Pretty uncomfortable.'

Sandy nodded, 'I can imagine. I once put mine out when…

well, never mind, it was a long time ago. It was jolly uncomfortable, though.'

Sarah asked, 'What happened?'

Sandy laughed lightly but her eyes bored into Sarah. 'There are those questions again! Well, if you must know, I fell off my bicycle in the rain.'

Sarah gripped her mug, 'Not dancing then?'

Sandy evaded her eyes, 'No. Why on earth would you think that?'

They both sipped some coffee.

Sandy brightened up. 'We saw Dom at the weekend.'

'Oh yes,' Sarah answered guardedly.

'He gave us a guided tour of his flat. It's really beautiful.'

Sarah felt her neck grow red; at least it wouldn't show through her neck brace. 'I'm sure it is.'

Sandy continued, 'He says that, if he keeps going the way he's going, he'll be Head of Chambers before long.'

Sarah closed her eyes. Counsellor Di was right; she needed to get herself a career.

Sandy patted her hand. 'You look tired, but don't worry; Dom will look after you. You needn't worry.'

A tear trickled down Sarah's cheek.

'There, there,' Sandy commiserated. 'You're still not well. You'd better get home.'

She bustled Sarah off her kitchen chair, into the hallway and into her coat. She stepped past Sarah and opened the front door. Roy was standing there with his key in mid-air.

He looked past Sarah, 'Are the children here?'

Sandy retreated and said, 'No. She just called in for a chat.'

Roy stepped into the hallway and loomed over Sarah. His eyes flashed dangerously.

Sandy said, 'You can let yourself out, can't you?' She turned and went back into the kitchen.

Roy hesitated and then followed her.

Sarah was alone in the hallway but whispered, charged words drifted in from the kitchen. She tiptoed back down the hallway and peeped in through the open door. Roy, his face like thunder, had his fists stuffed into his trouser pockets and Sandy was leaning against the sink, staring disconsolately into the garden, her cheeks gleaming with the trail of tears.

Sarah crept away and silently shut the front door behind her.

In the safety of her car, she burst into tears and allowed them to mix with the water of her inner pond. Even with the help of her inner glade she was never going to find out anything from her parents or from her ex-parents-in-law. She might as well give up her attempts to push conversations in that direction.

Whatever the big secret was, they were going to keep it; and maybe Di was right? Maybe the past was distracting her from the present – and just how awful her relationships with her parents' generation were.

Sarah sniffled away her tears, started her car and drove away.

A new thought struck her and she pulled into the side of the road and switched off the car's engine. Why had she visited Sandy? To find out about the past. Why did she usually visit Sandy and Roy? Because they were Josh and Minnie's grandparents. Not because she wanted to; not because she liked them; only because they were Josh and Minnie's grandparents.

The thought extended. What about her own parents? What about Margaret and Terry? Sarah began to cry again; she didn't like them either and only visited them because they were her parents. Some, tiny part of her, loved her mum and dad – but the rest of her hated Margaret and Terry. The little-girl part of her loved them, but the adult Sarah was living her life to please people she didn't even like. Was that fair? Was that right? Was that normal? No; it couldn't be!

Her tears became a torrent but she allowed them to water her inner forest and, when they subsided, she felt better.

Sarah laughed and exultantly honked her car horn. 'I know how I feel! I know exactly how I feel! Completely alone and completely determined! And I am going to make a new life – for me!'

CHAPTER TWENTY FOUR

'I can start now, if you like,' Sarah said.

Neil smiled across his kitchen island. 'That would be great. As long as you've recovered from your accident, that is?'

Sarah rubbed her neck, 'I'm fine. Now that the brace is off I don't, honestly, think that there was anything the matter.'

Neil's eyebrows rose. 'Really?'

Sarah nodded, glad to be able to. 'Really. I think they only put it on out of fear of being sued; you know, in case my neck was broken and they missed it and I sued them.'

Neil sighed, 'It's a strange world.'

Sarah nodded again. It was.

Neil found some papers in his briefcase. 'I hope you don't mind but I've had a contract drawn up, just in case you said: "Yes". If you just sign here and here, we can do this through the Calvi payroll. Here, have a look through the contract while I sort out the mail.'

Sarah read through the contract and her heart sank. She allowed the feeling to ooze into her forest glade.

Neil finished opening the pile of letters in front of him. 'All okay?'

She shook her head slowly but determinedly.

His face fell. 'What's the problem?'

She pointed out a clause near the bottom. 'This says that I get paid by Bank Transfer.'

Neil frowned, 'Is that a problem?'

Sarah closed her eyes; this was a conflict. It might not be much of a conflict but it was definitely a conflict. She let her desire to retreat sink into her glade and opened her eyes. 'I don't want to go into details, but I don't want my ex-husband to know about this…'

Neil frowned again, but it was a kind frown. 'And if your pay goes straight into your bank account he'll know about it?'

She nodded.

He raised his eyebrows. 'That sounds a little, um, unusual?'

Sarah could feel her cheeks going red, but she allowed her embarrassment to trickle into her glade.

Neil sucked his teeth. 'At the risk of intruding, you should probably discuss your financial arrangements with your solicitor. That's your business, though. Would it help if I paid you in cash?'

Sarah beamed. 'That would be brilliant!'

Neil smiled and reached for a pen. 'No problem.' He amended the contract, signed and dated the amendment and passed it to Sarah. 'There you go. Just make sure that you declare it to the tax man.'

She took the pen and signed the contract with a flourish.

He pulled off a yellow sheet from behind the sheet she had signed. 'That's your copy. Now, just refer to the other sheet I gave you; that one outlines your job.'

She looked through the sheet entitled: 'Job Description'. It was very clear and she would have no trouble with her duties; it was pretty much what she did at home anyway.

'Now,' he said. 'Let me show you where the vacuum cleaner lives and where everything else is kept.'

She followed him around the house while he gave her a guided tour. When they were back in the kitchen, he picked up a pile of letters, made his farewells, gave her a key and left for work.

Sarah made herself a cup of coffee and began work in the kitchen. She worked her way through the downstairs rooms and then, after cleaning the stairs, made a final assault on the bedrooms. Only the bathroom and master bedroom needed attention; clearly the other rooms were unused. Apart from a little light dusting there was nothing else to do.

When she had returned the vacuum cleaner to its cupboard she checked her watch. It was nearly lunch time. She washed up her coffee mug, put it away, closed the front door behind her and slid the key onto her key ring.

As she let herself into her own house, she looked around

sourly; now she would have to do it all again; but not until she had made herself some lunch!

It was a nice day so she took her sandwich into the garden and sat beneath the pear tree. Her garden was pretty unkempt compared to Neil's but it needed to be a space where the children, and especially Josh, could play; somewhere he could kick a ball around and let off steam. If their garden was remotely like Neil's she would be forever nagging Josh to keep away from this or that. She closed her eyes; Neil was very kind, and it had been a pleasant morning. She allowed her feelings of pleasure and gratitude to drift down inside her.

She breathed deeply and contentedly. He was a wonderful man and now she would have some money that was entirely her own. Also, even though his house was pretty tidy in the first place, now that she had cleaned it from top to bottom, the next time she went in her job would be much easier.

She sighed; life was good. Her inner forest glade was getting bigger all the time.

She paused as another feeling emerged coyly. She hadn't noticed at the time but, now that she thought about it, Neil's guided tour had been kind of intimate – as had cleaning and tidying for him… especially in his bedroom! She finished her sandwich and tried to define the feeling. When it wafted down inside her it added a rich and musky perfume. She shifted in her seat because the feeling had a surprising name. It was: 'sexy'.

A large bird fluttered in the tree above her and she squinted up through the branches to see what it was. Her movement must have alarmed it, because it flew off and landed on her television aerial. It was a wood pigeon and its weight made the aerial bounce; it would probably mess up the reception. She jumped up and flapped her arms and it flew off across her neighbour's rooftop.

She breathed deeply, enjoying the slight chill in the air, gathered up the remains of her lunch and went back inside. The kitchen looked okay, but she swept the floor and mopped it before cleaning the downstairs toilet. She then replaced the vacuum cleaner bag and pushed the machine around the living room, hall and study. She considered tidying the study but decided against it; it was her room now so she could be as untidy as she liked in here.

She cleaned the stairs and then did her best with the children's bedrooms. She didn't want to disturb their things, but she did need to keep the dust and fluff to a minimal level. She then focused on the bathroom and finally, her own bedroom.

As she walked in, she stopped dead as if she had walked into a glass wall. This was *her* room now, not, as she had always called it, *our* room. There was no *our* any more; Dom had gone; she was alone.

She sat down heavily on her chair. She had left a couple of folded jumpers on it but she didn't care; she felt something about this room, *her* room, and she needed to understand what it was.

She sat and waited and nothing happened; but her legs felt weak so something was going on. Was it just the thought of being alone? Was she lonely? Why would she feel lonely when she had the children to love? Surely she was beginning a new life? After all, she had a new job and–

Then it hit her.

Her house was just like Neil's house. They were decorated differently, of course, and they each had their own furniture, but they had been built to the same plan. As she sat in her bedroom she could overlay a picture of Neil's bedroom on top of it. In his bedroom she had felt sexy but as she stared at her own room she realised that she had never, ever, felt like that in here…

Grief rose within her and as she sat next to her bed, the symbol of her marriage, she clutched the vacuum cleaner handle as if it was the only solid thing in existence and sank, howling, into the pain of her loss.

Even as she descended into desperation her mind kept working. She opened an imaginary, inner sluice-gate and her pain became a tsunami in her forest glade, churning and drowning everything else.

She slipped down in her seat, accepted the agony that was tearing her apart and acknowledged the truth. She had not lost Dom when he left; she had never had him in the first place! This had never been *their* room; a place where they could share one another's lives; even when they were conceiving the children, she had always, in every way that mattered, been on her own.

She had never, in any real sense, had a husband at all, and, before Dom, she had lived with parents who didn't even like her. Her children loved her, and so did her grandparents, but apart from them, she had never, ever, been loved.

CHAPTER TWENTY FIVE

'I'm sure they'll be all right,' Nanna Gwen asserted.

Sarah squinted at the can of frankfurters in her hand. The writing on the label had faded and it was hard to read, but it looked as if the frankfurters were at least four years beyond their 'use by' date.

Nanna Gwen waved her walking stick dismissively. 'They only put these dates on to persuade you to buy more. During the war we expected canned food to last for years and years and years. Put it back; it'd be a waste to throw it out.'

Sarah swivelled on the chair she was standing on. Perhaps offering to organise Nanna Gwen's larder had been a mistake?

'Go on; put it back,' Nanna Gwen said.

Sarah did as she was told. At least if she returned it to the top shelf there would be no chance of Nanna Gwen getting hold of it; her days of climbing on chairs were over. She pushed the can into the furthest reaches of the shelf in case Nanna Gwen tried to hook it down with her stick. She got off the chair, carried it back to the enormous kitchen table and sat down.

'See?' Nanna Gwen said. 'I told you everything was shipshape and Bristol fashion!'

Sarah nodded. She would sort out her grandmother's larder another time; when Nanna Gwen was otherwise occupied. Hopefully, her efforts today would not be counter-productive; until she had offered to organise the contents of the larder, her grandmother had clearly forgotten what was in it. Now that she had been reminded, hopefully she wouldn't try and feed any of it to Poppa Jack!

Sarah sighed and looked around the familiar kitchen. It was very large but increasingly untidy. The nineteen-fifties kitchen units that were, in her memory, spotlessly clean and clear, were now piled high with cans, food packages and sundry piles of paper. The Aga, which was tucked into the vast fireplace, still provided the only constant source of heat in the house and, up on the high ceiling, between two ancient fluorescent lights, stiff towels and clothes hung from a clothes rail. Sarah sighed; the state of her grandmother's larder was the least of her problems – how long could she continue to look after Poppa Jack at home?

Nanna Gwen limped towards the table, leaning on her newly-acquired walking stick.

Sarah smiled sadly. She felt safe here; and loved; she recognised that now; but for how long?

Nanna Gwen sat down heavily and demanded heartily, 'So: what have you been up to?'

Sarah blew out her cheeks and imagined that she was blowing her negativity out through her mouth. 'Not a lot. Just the usual. Keeping an eye on the kids. Doing lots of housework. You know…'

Nanna Gwen tapped her stick on the floor. 'When Margaret was little we had a woman who came in three days a week to sort out the cleaning and the washing!'

Sarah smiled noncommittally. How would Nanna Gwen feel about her granddaughter becoming just such a woman?

Nanna Gwen grunted. 'We had this one woman; Kate she was called. Seemed to be very honest, even though she came from Palestine; down by the quay; but then, one day, I couldn't find my pearl ring!'

Sarah knew the story off by heart but said, 'Really? Did she steal it?'

Nanna Gwen tapped her stick. 'No idea; it was a damned coincidence, though. Anyway, as there was no evidence, The Captain made up some story and terminated her employment. The next woman was very good; I forget her name, though.'

Sarah smiled, 'I guess you only remember the bad ones?'

Nanna Gwen laughed. 'I suppose so. Take your Dominic, for example. You won't forget him in a hurry, will you?'

Sarah made a face and stared at the surface of the table. It looked sticky.

Nanna Gwen poked her gently with her stick. 'Jolly useful, this!'

Sarah smiled, 'And you're all right? After your fall?'

Nanna Gwen nodded. 'Oh, fine. Just missed my footing on the garden steps. The worst bit was landing in the bushes and then having to roll over and get up; still, at least there was something to hang on to! How about you?'

Sarah rubbed her neck. 'I'm fine – now that I don't have to wear that neck brace I'm fine. Shall I clean the table?'

'No need,' Nanna Gwen asserted.

Sarah stood up, crossed to the sink and found a relatively clean cloth. 'I know, but since it was me that spilled the tea, it ought to be me that cleans it up!'

Nanna Gwen shrugged; clearly this was an argument she accepted.

Sarah filled a bowl with soapy water and made a start on the table. The water soon turned an unpleasant shade of brown. She changed it and resumed her cleaning; she would never tell her grandmother that she had deliberately spilled the tea.

'How do you think Poppa Jack's doing?' Sarah asked.

Nanna Gwen pulled back from the table as some suds flowed in her direction. 'Oh, the same. Just the same.'

Sarah wasn't sure that this was true. Poppa Jack looked, somehow, to have collapsed further inside himself. She rubbed at a particularly stubborn lump of congealed something.

'He's a poor old soul,' Nanna Gwen sighed.

Sarah pursed her lips. The knife edge on which her grandparents lived was getting sharper all the time and when they were gone, this house would never be her refuge again. Her parents would inherit it and, if they sold it, it would become the home of strangers, but if they chose to live in it, she would never visit them here; ever.

'Still,' Nanna Gwen continued. 'We're both well past our threescore years and ten so we mustn't grumble.'

'Don't say that,' Sarah protested.

Nanna Gwen waved her stick. 'But it's true! My father only made it to seventy-two and Mother didn't fare much better. No; we've had a good innings so we mustn't grumble.'

Sarah finished cleaning the table, tipped the water away and rinsed the bowl. She was glad to be able to help them. She loved them and, even if they hadn't been related, she would have still liked them. How long could they remain independent, though? 'Nanna…?'

Nanna Gwen answered, 'Hmmm?'

Sarah sat down again. 'I've been meaning to ask you about that…'

'About what?' Nanna Gwen asked.

The door creaked open and Poppa Jack shuffled in.

Nanna Gwen used her stick and the table to stand up. 'Well come on in, you silly old sod. Don't go blocking out the light! Come and sit down!'

Poppa Jack headed for Sarah's chair and coiled into it. He definitely looked thinner and smaller.

Nanna Gwen sat down again and asked, 'Go on then, what did you want to ask me about?'

Sarah pulled another chair from beneath the table and considered the seat. 'I wanted to ask you about your threescore years and ten; about how things were then and about Mum when she was young.'

Nanna Gwen's voice changed subtly, 'Oh yes?'

Sarah fetched the cloth and wiped the chair seat. 'Yes. I've been looking in the local papers; you know, in the library. I hadn't realised how much things have changed since the nineteen-sixties.'

Nanna Gwen laughed, 'And I suppose that you want to ask me all about it before I pop my clogs?'

Sarah blinked, 'No! That's not what I meant at all!'

Nanna Gwen laughed again. 'Well we *were* talking about me being past my "use by" date weren't we?'

Sarah returned the cloth to the sink and was about to reassure Nanna Gwen that she had years of life left when she realised what had just happened – Nanna had changed the subject; seamlessly. Sarah had asked a question about her mother and suddenly they were talking about Nanna's impending death.

Sarah breathed hard. Is this what she did? With her counsellor? With everyone? She leaned on the sink and examined the window; it needed cleaning too but she could hardly spill tea over the windowpanes as an excuse to clean them!

'Don't you worry, my dear,' Nanna Gwen said firmly. 'I've had a good life and when my time comes I'll meet the Lord with no complaints!'

Sarah turned around. Was this going to turn into another of her grandmother's attempts to invite her to church?

Nanna Gwen continued, 'And don't you worry! When I shuffle off the coil, this will be yours!' She waved her stick in an arc.

Sarah stared. Why would she want her grandmother's stick?

Nanna Gwen chuckled and lowered her voice. 'I expect you thought it would all go to Margaret, but I'm not having your father getting his hands on any of it! Dear me no! And now that your Dominic has buggered off, it's all coming to you. You're the only one I trust – and it'll ensure the future for Josh and Minnie!'

Understanding crashed into Sarah's brain along with an appreciation of what her grandmother had just achieved. The news that she would inherit her grandmother's house was astounding but the timing of the revelation was masterful. How was she going to ask about Gerald Bailey or violence in the sixties now? She was tempted to give her grandmother a round of applause!

'No need to thank me,' Nanna Gwen said bashfully. 'It's the right thing to do.'

What was Sarah supposed to do now? Thank her grandmother or not?

Nanna Gwen poked Poppa Jack affectionately with her stick. 'We can't have our granddaughter going without, can we Captain?'

Poppa Jack chuckled contentedly.

Sarah crossed to the table and sat down. 'Nanna…?'

Her grandmother smiled warmly.

Sarah said seriously, 'You don't have to…'

Nanna Gwen hooted with laughter, 'I know *that*, but I want to! The poor old Captain hasn't got long and I don't suppose I'll be far behind him! It comforts me to know that, when we're gone, you'll be set for life and Dominic can just stew in his own juice!'

Poppa Jack chuckled amiably. 'Stew…'

Sarah said, 'Well; thank you.'

Nanna Gwen laughed again. 'Don't thank me too much – once Margaret and Terry find out, there'll be hell to pay! If I were you, I wouldn't tell them. Pretend you don't know and then, when we're dead and gone, let it come as a big surprise!'

Sarah eyed her grandmother.

Nanna Gwen laughed again, 'Oh, don't take life so seriously! Making a bit of mischief is half the fun!'

Sarah smiled and shrugged. She still had no idea what to say.

Her grandmother made a face and shifted uncomfortably on her chair. 'Now then, you'll have to excuse me. That's a sign of the advancing years; all this laughing has made me need the bathroom!'

Sarah rose from her seat, 'Can I help?'

Nanna Gwen grunted. 'Certainly not. If the time ever comes when I can't go to the toilet on my own, I'll stick a pistol in my mouth and pull the trigger!'

Sarah subsided back into her seat.

Nanna Gwen said to Poppa Jack, 'Don't you worry, Captain. I'll pop the top off your head first!'

Sarah chuckled dutifully; it seemed best to interpret her grandmother's comments as a joke – but what if she meant it? Did she actually have a pistol? It was entirely possible, especially if Poppa Jack had kept his navy revolver.

She glanced at her grandfather but he was gazing into the middle distance.

Nanna Gwen snorted and withdrew from the room. Her limp was definitely worse.

Sarah turned to Poppa Jack and put her hand on his.

His face swung round towards her as if he had only just noticed that she was there.

She said quietly, 'Astonishing; the way Nanna deflected my questions about the past.'

Poppa Jack made a vague noise, deep in his throat.

Sarah said, half to herself, 'And I never realised she felt that way about Dad. She's kept that a dark secret, hasn't she?'

Poppa Jack chuckled and his dry, bony fingers wrapped around hers.

Sarah smiled ruefully, 'I don't suppose I'll ever get to ask her about the past and, if I do, she'll just change the subject and avoid conflict; just like me.'

Poppa Jack murmured, 'Conflict…'

She patted his hand, 'Yes Poppa. You were no stranger to conflict, were you? It was your job; your life!'

He chuckled and again murmured, 'Conflict…'

She said, 'Yours was a different kind of conflict though, wasn't it? Not like the gang fights and the beatings and the robberies and all that.'

Poppa Jack tapped the table with his gnarled knuckles; 'Bad boys…'

'Bad boys?' Sarah said.

Poppa Jack's watery eyes found hers. 'Terry and Roy; bad boys.'

She caught her breath and willed him to say more but his attention seemed to wane. She said gently, 'Terry and Roy, Poppa Jack? Captain? Terry and Roy?'

His attention returned, his mouth became a firm line and in little more than a whisper he said, 'They went looking…'

Sarah leaned closer. 'Went looking for what, Poppa. Went looking for what?'

His attention receded and he gazed through her.

She patted his hand again, 'Terry and Roy, Poppa. What did they go looking for?'

He chuckled amiably and his attention dropped to the fingers of his other hand.

Sarah glanced towards the door; her grandmother would be back soon; this was her chance and she didn't have long. She bent sideways so that she could look into his face. 'What did they go looking for, Captain? Terry and Roy?'

He looked at her and for a moment his attention was back and then it receded again.

Beyond the kitchen, the sound of the toilet flush reverberated through the house. Nanna Gwen would be back in a minute. Sarah tried one last time. She said formally, 'Captain! What did Terry and Roy go looking for?'

Poppa Jack bowed his head and whispered a word.

Sarah stroked his hand. He hadn't answered her question; instead he had given his opinion of Terry and Roy. He had whispered, 'Buggers.'

Nanna Gwen limped back into the kitchen and sat down. 'There now; what were we talking about?'

Sarah made a wry face; 'We were talking about how you've decided to leave the house to me.'

Nanna Gwen hooted and slapped the table. She waved her stick in an arc again. 'Not just the house; everything! I said everything!'

Sarah gaped at her.

Nanna's laughter diminished to a chuckle. 'Now; let's have a really good chat about just, exactly, how angry my darling daughter is going to be!'

CHAPTER TWENTY SIX

Josh had gone to see who had rung the doorbell. Sarah clapped her hands to remove some of the flour that coated them and handed the mixing bowl to Minnie; she would probably have to shoo away a door-to-door salesman.

Josh's voice drifted quietly across the kitchen. 'Mummy!'

Minnie put the mixing bowl under the mixer, clicked it into place and the machine began to gently churn the cake mix.

Josh's voice was more insistent. 'Mummy!'

Sarah dusted the remains of the flour off her hands and turned towards the kitchen door. Josh was hovering just beyond the door frame; he looked tense and very pale. She said, 'Are you all right, Josh?'

His eyes became even bigger and his bottom lip trembled. 'Mummy – there's a policeman! At the door! A policeman!'

Sarah frowned. What had Josh been up to? She walked towards him and he drifted sideways into the hall and then hid inside her study. Sarah stopped and said, 'Josh…?'

He seemed to shrivel, 'I said sorry; you know I did; you were there – with Mrs Hopkins. I said sorry…'

Sarah hesitated. Should she stay with Josh or answer the door? She glanced up the hall; the front door was slightly open. She smiled reassuringly at Josh and went to find out why a policeman had called at her house. She pulled the door fully open and was greeted by DCI Driffield. He was standing, two steps down on the path but, even so, his eyes were level with Sarah's.

'Hello,' he said.

Sarah stared. 'Is there a problem?'

He frowned, 'Not as far as I know, why?'

Sarah frowned in return, 'Is this about my accident?'

His frown lifted. 'No, no. I was just passing so I thought I'd find out how you were getting on.'

Sarah said, 'And it's not about the children and no one's had a fatal accident or anything?'

He made a face, 'The copper's burden! We're not always the harbingers of doom, you know. I really was just passing and I really did just want to find out how you were doing.'

Sarah said, 'But how did you know where I live?'

He reached into his pocket and pulled out his police ID wallet. Clearly, in his mind, this explained everything.

Sarah paused; she must resist the urge to change compartments. How did she feel about Henry Driffield turning up on her doorstep? Actually, quite pleased… 'You'd better come in.'

She backed into the hall to give him space. Now that he was inside, he made everything look smaller. She said, 'Come into the kitchen. We're making cake.'

Henry beamed. 'Cake? I like cake!'

As they reached the kitchen door Sarah turned and said, 'Josh; this is Mr Driffield. He's the kind man I told you about; the one who stopped and helped me when I had the car crash. He's come round to see if I'm all right. Isn't that nice?'

Josh blinked, nodded and stared up at the detective. He must look absolutely terrifying to a boy of nine.

They went into the kitchen and Josh followed.

Sarah said, 'Minnie, this is—'

'I heard,' Minnie said. She dashed some hair out of her eyes with the back of her hand, leaving a trail of flour. 'Hello Mr Driffield.'

He smiled and said, 'Hello. Call me Henry.'

There was an awkward pause when no one said anything.

'Please, Sir?' Josh said.

Sarah, Henry and Minnie swivelled together. Josh was back to his normal self; the colour had returned to his cheeks and he looked enthusiastic and excited. He said, 'Have you got a Taser?'

Henry's laugh rumbled around the kitchen, 'Not on me, no! When we go into certain situations we carry them.' He cocked his head and lifted one eyebrow, 'Not when we visit people's kitchens, though!'

Minnie laughed and returned her attention to the mixer but Josh continued undeterred. He mimed shooting someone and cried, 'But, shoom; you zap 'em, don't you?'

Henry grinned but answered seriously, 'We warn them and if they pay no attention we warn them again. If they continue to pay no attention, though…'

Josh looked expectantly at the policeman.

Henry winked, mimicked Josh's mime and said, 'Shoom; we zap 'em!'

Josh crowed with delight and rushed out of the kitchen. His cries of 'Shoom,' retreated upstairs.

Sarah chuckled. 'Tea?'

Henry grinned. 'Please.'

She went over to the kettle while he drifted over to Minnie and asked her about cakes. When the tea was ready Sarah found the largest mug in the cupboard and handed it to him.

He took a large gulp and watched as Minnie poured the cake mix into a baking tin. She paused and asked him, 'Doesn't that hurt?'

He looked perplexed.

Minnie said, 'Drinking hot tea like that. Doesn't it hurt?'

He regarded the contents of his mug. 'Never really thought about it.' He swilled the tea, took another enormous gulp and made a face. 'Actually, yes; it does!'

She giggled, 'You're mad!'

He leaned towards her and said confidentially, 'To be honest, in my job, it helps!'

Minnie giggled again and glanced at him through her eyelashes.

Sarah sipped her tea; Minnie was definitely growing up…

Henry took another gulp of tea, made another pained face and then stood back as Minnie opened the oven door and slid the cake tin inside. She set the timer, smoothed her hands on her apron and took it off. She glanced from Henry to Sarah and smiled sweetly, 'I'll be back in ten minutes. I'm sure you have a lot to talk about.'

Henry chuckled as she left the kitchen, 'Nice girl.'

Sarah nodded; that was a compliment. She let it settle inside her beside the pleasure of Henry's presence.

She nodded towards the kitchen table. 'Have a seat.'

He pulled out a chair and sat down. He was wearing the same black coat that he had been wearing on the day of the crash but his hair was a little shorter; perhaps he had recently had it cut? He smiled and asked, 'So; how's it going?'

Sarah sat down opposite him. 'Fine. I had to wear that neck brace for a week but there was nothing wrong. It was like you said; just a precaution.'

He pulled his thick coat open and flapped it, 'Do you mind if I take this off? It's hot in here.'

Sarah said, 'Make yourself at home.'

He shrugged out of his coat and let it drop over the back of his chair. His suit was good quality but showing signs of wear; perhaps it was his 'on duty' suit? Presumably he *was* on duty? He sat very upright, as if ready to spring into action at any moment and his eyes flicked around the room. His eyes settled on Sarah as he asked, 'And how about the insurance and so forth?'

Sarah smiled, 'My insurance company has written to say that the accident wasn't my fault. Hopefully they'll follow up with a cheque at some point so that I can buy another car! I'm not really sure about the "so forth" though?'

Henry glanced at her and chuckled. 'I guess that remains to be seen…'

Josh burst into the kitchen. He was carrying a small cereal box in one hand. He had stuck two cocktail sticks into the top, tied a length of cotton to them and attached a blob of blu-tack to the other end of the cotton. He shouted, 'Shoom,' and jerked the cereal box forwards. The cotton snaked out and the blu-tack hit the fridge with a dull thud and dropped to the floor.

Henry leaned sideways and retrieved it. 'You need something stickier.'

Josh made a face, 'It worked upstairs.'

Henry examined the blu-tack professionally. 'It's got fluff on it. You definitely need something stickier.'

Josh reeled in the cotton and said enthusiastically, 'I've got some silly putty. That might work.'

Henry nodded but kept hold of the blu-tack. 'There's one more thing, though.'

Josh continued to reel in the cotton, walking towards the detective as he wound it around the cocktail sticks.

Henry handed him the blob of blu-tack. 'Before you Taser the fridge, you have to warn it!'

Josh frowned and pursed his lips.

Henry dropped his voice confidentially; 'I suggest you tell it to move. If it doesn't, Taser it!'

Josh's face lit up and he rushed from the room.

Sarah sipped her tea. 'Your kids must love you.'

Henry looked at her in surprise. 'I don't have any; I'm not married.'

She continued to look at him. Why was he telling her that?

He shrugged. 'And no partner, either. I'm just a good uncle; well, from the kids' point of view I am. I'm not sure that my brother's wife appreciates me winding them up…'

Sarah smiled. His sister-in-law must be particularly anal if she objected to him horsing around with her children. She said, 'I'm sorry that I didn't get round to calling you.'

He sat back in his chair and grabbed his chest as if pained.

Sarah laughed, 'Yeah; right!'

There was a pause when neither of them said anything; but it was a comfortable pause.

He put his empty mug down on the table, glanced around the room again and asked, 'Do you enjoy living here, in Twisle Drift? I know someone who lives up the road from here…'

She kept her expression neutral; it might be a policeman or a criminal… She said, 'It's good for the children, and it's nice and quiet, too.'

He smiled. 'That sounds like a justification?'

Sarah sighed; she was quoting again. 'It was Dom who wanted to live here, really, not me.'

'Dom?' he asked gently.

She made a wry face. 'My ex-husband.'

He said, 'Ah. That explains it.'

She glanced at him. 'I'm sorry; explains what?'

He nodded towards her left hand. 'No rings.'

She examined her fingers. She had removed her rings the day that she had received that letter; the one that said that she had been divorced for a fortnight.

His voice dropped sympathetically, 'Oh, I'm sorry. I didn't mean to upset you.'

She was tempted to change the subject but she might as well experiment with acknowledging her feelings with a stranger; with a professional who had no personal interest in her. She waved her hand to show that it was all right, allowed her sense of loss to sink down inside her, fished out a tissue and dabbed at her eyes.

They sat in silence and the detective showed no sign of moving. He had probably been trained to put up with the ridiculous emotions of others.

Josh rushed back in and shouted, 'Fridge! Move!' He glanced at Henry.

Henry said, 'Clear defiance! Hasn't moved an inch!'

Josh shouted, 'Shoom,' and the cotton snaked from his hand. The silly putty landed on the fridge door with a satisfying splat and stayed where it was. Josh shouted, 'Zzzzzzz,' retrieved the putty and ran upstairs shouting, 'Min! Min!'

Henry grinned and said casually, 'Your documents said that you were Sarah Price?'

She nodded. He must mean her driver's licence and insurance note. He had checked them on the day of the accident. That must be where he had got her address from; he must have a prodigious memory.

He drummed his fingers on the table. 'And you say that your ex-husband is called Dom? Would that, by any chance, be Dominic Price, the barrister?'

She nodded again. Henry must have come across Dom in court.

He blew out his cheeks.

She glanced at him and caught his gaze. 'What?'

His face became inscrutable, 'I'm just surprised; that's all.'

She held his gaze and raised her eyebrows.

He said, 'It's just that I'd always assumed that Dominic Price was, um, single?'

Sarah dropped her gaze to her fingers. Her ringless fingers. Oh God – was she the *only* one who hadn't realised that Dom was gay?

Henry said softly, 'You have wonderful children.'

She sighed; she might as well answer his unspoken question but why did he want to know who the father of her children was? She shrugged. It was a probably a police thing. She said, 'We do. Dom and I. Our children.'

Silence descended again but he still showed no sign of leaving. Maybe he was on a case and needed to kill some time somewhere out of public view? That would explain why he had turned up so unexpectedly.

Sarah made a decision; it was time to change compartments. He was a policeman so maybe she could make use of that? 'Can I ask you something?'

Henry rubbed his eyes lazily. 'Of course.'

She said, 'You know these TV dramas about crimes from the past?'

He nodded, 'You mean cold cases?'

She nodded in return. 'Are there really police departments that look into them?'

He shook his head slowly, 'Not as such. What you see on TV is fiction. Usually, when a cold case is of interest, a team is set up to investigate it or re-investigate it. Once the investigation is over, everyone moves on.'

Sarah's face fell. 'Oh.'

He asked, 'Why?'

She glanced at him. He looked interested so she said, 'Well, I recently found out that Dom's mother had a husband before she met Dom's father. I went to the library and looked through the press cuttings.'

He said; 'That doesn't sound like a cold case.'

She said, 'The thing is; his name was Gerald Bailey. He lived in Pentonville, in London, and he was mugged in an alley near his flat; in nineteen sixty-nine; on October the eighteenth; and he died. I found this newspaper article about it but I don't know what happened next – if anyone was ever arrested or what happened to them; that sort of thing.'

He frowned. 'Have you asked your family about it?'

She made a face. 'No one talks about it; that's why I went to the library.'

He regarded her sceptically.

She said quickly, 'I understand why. It's because Gerald was a successful actor; Dom's father is very ordinary, so no one talks about Gerald. I just wanted to know a bit more about it, that's all. You know, so that I can tell the children the family history some time.'

The detective seemed to consider what she had told him.

She said, 'Not to worry, though. It doesn't matter.'

He came to a decision, pulled out a notebook and jotted down the details. 'No problem. It's probably not a cold case as such but I'll get someone to look in the files and let you know what happened.'

They sat in silence again.

The oven timer pinged and Minnie clattered back into the kitchen. She glanced from Henry to Sarah and asked, 'Having a nice time?'

Henry smiled broadly and tucked his notebook away. 'Yes, but I need to make a move.'

Sarah stood up, 'Well, thank you for calling in. It was very kind of you.'

He stood up and she escorted him into the hall, opened the front door and squeezed herself against the wall so that he could get past.

As he stepped outside, he turned and smiled. 'It was good to see you.'

She smiled back. 'Thank you, again.'

He patted the pocket where he had put his notebook. 'I'll be in touch.'

'Thank you; you're very kind.'

He turned and walked away; he had the same air of confidence and power that she had noticed in the hospital. At the end of her drive he turned right and walked up the road. Perhaps he was going to call on the other person he knew in Twisle Drift? The policeman; or the criminal...

She shut the door, went back to the kitchen and began to wash up.

Minnie joined her, cloth in hand. 'So that's Mr Driffield?'

Sarah nodded. Should she have that mother-daughter talk about flirting with older men? Maybe another time; Minnie was learning to handle her first period and her emotions were somewhat random at the moment.

Minnie dried the mixing bowl carefully. 'Do you like him?'

Sarah paused, washing-up brush in mid-air, 'He's been very kind.'

Minnie snorted.

Sarah let the brush, and her hand, drop into the soapy water. She turned to her daughter. 'What does that mean?'

Minnie picked up the mixing spoon and began to dry it. She glanced at Sarah. 'Mum; why do you think he came?'

Sarah said, 'He wanted to make sure that I was all right after the accident. As he said, he was passing so he just popped in.'

Minnie gave Sarah an old-fashioned look.

Sarah frowned. Perhaps she *should* talk to Minnie about older men now...

Minnie peered into her face, 'Mum?'

Sarah frowned, 'Hmmm?'

Minnie said, 'You do know – don't you?'

Sarah's frown deepened, 'Know what?'

Minnie said, 'That he came here to see you?'

Sarah nodded. 'Of course; after the accident.'

Minnie rolled her eyes. 'Mum; the accident had nothing to do with it!'

Sarah tried to make sense of this.

Minnie said, 'Mum! For goodness sake! He was here because he fancies you something rotten!'

CHAPTER TWENTY SEVEN

The creature stood, face to the wall, refusing to move and refusing to speak.

Sarah sighed and said to Minnie, 'Take your bag and go and wait in the car, will you?'

Minnie hesitated.

Sarah smiled and sat down at the bottom of the stairs. 'Go on. I need to talk to Josh – and if you hear screaming, just stay in the car.'

The creature moved fractionally.

Minnie glanced from Josh to Sarah, picked up her bag and left the house.

Sarah studied the creature. She understood, now, that he wasn't a creature; he was Josh. She had only called him *the creature* to rationalise his behaviour; to put him in a compartment that she could cope with; but he wasn't a creature, he was a little boy who hated what had happened to his life. He was very different to her as well; he had no compartments; he was just Josh and he needed her help.

She knew what she had to do. She got off the stairs, hugged him and forced him to face her. 'Josh. I know how you feel.'

He refused to meet her gaze.

She said. 'And I'm going to show you how I feel.'

His eyes flicked briefly to her face.

She smiled and pushed him gently against the wall. 'You just stand there and watch and listen.'

She stepped back and he began to tremble. He looked very small and frail. She smiled reassuringly; 'Don't be frightened. I've never shown you how I feel – about Daddy leaving – but now I'm going to. Don't be scared. This is about me; not you!'

She closed her eyes and found her forest glade. Should she do this? Was it right for a parent to do what she was about to do?

She batted the thought away; she was in the right compartment and she wasn't about to change it for another one.

She found the ooze that festered in her pond and allowed it to become a geyser. It forced its way up her throat and she threw back her head and howled like a banshee. Tears flooded from her eyes, pain clawed at her stomach and she doubled over and sank onto her knees on the hall rug, screaming, weeping and gasping.

She became aware of a hand on her hair, gently stroking and caressing.

Josh whispered, 'Mummy?'

She allowed her emotions to drain back into her pond and sat back on her heels.

Josh stared at her. He was crying too. 'Mummy?'

'Yes,' she said. He was right; she wasn't a creature any more than he was; she was his mummy and she needed him as much as he needed her. She held him tight and he pushed himself against her as, together, they wept.

Sarah sensed that it was time to move. She blew out her cheeks, found a tissue and dried her eyes and his. 'Let's go and sit on the stairs for a bit. My back is killing me, kneeling here!'

They sat together at the foot of the stairs. Her arm was around his shoulders as she asked, 'Were you frightened? I'm sorry if you were.'

He shook his head, 'A bit; at first. Then I was just sad.'

New tears arrived in her eyes. Had she made things worse? 'Sad?'

He nodded, 'You feel just like me and it's horrid! I hate that you feel like me!'

She pulled him close, 'Oh Josh, I'm sorry.'

He wept into her chest and muttered vehemently, 'It's not your fault!'

She said, 'But I showed you – and it made you sad!'

He pressed closer to her, 'But it's not you! It's Daddy!'

What was she supposed to say? That grown-ups sometimes didn't get on? That it was as much her fault as Dom's? That it was all her fault for marrying Dom in the first place? No; for better or for worse she needed to tell the truth. 'Yes,' she said. 'You're right. It's his fault.'

Josh stopped crying and wiped his nose with the back of his hand.

Sarah said, 'But life is complicated and we all do things we shouldn't.'

He stared straight ahead. 'Like me fighting Ryan?'

She stroked his shoulder and nodded, 'Like you fighting Ryan.'

His breathing became ragged, 'And like wishing Alex was dead?'

Sarah forced herself to breathe normally. 'Daddy loves Alex and we shouldn't wish for anyone to die.'

Josh became rigid, '*I* do; I wish he was dead.'

Sarah waited for a moment; what would Di say to that? She said gently, 'I don't know if you'll understand this, Josh, but have you noticed that coins have two sides? There's a picture of the Queen on one side and something else on the other?'

He relaxed a little and nodded.

She said, 'Well, the way we feel is a bit like a coin but on one side there is love and on the other side there is hate. You can't have one side without the other; everyone loves and everyone hates.'

After a few moments he asked, 'So do I hate Alex because I love Daddy?'

She kissed the top of his head. 'In a way, but people are more complicated than coins…' She was in deep water – what if he asked if he hated Dom because he loved her?

He nodded, 'Is it all right to hate people?'

Sarah dredged up a conversation she had had with Di, 'It's neither right nor wrong. It just is. What matters is what we do about it.'

After a time he asked, 'Do I have to pretend that everything's all right?'

She pulled him close. 'I don't think you do. At bed time, and when we go to Daddy's, you show exactly how much you hate what's happened.'

He wriggled beneath her arm. 'I pretend at Daddy's.'

Sarah considered what she should say: she asked, hesitantly, 'Perhaps you shouldn't?'

He became very still, 'You mean…'

She squeezed his shoulders, 'Yes. I mean just be yourself. When you're at Daddy's. If you want to cry; cry. If you want to jump up and down and scream; do it. Just be yourself.'

He fiddled with his fingers, 'Won't Daddy mind?'

She laughed. 'I expect he will!'

Josh faced her and grinned, 'But I should still do it?'

She kissed his forehead. 'It's what you do at home and I still love you. Why would it be any different at Daddy's?'

Josh thought this over. 'Because *you're* different.'

She stared at him. 'Do you know what, Josh? You are a very wise young man…'

He smiled proudly.

She said, 'I can't tell you what to do or not to do. All I can tell you is that if you pretend with Daddy and Alex, no one can sort anything out. If you're honest, we can. I don't know what Dom will do if you throw a wobbly in his flat, or at the zoo, or wherever you go together, but what I want you to understand is this: if you *do* behave badly when you are at Daddy's, you won't get into trouble with me.'

He nodded. 'Because you feel like me?'

She kissed his forehead again. 'Because I feel like you. Now, let's get your bag and go to Daddy's.'

He jumped off the stair, grabbed his bag and rushed out to the car shouting, 'Min! Min! You'll never guess what Mummy just did!'

Sarah set the alarm and closed the door behind her. Had she done the right thing or just sent Josh back to square one? She had no idea, but she had to do something. Di was always saying how important it was to take risks; well she had taken one and with no one to counsel Josh she just had to do her best.

She had almost reached her car when she noticed Neil, over the hedge, in his front garden.

He straightened up, gardening fork in hand. 'Is everything all right?'

She smiled and waved at the car, 'Just taking the children to their father for the weekend.'

He said, 'Ah…'

She asked, 'Why?'

He looked embarrassed. 'It's just that I heard shouting…'

Sarah breathed deeply and said lightly, 'Just a domestic.'

He said, 'Ah…'

She smiled, 'Nothing to worry about. Sorry if we disturbed you.'

He nodded sympathetically and returned to his gardening.

Sarah was very grateful that he had turned away from her; the look on his face made her want to cry.

Sarah pulled up outside Dom's building and sang out, 'Here we are.'

Dom bounded down the steps onto the pavement and greeted the children loudly. 'Guess what we've got lined up this weekend?'

Minnie muttered, 'Can't wait,' as she climbed out of the car.

Josh stood on the pavement and said, 'What?'

Dom danced like a boxer and punched him playfully, 'I said: "Guess." So go on: guess!'

Josh glanced at his shoes and then back at his father. 'No.'

Dom stopped dancing around and glared unhappily at Sarah.

She said, 'Well go on; tell him.'

Josh flicked a grateful glance at her.

Dom stood up straight and said heartily, 'We're going down a mine!'

Josh was clearly interested but he watched his father carefully and asked; 'Why?'

Dom seemed to shrink slightly. 'Because it'll be fun!'

Josh thought this over, 'Who for?'

Dom snapped, 'Get your bag and go inside. I want a word with your mother.'

Josh turned hunted eyes on Sarah.

She smiled reassuringly. 'Do as Daddy says. He won't be long.'

Josh collected his bag and went inside with Minnie.

Dom loomed over her, 'What's the matter with him? What have you been saying?'

Sarah accessed her forest glade. 'Nothing and the truth.'

Dom stepped even closer.

She dipped into her glade and said firmly, 'Will you step away from me please.'

He stayed where he was.

She delved deeper into her forest glade and connected with the name she had given it right at the beginning: 'Sarah'. She deserved better than this. 'In that case, Dom, this conversation is over.'

He grabbed her arm.

Fear lanced through her and then rage. How dare he? From the corners of her eyes she could see that there were other people in the street so she screamed as loudly as she could and a woman with a small dog stopped. She looked vaguely familiar and she asked anxiously, in a curiously foreign accent, 'Is everything all right?'

Sarah called, 'No. This man has grabbed me. Call the police!'

Dom let go, turned to the woman and flicked on his charm. 'It's all right, she's my wife.'

Sarah said defiantly, 'No I'm not. Call the police.'

The woman backed away and pulled out a mobile phone.

Dom hesitated in the space between Sarah and her new ally. He was clearly weighing his present predicament against his future career.

Sarah said softly, 'If you don't want her to call, back off!'

He retreated a few paces and said, 'I'm sorry.'

Sarah walked towards the woman. 'It's all right. You don't need to call them. I can sort this out.'

The woman paused, fingers on her phone keys, 'Are you sure?'

Sarah nodded, 'He's just a bully who needs putting in his place. I'll be fine now.'

The woman looked uncertain. 'Do you want me to stay?'

Sarah laid a grateful hand on the woman's arm. 'Would you?'

The woman smiled, 'Of course; it's not as if we don't know each other.'

Sarah's memory clicked. Of course, it was the librarian! 'Thank you, Ruth.'

She beckoned to Dom and he approached cautiously. 'Now. I haven't done anything to Josh. It's just that he hates what's happened and until now he's kept how he feels a secret from you. When he comes to stay he pretends that everything's all right, but it isn't and it's tearing him up. I've just told him that he doesn't have to pretend any more.'

Dom opened his mouth but she interrupted him; 'I love Josh whether he's good, bad or ugly. I've told him that you do too.'

Dom glared at her. He rocked forwards as if he were about to take a step, glanced at Ruth and stopped.

Sarah said, 'So prove me right or prove me wrong. It's up to you.'

His face went blank, he turned on the spot and stalked away, up the steps and into the building.

Ruth let out a rush of air, 'Hell's teeth; he's petulant!'

Sarah sagged; 'You have no idea!'

Ruth gently pulled on her dog lead and the small white terrier beside her obediently sat down. She asked, 'Would you like Rex to poo on his doorstep?'

Sarah laughed. The librarian clearly had a sense of humour; why else would she name such a tiny dog Rex? She said, 'No; it's fine. It's not just *his* doorstep so it wouldn't be fair on the other people who live in the building.'

Ruth smiled.

Sarah smiled back, 'Thanks for offering, though.'

'No problem. Are you sure you're all right?'

Sarah shrugged, 'Like I said, he's just a bully. Thank you for bringing up the reinforcements!'

'No problem. Well. If you're sure that you're all right, I'll get Rex down to the beach. See you at the library sometime, I expect.'

Sarah smiled and watched her go. She needed some time to think; about what she'd just done and about what she'd just said. Until she'd said it, she'd never realised it before, but Dom was a bully. It was true, and she knew it was true, but what did it mean? Had she, for example, as she had always thought, married him because she wanted to or because he had bullied her into it?

She needed to think about that and the key was probably to access her feelings – but she had no idea where her old feelings about Dom were. She could access her recent feelings about him because she had tipped them into her pond; but her old feelings? Where were they?

However, she had again chosen conflict with Dom and this time she had accessed her forest glade! Actually, she needed to start thinking of it as her 'Sarah' compartment. But, whatever she called it, astonishingly, her feelings had strengthened her, not weakened her, and she had stood up to Dom! Good God – she had even threatened him!

Sarah laughed aloud.

'What's funny?' asked Minnie.

Sarah did a double-take. 'What are you doing here?'

Minnie opened the car boot, grabbed a small bag and declared: 'I forgot my makeup.'

Sarah stared. 'Makeup? You don't wear makeup!'

Minnie straightened up. She was almost as tall as Sarah now and she said defiantly, 'I do when I'm at Daddy's!'

Sarah chuckled. 'Fair enough – but we'll talk about it when you get home.'

Minnie tensed, 'Why?'

Sarah kissed her on the cheek. 'Because we want to make sure you're using the right foundation for your colouring.'

Minnie threw her arms around her and hugged her. 'I love you, Mum!'

Sarah hugged her back. 'And I love you too.'

Minnie pulled away and bounced up the steps. At the top, she turned and said, 'By the way; have a nice time.'

Sarah frowned.

Minnie said innocently, 'Wherever you're going. Have a nice time!'

Sarah questioned her with a look.

Minnie pointed towards the boot of the car. 'Wherever you're going with that case. The one under the blanket in the boot. Have a nice time.' She grinned and went into the building.

Sarah grimaced. So much for subterfuge.

CHAPTER TWENTY EIGHT

Sarah emerged from the Yacht Club toilets, overnight bag in hand and feeling rather self conscious. Almost without thinking, she let the feeling slide down into her inner, Sarah compartment. She caught sight of herself in the mirrored wall of the Yacht Club entrance lobby and smiled. The hours she had spent trawling the internet for makeup tips had paid off and she had made good use of the samples Neil had given her; she looked very nice. Her new, blue, pencil skirt complimented her lighter blue vee-neck sweater, her new, white blouse, and her black shoes. Sarah smiled; now that she had her own money it felt good to spend it. Her heels clicked confidently as she walked and her green-flecked moonstone pendant nestled in her cleavage. Her breasts were smaller than Ruth's, but so was her pendant.

She walked out of the Yacht Club, put the case, which now contained her jeans, her old sweater and her trainers, in the boot of her car and pulled on her rain coat. There: she was ready. She locked the car and walked along the quay side.

Several men, working on boats, watched her as she walked by. She hid her grin. She had been right about Ruth's sense of style and right to copy it – and what a coincidence that she should meet the librarian when her new ensemble was hidden in the boot of her car! At least, she *thought* it had been hidden but Minnie was a sharp cookie! She smiled sourly; never mind. They could have a girlie chat about clothes and makeup on Sunday night; or whenever.

Someone whistled and Sarah glanced around in surprise. A workman leered at her and she allowed the mixed feelings of pleasure and disquiet to slide down inside her.

She turned onto the pier where Ewan's boat was moored. He was waiting and her confident steps faltered. He was wearing a bright blue jacket and a bobble hat. He looked as if he was ready to go sailing…

She reached his boat and glanced at the sail; it was still furled.

He said, 'You look wonderful.'

She eyed him suspiciously. Maybe it wasn't her getting it wrong? Maybe it was him?

He burst out laughing. 'Just a joke!' He pulled off the bobble hat and the jacket to reveal smart-casual clothes.

'Oh: ha ha!' Sarah said, but she couldn't help smiling.

He jumped onto his boat, opened a hatch, tossed his things inside and landed back beside her on the pier. He offered her his arm, 'Shall we?'

She settled next to the rhythm of his stride and listened while he pointed out yet more boats that interested him. When they reached the Yacht Club, he escorted her to the restaurant, guided her to a table, held her rain coat as she slipped out of it and held her chair for her. When they were seated, he said, 'You're very quiet. Not my little joke, I hope?'

Sarah shook her head, 'No; just a busy week, that's all.'

He nodded, 'Me too.'

Sarah could feel herself sinking; clearly there was more to a date than dressing attractively. She deliberately changed compartments. She was determined to enjoy herself. 'You said that you work with computer software?'

He nodded, 'I want to specialise in digital music but at the moment I'm designing games for smartphones.'

'Oh, really?' Sarah said, trying to sound interested.

He nodded again. 'It's the next big thing; applications for smartphones; apps; they're going to make a fortune!'

Sarah made an indeterminate noise.

His nodding became enthusiastic. 'My latest app is a zombie game but the twist is that it runs in tandem with a pulse monitor. The calmer you are, the greater the carnage!'

Sarah said, 'It sounds, er, wonderful?'

He grinned, 'It's brilliant; gore and guts all over the place. It'll make a mint but we need to sort out a suitable title for it first.'

Sarah nodded sympathetically. No doubt the title: 'Complete Crap' had already been considered and dismissed?

'How about you?' he asked. 'What do you do?'

She almost said: 'nothing' but stopped herself. She was not about to admit that she was a full-time mother and a part-time cleaner. 'I'm self-employed at the moment.'

He sounded interested, 'Doing what?'

She smiled wearily, 'Look; do you mind if we don't talk about work? It's been a long week…'

He grinned. 'Good idea. Let me get you a drink and then we'll order some food.'

She watched as he made his way to the bar. He was a nice man, and she'd really been looking forward to this evening, but now that she was here, she wasn't sure that this was where she wanted to be. She sighed; that was the problem with feelings — they were so unpredictable!

She closed her eyes. When she was married, everything was simple; it was just Dom, her and the children. Well, and her parents, and his parents, of course, and their friends too…

Her eyes flicked open. Except — they weren't *her* friends, were they? The couples they had welcomed into their home; the people who had reciprocated their invitations. All those dinner parties and weekend visits, and those people weren't *her* friends at all; if they had been, they would have been in touch when Dom left, but they hadn't! Oh, there had been phone calls and letters to say how sorry they were, but nothing more. Nothing that could be called real friendship.

She nodded to herself. It was obvious, really. They were Dom's friends, not hers, and when it came right down to it, she had lived in his shadow for years — and now that she had emerged from it she didn't really know how to make new friends, let alone new relationships! Supposedly, people just met each other and got on. Was it really as easy as that?

She watched as Ewan returned to their table. That was what

this evening was about; getting to know one another; finding out if they got on…

Unexpectedly, panic began to rise out of her Sarah compartment. She swallowed hard and slammed that particular compartment shut. If she was going to find out if she liked Ewan she would have to change compartments; she had no other choice – or her feelings would ruin everything!

He handed her a drink and sat down. 'So what have you been watching on TV lately?'

Sarah stopped herself from grimacing; she was not about to admit that she mostly watched cartoons with Josh. 'I haven't had time to watch much, lately.'

He nodded sympathetically. 'I know what you mean; guess who I bumped into last week!'

She gazed at him blankly and asked, 'Who? John Logie Baird?'

He seemed not to notice. 'Josie Tasker! I bumped into her, literally, coming out of a pub in Binderfield! I've been watching those Sunday night reruns on TV; and there she was as Nancy in Oliver Twist and then, thump, I walk straight into her coming out of a pub in Binderfield!'

Sarah resisted making a face. Was colliding with an actress that exciting? Really? Ewan seemed to think so. 'What did you say?'

Ewan opened his arms; 'Well, I said sorry!'

That seemed to be the end of the anecdote. He had walked into a celebrity and apologised; it seemed unlikely that he would be invited onto a chat show to share his experience! Sarah forced a smile.

He nodded sagely. 'Pity everything's gone so badly wrong for her.'

She nodded and offered: 'Wasn't she involved in some sort of scandal?'

Ewan paused and then shook his head. 'I don't think so.'

She said, 'I thought she'd gone to America? Or am I thinking of someone else?'

He glanced at her ruefully. 'Yes. I think you're probably thinking of someone else…'

Sarah leant against her inner compartment to keep it shut. It was threatening to burst open and demand, why, exactly, she was here with Ewan.

Ewan stopped beside Sarah's car and she slid her arm from under his.

He said, 'It's been a terrific evening!'

She smiled cautiously, 'Yes, it has. Thank you.' Apart from him going on and on about Josie bloody Tasker, that was. The woman was a decent enough actress, Sarah conceded that, but once the theatrical makeup was stripped away was she even, actually, that attractive? And, for all anyone knew, in private, she was probably a complete bitch! Why would Ewan want to slobber over a fantasy woman when he had a flesh and blood one with him?

His arms slipped around her. 'Would you like to come back to my place for coffee or shall I come to yours?'

Sarah desperately searched for the right compartment, but there wasn't one.

He leaned towards her and kissed her tenderly.

She could feel her body responding and she longed to feel a man beside her, with her, inside her. Did it matter if it was Ewan? He obviously wanted her.

She opened her eyes – his were shut. Did it matter to him that she was Sarah? Inside his head, was he actually kissing his favourite actress?

She tiptoed around the outside of her Sarah compartment. She was sure that there was something inside, trying to get out, but she was nervous about what might emerge...

Ewan began to kiss her more enthusiastically.

Should she sleep with him? It would, if nothing else, confirm her femininity…

She had to do something! She had to make a choice and she had to say something out loud! She allowed her inner compartment to open and what emerged surprised her; she had hoped for a hot rush of passion and feared the cold chill of jealousy but the feeling that appeared was simply a feeling of hollowness. Nothing else; just hollowness. She felt aroused, and attractive, and uncertain, and guilty, and anxious; but below all of those feelings she just felt completely and utterly hollow.

Whatever her feelings for Ewan were, they weren't enough. Not nearly enough. He was a man she could cope with – and she had travelled that road before…

She stopped returning his kiss.

He pulled his head away and searched her eyes. 'Is something wrong?'

She put her hand on his chest. 'Ewan; I'm only just divorced. I'm not ready.'

His hands slid to her hips and he kissed her forehead just as she, a few hours ago, had kissed Josh. He smiled. 'That's all right. I can wait; but I can call you again, can't I?'

She let her hand drop and his eyes searched hers desperately. How could she say: 'No'? It would be so cruel! She changed compartments, smiled and said, 'Of course!'

He brightened and put his hands in his pockets. 'Brilliant! It's been a terrific evening!'

She pecked him on the cheek. 'Thank you again. Goodnight.'

He held the car door open for her and, as she got in, he shut it carefully.

She started the engine and as she drove away she glanced in her rear-view mirror.

Ewan was waving enthusiastically and doing a comedy jig. He was obviously very happy.

Sarah concentrated on the road; if she was going to get back to Twisle Drift safely she needed to ignore her feelings. When she got home she would probably cry all night.

CHAPTER TWENTY NINE

Sarah watched from her bedroom window as Neil's car nosed down his driveway and out onto the road. She felt terrible. She had slept badly and regretted not telling Ewan that she didn't want to see him again.

'Listen to me!' she said aloud. 'I *regret!* I am the queen of feelings!'

She wasn't, though. If she was, she would have listened to that feeling last night. She grimaced; she hadn't expected her date to end in conflict – Ewan wanted to see her again but she didn't want to see him; that was conflict; and she had reverted to her old self and displaced her feelings and run away.

She swore loudly but it didn't help. The pending conversation with Ewan felt like an avalanche waiting to begin, creaking above her. If she was very quiet, would it just stay where it was?

Sarah blinked her gritty eyes. She needed something to do; if she moped around under the avalanche, tonight would be even worse than last night! She sneered sourly at her overnight case; Minnie had hoped that she would have a nice time, but she hadn't and it wasn't fair.

She shook her head. She was just going round in circles. She needed a change of scenery. She picked up her keys, left her house and went next door.

As soon as she was in Neil's hall the absurdity of what she had just done hit her. She had wanted a change of scenery but his house was exactly like hers! She laughed mirthlessly. Never mind; now that she was here she might as well do her job.

She started in the sitting room. Neil was a very tidy man and there wasn't much to do but she flicked a duster around and pulled an empty peanut packet out of the bin. She went through to the kitchen and squirted some liquid cleaner into the stainless steel sink. Again, it didn't really need cleaning but it was something to do.

When she'd finished dusting and tidying she fetched the vacuum cleaner and pushed it around every downstairs room. She changed the bag, mopped the kitchen floor and started to vacuum the stairs. When she reached the landing, she left the vacuum cleaner where it was, fetched the duster and worked her way through the bedrooms. She cleaned the bathroom, mopped the floor and ended, as she always did, by cleaning Neil's bedroom.

He, like her, had a chair on which he kept discarded clothes; did everyone? Her knowledge of bedrooms was limited…

She moved the clothes onto his bed and sank down on his chair. If she had gone with Ewan last night, she would have seen his bedroom. Did he have a chair?

Grief rose up within her and she allowed it to pour out into the silent bedroom. It was all so unfair. Ewan was a nice man and he was attracted to her; so why wasn't she attracted to him? Why couldn't she be the kind of woman who was happy to have sex with a man she felt nothing for?

Her grief shut off as she realised that she was, in fact, *exactly* that kind of woman. She had never, really, been attracted to Dom, but she had had sex with him anyway! So why couldn't she just have sex with Ewan?

She held her head in her hands. Everything was so complicated! She needed to think.

Why had she married Dom? Because she loved him? Sort of, but now, when she thought about it, her love for him was pretty much the same as her love for her parents. It wasn't, actually, as strong as her love for her grandparents and it was nothing like as deep as her love for Minnie or Josh – and wasn't a lover's love supposed to be stronger? Books always talked about that kind of love as the strongest love there was, so shouldn't it be different even to the kind of love she had for her grandparents and children? Deeper? Stronger? More intense?

Of course, the books might be wrong. Romantic love might just be a fiction; perhaps, in reality, people just got along with each other and had sex? Perhaps there was no such thing as love? But if there wasn't, it meant that when people spoke of their love for other people – at anniversary celebrations and at funerals – they were lying. They couldn't all be lying, could they?

No. Romantic love must exist; it was just that she had never experienced it. The truth was that she had never had much luck with relationships and she had married Dom because it was the safe option. Theirs had been a love she could cope with but now that she was beginning to access her feelings she realised just how hollow it had been. Years and years of hollowness.

She wept again, not for the loss of Dom, but for all that she had lost by being with him.

When the flurry had passed, she dried her eyes and stared at Neil's bed; that was another thing; beds. Last night, when she had come home, she had realised that Ewan would never sleep in her bed. She could imagine going to his house, or flat, or wherever he lived, and sleeping with him in his bed, but she could never imagine him lying in her bed. Not with Minnie and Josh in adjoining rooms; not with them knowing what she was doing.

With Dom it had been different. He had been their father and they, like most children, probably thought that their parents never had sex. Sarah smiled wryly; if that's what Minnie and Josh thought, they weren't far wrong! If she brought a new man home, though, overnight, they would know exactly what was going on! Could Ewan be that man? No! Why? Because Minnie would ask her: 'Do you love him, Mum?' And she would have to say: 'No.' And when she did, she wouldn't be able to live with the look Minnie would give her.

Sarah closed her eyes. She would have to call Ewan and tell him – or should she arrange to meet him and talk to him?

Rage zig-zagged out of her. She didn't want to do anything! She just wanted Ewan to go away!

She rubbed her eyes. She needed to talk to Di. This was all, just, too complicated!

She opened her eyes and stared morosely at Neil's bed. If she told Di about Ewan, though, she would just have to answer awkward questions. She needed to do some more thinking!

So: Ewan was a nice man but she wasn't going to go any further with him than their kiss last night. What about Henry? If Minnie was right, Henry would want to see her again; how did she feel about *him*?

She bit her lip. He had liked Minnie and Josh and they had liked him. In many ways, Henry would fit seamlessly into their family – but there was something about him; he was dangerous. There was no other word for it; he was dangerous. If Sarah let him into her life, she would never be able to cope with him and, more to the point, could she imagine making love with Henry? Not really; he was just too, well, dangerous.

She stared at Neil's bed and her eyes widened. At first, she had thought that Neil liked her, and then she had realised that he only wanted to help her – but what if her first thought was correct? What if he had been kind to her because her first instinct had been right and he *was* attracted to her? He had certainly been very concerned yesterday, when he had heard her screaming, and he was always very friendly with the children…

She stood up, folded his clothes and put them back on his chair. She then, very carefully, lay down on his bed. Could she imagine herself here, naked, with Neil? Yes. Could she imagine moving in with him here? Yes, she could; and could she imagine him moving in with her and the children?

She needed to go home and find out!

She swung her legs off his bed and straightened the covers. She sorted out the vacuum cleaner cable, returned the machine to its cupboard downstairs, and tidied up the rest of her cleaning implements.

She closed the door behind her and almost ran home. She went into her living room. Could she imagine Neil in here? Yes.

She went into the kitchen. Could she imagine him in here? There was no need; he had already been in here several times and he fitted right in!

She went upstairs, plucked up her courage, went into her bedroom, and asked her question. Could she imagine Neil in here? With her? She sank down onto her chair and smiled. Yes she could!

Sarah nodded. It wasn't Ewan she wanted, and it certainly wasn't Henry; it was Neil!

She could imagine being here, in bed with Neil, with Minnie and Josh knowing; and she could imagine Minnie asking her question: 'Mum, do you love him?'

Sarah smiled and whispered, 'Yes!'

She sat up as a new thought hit her: and what about her parents? Could she imagine telling them about Neil? What would they think?

She laughed aloud and sank back in her chair; frankly, she didn't care.

CHAPTER THIRTY

Sarah usually enjoyed browsing in 'Berty's', or, to give it its proper name, Bertram and Sons, Yelmouth's leading department store. Today, though, she was not the one who was browsing; Margaret was, and this meant that Sarah had been consigned, effectively, to the role of Sherpa. On this shopping expedition she was expected to act as guide, carry the bags, and offer flattery. Sarah suspected that if the escalators were to break down she would be expected to carry her mother upstairs.

Should she insist that Margaret carry her own bags? Counsellor Di said that choosing confrontation was important but it was also very costly — and so were the emotions that seemed to flutter around every skirmish. It was like being followed by an invisible flock of birds; at some point they would swoop and attack but she never knew when it would happen. At least, now that she had located her Sarah compartment, she had somewhere to shoo these bird-like feelings, but life, surely, was easier if she didn't argue and just went with the flow?

She closed her eyes briefly; she was exhausted. She sighed, regarded her mother, and asked despondently; 'Do you really need it?'

Margaret pursed her lips and studied her reflection in the mirror. The ridiculous turquoise fascinator perched on the back of her head while its feather bobbed in front of her face every time she moved. It made her look like a deep-sea angler fish. 'I might need it; you never know.'

Sarah resisted the urge to suggest that her mother might use the fascinator as bait. 'Isn't it irritating? The way it moves around in front of your face?'

Margaret moved her head experimentally and then bent her knees, ducking down and straightening up again, several times.

'I see what you mean. Oh well; perhaps not…' She removed the fascinator and placed it reluctantly back of the foam head which had been a silent, unseeing, unsmiling witness to her remarkable physical demonstration.

Sarah sighed.

Margaret cast one last, longing look at the millinery display and said, 'Shall we go for a cup of tea?'

Sarah smiled and picked up the bags. They contained a new pan with, as Margaret insisted, 'a lid that fitted', new cotton sheets, a pair of slippers, a gardening trowel, a pair of gardening gloves, a jar of honey and a china house. Clearly it was not enough for Margaret to live in a house; she needed an ornamental house too…

Margaret marched off towards the escalators. 'Thank you so much for helping. You know I can't carry anything myself; not in my condition.'

That would be the mysterious medical condition that allowed her to march about, garden by herself when no one else was around to do it for her, do knee-bends in a fascinator, but not carry a bag… Sarah set off after her.

They rode the escalators to the top of the building in silence, went into the restaurant and found an empty table. Sarah arranged the bags between her chair and the wall and sat down while Margaret marched off to the self-service counter.

Sarah glanced around the restaurant. It was surprisingly full and, as usual, the clientele was almost exclusively female. She tried to work out how many of the women at other tables were mothers and daughters and whether they looked happy in each other's company. Most of them seemed to be enjoying their conversations and Sarah felt a stab of jealousy. She shoved the sharp, spiky feeling into her Sarah compartment and then allowed the follow-up feeling of sorrow to follow it.

Would she ever be able to say what she really thought to her mother? Or was she consigned to a lifetime of responses only in her head? Was it worth saying what she thought when every comment seemed to lead to conflict – and did she want conflict in a public place like Berty's? Was conflict really the way forward? Was Di right or wrong?

'Here we are,' Margaret announced. She put the tray between them. On it were two Berty's design floral teacups and saucers, a couple of plates, a teapot and a milk jug. There was also a stainless steel, lidded jug with extra hot water and a plate brimming with a variety of cakes. 'Shall I be mother?' Margaret joked.

Sarah offered the response expected of her and received her cup of tea from her mother's hand with a murmured, 'Thank you.'

'Cake?' Margaret offered.

Sarah took a plate, considered the selection and reached for a chocolate fairy cake.

Margaret's face fell.

Sarah reached past the chocolate cake and picked up a plain slice of Victoria sponge.

Margaret took a plate for herself and selected a blueberry mini-muffin. She was, evidently, saving the chocolate cake for later.

'I must say,' Margaret said. 'You're looking much better. You've been eating properly, haven't you?'

Sarah nodded and nibbled her cake. Her mother wasn't really interested in her reply.

Margaret finished the mini-muffin, reached for a slice of Battenberg, and nodded in satisfaction. 'That's what I always say. With a good meal inside you, your troubles just melt away!'

Sarah resisted pointing out that while troubles might melt away, the pounds of fat didn't…

'How are the children?' Margaret asked.

Sarah said, 'They're fine. Josh is still learning his lines for the school play and Minnie has joined the school athletic club.'

Margaret declared, 'That'll do her good. A bit of extra exercise.'

Sarah allowed the conversation to taper into silence.

Margaret helped herself to a fondant fancy and munched it with relish. She then considered the chocolate fairy cake and a vanilla macaroon, the two remaining cakes on the plate. She shot a glance at Sarah. 'And you haven't had any more foolish ideas about men?'

Sarah shook her head. She hadn't; all her ideas about men had been entirely sensible!

Margaret picked up the macaroon. 'So; what have you been up to?'

Sarah sipped her tea; not a lot – apart from her relationship with Neil. She put her cup down and said, 'You know next door's been empty? Well someone's moved in.'

Margaret finished the macaroon and reached for the chocolate fairy cake. 'Oh yes; are they nice?'

She answered deliberately, 'It's not a *they* it's a *he.*'

Margaret paused, the fairy cake half way to her mouth. 'That's a bit unusual, isn't it?'

Sarah ducked her head. 'He's a widower; he's on his own.'

Margaret put the fairy cake down and said casually, 'And is he nice?'

Sarah nibbled some more of her slice of Victoria sponge. 'Seems to be. He asked me about the rubbish collections the other day and a lady goes in to clean for him a couple of times a week.' Best not say who, exactly, that was…

Margaret became even more casual. 'What does he do?'

Sarah sipped some more tea, 'He works in cosmetics.'

Margaret glanced from her cake to Sarah and back again. 'Oh yes?'

Sarah finished her cake.

Margaret lowered her voice; 'Men like him; like Dominic…'

Sarah chuckled to herself. Nanna Gwen was right; mischief was fun! 'Oh! He doesn't *wear* cosmetics; he makes them.'

Margaret looked sourly at her fairy cake and then back at Sarah.

Sarah continued, 'His name's Neil. Neil Godley.'

Margaret's brow furrowed and her attention turned inwards. 'I know that name. Where do I know that name from?'

Sarah said casually, 'He owns Calvi.'

Expressions scooted across Margaret's face like clouds across the sun. Her attention was now on Sarah and she examined her as if she were an item for sale. She leaned forwards; 'And he's moved in next door to you?'

Sarah nodded. 'We've chatted a couple of times. He's just there temporarily while he looks for somewhere more permanent.'

Margaret considered her fairy cake.

Sarah continued slyly, 'Minnie and Josh have got to know him, too.'

Margaret looked up, through her eye lashes.

'They seem to like him,' Sarah concluded.

Margaret's eyes were calculating as she said, 'He sounds like a nice man.'

'He seems to be,' Sarah agreed. She poked a few crumbs on her plate and then sucked her finger.

Margaret relaxed, picked up her chocolate fairy cake and said in the tone of an intellectual imparting wisdom: 'It's always good to have nice neighbours.'

'Isn't it?' Sarah agreed.

Margaret flicked a calculating glance in Sarah's direction, 'And you've had your hair done, I see?'

Sarah nodded, 'Nanna Gwen suggested it.'

Margaret's inquisitorial persona crumbled and she simpered, 'Neil Godley; well, well! I can't wait to tell Terry! He'll be so excited!'

Sarah smiled. She knew from long experience that it didn't matter what her father thought; her mother would tell him what he thought.

Margaret finished her cake and drained the tea in her cup. She made a show of checking her watch. 'Well, drink up; you ought to be getting home.'

Sarah nodded; back home to her house and her next door neighbour; who just happened to be a very rich, available, widower.

Sarah stood up, picked up her mother's bags and hid her smile. Conversation was overrated – and so was Di's much vaunted confrontation. With a bit of judicious manoeuvring, angry words and horrible feeling could be side-stepped.

With just a few oblique remarks from Sarah, Margaret had answered her unspoken question. She had no further need to discuss her future, or her relationship with Neil, with her parents. However negative they had been previously about their daughter meeting another man, and whatever their expressed opinions about her priorities, which were, of course, Margaret's expressed opinions; when it came to matters of the heart, as far as her mother was concerned, money talked – and, seemingly, it spoke in a very loud voice indeed.

Sarah followed Margaret to the escalator. There was no doubt about it, keeping quiet was much easier than fighting her corner, and being clever with words was infinitely preferable to being honest.

CHAPTER THIRTY ONE

Di said, 'I don't agree.'

Sarah said in surprise, 'Really? But surely, reasoning things out is better than weeping uncontrollably and making wrong decisions!'

Di grimaced with frustration, 'But you don't have to do one or the other! It's not a choice! You can do both! When you pay attention to your feelings, they inform your reasoning but when you don't, that's when you make choices with no idea of how you feel about them!'

Sarah frowned. 'But the feelings are horrible; and hurtful; and exhausting! It's much easier to reason things out than to have arguments all the time.'

Di clucked with exasperation. 'But easier isn't always better! Look, sometimes it's important to argue and to stand up for yourself; sometimes it's important to keep quiet and, sometimes, it's important just to go with the flow. That's how human beings interact! The point is this: whether you speak up or keep quiet you will have feelings. The point is: as long as you acknowledge your feelings, you won't lock up.'

'Even if I keep quiet?' Sarah suggested.

'Even if you choose to keep quiet,' Di confirmed. 'It's not about what you say or don't say; it's just about acknowledging how you feel.'

Sarah could feel her neck growing red.

Di asked, 'What are you feeling right now?'

Sarah asked, 'Do I have to tell you?'

Di smiled, 'Not if you don't want to. As long as you understand what you feel. That's the important thing. It's up to you whether you tell me, or anyone else.'

Sarah nodded. That made sense; if she didn't want to, she didn't need to tell Di that, right now, she felt like a stupid toddler who was being told off…

'It's not about whether you argue or not,' Di continued. 'It's just about acknowledging how you feel.'

Sarah made a face. 'I got that wrong didn't I?'

Di made her clucking noise again. 'No! It's not about getting it right or wrong, either!'

Sarah held up her hands as a sign of peace and grinned. 'I know – it's about acknowledging my feelings!'

Di blew out her cheeks and then laughed; 'Yes.'

Sarah laughed with her and allowed her soaring, gliding pleasure to follow her sharp-pecking feeling of stupidity into her Sarah compartment.

Di said, 'We also need to talk about your "Sarah" compartment.'

Sarah said in surprise, 'That's a coincidence!'

Di grunted, 'Let's not change the subject. It started out as a forest glade, is that right?'

Sarah nodded. 'With a pond in the middle. But, as I got more used to tipping my emotions into it, it seemed a bit stupid so I just started calling it my Sarah compartment.'

Di made a sour face.

Sarah sat forward and asked, 'Have I got that wrong too?'

Di clucked and flapped her hands. 'No! None of this is about right and wrong! It's just about things that help and things that don't!'

Sarah hung her head; so she *had* got it wrong! Again!

Di said firmly, 'Sarah!'

Sarah sat up.

Di continued kindly, 'Sarah – you are not in trouble. We are both adults and I'm here to help you.'

Sarah reached for a tissue and dried her sudden tears.

Di continued, 'To be honest, when I suggested that you create a new compartment for your emotions I was taking something of a risk. From what you've told me, when you were thinking of it as a forest glade it was working as it was intended–'

'Which means it isn't now?' Sarah interrupted.

Di nodded thoughtfully. 'The thing is, when you thought of it as a forest glade, it was a location inside you. Yes?'

Sarah nodded. 'Yes. That's what it felt like.'

Di continued, 'But now that you've renamed it your Sarah compartment, how can you have a "Sarah compartment" inside Sarah? You *are* Sarah; not a small compartment inside yourself!'

Sarah frowned and said, 'Oh.'

Di said, 'Do you see? By renaming it "Sarah", you've managed to divorce your feelings from the rest of you – which is pretty much where you were to start with – and now that you're letting your Sarah compartment deal with your feelings, the rest of you, the actual Sarah, has gone back to relying on reason!'

'It *is* easier, though,' Sarah protested.

Di said with enforced calm, 'I know that it *seems* easier at the time, but in the long run it will lead to you making choices that are disconnected with your feelings.'

Sarah fidgeted with her fingers. 'Like marrying Dom.'

Di sighed, 'Like marrying Dom.'

Sarah felt her energy drain away.

Di said kindly, 'Don't be despondent. You've made enormous progress. For the first time since you were a small child you know how you feel. We just need to make sure that you don't dissect and mount your feelings in a sterile environment. We need to make sure that your feelings inform your adult decisions.'

'Because they are part of me?' Sarah asked.

Di shook her head. 'No. Because they *are* you; as much as your logic and your choices are you.'

'And I don't have a Sarah compartment?'

Di smiled, 'You don't have *any* compartments. Not really. That's just using your imagination to get a handle on life.'

Sarah nodded slowly. It made sense and it explained why she had reverted to feeling like a child.

'And,' Di chirped, 'it's all very positive!'

Sarah made a face. 'It doesn't feel very positive! Most of the time I have no idea what I'm doing!'

Di mirrored Sarah's expression. 'Welcome to the human race –
but did you hear what you just said?'

Sarah frowned, 'Not really.'

Di smiled, 'You said that it doesn't *feel* positive. You see? You
are connecting with your emotions!'

Sarah shifted in her seat. 'I can see that but I still have no idea
where anything will lead.'

Di laughed. 'None of us do. We just launch out into what we
hope is the right direction and see what happens.'

Sarah frowned again, 'So is it wrong to have a plan?'

Di sighed, 'Of course it isn't wrong to have a plan, but life isn't
like a train that runs on rails. It's more like a sailing boat on the
ocean. We have to make constant course corrections.'

Sarah nodded with relief. Finally, they could stop talking about
her feelings and where they were located and talk about
something more useful. 'That makes sense. Being with Dom was
like being on rails…'

Di cleared her throat, 'And we know where *that* led! But now
that we're on the subject of Dom, there's something else we need
to talk about.'

Sarah pursed her lips. 'About our marriage?'

Di said, 'No. About Dom.'

Sarah screwed up her face and then relaxed. 'Sorry – you've
lost me.'

Di said gently, 'You've never said anything about things from
Dom's point of view.'

Sarah replied in surprise, 'Why would I?'

Di answered, 'Because it may help you to think about how
complex life is.'

Sarah said firmly, 'I know how complicated life is. That's why I
told you about Ewan!'

Di crossed her legs. Today she was wearing a heavy, russet
skirt and a matching sweater with a gold chain. She looked good;
would something like that suit Sarah?

Di said, 'I meant complicated for Dom and the children.'

Sarah blinked. 'Oh. Okay. I see; I think…'

Di smiled encouragingly. 'Let's think about Dom. What was your marriage like from his point of view, do you think?'

Sarah puffed out her cheeks. 'I don't know if I can answer that.'

Di settled back in her chair. 'Try. And try to be objective. You're good at that. Put yourself in his shoes.'

Sarah tried to think back. 'I suppose our marriage was somewhere for him to hide; no, that's not right; from his point of view, I think he thought that he *had* to hide.'

Di suggested, 'Because he was gay?'

Sarah nodded. 'When we were growing up, I knew about gay people and he must have too. But, living where we lived, there just weren't any gay people. At least, there must have been; but I suppose they either moved away or hid inside themselves. I mean, according to the newspapers and the TV there were gay issues, and discussions about gay rights, and gay people everywhere, it was just that there didn't seem to be anyone living near us – so it was all a bit, sort of, hypothetical.'

Di nodded and waited.

Sarah continued, 'So I guess Dom thought he was the only one. There must have been a Gay Society at his university but maybe he wasn't interested in the kind of men who joined it? Or, perhaps he was frightened that if his course tutors found out they wouldn't approve? I think he worked out that if he was going to make a success of the Law, he would need to blend in and get married.'

Di paused and then asked, 'Was there a religious element to it?'

Sarah frowned. 'How do you mean?'

Di said, 'I just wondered – with him being called Dominic?'

Sarah nodded. 'Oh, I see what you mean. Maybe; sort of. His mum, Sandy, was brought up as a Roman Catholic but Roy's pretty much an atheist and religion doesn't figure in either of their lives.'

Di made a note in her notebook.

Sarah continued, 'Thinking about it, though, maybe religion was at the heart of the family split? I mean, maybe Sandy lost her faith when her first husband died and maybe her first marriage caused a lot of rows? If her family were big on religion, maybe that's why Dom never met his grandparents? I can't see why any of that would cause a rift with my family, though.'

Di said firmly, 'Let's not change the subject. I was asking about *your* marriage. Do you think he loved you?'

Sarah hauled her attention back to her marriage; 'I've been thinking about that and I think he did – not as a man loves a woman, though. I think he loved me as a friend.'

Di said, 'Do you think he loves Alex like that?'

Sarah spat back, 'I have no idea!'

Di waited.

Sarah found her Sarah compartment, paused, rebranded it as her inner forest glade, calmed herself and said, 'I'm sorry. It's just that I find it hard – thinking of them together. It makes me feel… inadequate. Totally, completely inadequate!'

Di suggested, 'Because you couldn't be the man Dom wanted?'

Sarah determinedly stayed in her glade. 'Yes. No. I don't know!'

Di waited for a moment and then asked, 'Do you think it would have been different if Dom had fallen in love with another woman?'

Sarah shrugged hopelessly, 'I've thought about that too, but I just have no idea and I can't work out how it would feel. It's too hypothetical even for me!'

Di chuckled. 'Fair comment. Let's get back to reality. Do you think that you could ever be happy for Dom?'

Sarah's neck began to burn and she clasped her hands together tightly. 'I don't know. I really don't know.'

Di waited and then said, 'It's complicated, isn't it?'

Sarah nodded.

Di said, 'Let me ask you something else. You were married to Dom for twelve years. Do you think, before he married you, that Dom should have told you how he *didn't* feel?'

Sarah nodded vigorously. 'Definitely!'

Di continued softly, 'And are you going to tell Ewan how *you* don't feel?'

Sarah felt as if she'd just been kicked in the chest. 'I have to; don't I?'

Di said, 'That's up to you. The reason I mentioned it is because we usually resent most deeply the shortcomings in others that we are most aware of in ourselves.'

Sarah chewed her lip. 'Can you just say that again?'

Di repeated, 'We usually resent most deeply the shortcomings in others that we are most aware of in ourselves.'

Sarah considered this. 'You mean that what I hate about Dom is what I hate about myself?'

Di said quietly, 'It's something to think about.'

Sarah nodded. Di was right. She was as guilty as Dom of allowing their relationship to become a marriage. She had taken what looked like the safe road and it had turned out to be a disaster. 'I'm just like him, aren't I?'

Di cleared her throat. 'No; as we've said before, you are Sarah. The only person you're like is yourself.'

Sarah frowned, 'What about birds of a feather flocking together?'

Di laughed, 'All right. I'll let you change the subject – for now. It's true that some people are similar; it's also true that opposites attract. A good rule of thumb for any relationship is for you to be similar enough to get on and different enough to make it interesting!'

Sarah nodded; like her and Neil!

Di said, 'Now, let's get back to looking at this from Dom's point of view. You say that you think he deliberately avoided sex. How do you think he felt about that?'

Sarah said immediately, 'Well he didn't want to have sex with me so it's pretty obvious how he felt. He found the idea repulsive.'

Di said, 'That's not what I meant. Picture Dom at work. He's packing up and getting ready to come home. He knows that he ought to make love to you but he doesn't want to. He wants to be a good husband but he can't be. How do you think he feels about that?'

Sarah tried to put herself in his position. What if she'd married a woman? What if she'd married Di? They got on and she could imagine their friendship. Di probably wasn't a lesbian, but she could be prickly about any intrusion into her private life so, for the sake of argument, what if she was? What if Sarah had to go home with Di tonight and make love? What would she do?

Sarah nodded slowly, 'I understand. It must have been desperately hard for him.'

Di said, 'Just like it was hard for you; although for different reasons.'

Sarah stopped nodding; 'You're right. I've never thought about it before.'

Di waited.

Sarah said quietly, 'I still don't know that I can ever forgive him, though.'

Di shrugged, 'Maybe you can; maybe you can't. If you are able to understand him it's a start.'

Sarah said, 'I guess; but even that seems like a big ask.'

Di nodded. 'It is, because it means facing up to your feelings, and you may not be proud of how you feel. The thing is, though, unless you can understand Dom, and what he's done and why, the chances are that you will take sides. You will then, naturally, want the children to be on your side and you will, in effect, ask them to choose between their mother and their father. How can they do that?'

Sarah scratched her neck; it was prickling. She had worked very hard to appear neutral in her opinions so that the children would not see her blaming Dom. Was that the same as not taking sides?

Di said, 'You mentioned that you let Josh see how you felt about the divorce?'

Had that been a mistake? Sarah's neck was getting worse.

Di said, 'It's important that your children know how hurt you are. If you hide it from them they'll think that you don't care and they'll think that their own pain is abnormal.'

So she *had* done the right thing, had she?

Di continued, 'Not taking sides is about letting them make up their own minds about who did what and who hurt who.

The more you talk about it with them, the more you give them permission to acknowledge their own pain.'

Sarah burst into tears. She hated to think of Josh and Minnie in pain. What could she do though? She dried her eyes; she could do what Di said.

Di passed a fresh box of tissues. 'It's very hard and there are quite a few couples going through what you're going through. It may be different for the next generation, and the next, but it's surprising how many gay people of your age have denied their sexuality and tried to live heterosexual lives.'

Sarah blew her nose and glanced at Di. Was she saying that she *was* a lesbian?

Di said, 'But if you can imagine what the marriage was like for Dom, it may help you to know what to say when your children ask questions.'

Sarah became suddenly still. Neither Minnie nor Josh had ever asked her anything personal. They had only asked about the practicalities of what was going to happen, where they would live and that sort of thing; they had never asked anything personal. Was that because she had made it clear that they mustn't? Had she squashed down their questions from her own inability to cope? Was she, actually, a terrible mother?

Di began to tidy up her papers. 'I think you've probably got a lot of reflecting to do before the next session. And remember, stick with the forest glade!'

Sarah nodded. She didn't trust herself to speak.

Di said, 'It may help if you can talk things over with someone else. You never mention your friends but friends help us to cope. Is there someone you could think things through with?'

Sarah nodded with relief. There was. Neil.

CHAPTER THIRTY TWO

'I'm glad you came,' Neil said.

'So am I,' Sarah agreed. She had taken a chance and arrived early, hoping that she might be able to talk things over with Neil before her cleaning duties began. He had welcomed her into his home as if she had never visited before and he had made a fuss of her, insisting that they sit together and share some tea and cake.

For the last half hour she had resolutely stayed within her forest glade, and poured out her troubles to him while he listened attentively and prompted her with occasional questions. It had been an emotional experience but Neil had responded by sharing some of the intimate details of his own bereavement and Sarah was very glad that she had risked this conversation. He clearly liked her and trusted her, so she was right; he had offered her a job out of more than just compassion!

'Oh look!' Neil said. He pointed through the French window to the apple tree beyond the patio. A woodpecker had landed on a low branch and was eyeing up a bird feeder that hung beneath it. The bird's head flashed red as it twisted from side to side.

'How lovely!' Sarah agreed. They were sitting in his dining room, but the table had been pushed back towards the door and they sat on either side of the French window, in comfortable chairs, looking out into the garden. Sarah decided not to mention that the woodpecker was a regular visitor in her garden too.

She slid a sideways glance towards Neil. He was smiling through the window. The woodpecker dropped to the feeder, missed its footing and flew off in a burst of colour.

He sighed and turned towards her, 'Do you mind if I say something?'

Her heart thudded in her chest; what was he going to say? Was he about to confess that he liked her? She said shyly, 'No. Say whatever you want to say.'

He shifted in his seat. 'It doesn't sound very conventional; to me.'

Sarah tried to make sense of this and failed.

He continued, 'And I suspect the conventions are there for a reason.'

What was he talking about?

He sat up a little. 'I mean, it sounds very generous of your ex-husband to fund you to stay next door, but doesn't it make you somewhat dependent on him?'

Her heart thudded again; was he about to ask her to move in with him?

He leaned his elbows on his knees. 'Having a joint bank account, too. If you don't mind me saying; it doesn't really sound that healthy.'

Sarah had to say something so she said, 'Oh?'

He nodded. 'Usually, when couples divorce, the court specifies the assets and there is absolute clarity about the finances, custody of the children, access to the children for the absent parent and that sort of thing. Did your divorce settlement not specify all that?'

Sarah nodded, 'I'm sure it did.'

He glanced at her and smiled encouragingly, 'And did your solicitor explain everything to you – in plain English?'

Sarah rubbed her knees, 'Actually, I didn't have a solicitor.'

Neil stared at her.

She said quickly, 'What with Dom being a barrister, he said that it was a waste of money; he did everything and, as he was so generous, everything worked out fine.'

Neil sucked his teeth and made a face as if something was stuck in them. 'Again; it doesn't sound very conventional.'

'Does it matter?' she asked.

'It might,' he answered. 'Look. Would you give me permission to ask a solicitor in our legal department to look into this?'

Sarah frowned, 'I can't, really, see the point…'

He smiled winningly, 'For me?'

She chuckled, 'Oh well; if you put it like that!'

He nodded, 'Thank you. It's just that…' he made his something-stuck-in-his-teeth face.

'It's just that: what?' she asked.

He nodded his head from side to side, 'It's just that something doesn't sound quite right and I think you deserve better.'

Warmth pooled in Sarah's abdomen. What a lovely man he was. Of course she deserved better than Dom…

He smiled, 'And don't worry, my guy will be very discreet. If you let me have copies of whatever divorce documents you have, and your bank details, he'll be able to track down all the information. And, as I say, don't worry, your ex-husband will never know.'

Sarah settled deeper into her chair. It was just like being hugged.

Neil slapped his knees. 'Well, I'm really glad you came, but I need to get on with something. I'm expecting some visitors in just over an hour's time – it's a work thing and I need to get organised.'

Sarah collected her teacup and plate and followed him into the kitchen. She piled her things in the sink and took his from him. Their hands touched and he smiled. He looked deeply into her eyes and said gently, 'Sorry I have to rush off. Is that all right?'

She smiled contentedly, 'Of course.'

He hesitated.

Was he going to kiss her?

She pushed his chest gently, 'Go on! Get ready for your meeting!'

He returned her smile, turned, and walked out of the kitchen. For a tall man, he moved with great grace and poise.

Sarah turned to the sink and looked through the window into the garden. She opened her eyes wide and grinned broadly. Blimey! He really did like her! She sang as she filled the sink with soapy water and washed up the crockery.

When everything was dried and put away, she lugged the vacuum cleaner out of its cupboard and pushed it round the kitchen floor. If Neil had a meeting scheduled for an hour's time, she would be able to complete the vacuuming before his visitors arrived.

Her song turned into a whistle as she vacuumed the dining room and then made her way into the hall. She was right by the doorbell chime when it hurled its cacophony into the air. In spite of the rumble of the vacuum, the hideous electronic rendition of the William Tell Overture almost made her jump out of her skin.

She could see a shadow through the frosted-glass panel in the front door. It was probably the postman. She toggled the power button on the vacuum cleaner and it droned into silence.

She opened the door and said, 'Yes?'

A very attractive and very familiar young woman said uncertainly, 'Oh, hello, I'm sorry to bother you–'

Sarah beamed. What a wonderful day! She and Neil had begun a new relationship and now she would be able to catch up with an old friend! 'Hello! I haven't seen you for ages? How are you?'

'I'm fine, thank you. How are you?' the woman replied with a friendly smile.

'Fine,' Sarah said; but something wasn't fine. Something was nagging at her memory; she had forgotten just how beautiful her friend was; and she had also forgotten her name; who was she? How did they know each other? Was it from school or from somewhere else?

'Sarah?' Neil's voice intruded. He was standing in the study doorway.

'It's–' Sarah called back over her shoulder. Who was it? 'It's...'

'Josie Tasker,' said the woman on the doorstep. 'Look, there's been some sort of mix-up, I'll leave you to–'

'Josie!' Neil said over Sarah's shoulder. 'How lovely to see you again. You're early. Come in.'

Sarah almost ran to the vacuum cleaner, pushed it into the sitting room and shut the door. She toggled the power button on and the vacuum roared into life. 'You idiot!' Sarah hissed to herself under the steady hum of the machine. How could she be so stupid as to mistake Josie Tasker for a friend? She was a celebrity, for God's sake, and Ewan had been droning on about her only a few nights ago! No wonder she looked familiar!

Her neck burned and she began to shove the vacuum cleaner around the floor. That way, with any luck, her whole face would become hot and sweaty and cover her embarrassment.

She could hear Neil and Josie Tasker talking together in the hall and her recent thoughts about Josie returned to her; she had been completely wrong. Even without her theatrical makeup, there was something exquisitely beautiful about the woman; something that took even Sarah's breath away. She pushed the vacuum cleaner with even more gusto as an unwelcome blast of shame rocked the trees around her inner forest glade.

The voices in the hall receded. It sounded as if they had gone into the kitchen. Sarah left the vacuum cleaner running, standing upright in the middle of the sitting room. What should she do? Follow them into the kitchen and apologise? For what? Maybe Josie hadn't noticed her gaffe?

She pulled the extension tube out of the machine, fixed a fine nozzle on the end and flailed it around under the settee. After a few minutes of aimless vacuuming, she stood up, fixed a small brush attachment to the tube and began to clean the curtains.

'Sarah?' Neil asked loudly.

Sarah gave a small shriek and almost brained herself with the extension tube.

'Sorry,' he half-shouted. 'I didn't mean to make you jump.'

Her heart began to normalise. Never mind, at least, if she looked flushed now, he wouldn't know why.

He called. 'I probably should have told you that Josie would be one of my visitors.'

Sarah shrugged. He probably had high-powered meetings with celebrities all the time.

He gestured towards the vacuum cleaner and she turned it off.

'That's better,' he said. 'She's just early. The others will be along a bit later. Maybe if you concentrate on the bedrooms and the bathroom today?'

Sarah nodded and pulled the brush attachment off the hose.

Neil stepped closer and searched her eyes. 'Are you all right? Josie says that she gets recognised all the time – by people who think they know her, and greet her as an old friend, and then get embarrassed when they realise that they don't, actually, know her in any personal way.'

Sarah made a face. 'That's just what I did…'

He gathered her in his arms and hugged her. 'Don't be embarrassed. If you like, just pop in when you've finished and I'll introduce you. Then you really will know her!'

She leaned against him and then pushed him away with a coy smile. 'Go on! Go and have your meeting!'

He grinned and his eyes sparkled. He half waved and left the room.

Sarah started to sing again as she smoothed the curtains with her hands, but as she went upstairs, she stopped. Josie Tasker had started her career as a singer; what must she think of Sarah's warbling?

She pushed the vacuum around the upstairs rooms and then cleaned the bathroom, but as she worked something new nagged at her. It wasn't a memory, though, it was a feeling and Sarah wasn't exactly sure where it was. It wasn't in her forest glade and it didn't seem to be anywhere else, either. She sat on the edge of the bath and tried to work out what it was. She could identify its source – it had appeared when Neil had grinned and his eyes sparkled; but the feeling itself was a mystery.

She shrugged and finished off the bathroom, tidied up and went back to the kitchen. She returned the cleaning equipment to the appropriate cupboard and jotted down a few things on Neil's shopping list.

She washed and moisturised her hands and went into the hall. She found her coat hanging next to Josie Tasker's jacket. She had a quick peek at the label; it must have cost a fortune! She was tempted to try it on, but she resisted the urge and pulled her own coat on instead.

She could hear voices coming from the dining room, so she headed for the door, but as she crossed the hall, a feeling of dread surged around her. What feeling was this?

She tipped it into her forest glade and opened the dining room door. Neil was sitting where he had sat earlier and Josie Tasker was sitting where Sarah had sat.

Sarah smiled but, for some reason, it was an effort. 'I'm finishing off now. I've left a list in the kitchen – you're running out of kitchen towels and floor cleaner.'

Neil stood up. 'Right you are. I'll see you on Monday then shall I?'

Josie Tasker stood up too. She walked gracefully across the room and held out her hand. 'It was nice to meet you. And please don't worry about thinking I was an old friend. It happens to more people than you'd expect.'

Sarah shook her hand; it was warm and smooth, her nails were beautifully manicured and the bracelet on her wrist sparkled with gem stones; in comparison, Sarah's hand looked rough and blotchy. She said, 'Thank you. It was nice to meet you too.'

Josie's beautiful face smiled kindly. 'You too.'

The rogue feeling that Sarah had been unable to identify earlier landed in her gut. She managed to say, 'Bye then,' pull her hand free, and make a dignified exit from the room.

She let herself out of the house and, with determined self-control, walked sedately down Neil's drive and half way up her own before she collapsed, trembling, against her car. She couldn't bear to go inside her house, alone. She needed to go somewhere; anywhere but here…

She unlocked the car, flopped inside, turned the key and stalled the engine. She tried again; and again. Eventually, the engine coughed into life and she set off through Twisle Drift. She turned on the windscreen wipers and then realised that it wasn't raining. She turned two corners and pulled her car into the gateway to a field and gave in to the storm within her.

What an idiot she had been! Neil's grin and sparkling eyes had begun the feeling of dread inside her but when she had seen him with Josie Tasker the feeling of dread connected with reality. Neil was interested in Josie! Of course he was! And why wouldn't he be? She was everything that Sarah wasn't; she was beautiful, rich and famous, and, worst of all, she was really, really nice!

How could Sarah have been so stupid as to think that Neil had been interested in *her?* Why would he even look at her? She was a woman who had meekly allowed herself to be locked up in a loveless, sterile relationship! A woman who needed counselling! A woman who was a complete mess! Why would he want her when he could have a sorted out woman like Josie Tasker?

In fact, how could she have been so stupid as to think that any man would want her? Even Ewan didn't really want her! For him, an imaginary Josie Tasker was better than a real live Sarah; so how could she possibly compete with Josie Tasker in the flesh? Of course Neil was interested in her! Of course; of course; of course!

She tried to direct her grief into her forest glade but it didn't exist. As Di had said, it was only, really, in her imagination. She was alone with her grief. *Her* grief.

She put her head in her hands and wept until she was sure that her body must split and fall to pieces – and even then she couldn't stop.

CHAPTER THIRTY THREE

Sarah woke with a start, grabbed her mobile phone and said blearily, 'Hello?'

A male voice rumbled, 'Is that Sarah? Sarah Price?'

Sarah blinked hard to clear her eyes. Her thumb hovered over the 'end call' button: it was probably someone wanting her to upgrade her phone. 'Who's this?'

The male voice said, 'Oh, sorry. It's Henry. DCI Driffield.'

Sarah moved her thumb and laughed but it sounded brittle, even to her.

Henry said gamely, 'Glad I was able to cheer you up!'

Sarah frowned, 'How did you know I needed it?'

Silence tapped in the phone's earpiece.

He said, 'How did I know that you needed what?'

Sarah moved her phone in front of her face and stared at it. The easiest thing would be just to end the call.

Henry's voice, sounding thin and tinny said, 'Hello? Hello?'

Sarah made a face and put the phone back by her ear. 'Hello. Look, sorry, you just woke me up.'

The jaunt was back in his voice. 'Afternoon nap?'

She glanced at the clock and leapt to her feet. 'I have to collect the children.' She ended the call, ran out of the house and ducked down, below hedge height, as she headed for her car. After her ridiculous performance with Josie Tasker, she had been avoiding Neil all week. She set off on the school run, slowing only to avoid speed cameras.

Josh and Minnie were waiting just inside the school gate but at least the road was clear of cars. They saw Sarah, waved, and bundled themselves into the back seat.

'Sorry I'm late,' Sarah said.

'Where were you?' Josh demanded.

Sarah glanced over her shoulder, 'I fell asleep. On the sofa.'

Josh opened his mouth but Minnie said, 'That's all right. You weren't very late and we've been playing "Picky-Pooty".'

'Min's been teaching me!' Josh cried happily.

'Picky-Pooty?' Sarah enquired. She let the explanation wash over her as she drove home. Clearly Picky-Pooty was a new craze; it sounded like a complicated game and winning had something to do with little fingers and standing on one leg at the vital moment. As Sarah was unlikely ever to play it, she put on an 'interested' expression and just let the children talk.

She pulled into Twisle Drift and slowed down as she reached home; there was a car parked in their driveway.

'Who's that?' Minnie asked, craning her neck.

Ewan, who had been waiting at the front door, turned and waved. He was wearing a brown suit with a red tie that sagged below the open top button of his white shirt.

'He's a friend of mine,' Sarah said. She could feel her cheeks beginning to burn.

Minnie said saucily, 'He looks nice.'

Josh jumped out of the car and ran towards the house, his school bag flapping against his hip. 'Hello; I'm Josh!'

Ewan offered his hand. 'Hello; I'm Ewan.'

Josh shook hands solemnly and said proudly, 'Min's been teaching me Picky-Pooty!'

Ewan immediately leapt into an extraordinary pose and with his arms stretched out like aircraft wings and one leg out behind him. He crowed like a cockerel and bawled, 'Pooty!'

Josh collapsed into laughter, waggled his little fingers and declared, 'I win – I never even did *Picky*.'

Ewan looked aggrieved; 'It's one-nil to you then!'

Josh was still giggling when Sarah and Minnie caught him up.

Sarah said, 'How come you're a Picky-Pooty expert?'

Josh hooted, '*He's* not an expert; *he* just lost!'

Sarah caught his eye, 'Josh…'

He dropped his gaze and muttered, 'Sorry.'

Ewan mussed his hair, 'No worries.'

Minnie glanced from Ewan to Sarah and back again; her eyes alive with curiosity.

Sarah sighed and gestured towards Ewan. 'This is Ewan. Ewan; this is Minnie and this is Josh.'

Ewan smiled, 'Hello. Nice to meet you.'

Josh squinted up at him, 'Are you coming to tea?'

Ewan looked quizzically at Sarah.

She said, 'Well; a *cup* of tea…' She opened the door and led the way inside, closely followed by Minnie, Josh and Ewan. The children dumped their bags and coats and headed for the stairs while Sarah indicated that Ewan should follow her into the kitchen.

As she filled the kettle with fresh water she said, 'You didn't explain how you know Picky-Pooty.'

Ewan leant against a worktop and crossed one ankle over the other. 'I have nephews.'

Sarah nodded. 'Ah.'

Ewan looked around the kitchen. 'Have you just moved in?'

She pushed the button on the kettle and shook her head, 'No; why?'

He shrugged, 'I just thought; the kitchen looks new and with you being divorced, doesn't that usually involve getting a new place?'

Sarah inspected her nails. 'I suppose so; but *usually* isn't always what happens.'

He shifted his weight and crossed his ankles the other way.

Crashing on the stairs heralded the arrival of Minnie and Josh. They had both changed out of their school uniforms and were now wearing jeans and slippers. Minnie's eyes looked very big.

Josh held out a plastic dinosaur. 'Do you like dinosaurs?'

Ewan shrugged, 'Only on toast.'

Josh paused and then laughed, 'This is Tyrannosaurus Rex. He'd have *you* on toast!'

Ewan grinned and studied the plastic figure, 'Not if he was only that big, he wouldn't.'

Josh laughed again and then, making his dinosaur walk in the air, rushed out of the kitchen, roaring.

The kettle clicked and Sarah prepared a pot of tea.

Minnie said politely, 'Would you like to sit down?'

Ewan sat by the kitchen table and Minnie sat down next to him. 'How do you know Mum?' she asked with apparent interest.

Sarah stopped, with the teapot in mid-air. What would Ewan say? That he'd noticed her blubbering in her car? That he'd picked her up on the esplanade?

'We met at the yacht club,' he said.

Minnie looked at Sarah. 'I didn't know you belonged to the yacht club!'

Sarah put the teapot on the table and fetched some mugs and milk. 'What do you think I do all day, or when you're at Daddy's? Stay here and hide in the cupboard under the stairs?'

Minnie looked thoughtful. 'I don't know; I've never thought about it and you never say…'

Sarah sat down at the table, opposite Ewan. 'Well, sometimes I go to the yacht club.'

Ewan spooned some sugar into his mug.

Minnie waited; an appraising expression on her face.

Sarah continued, 'With friends.'

Minnie asked innocently, 'Like Ewan?'

Sarah could feel her cheeks starting to burn but she nodded firmly, 'Like Ewan.'

Minnie smiled a private smile and rose gracefully, if theatrically, to her feet, 'Well; I'll leave you to *chat* then.' She grinned pointedly at Ewan and left the room.

'Nice girl,' he said.

Sarah nodded; he didn't know the half of it. She suggested, 'Well; this is a nice surprise.'

He grinned. 'Good; I wasn't sure how you'd feel about me just turning up.'

Sarah nodded; neither was she. She knew that she definitely had feelings about him just turning up, but she wasn't quite sure what those feelings were or where they might be…

He smiled, 'But then, faint heart fair maid never won!'

Sarah forced herself to smile, 'I'm not exactly a maid.'

He looked at her blankly.

She said, 'I have two children – so I'm not exactly a maid, am I?'

His blank look faded into a sly smile; 'Are you talking about dressing up?'

Sarah put her mug firmly on the table. 'No; look it up!'

He shrugged but his eyes suggested that his imagination was elsewhere.

She said, 'It was nice of you to, er, drop in.' She had almost said, 'come' but that would be inappropriate – given the direction of the conversation.

'I wanted to see you,' he said simply.

Sarah closed her eyes; she didn't want to see him and she needed to tell him…

He continued, 'I thought we might go to the theatre. On Saturday. If you're free?'

She opened her eyes and said gratefully, 'Sorry, but I have the children this weekend.'

His face dropped a fraction, 'Oh. Can you get a baby sitter?'

She shook her head, 'I don't think so; not at such short notice.'

His expression brightened, 'I could probably get one. My sister knows loads of people and never seems to have a problem. I could ask her!'

Sarah examined her nails, 'That's very kind but I wouldn't be comfortable with a stranger.'

Ewan paused and then said, 'Well; how about if we all go? I could get tickets for the children too!'

Sarah closed her eyes; how was she going to get out of this? Didn't he understand that she wasn't interested in him?

Josh said, from the kitchen door, 'Tickets for what?'

Ewan said, 'To the theatre. I thought we could go to a play.'

Josh held up his hands; he had a plastic brontosaurus in one hand and a stegosaurus in the other. 'Has it got dinosaurs in it?'

Ewan shook his head. 'No, just people.'

Josh snorted, and wandered away, down the hall.

Sarah disguised her relief. 'Sorry; it was a lovely idea but I don't think it'll work out.'

Ewan opened his mouth but the doorbell rang and Minnie shouted from upstairs, 'I'll get it!'

She crashed down the stairs and her voice mixed with a new one while Josh shouted, 'Look! Dinosaurs!'

The babble of voices approached and Minnie appeared, her face flushed with excitement; 'It's Mr Driffield and he says I should call him Henry!'

Sarah forced every feeling into the nearest compartment and slammed it shut. 'Hello Henry.' She stood up and indicated a free chair. 'Tea?'

He crossed the kitchen in two strides and sat down.

Ewan, beside him, looked tiny.

Josh plonked his dinosaurs on the table and slouched next to Henry. 'Would a taser knock a dinosaur out?'

Henry said, 'I doubt it. You could try two though, maybe three?'

Josh nodded, collected his models, said, 'Thanks,' and wandered thoughtfully out of the kitchen.

Minnie sat down and looked expectantly from Henry to Ewan.

Sarah smiled at Henry, 'Just passing?'

He nodded, 'Thought I'd call in.'

Sarah ignored Minnie and introduced Henry and Ewan to each other.

Henry turned his attention to Sarah; 'Sorry I woke you earlier…'

Minnie gaped.

Ewan looked constipated.

Sarah continued to ignore Minnie and smiled at Ewan; 'I fell asleep on the sofa and Henry phoned me. His call woke me up.'

Henry said easily, 'Yes; sorry about that.'

Silence descended. Henry gulped some tea, Ewan fidgeted, and Minnie's eyes grew even rounder.

Josh wandered back into the kitchen and stood in front of Henry. 'Can I ask you something?'

Henry gulped more tea and nodded.

Josh said, 'You know you're called Henry?'

Henry gave his full attention to Josh and nodded again.

Josh continued, 'Well I'm Joshua, but everyone calls me Josh.'

Henry regarded Josh seriously.

Josh said, 'Do people often call you "hen"?'

Henry's face became frighteningly blank. He leaned forward and said meaningfully, 'Not *often*, no. They usually only do that *once!*'

A sense of menace rippled out through Henry but he winked, his eyes twinkled and the threat evaporated.

Josh howled with laughter, launched himself at the detective and sat on his knee.

Minnie's eyes swivelled from Henry to Ewan.

Ewan coughed. 'Well, I think I'd better be going.'

Sarah stood up and escorted him to the front door.

He shifted nervously from foot to foot on the doorstep. 'Can I call you?'

Sarah took a deep breath, 'I don't think that's such a good idea. I'm sorry.'

He glanced past her towards the kitchen. 'Because of… is he…?'

She hid her relief; this was her way out. She nodded.

He seemed to deflate.

She kissed him on the cheek. 'You'll find someone; I'm sure you'll find someone…'

His eyes glistened, 'Just not you?'

She nodded sympathetically, 'Just not me.'

He puffed out his cheeks, 'Well, thank you for telling me. At least I know now; rather than… rather than…'

She nodded and began to close the door.

He rubbed his eyes. 'I'm sorry.'

She smiled sympathetically, 'So am I.'

He turned away and she shut the door and leant on it. All kinds of feelings were pecking and swooping around inside her but she pushed them all away. She needed time to think.

CHAPTER THIRTY FOUR

Minnie appeared in the hall and walked towards her.

Sarah shoved her tangled thoughts after her feelings; she would have to think about things later.

Minnie arrived in front of her and said mischievously, 'I'll leave you to chat with *Henry* now, shall I?'

Sarah said bluntly, 'Yes, and you can stop *that* too!'

Minnie rocked backwards. She looked as if she'd been slapped.

Sarah reached out and embraced her. 'Sorry Min, but today's turning out to be much more complicated than I expected. I need you to be grown up and not do the nudge-nudge wink-wink thing.'

Minnie sobbed unexpectedly, 'But I *am* being grown up, Mum. I do know about men and women, you know!'

Sarah kissed her. 'I know you know, but you being excited isn't helping.'

Minnie pushed herself away and rubbed her eyes. 'It's all right, you know. You having boyfriends. I've talked to Josh and he's fine about it too. We both are.'

Sarah gaped.

Minnie blew her nose. 'I think, we think, that if Daddy can have a boyfriend, so can you.'

Sarah protested, 'But I haven't got a boyfriend!'

Minnie looked confused.

Sarah said, 'And I'm not sure that I even want one.'

'But what about Ewan?'

Sarah said, 'He was just someone I met. A friend. It's complicated. He wasn't my boyfriend.'

'Wasn't?' Minnie asked tentatively.

Sarah made a face. 'He wanted to be, but I've just told him that I don't feel that way about him.'

Minnie glanced towards the kitchen.

Sarah said, 'And he's not my boyfriend either.'

Minnie looked uncertain.

Sarah hugged her again, 'He's just a policeman who helped me when I had my accident. That's all.'

Minnie muttered, 'But he likes you. Ewan does – did – too. What's so complicated?'

Sarah shook her head and smiled, 'Go and make a start on your homework; we'll talk about it later. I need to go and see what Detective Chief Inspector Driffield wants.'

Minnie drifted up the stairs and Josh came racing down the hall and followed her. Sarah headed determinedly for the kitchen.

'Everything all right?' Henry asked.

Sarah sat down and nodded. 'Just a domestic.'

Henry grunted, 'Well, as domestics go, you've got off lightly. Believe me, over the years, I've seen some domestics that would put you off families for life!'

Sarah laughed. 'Thanks; that's put things into perspective.'

He saluted smartly, 'As the Americans say, that's what we do: protect and serve!'

Sarah laughed again, 'You know, most of the time, I completely forget that you're a policeman!'

He smiled back, 'That's another thing they say, isn't it?'

Sarah said, 'What's that?'

He grinned broadly, 'That flattery will get you everywhere.'

She poured some more tea. 'Thank you for calling in; actually, you couldn't have called at a better time.'

He drank some tea and then raised his eyebrows.

She leaned forward and lowered her voice, 'I wasn't sure how to get rid of Ewan.'

His eyebrows rose again, this time in surprise.

Sarah nodded, 'So your arrival was timely. Thank you.'

He shrugged.

She continued brightly, 'So anyway, did you want to tell me something else about the accident?'

Henry glanced towards the open kitchen door. 'No. You asked

me about the death of Gerald Bailey and I've done a bit of digging. Can we go somewhere a bit more private?'

Sarah followed his gaze; he was right; it wasn't appropriate for the children to hear this. 'We could go into the garden. It's a bit chilly, but would that do?'

He nodded and stood up.

Sarah stood up too. 'Hang on; I'll just get my coat.' She went into the hall, collected her coat and called up the stairs, 'I'm just going to show Henry the garden.'

'Can I come?' Josh called back.

'No,' Minnie said firmly.

Sarah smiled and returned to the kitchen.

When they were near the top of the garden, she brushed some leaves off the garden bench and they sat down.

Henry pulled some papers out of his inside pocket and became business-like. 'How much do you already know about Gerald Bailey?'

Sarah scratched her ear. 'I know that my ex-mother-in-law was married to him but apart from that I only know what I read in the paper; that he was an actor, a rising star, and that he was mugged on the way home from a performance.'

Henry sucked his teeth.

Sarah rested her hand on his arm, 'What?'

He glanced at her, as if he was making up his mind about something. 'And you want to know everything?'

She nodded, 'I do. Why?'

He sucked his teeth again. 'Knowledge isn't always what it's cracked up to be. Sometimes secrets are secrets for good reason.'

Sarah felt a cold mist form in her stomach, 'What are you saying?'

Henry glanced at her again, 'It might be best if you just leave it alone.'

She sat back from him and the cold mist solidified inside her. 'Well that's no good is it? I mean, if I was better off not knowing, you should have just told me that there was nothing to know, or just never got back in touch with me. But now, you've basically told me that there's something else to know, so you can't leave me not knowing it; can you?'

He blinked and then smiled. 'Fair point.'

She waited.

His smile broadened and he looked her in the eye, 'I'll tell you what, though.'

'What?' she asked.

He patted her arm, 'I really *do* like *you!*'

She pointed at the papers in his hand.

He shuffled them and became business-like again. 'Okay, you know that he was murdered on his way home from the theatre?'

The chill inside Sarah moved up into her chest. Until now she had not named Gerald's death as 'murder'; but that's what it was.

Henry cleared his throat, 'What you don't know is that he was known to the police.'

Sarah said in surprise, 'What does that mean? "Known to the police"?'

Henry kept his attention on the papers, 'It means that there was a file on him. Before he died there was already a file on him.'

Sarah said, 'You mean that he was a criminal?'

Henry shook his head, 'No; the file contains specific details of meetings with other men who were also known to the police. But he was never arrested.'

Sarah said, 'You mean that he was under surveillance for some reason? Are you saying that he was a spy or something?'

Henry sighed, 'No; nothing like that. *He* wasn't under surveillance; it was the places he went to that were under surveillance; certain parks and public lavatories. From time to time, Gerald Bailey frequented those places and someone made a note in his file.'

Sarah said, 'I'm sorry but I don't understand.'

Henry lowered his voice. 'You have to remember that this was the nineteen-sixties; things were very different to how they are now.'

Sarah nodded. That was true; people were much more violent.

Henry continued confidentially, 'And homosexuality had only just become legal. In private…'

Henry's words tumbled into shape and Sarah blurted out, 'Are you saying that Gerald was gay?'

Henry nodded. 'But you need to understand how it was, back then. In nineteen sixty-seven it became legal for consenting adults, over the age of twenty-one, to engage in homosexual acts in private. Meeting like-minded men in public places was still illegal, though, and while some police forces prosecuted gay men who visited pick-up points, others kept more of a watching brief – if all they did was meet and then go off somewhere private.'

Sarah said faintly, 'And they were watching Gerald?'

Henry nodded and glanced at her. 'As I said; he came to their attention. Are you coping all right with this?'

'I don't know,' she answered quietly.

'We could stop?' Henry said gently.

Something was nagging at her, but she shoved it aside. 'No; I'm fine; I just never realised that I had so much in common with my mother-in-law!'

Henry grunted, 'Okay; but I'm afraid there's more.'

Sarah waited.

He became business-like again. 'The thing is, in the gap between political discussion and changes in the law, some people took direct action.'

Sarah whispered, 'I'm sorry, but I really don't understand…'

Henry became very matter-of-fact. 'They called it "queer-bashing". Gangs of men went looking for gay men and beat them up.'

Something new nagged at Sarah but she ignored it. She needed to understand what Henry was telling her. 'Are you saying that Gerald was killed because he was gay?'

Henry folded the papers. 'The formal report says that his wallet was stolen so it was recorded as a death following a robbery.'

Sarah said quietly, 'But there was an informal report?'

Henry nodded. 'The alley where Gerald Bailey died was a well known pick-up point for gay men. Informally, the police did not believe that Gerald was on his way home; they believed that he was in that alley to meet men.'

Sarah rubbed her forehead, 'But why didn't they tell anyone?'

Henry sighed, 'Like I said, it was a different time. By keeping quiet about their suspicions they hoped to save the family from shame.'

Sarah was horrified, 'But that's terrible!'

Henry nodded, 'I agree – but, as I said, it was a different time.'

Sarah shook her head slowly. She had too much to think about.

Henry rested his hand on her arm. 'Should I stay, or go?'

Sarah stared at her feet. 'Would you mind, awfully, if you went?'

He stood up. 'Not at all. You stay where you are; I'll tell the kids that you have some stuff to think about and let myself out.'

She watched as he walked down the garden and let himself in through the kitchen door. She leant back and stared up through the branches of her pear tree. Part of her wished that she didn't know; about Gerald; about his terrible, vile death; about anything. And yet she was glad to know. Finally she understood why Sandy had never said anything to anyone about her first marriage.

She sat forwards on the bench and clasped her hands. When Dom had left her, when he had told her that he was gay, she had wished him dead. How terrible if Sandy had found out about Gerald and wished the same fate on him; only to have her wish granted by a gang of men who kicked him to death.

Sarah took a ragged breath. There were no words to express her abhorrence at what had happened to Gerald – and it was almost unthinkable that, only one generation ago, attitudes about sexuality had led to such an atrocity. At least, in her own generation, that had changed, and Dom could live his life without fear of violence. He deserved to be happy. In fact everyone deserved to be happy.

A new memory nudged into the forefront of her mind. It was a memory that was less than an hour old; it was the look on Ewan's face when she let him believe that she was in a relationship with Henry. When Dom had left her he had been as kind as he could be, but he had still left her. She, in her turn, had been kind to Ewan, but she had still done to him what Dom had done to her…

Yes; everyone deserved to be happy; but who was?

Her tears arrived and she gave in to them, hoping that Di was right – that they would help her to be a better person and that she would, in turn, be able to make the world a happier place for others.

CHAPTER THIRTY FIVE

'You're being very attentive,' Sandy said suspiciously.

Sarah smiled happily; it was amazing how close she felt to her ex-mother-in-law. She smiled again – happiness was a feeling and she knew exactly where it came from and exactly where it belonged. 'I'm just really happy that we're redecorating together.'

Sandy looked her up and down.

Sarah chuckled, 'Sorry; I must look a mess!' She could feel wallpaper paste drying in her hair, across her face and on her knees where she had inadvertently knelt on a patch of pasty tarpaulin.

Sandy ignored her and began to paste a new sheet of wallpaper.

Sarah said, 'It's really good of you to help redecorate Josh's room.'

Sandy shot a guarded glance across the pasting table, 'Well it's not as if Roy can do it, is it?'

Sarah smiled, took the sheet of freshly pasted wallpaper and climbed the step-ladder. She allowed the wet paper to flop down the wall, adjusted the top and then located it next to its neighbour. She reached behind her, pulled the decorator's brush out of her back pocket and used it to smooth out the air bubbles. She sliced off the waste at the top, climbed down the ladder, sliced off the waste at the bottom, stood back, and examined her work critically. The paper was a fluorescent green colour. In her opinion it was hideous but Josh liked it.

'Have you overlapped it?' Sandy asked pointedly.

Sarah nodded. She had done exactly what Roy had told her to do; she had begun in the corner furthest away from the window and slightly overlapped each sheet. He was right: the light disguised the join and the finish looked smooth.

'How long will Roy be out of action?' she asked.

Sandy snorted derisively, 'Until he gets a "sensible" transplant I expect.'

Sarah smiled sympathetically. Roy had been in the high street and had stepped off the curb without looking. He had twisted his ankle on a crooked drain cover and ended up in the Accident and Emergency Department of Yelmouth Hospital. X-rays had confirmed that his swollen ankle was only sprained but he was struggling around on crutches and finding stairs almost impossible. She said, 'Poor Roy.'

Sandy handed her another piece of pasted paper and muttered, 'Silly bugger, Roy, more like.'

Sarah took the paper and hung it from the top, smoothing out the wrinkles with her brush. 'Are you sure he'll be all right, downstairs, with the children?'

Sandy glanced out of the corner of her eyes. 'He'll be fine. He's always been soft with children; they won't come to any harm.'

Sarah said, 'Actually, I was thinking of him. I wouldn't want the children to bash his ankle.'

Sandy snorted. 'He'll be fine. If they jump all over him, it serves him right!'

Sarah sat on the step-ladder. It was hard to believe that she was getting on so well with Sandy. Now that she understood the past, though, now that she understood what Sandy had gone through, it changed everything. It explained why her ex-mother-in-law was so tetchy and defensive; it also explained why she was so abrupt with Roy and why she found it so hard to talk about the reality of Dom's decision to live with Alex. That must be like a ghost from the past, haunting her – and how strange that Dom, like her first husband, should be gay…

Something tapped at Sarah's memory but it was faint and hard to locate.

'Here you are,' Sandy pronounced.

Sarah took the pasted paper and hung it next to the previous piece, this time turning the corner of the room. Once she had hung two more pieces, she would begin again on the opposite wall, in the other corner away from the window. She smoothed the paper flat into the corner and said, 'And are you coping? I could come and sit with Roy if you want to go out for a bit.'

Sandy paused, paste brush in hand, 'You're being very attentive.'

Sarah shrugged, 'Not really, I just want to help.'

Sandy stared at the brush in her hand and then continued pasting. A peal of laughter erupted from the sitting room below them.

'Should I make sure that everything's all right?' Sarah asked.

Sandy looked at her as if she was mad; 'Don't bother.'

Sarah continued to hang the paper in silence. It was very hard not to tell Sandy that she knew all about Gerald and his terrible murder. Several times she had considered broaching the subject but there just didn't seem any way to approach it obliquely and, given Sandy's bad mood, coming straight out with the truth didn't seem like such a good idea.

Sarah decided that she needed to make a choice. She finished hanging another piece of paper and asked casually, 'Have you been over to Dom's new place recently?'

Sandy paused again, brush in hand, 'Mmmmm?'

Sarah said, 'I just wondered. A few weeks ago, when I was dropping the children off, he asked me in for a chat but I didn't think it was appropriate for me to intrude on his time with the kids. I just wondered what his new flat was like, and you mentioned a while ago that you'd been over?'

Sandy began to paste again. 'Have you asked the children?'

Sarah said, 'Well, no; I didn't think that was appropriate either.'

Sandy snorted, 'And asking me *is?*'

Sarah could feel her cheeks prickling; so much for choosing to be subtle. Should she just go for it? She glanced at Sandy and took a deep breath, 'What do you think of Alex?'

Sandy stopped pasting and shot a calculating look across the room. 'Talking of appropriate; I don't think that's an appropriate question – do you?'

Sarah could feel her inner compartments slamming shut. On one level, she and her ex-mother-in-law were decorating a child's bedroom but, on another level, she was fighting for her life.

She gave in to her familiar defences and followed the strategy she was so used to; she backed down. 'Sorry; no.'

Sandy nodded with satisfaction and returned her attention to the paste table.

Sarah opened her inner forest glade and pushed her shame and disappointment inside. She would deal with her feelings later.

'Blimey!' Minnie said from the doorway.

Sarah sighed with relief, glad of the interruption.

Minnie chortled, 'It's like being inside a frog!'

Josh pushed past her and declared fiercely, 'Well I like it!'

'Watch where you're treading!' Sandy shouted.

Both children stopped in their tracks and then moved with exaggerated care, placing their feet as if crossing a minefield.

Sarah laughed but stopped when Sandy glared at her.

'You really like this?' Minnie asked.

'Yes,' Josh said stubbornly.

Minnie shrugged, 'Well it's you that has to sleep in here, not me. So good luck with that!'

Josh smouldered in the middle of the room.

Sarah crossed the space between them and rested her hand on his shoulder. 'I think it's very nice.'

Josh glanced at her gratefully but she could see the uncertainty in his eyes. Never mind, when the paper was dry they could always paint over it…

'So do I,' said a new voice.

Sarah glanced towards the door and was surprised to see Neil.

Josh poked Minnie, 'See? It's a *man* thing!'

Minnie poked him back, 'And you know what they say about men and taste, don't you?'

Josh looked worried, 'No…'

Minnie smiled at Neil, 'No offence!'

Neil held up his hands, 'None taken.' He continued his gesture to indicate the room, 'I think it's very nice; very, um, vibrant.'

Josh nodded vigorously; 'Vibrant!'

Minnie glanced from Neil to Josh and then back to Neil. She looked as if she was about to laugh.

Sarah interjected, 'Anyway, we've nearly finished; then we can all have tea. Later on, we can clear up and tomorrow, when the paper's dry, we can shift all of Josh's things back in and it'll look quite different then.'

Josh nodded again, 'Vibrant!'

Minnie rolled her eyes.

Neil said, 'Do you need a hand; tomorrow?'

Sarah smiled, 'Would you?'

He smiled back and nodded.

Sarah said, 'Would you like to stay for tea? We've nearly finished so we won't be long.'

Neil said, 'Oh, thank you, but no. I just dropped in to see you but you're obviously busy. Give me a call when you're free and we can meet up.'

'Right-oh,' Sarah chirped.

He said to Minnie, 'Thanks for bringing me up but I'll see myself out; it's not like I don't know the way.'

Sarah laughed, their houses were identical; her house must be as familiar to him as his was to her. 'I know – this is your guest room and my bedroom is your bedroom too!'

He smiled at Sarah and said, 'Bye then.' He turned away and his footsteps receded down the stairs.

Sarah glanced at Minnie, who was staring at her wide eyed.

'What?' Sarah asked.

Minnie just said, meaningfully, 'Mum!' and left the room.

Josh charged after her and Sarah smiled at Sandy; she was standing with her mouth hanging open.

Sarah frowned. 'Are you all right?'

Sandy closed her mouth slowly and nodded to herself. 'I see…'

'Pardon?'

Sandy's expression hardened. 'Now I understand – why you were blethering on about Dom's new flat and Alex. Now I see!'

'Do you?' Sarah asked; because she didn't.

Sandy waved the pasting brush to indicate the room and a blob of paste plopped onto the tarpaulin. 'You know all this is Dom's generosity, don't you?'

Sarah nodded. Dom was paying for the wallpaper just like he paid for everything else.

Sandy slapped the brush on the paste table. 'You only get to live here because Dom lets you, you know!'

Oh – she was talking about the house. Sarah nodded again.

Sandy lowered her voice and narrowed her eyes, 'He who pays the piper, young lady! He who pays the piper!'

'I'm sorry but I'm not sure that–'

Sandy threw the paste brush on the floor. 'So Dom can live with who he pleases – but you can't! I can't believe how low your standards have sunk – and in front of my grandchildren too! You should be ashamed of yourself!'

She stalked out of the room and down the stairs calling, 'Roy? Roy! We're going!'

Sarah gaped and tried to make sense of what had just happened but her brain didn't seem to be working. She tried to find her feelings, but they had gone absent without leave too. She shrugged; she had offered an olive branch to Sandy and it had been thrown back in her face. Maybe they had nothing in common after all?

She picked up the pasting brush and completed another strip of wallpaper. Right; finishing the room was what mattered; she would think about what had happened later.

She let her mind go blank and got on with the job. As she smoothed the final piece of paper into place, she heard footsteps behind her. It was Minnie.

Sarah smiled, 'There. What do you think?'

Minnie looked uncertain, 'About what?'

Sarah replied, 'About the room, of course!'

Minnie looked around and made a face. 'It's horrible.'

Sarah sighed; 'You don't have to like it…'

Minnie looked uncertain again. 'Are we talking about Josh's room or something else?'

Sarah attempted to kick her brain into action but it just sat inside her head. She rubbed her forehead and said wearily, 'I'm sorry Min, but I have no idea what you're talking about.'

Minnie came to her and hugged her. 'It's all right Mum. It's like I said; it's fine with me and Josh.'

Sarah hugged her back. 'What is?'

'You having a boyfriend,' Minnie answered.

Sarah considered this. 'I know; but I haven't got a boyfriend.'

Minnie drew back from her and stared into her eyes. 'What about Neil?'

Sarah blinked. 'What *about* Neil?'

Minnie looked confused. 'Isn't he your boyfriend?'

Sarah stared, 'No; why would you think that?'

Minnie said, 'Because you're going to bed with him.'

Sarah stopped breathing, 'Where did you get that idea?'

Minnie said, 'You said so?'

Sarah cudgelled her brain but it still sat, useless, inside her head. 'I said so?' When had she said that? What had she said? It was true enough that she'd fallen for Neil but he had no interest in her; he was probably off chasing Josie Tasker.

Minnie smiled knowingly, 'You know: when you said "my bedroom is your bedroom"?'

Sarah burst out laughing, 'I just meant that our houses are exactly the same; all the rooms are the same so his bedroom is the same as mine!'

Minnie frowned, 'But how do you know?'

Sarah stopped laughing; she hadn't told the children about her cleaning job so why would she know about Neil's bedroom? She said lightly, 'Everyone knows. It's the way these houses were built! Every house in the road is the same!'

Minnie hugged her again, 'So Neil's not your boyfriend?'

Sarah hugged her back, 'No.'

Minnie mumbled, 'And you aren't going to bed with him?'

'No,' Sarah said firmly.

Minnie said, 'It would have been fine if you had.'

Sarah resisted the urge to say: 'It probably would!' Instead she hugged Minnie again. 'Thank you.'

Minnie disentangled herself and went towards the door. 'We like Neil.'

Sarah nodded. 'So do I.'

Minnie stopped and frowned, 'But he's not your boyfriend?'

Sarah sighed, 'No, and he never will be.'

Minnie caught her eye, 'And Ewan's not your boyfriend either?'

Sarah shook her head.

Minnie asked, 'What about–'

Sarah interrupted firmly, 'Min, I don't have a boyfriend. If I did I'd tell you.'

Minnie considered this and nodded.

Downstairs, the front door slammed and a car engine roared into life.

Minnie said, 'And you'd better tell Grandma that Neil's not your boyfriend too.'

Sarah muttered, 'Oh crap.'

She began to clear up the decorating equipment. She'd better ring Sandy later and explain what she'd meant.

Without warning, her feelings emerged and left her breathless. Actually, why should she? Sandy had treated her like dirt all afternoon so if she wanted to believe that Sarah was sleeping with Neil, let her! She smiled wryly; in the grand scheme of things, choosing to let Sandy believe an untruth wasn't much of a choice, but at least it was a choice! And if Sandy was determined to be a vicious old hag then she could choke on the idea of Sarah making whoopee with someone as wonderful as Neil!

She began to fold up the tarpaulin and something started nudging at her memory again. It was something about Dom. She really must find time to sit and think...

CHAPTER THIRTY SIX

Sarah walked into Yelmouth library and literally bumped into Ruth. Two books fell from the pile the librarian was carrying and landed with loud thumps on the highly polished wooden floor.

Sarah stooped to pick them up and said, 'Sorry!'

Ruth briefly bent her knees as Sarah replaced the books on her pile and answered in her enigmatic accent, 'Not a problem; you look nice!'

Sarah smoothed her russet skirt and adjusted her matching sweater; the outfit had suited Di, but did it suit her? 'Do you really think so? I wasn't sure if these are really my colours.'

Ruth said, 'Hang on.' She slid her feet across the smooth floor, put the pile of books on the reception counter and turned around.

Sarah took her coat off and held her arms away from her sides. 'What do you think? Be honest…'

Ruth looked at her critically, 'I see what you mean. You're a bit blonde for those autumn colours, really.'

Sarah let her arms fall to her sides.

Ruth continued, 'It's a good look, though, and the bias cut looks great. Have you thought of, maybe, tying your hair back?'

Sarah gathered her hair in her hand at the back of her head, 'Like this?'

Ruth snapped her fingers and grinned, 'That's great; you'll knock him dead!'

Sarah almost said: 'who?' but stopped herself. 'I'll stop off on my way home and get some scrunchies or something.'

Ruth reached over the counter and offered a yellow rubber band. 'You can experiment with that, if you like. The Ladies is just over there.'

Sarah accepted the circle of elastic and went into the Ladies. She stood in front of the mirror and experimented with her hair. Ruth was right; the russet sweater looked much better against her skin when her hair was out of the way. The colours were just right for Di's darker complexion but with Sarah's blonde hair minimised, they worked fine on her too. She looped the rubber band to make a splayed bun and smiled. She looked good with her hair up; she should wear it this way more often. She made her way back to the reception desk, relishing feeling good about the way she looked. Now she had two outfits that made her feel great; her 'Ruth look' and now her 'Di look'.

Ruth stamped the flyleaf of an open book and looked up, 'So; what are you after this time?'

Sarah smiled. 'I'd like to use the internet.'

'We still haven't got the newspapers on the net, yet,' Ruth apologised.

Sarah grinned; 'The: "netyet"?'

Ruth grinned back and in an impressive impersonation of Miss Piggy said, 'The netyet!'

Sarah chuckled. 'Not to worry, I don't want to look at the papers, this time. It's a birth certificate I'm after.'

Ruth stood up and resumed in her normal voice, 'Come on, then. I'll log you on with our code, but I'm afraid you'll have to pay to access the records. They're on the national database so they're not something we hold here. Have you got a credit card?'

Sarah nodded and walked with Ruth to the now familiar reference room and sat down at the table Ruth indicated.

The librarian accessed the appropriate web page and pointed to the computer screen. 'You input information in here, here and here, click this and a list of possibilities will come up. You pick the one you think is correct and then you'll go to a screen that asks for your credit card details. If you register an account, you don't have to go through the payment options each time. Just be aware that, once you've set up an account, every time you click on a record, it costs you money. Sorry.'

Sarah smiled, 'Don't worry, I won't get carried away.'

Ruth straightened up, 'I'm sure you won't, but some people do and then, when their credit card bills arrive, they come screaming and shouting at us!'

Sarah hesitated and then said, 'Ruth, can I ask you something?'

The librarian looked at her quizzically.

Sarah said, 'I love your accent; I really do; but I've been trying to place it and I just can't. Is it Scandinavian?'

Ruth laughed aloud and then glanced around and lowered her voice. 'Ach no; I'm a Highlands girl; north of Scotland.'

Now that Sarah knew where Ruth was from, she could hear the accent clearly. She watched as the librarian walked away; today she was wearing black, tailored trousers, a plain, red, vee-necked sweater and what looked like the white blouse she had worn with the pencil skirt and the same shoes. She also had a small, enamel daisy on a hair slide just above her left ear. She looked good – maybe, next time Neil paid her, Sarah would add her earnings to the money she had started to squirrel away without telling Dom and explore a similar outfit?

She pulled a sheet of paper out of her bag and found her pen. She reminded herself of the dates on her sheet. The first date was February the eleventh, nineteen sixty-seven; that was when Sandy had married Gerald. The second date was October the eighteenth, nineteen sixty-nine; the day of Gerald's murder.

Sarah looked at the list; it was very short. There was so much that she didn't know but there was something about those two dates that nagged at her, along with some of the comments that Sandy had made in the last few months. She tapped her pen on the paper and considered the screen in front of her. The cursor was blinking in the first information box.

Should she be doing this? She sat back; why shouldn't she? After all, records of births, marriages and deaths were public documents. She had as much right as anyone else to look at them. She interlaced her fingers; that wasn't the point, though, was it? The records might be public, but she was about to pry into her own relatives' pasts. Should she be doing this?

She couldn't decide; she needed to go on her gut instinct and, now that she was finally listening to her feelings, her gut instinct was telling her to proceed. She sat forward but paused; her hands on the keyboard; it had been a difficult few days. After the decorating debacle, her misunderstanding with Sandy had prompted her to reflect on a lot of recent conversations and, the more she reflected, the more she noticed the misunderstandings and anomalies.

Sarah made up her mind and entered the information. In the first box she typed in Dom's full name, in the second, his date of birth and, in the third, 'Yelmouth'. She paused with the curser hovering over the 'OK' button and clicked it. As Ruth had predicted, she was taken immediately to a screen that asked if she wanted to register a new account. She clicked the 'Yes' button and spent the next few minutes inventing a user-name and password and entering her credit-card details. Eventually, a friendly blue screen welcomed her and asked her if she wanted to take a tour of the website. She clicked, 'later' and stared at a blank screen. She had just paid to find out nothing!

She scrolled up the screen and was informed that no records matched her search criteria and asked if she wanted to widen the search parameters. Sarah had no idea what that meant so she backtracked through the screens and clicked the button that started the tour. Ten minutes later she understood what she was supposed to do and found the search screen again. This time she typed in Dom's full name, but next to the *date* box she found the parameter button and entered 'plus or minus one year'. In the final box, she again typed in: 'Yelmouth.'

This time, when she clicked the 'OK' button, a list of three identical names appeared. She scrutinised the list and decided that the child located up near the Quarry was her best bet. She clicked on the name and a box appeared, asking her if she was prepared to pay fifty pence for the information. Clearly she had been wrong about paying for the blank screen. She clicked; 'OK' and a document appeared on the screen.

She scrolled across it but it wasn't what she was looking for. The names of the father and mother meant nothing to her. She returned to the input screen and, this time, changed the final box from: 'Yelmouth' to: 'England'.

Immediately, a list of thirty-four names appeared. She considered all of them, but one in particular caught her eye. This Dominic Price had been born in Finsbury – wasn't that near Pentonville where Sandy and Gerald had lived? She clicked on the name, confirmed that she would pay for the information and the document appeared on the screen. There it was; Dom's birth certificate. He had been born on the ninth of June nineteen-seventy; Sarah knew that already. She also knew that his mother was Alexandra Price and that his father was Roy Price. What she didn't know, though, was why his birth had been registered in Finsbury, London, rather than in Yelmouth.

She went back to the home screen and changed the search to the marriage registers. She entered Sandy and Roy's names, left the date blank and entered: 'England' in the final box. To her surprise, only two options appeared on the screen and one was located in Yelmouth. She clicked it, agreed to pay, and the document appeared in front of her. It was the record of Roy and Sandy's marriage, and it was dated the twenty-fourth of January nineteen-seventy.

Sarah sat back in her chair. She was right. Roy and Sandy had married only three months after Gerald's death, but, just as importantly, when Sandy had been four months pregnant with Dom – no wonder she had worn her original wedding dress again! On the first occasion, when she had married Gerald, it had been a theatrical wedding, but when she married Roy, that high-waisted Regency dress, on a woman as slim as Sandy, would have disguised her pregnancy from the wedding guests.

Sarah made a note of the date on her sheet and then blew out her cheeks as she saw it in the context of the other dates. She counted on her fingers and there was no doubt about it; unless

Dom had arrived early, he had been conceived in September nineteen sixty-nine – four to six weeks before Gerald's death.

Roy clearly believed that Dom was his son, so he and Sandy must have been having an affair before Gerald was murdered. So much for Sandy's holier-than-thou attitudes!

A new thought hit Sarah like a blow to the head: *unless...*

She blew out her cheeks again; it was the oblique remark that Sandy had made about Josh's school play that had nagged at her and caused her to wonder. Sandy had talked about Dom's childhood appearances in school plays and had quoted the old saying: 'Like father, like son'. At the time, Sarah had assumed that Sandy had meant Dom and Josh, but what if Sandy had meant Gerald and Dom? What if, regardless of her affair with Roy, Dom's father was actually Gerald?

She had also described Dom as 'her' son; not as 'our son'. Was that a tacit admission that Dom was not Roy's son? And yet, Roy clearly believed that he was, otherwise why would he have been so aggressive when he asked about Dom being Josh and Minnie's father?

She went back to the birth certificate and scrolled across it to make sure. It definitely said that Roy was Dom's father, but it would, wouldn't it? Especially if Sandy had given him every reason to think that it was true. A certificate didn't make Dom Roy's son though, and it might explain why they were so very different!

Another thought hit Sarah like a sledgehammer. Oh God! What if Dom was *exactly* like his true father? Gerald had been gay and so was Dom. What did that mean for Josh?

She accessed her inner glade. Whatever it meant, at least Josh would grow up in a generation where homosexuality was acceptable. He would live in a time when his rights were protected; where he could make his own choices without being murdered in an alley in London. Homosexuality might have been illegal in her parents' generation and socially ambiguous in her own; but if Josh was gay she would do everything she could to make sure that his life was happy and fulfilling.

She stared at the screen and moved the curser. A box appeared asking her if she wanted to print the certificate. She clicked the 'No' button.

She sat back and noted the date of Sandy and Roy's wedding on her list. There was no mistake. Gerald could well be Dom's father and when Roy had married Sandy, he must have married a woman with whom he was already conducting a clandestine affair. After the wedding, they must have moved to Finsbury for a while, had Dom, and then moved back to Yelmouth and fudged the dates. If Sandy's first marriage had been a family secret, then everyone would have assumed that Dom was Roy's anyway, but although the sixties were regarded as progressive, they evidently weren't as progressive in Yelmouth as they were in London!

Sarah closed down the site and collected her things.

Ruth smiled brightly from the reception desk and said in her beautiful, lilting accent, 'Did you find what you were looking for?'

Sarah sighed heavily, 'Yes and no. I found what I was looking for, but I'm not sure that I like what I found.'

Ruth made a sympathetic face, 'I'm afraid family trees can be a bit like that.'

Sarah waved dispiritedly and left; wasn't that the truth. Her counsellor, Di, had been right; she should have left the past where it was – in the past.

CHAPTER THIRTY SEVEN

Di said, 'To be honest, I think that's all pretty impressive!'

'Really?' Sarah asked. She had avoided talking about Neil but she had told Di about her conversations with Ewan and her misunderstanding with Sandy. This had involved telling Di about her trip to the library to give some kind of context to the conversation and, although she had only given an edited version of the truth, she had expected Di to remonstrate with her for spending time raking over the past instead of concentrating on the present.

Di nodded. 'You've discovered that life, and family life in particular, isn't cut and dried. It's about people, and because people are complicated, so is family life. That's what you know, though. What I think is impressive is the way that you've handled your emotions. Well done you!'

Sarah felt slightly guilty. Should she have told Di everything?

Di smiled. 'Think of it this way: when we first started these sessions we were talking about layers of life, the two-sided coin of emotion and your prime motivation being your desire to cope – and what you meant by that was: getting rid of negative feelings.'

Sarah nodded. That was true.

Di continued, 'Then we moved on to think about the way your emotions made themselves known and then disappeared; what I called the *whoomph-woosh* thing. Then we moved on to think about you choosing to face negative emotions and your inner life; your compartmentalisation.'

Sarah nodded again. That was true, too.

'Di said, 'But now that you are connecting with the right imaginary compartments, you are taking responsibility for your own actions, recognising when the responsibility lies with someone else, choosing confrontation when necessary and starting to think about things from other people's viewpoints. I'd say that was pretty impressive – wouldn't you?'

Sarah grinned, 'Now say all that without referring to your notes!'

Di laughed, dropped the sheets she had been skim-reading onto the coffee table and briefly poked out her tongue. 'Do you fancy a coffee?'

Sarah blinked. Was this a new level in the counselling relationship? Di had never offered coffee before! 'Yes, actually; thank you.'

Di stood up. 'I won't be long. While I'm gone, I want you to think about why you first started these sessions – you said it was because you wanted to cope and because you wanted to know how you had managed to marry a gay man without noticing. Well, it seems to me that both of those goals have been reached. When I get back with the coffee, we can think about what else you want from these sessions.'

Di left the room and Sarah gripped the arms of her chair. Di was going to end the sessions! She was going to leave Sarah to struggle through on her own! But these sessions, and Di, were her lifeline! Surely Di wouldn't abandon her? This gloomy little room had become her one safe place in the shifting miasma of her life and Di was the only person who truly understood her! If the sessions stopped, what would she do? Where would she go? Who would she talk to?

Panic gripped her and her mind went blank.

'Here we are,' Di said. She put a tray on the coffee table, handed a mug to Sarah and sat down with another. 'Help yourself to milk and sugar.'

Sarah fought with her breathing.

Di smiled. 'How are you doing?'

Sarah made a vague noise in the back of her throat.

Di's smile became sympathetic, 'Not so good, then?'

Sarah managed to shake her head.

Di nodded, sat back, and sipped her coffee.

Sarah ran around inside herself, but the only compartment she could find was her forest glade. She blurted out, 'I don't want to stop coming!'

Di toasted her with her coffee cup. 'There you go: you know how you feel.'

Sarah forced her breathing into some kind of rhythm. 'And I'm not nearly ready to sort things out on my own.'

Di said nothing.

Sarah could feel her cheeks burning. She shouted, 'It's not fair. You have no bloody right to kick me out!'

Di smiled, sipped her coffee and said sincerely, 'Fantastic: emotion and confrontation. Well done!'

Sarah could feel confusion settling on her like a damp summer mist.

Di rested her mug on the arm of her chair. 'My apologies for the shock tactics, but there was no point raising the issue in an objective way with you.'

Sarah stared at her.

Di said, 'My apologies, again, but if I'd suggested that we were coming to the point of drawing these sessions to a close, we'd have had a careful, objective discussion for half an hour. This way, you get to see what you feel and where you are.'

Sarah said faintly, 'I'm here – and here is where I need to be.'

Di sipped some more coffee. 'I'm not sure that's true. Not any more.' She gestured towards the tray on the coffee table. 'Are you going to have some milk or sugar?'

Sarah sat up and, although it felt like dream, poured some milk into her mug.

Di smiled confidently. 'Is that better?'

Sarah took a sip of coffee, sat back in her chair, and nodded.

Di said, 'Good. I think that these sessions have been very productive, and I think you do, too. But it's important that you don't become dependent on me. These sessions are just a temporary part of your life. At some point, and that may be soon, they should come to an end.'

Sarah made a decision. 'Do I get a choice – in when these sessions finish? Do I get a choice?'

Di cocked her head on one side. 'It's mutual; it's a decision we come to together. That's why I asked you to reflect on the goals you've already achieved and to think about what else you want to gain from these sessions.'

Sarah began to relax, 'So it wasn't just shock tactics?'

Di laughed, 'No. Now: have a think about my question. What else do you want to achieve through these sessions?'

Sarah considered the question. 'I hadn't realised it, but you're right. I wanted to cope and I'm coping – I just hadn't noticed because coping has turned out to be different from how I expected it to be…'

Di sipped her coffee again and said, 'Go on.'

Sarah stared at the liquid in her mug. 'You're right, when I first came here I thought coping meant avoiding crap, but now I understand that it's about dealing with crap.'

Di said, '*And* whatever the opposite of crap is: the good stuff.'

Sarah nodded. 'Yes, and I also understand about the coin and about compartments and about love and hate and all of that.'

Di sipped her coffee.

Sarah continued, 'And I also know that life is about being happy and unhappy and excited and fearful and so on and so forth.'

Di said, 'And you don't just know it either; you feel it!'

Sarah nodded sourly, 'Yeah. Like just now!'

Di nodded in return, 'Like just now.'

Sarah put her mug down on the table, 'And I also understand how my compartments got there and why I developed the strategies I did to avoid confrontation and how all of that led me into my marriage with Dom.'

Di said, 'So there we are; goals reached.'

Sarah could feel tears in her eyes, 'It was just a shock; thinking of not coming here any more. Just a shock…'

Di pushed the box of tissues across the table, 'I know.'

Sarah blew her nose and dabbed at her eyes.

Di sipped her coffee and waited.

Sarah picked up her mug and sucked in some of the brown liquid; it was tepid.

Silence descended.

Di finished her coffee and said, 'So there we are. It's nice to sit together and have coffee but that's not why we are here. You still haven't answered my question.'

Sarah pursed her lips, 'Mmmm?'

Di smiled, 'Is there anything else you want to get out of these sessions?'

Sarah thought hard, 'Yes.'

Di picked up her notebook and her pen and said, 'What's that.'

Sarah said, 'I want to be sure that, when these sessions finish, I'll be all right on my own.'

Di made a note and closed her notebook. 'That sounds like a very sensible goal to me. You reflect on that for the next couple of weeks and, when we meet again, we'll work out how to reach that goal.'

Sarah sighed with relief. 'Thank you.'

Di continued, 'And, in the meantime, if it's at all possible, try and work out if there's anyone in your family you can talk to.'

CHAPTER THIRTY EIGHT

'You didn't need to come,' Nanna Gwen said briskly. The hospital visitor's room was small but, hunched in a corner of the settee beside the window, Nanna Gwen looked tiny.

Sarah moved closer to her grandmother and held her hand; her skin was dry and papery. 'I know, Nanna, but I wanted to.'

Nanna Gwen nodded; she looked exhausted. 'You're a good girl but he's sleeping at the moment and even when he's awake he won't know that you're here.'

Sarah stroked her grandmother's fingers, 'I know; but I will.'

Nanna Gwen nodded again. 'You're a good girl.'

Sarah looked around the room. It was scruffy and bleak; if it was there to cheer visitors up, it failed miserably. Sarah sighed; no doubt hospitals had more pressing financial priorities than paint and pictures.

She said, 'You look tired, Nanna. Why don't you go home and get some sleep? I'll stay here with Poppa Jack and call you if there's any change.'

'Silly old sod,' Nanna Gwen grunted.

'I know,' Sarah commiserated. 'But he can't help having a stroke, can he?'

Nanna Gwen's lower lip quivered.

'Oh Nanna,' Sarah said, drawing the old lady into her arms. 'I'm so sorry.'

Nanna Gwen clutched her briefly and then pushed her away. 'It was bound to happen,' she said bravely. 'Sooner or later, something like this was bound to happen.'

'I know,' Sarah sympathised. 'But why don't you go home and get some rest?'

Nanna Gwen's hunted eyes stared at her, 'But what if… while I'm not here?'

Sarah held her hand in both of hers, 'I know – but as you said, he doesn't know if we're here or not.'

Nanna Gwen considered this and then made up her mind. She creaked to her feet and said, 'All right; seeing as it's you; but I wouldn't trust anyone else and you'll call me if there's any change?'

Sarah stood up, 'I will, and I'll sit with him all the time you're gone.'

Nanna Gwen hesitated. 'And you'll call me?'

Sarah said, 'I'll call you.'

Nanna Gwen seemed satisfied. She limped out of the visitor's room, leaning heavily on her stick, and walked up the ward towards the cubicle where Poppa Jack lay on his back with a sheet pulled up to his chin. The nurses had removed his false teeth and his face looked hollow. His breathing was very slow.

Nanna Gwen kissed him on his forehead and whispered, 'Silly old sod.'

Sarah watched as her grandmother attempted to march away but her limp made it impossible. She probably shouldn't still be driving, but who had the courage to tell her to stop? Not Sarah…

Nanna Gwen pushed through the double doors at the end of the ward without looking back and Sarah sat down next to Poppa Jack's bed. She found his hand under the bed clothes and held it. Poor Poppa Jack, and poor Nanna Gwen. They had lived on a knife edge of independence for years and now it was all over. If he recovered, Poppa Jack would have to go into nursing care and if he didn't make it; if this was the end; without Poppa Jack to look after, would Nanna Gwen cope?

Sarah found a tissue and wiped her eyes. She couldn't bear to think of either of her grandparents in a nursing home – but what other choice was there?

She found Poppa Jack's hand again, squeezed it and said, 'I'm here, Poppa.'

Poppa Jack continued to breathe slowly.

Sarah fished out the novel she had brought with her and attempted to read it, but it was impossible. Her thoughts raced from Poppa Jack to the past to old age to her family to death to funerals to the past and back again in a relentless circle. She shoved the book back in her bag and let her thoughts race wherever they wanted to go.

She woke up with a start; she must have dozed off. She blinked to clear her eyes; Poppa Jack's breathing had changed; it was faster and stronger.

'Poppa?' she said tentatively.

He opened his eyes and stared at her.

She leaned forwards, 'Poppa?'

He mumbled something but without his teeth the words were slurred.

She leaned closer and he mumbled something again; it sounded like: 'Dadda.'

Sarah squeezed his hand again; what else could she do? She wasn't his dadda.

He looked content and closed his eyes.

Sarah hurried back to the visitor's room, grabbed the public phone and called her grandmother. After half a dozen rings, Nanna Gwen's bleary voice said, 'Hello?'

Sarah said in a tumble of words, 'Nanna, it's me. He's awake.'

'Stay there,' Nanna Gwen commanded. 'I'm coming.'

The line went dead. Sarah replaced the receiver and hurried back to Poppa Jack's cubicle. He had struggled up towards the bedhead so Sarah helped him into a more comfortable position and put some more pillows under his head and shoulders.

He said, more strongly, 'Maggie?'

'Sarah,' she said.

He stared at her blankly.

'Oh,' Sarah said. Now she understood. He thought that she was his daughter not his granddaughter – he thought that he was *her* dadda.

Tears began to trickle from the corners of his eyes and he pulled his hand away from hers. He began to thrash feebly in the bed and he looked increasingly distressed.

Sarah reached for the alarm button and pressed it. A moment later, a nurse came into the cubicle and took his pulse. She soothed him with a constant string of words and then turned to Sarah. 'There's nothing to be done – is there anyone you should call?'

Sarah recognised the cold chill that lanced through her stomach; it was fear. 'Are you saying…?'

The nurse smiled kindly. 'It may not be long, so if there are other family members who should be here?'

Sarah exhaled hard, but the chill remained where it was. 'I already have.'

The nurse smiled gently. 'Then stay here, with him, and talk to him.'

Sarah nodded and the nurse left. She stroked Poppa Jack's hair; surely the kindest thing to do was to enter his world? She said gently, 'It's me, Dadda; Maggie.'

His eyes snapped to her face and he whispered, 'Forgive me.'

Sarah wiped away his tears and whispered, 'Of course; but there's nothing to forgive, Dadda. Nothing.'

He took a ragged breath, 'But you don't know…'

He looked deeply troubled so Sarah said, 'It doesn't matter. I forgive you anyway'

He struggled to sit up but she held him gently against the pillows. He relaxed and whispered, 'I'm sorry, Maggie; I'm sorry…'

'It's all right,' Sarah soothed, her voice breaking. 'Everything's all right.'

He shook his head on the pillow and his voice was faint but firm, 'It isn't! They went looking! I never told you, but they went looking and I knew and I never told you. Forgive me… forgive me.'

Sarah stared at her grandfather as pieces of past conversations began to connect. Her feelings told her to ignore his words, to let them go but she made a choice and ignored them. 'Tell me Pop–, Dadda; tell me now.'

He closed his eyes. 'I knew; that they were going. I knew…'

Sarah fought with her feelings and whispered, 'And you never said anything?'

His head rocked away from her and then back again. New tears trickled down his cheeks, 'For buggers... they went looking...'

Something in her memory clicked; he had said this before. She had thought that he was passing judgement on Terry and Roy but he wasn't; and now she understood! It was a violent time; they were bad boys. He had been using the language of his past to tell her that Terry and Roy had gone looking for gay men; they were 'queer-bashers'!

He mumbled again, 'They went looking; for buggers...'

Her feelings screamed at her that she shouldn't be doing this; that she was an evil person; that she was taking advantage of a dying man. She shoved them away and whispered, 'For Gerald?'

His nod was slight but definite.

It wasn't enough; it wasn't certain. She trampled her feelings into submission, leaned close to his face and asked, 'Was it them?'

He nodded again.

She needed to be sure before her inner tide turned and drowned her. 'Who was it? Who went looking?'

He whispered, 'Roy; and Terry; they went looking for buggers and they found him; Gerald; they found him. Forgive me, Maggie. Forgive me...'

Sarah grabbed her feelings and hurled them into the nearest compartment. She kissed her grandfather and said gently, 'I forgive you.'

He sighed contentedly and the tension went out of his body. The distress faded away and his breathing became slow and intermittent.

Sarah pressed the alarm button and a nurse came back into the cubicle. She checked Poppa Jack's pulse and said, 'I'll get the doctor.'

The doctor was still listening to Poppa Jack's chest when Nanna Gwen arrived, breathless and flushed.

'Is he...?' she asked.

The doctor removed his stethoscope. 'It's good that you've come.'

Nanna Gwen sagged and then stood up straight. 'Thank you, doctor. I'm here now.'

The doctor smiled sympathetically at Sarah and left the cubicle.

The nurse paused on her way out; 'Let me know if you need anything.'

Sarah put her arm around Nanna Gwen.

The old lady sat in the chair by the bed and stared at Poppa Jack. 'You said he was awake.'

Sarah moved behind her grandmother and laid her hand on her shoulder. 'He was; for a little while.'

Nanna Gwen stared at Poppa Jack as if mesmerised by his slow, ragged breathing. 'Did he say anything?'

Sarah paused; should she say something or say nothing? She had another choice to make but she was determined to be objective; dispassionate.

Nanna Gwen twisted around in her chair. 'What did he say?'

Sarah caught and held her grandmother's gaze. She was the one person Sarah could talk to – but how could she ever share what she knew; what Poppa Jack had known? She said 'Nothing really; he was just rambling about the past.'

Nanna Gwen dropped her eyes, 'About when he was young?'

Sarah said, 'I think so.'

Nanna Gwen sighed deeply and patted Sarah's hand. She turned back to Poppa Jack, 'I suppose, in your head, you're ten years old again and running through the fields…'

Sarah felt completely devoid of emotion, 'I suppose so.'

Nanna Gwen patted her hand again. 'Now; I want to be alone with Jack. He might wake up again. Will you excuse us?'

Sarah left the cubicle and made her way back to the visitor's room. Her brain was in overdrive as pieces from the past fell into place. The nineteen-sixties; Roy telling her that in the past families had sorted out their own problems; the hideous practice of queer-bashing; the fact that her parents' generation even *used* phrases like that; and Roy and Terry looking for gay men to beat up and finding Gerald Bailey…

Sarah shook her head. How could she accept that her dad and Roy were responsible for the murder of Sandy's first husband? And yet, how could she *not* accept it? Poppa Jack had told her. This must be why the friendship between her father and Roy had ended. This must be the secret at the heart of the family rift; the murder of Gerald Bailey…

What should she do? Tell Henry? Have the case reopened? Give testimony against her own father? But on what evidence? The muttered words of a senile, dying old man? Would all of her family be interviewed by the police? Would Nanna Gwen? Did any of them, apart from Terry and Roy, know the truth?

What should she do? What could she do? Perhaps she had made a massive mistake? Was it even true?

Then she remembered Poppa Jack's distress and the look on his face as he muttered his confession – and the look of relief when he had finished. Sarah's head drooped lower; it was true; of course it was true!

Her head jerked up. It wasn't fair! She had come to the hospital because her grandfather was ill; because this might be her last ever visit. She had come because it was the right thing to do. She had come because she loved him but she had been handed an evil, repulsive burden. Her life had just been getting onto a new track – and now this! It wasn't fair, any of it, and from this day on she would have to face her family, knowing what she knew.

The inner compartment where she had slung her emotions burst open. She almost fell into the visitor's room and managed to reach the couch just before her legs gave way.

CHAPTER THIRTY NINE

'I don't care,' Sarah screamed. She had made her choice and she wasn't about to back down. 'Put your socks in the wash!'

Her words echoed off the kitchen walls and Josh stood rooted to the spot, terrified. Even Minnie pressed herself against the wall as if trying to dissolve through it.

Sarah stepped sideways, imagining that her anger remained in the space she had just left. She wagged her finger and said calmly, 'This is called a row. The idea is that you shout back at me.'

Josh glanced frantically towards Minnie.

Sarah said reasonably, 'Well go on then, shout back!'

His eyes became even wider, but then he grinned, 'You mean, like a game?'

Sarah shrugged. 'Sort of, but it's more like a *practice*. That's why families row – to practice sorting things out with people they love so that they can sort things out better with everyone else.'

Josh said, 'That sounds weird.'

Sarah nodded. 'I know, but think about it: when you play football, you practice with your own team and then play against strangers. Having a row at home is like that; it's practice with your own team.'

Josh said, 'But what do I do, Mummy?'

Sarah said, 'I'm going to step back to where I was and I'm going to scream again. Then you scream back.'

Josh scratched his head. 'What do I scream?'

Sarah wagged her finger again. 'Whatever you feel like. Ready?'

She stepped sideways, connected with her anger and screamed, 'I said: "Put your socks in the wash," you lazy toad!'

Josh flinched and then hurled back at her, 'I hate you!'

'Well boo hoo; I don't care,' Sarah screamed.

Josh shouted, 'It's not my job!'

'*What's* not your job?' Sarah flung back.

'My socks!' he yelled, red in the face.

'Is it mine?' Sarah shouted.

'Yes,' he bawled. 'You're my Mummy so you have to pick up my socks!'

'Oh I don't think so,' Sarah hissed dangerously. 'I think you'll find that because I'm your Mummy I get to tell *you* what to do!'

His mouth opened but nothing came out.

Sarah pointed towards the door and commanded, 'Go upstairs now, collect all your festering, putrid socks, bring them down here and PUT THEM IN THE WASH!'

He moved towards the door as if in a trance.

'Wait just one minute,' Sarah snapped.

He stopped.

'What do you say?' she demanded.

Various expressions crossed his face and then he said, 'Sorry...?'

Sarah allowed her anger to flow down her body, into her legs and into the floor. 'Good boy.' She held out her arms and he came to her and hugged her.

'Sorry, Mummy,' he said.

She kissed him and said, 'That's all right.'

He disentangled himself from her, took a step towards the door and stopped. 'Mummy?'

'What?'

'Is the row over?'

She nodded. 'Rows usually end when someone says sorry.'

He nodded thoughtfully. 'So does that mean I don't have to get my socks?'

She slapped him lightly on his bottom. 'Don't push it!'

He yelped, giggled and ran off, upstairs.

Minnie peeled herself off the wall and strolled rather too nonchalantly to the other side of the kitchen table. 'Mum?'

'Yes, Min?'

'What was that about?'

Sarah shrugged, 'That was a row.'

Minnie rolled her eyes, 'Well I know that – but you don't do rows!'

Sarah pulled a kitchen chair out from under the table and sat down. 'I do now. I've come to realise that I should.'

Minnie looked confused.

Sarah said, 'Let's sit down.'

Minnie pulled out a chair and lowered herself warily onto it.

Sarah took a deep breath. 'Min, since your daddy left I haven't been coping so I've been going to see a counsellor. I didn't tell you because I didn't want you to worry.'

Minnie said tentatively, 'Uh huh?'

Sarah smiled. 'It's been very helpful – it's helped me to understand what I'm like. I've found out that I wasn't really coping even when your daddy was here.'

Minnie frowned, 'But you always cope.'

Sarah nodded. 'That's sort of true but the way I've been coping has been a, sort of, act. I've ended up being lots of different people – a mum, a wife, a daughter – but none of them is exactly me. Have you any idea what I'm talking about?'

Minnie nodded slowly, 'You mean like me being different with my friends and different at home?'

Sarah blinked, 'Are you?'

Minnie looked at her as if she was mad.

Sarah coughed, 'Yes; just like that.'

Minnie looked thoughtful. 'And your counsellor has told you that rowing will make you more the same with everyone?'

Sarah dropped her hands into her lap. 'Do you know what, Min?'

'What?' Minnie said.

Sarah shook her head slowly, 'You are a heck of a lot cleverer than me.'

There was an almighty thump from upstairs. Either Josh had jumped off something or a light aircraft had just crashed through the roof.

Minnie said. 'Mum?'

Sarah gazed at the ceiling, amazed that it was still there. 'Mmmm?'

'This having rows thing…'

There weren't even any cracks in the plaster. 'Mmmm?'

'Are you planning to row with me?'

Sarah laughed and smiled at her daughter, 'I'm not *planning* on it, but I expect it'll happen.'

Minnie's frown deepened, 'To help you be more the same?'

Sarah smiled, 'And you.'

Minnie's frown retreated. 'Oh. I hadn't thought of that. I'll have to think about that.'

Sarah nodded. 'There's something else for you to think about, too.'

Minnie raised her eyebrows.

Sarah said, 'When we row, it'll be because I love you.'

Minnie's eyes filled with tears and Sarah got up and went around the table to her. 'What is it? What's the matter?'

Minnie flung her arms around her neck and burst into tears.

'What is it?' Sarah asked. 'Min, what's the matter?'

Minnie choked out, 'Mum; does Daddy love me?'

Pain lanced through Sarah's chest and she felt tears on her own cheeks. Here was another choice; run from the pain or accept it.

Minnie held her tight. 'Does he, Mum? Does he?'

Sarah felt her own tears arrive. What could she say? That he did? That he didn't? That his idea of love seemed different to everybody else's? That he was a damaged child of secrets? That his step-father had murdered his real father? How could she say any of that? All she could do was to be here with her daughter. They wept together until Sarah became aware of another hand on her back. She gently pulled away from Minnie and dried her eyes.

Josh was next to her with pile of old socks clutched to his chest. He looked at his mother and sister and nodded wisely, 'Have you had a row too?'

Minnie blew her nose and shoved him. 'Twit!'

Sarah said, 'No. We were just sad together.'

He looked unconvinced.

Sarah said, 'It's a girl thing. Now, put your socks in the washing machine and then we'll get some ice cream.'

He went into the utility room and Minnie said softly, 'Thanks, Mum.'

Sarah said, 'What for?'

Minnie put her tissue away. 'For listening.'

The doorbell chimed and Josh shouted, 'I'll go!'

He rushed through the kitchen and Minnie reached for Sarah's hand. 'Does he love me, Mum? Does he?'

Sarah dropped her eyes, 'Honestly Min? I don't know; I just don't know.'

'Hello,' Margaret announced as she marched into the kitchen. 'We were just passing so we thought we'd call in for tea.'

Sarah regarded her mother and father. A moment ago she had been a mother herself, like Margaret; now she was just a little girl – if she allowed herself to be. She had another choice to make...

'We haven't interrupted anything, have we?' Margaret's tone made it impossible to disagree.

Sarah stood up and the little girl inside her trembled. She glanced at Minnie; she needed space, not grandparents, and she needed to see that it was all right for her to stand up to her own mother. She glanced at Josh; he needed to learn how to deal with difficult situations. There was no choice, really; it was obvious what must happen.

Sarah acknowledged the petrified child inside her, but swallowed hard. 'As a matter of fact, you have.'

Margaret looked as if she had been slapped. 'Pardon?'

Sarah cleared her throat and her voice became clearer. 'I'm sorry, but yes, you have interrupted something.'

Margaret stood a little straighter, 'Well!'

Sarah walked towards her, 'This isn't a good time for you to drop in.'

Margaret glanced nervously over her shoulder, 'Terry?'

Terry barked, 'Now look here–'

Sarah held his gaze. Inside, a little girl's voice cried for attention but she ignored it. 'No. *You* look here! You know that you're always welcome, but if you don't let us know when you're coming, you'll have to take us as you find us. And now is not a good time, so it's best if you go on to wherever it is you're going.'

Terry said, 'But we aren't going anywhere!'

Sarah's inner child was writhing in agony. She stepped sideways and imagined the child was next to her. She glared at her mother; how dare she make her feel like this? 'You said you were passing, so you must be going somewhere!'

Margaret glared back but there was uncertainty in her eyes, 'I don't think that's any of your business!'

Sarah was aware of her inner child standing beside her. It would be so easy to allow her back in; to become her; to back down and accept her mother's domination. Sarah gasped; that was what it was! Domination! In her imagination she held the child's hand tightly. She said, 'Neither do I. So off you go.'

Terry bristled, 'Don't you talk to your mother like that — especially when her father's dying!'

Sarah squeezed the imaginary hand in her own and screamed, 'And don't you dare talk to me like that either! You've only been to see him once and that was only for ten minutes! Don't you dare make out that this is about him!'

Her father shoved Margaret as he took a step towards her.

Sarah stood her ground and held onto the imaginary hand. She lowered her voice but allowed her knowledge of her father's past to fill her words, 'And what will you do, Dad? Put me out of the room? Go looking for me?'

He stepped back, as if she had struck him and his eyes darted around everyone present.

Sarah took another step towards them and they both backed away. She said, 'I love you both, but this isn't a good time for you to drop in. I'll phone you later.'

Margaret turned imperiously, 'Come on Terry. We won't stay where we're not wanted.'

Sarah's vision shifted and her parents looked suddenly elderly and small. She almost laughed. 'Don't be ridiculous, Mum.'

A small hand took hers and she looked down in surprise. The imaginary little girl had gone but Josh was there, and his eyes were alive. He said, 'This is a *row* grandma and it's like football practice!'

Minnie burst out laughing and Sarah joined her.

The door slammed as Sarah's parents left with as much dignity as they could muster.

'Mummy?' Josh asked.

Sarah leaned against the doorframe and breathed hard. Her heart was racing and she knew that she would have to rebuild some bridges but she felt good. Something had just changed for the better. 'What is it, darling?'

His face screwed up in concentration, 'It *was* a row, wasn't it?'

Sarah nodded.

He said, 'And was it about tea?'

She drew him to her and hugged him. 'No, not really.'

He hugged her back. 'What *was* it about?'

It was about being forty; not four. 'Lots of things.'

He pulled free from her. 'Like socks?'

Sarah laughed, 'No, not like socks. Socks was about socks; this was about all sorts of other stuff.'

He considered this. 'But was it practice?'

Sarah smiled. 'No. Not this time. That was the real thing.' And it was long overdue.

He thought about this, shrugged and said, 'What about the ice cream?'

Sarah laughed again, 'Go and get the tubs.'

He went into the utility room and the freezer door banged open.

Minnie asked, 'Are you all right, Mum?'

Sarah slid her arm around her daughter. She tried to find her inner, fearful child, but the little girl seemed to have gone. 'Do you know, I think I'm more all right than I've ever been.'

Minnie hugged her. 'I know why you did that.'

Sarah said, 'Do you?'

Minnie leaned against her. 'Yes; because you love me.'

Sarah kissed her and Josh appeared, carrying a pile of tubs.

Sarah said, 'Right, let's get some bowls and spoons and find a DVD to watch.'

They made exotic ice cream concoctions and then the children took their brimming bowls into the sitting room. While the DVD player grunted through its start-up menus, Sarah tidied the tubs back into the freezer and then joined them.

'Mummy?' Josh said, spoon in hand.

'Mmmm?' Sarah sat between them and poked at the remote control.

'Are you going to row with everybody?'

It was a good question, and a perceptive one. He evidently understood just how important it was for people to sort out their differences rather than let them sit, unattended and grow into unspoken, unresolved problems. 'I suppose so, why?'

Josh waved his spoon, 'Good. Because if we get ice cream every time you row, you should!'

CHAPTER FORTY

'Just sign here,' Neil said.

Sarah signed her wages sheet and slipped her pay into her bag. 'Thank you.'

He waved his hand, 'No; thank *you!* This place has never looked better.'

Sarah smiled; he was right; even his dining room looked better. Cleaning was a lowly job, but doing it well was an achievement and the compliment made her feel good. She tipped the good feeling towards her forest glade and almost fell against Neil's dining room table. Her inner glade wasn't there; just like it hadn't been there when she realised that Neil had no interest in her.

'Are you all right?' he asked anxiously. 'Here, sit down for a minute, I'll get you a glass of water.'

She allowed him to help her into one of the easy chairs that faced the French windows. His arm felt strong and muscular – what a pity he wasn't interested in her!

He left the room and she stared at the garden. Tentatively, she searched inside for her forest glade – it definitely wasn't there and the shock of finding it gone had knocked her sideways; literally. Where was it?

Neil returned with a glass of water and she took a sip.

He sat down in the other chair. 'Are you all right?'

She smiled and sipped some more water. 'I'm fine; it's just been a rather hectic few days.'

He frowned. 'You should have said. You didn't have to come in and clean today.'

Sarah shrugged, 'I said I would.'

He nodded and sat back in his chair. 'Are you sure you're fine?'

She finished her water. 'Absolutely. I'll get off and leave you be.'

He leaned forward, 'Actually, I was rather hoping we could have a chat. Have you got a minute?'

She put the glass down on the occasional table beside her chair. 'Of course.'

He stood up; 'Just a minute.'

She watched him leave; he walked with grace and fluidity – it was such a pity he didn't like her! She wanted to tip her feeling of abandonment into her glade but it wasn't there; it wasn't there…

He came back with a blue file and sat down.

Sarah frowned; what was this?

He looked across the file at her. 'Now, Sarah, you've been working for me for just over three months now…'

Sarah closed her eyes as her stomach sank. He was going to fire her; that was what this was about. It was a horrible feeling, but where could the horrible feeling go?

She opened her eyes and forced herself to nod.

Neil smiled, 'And you have been a conscientious, honest worker. I have no idea how many hours you've put in, but I'm pretty certain you've done more than I've paid you for.'

Sarah could feel her cheeks beginning to burn. What he said was true, but she liked him…

His smile broadened. 'You said, when we first met, that you used to do office work?'

Sarah said in confusion, 'Did I?'

He nodded and picked several sheets of paper out of the file. 'Sarah, I'd like to ask you if you'd consider working for Calvi.'

He handed her the papers and she stared at them, stupidly. 'I'm sorry?'

He gestured towards the papers. 'That's a job description, terms of service and an application form. You'd be working part-time at our office in Yelmouth. You can see from the hours that you would be able to fit the job around caring for Minnie and Josh and, during school holidays, they could join our employee child-care scheme if you're not happy to leave them at home by themselves or are not able to make use of grandparents or such like.'

Sarah became aware that her mouth was hanging open. 'But what would I do?'

Neil leaned across and turned the page in her hand. He indicated the sheet. 'It'd be general office work to start with, but I've got a new scheme in mind. I can't go into any details right now, but if it gets off the ground, I'd like people like you involved at every level.'

'People like me?' she stuttered.

He nodded. 'Conscientious, honest people who work hard, get on well with people and know how to keep confidences.'

Sarah gaped at him; is that how he saw her?

He sat back in his chair. 'What do you think? Are you interested?'

She attempted to bully her brain into action. She stared at the 'Job Description' sheet and one line swam into focus. 'It says I need IT skills?'

Neil smiled. 'You use a computer at home, don't you?'

Sarah nodded.

'What programmes do you use?'

She told him.

He smiled again. 'Well, you're more than half way there already. We have a "Re-entering the Workplace" course for people who've had a career break to raise a family. You'd go on that; you'd soon be up to speed. So, what do you think? Are you interested?'

Sarah gazed at the papers on her lap. She might as well be honest. 'I don't know. I really appreciate you asking me, but I'll need to sit down and think about it.' She would also need to work out how she felt about it; and where her feelings were…

He nodded seriously. 'Of course, but just be aware of the deadline. If you decide to go for it, fill in the application form; that's the pink sheet; and drop it through my letter box. You'll then be invited for interview and, my advice is: just be yourself and you'll ace it.'

Sarah turned to the pink sheet; the deadline was next week so she had time to think this through. Another section of the application form caught her attention. 'It says here that I need to get a reference from my last employer. I'm not sure that the firm's still trading and, even if it is, my old manager may not be working there any more.'

Neil laughed. 'You have to supply the name of your *last* employer!'

Sarah blinked; what had she missed?

Neil tapped his chest and grinned. 'That's me!'

Sarah dropped the papers onto her lap. 'Oh.'

Neil chuckled, 'I can tell you what my reference will say now, if you like?'

Sarah blew out her cheeks. 'No need.'

'Will you think about it?' he asked.

She nodded.

'And I'm not doing you a favour,' he said. 'I think you're an excellent candidate and Calvi would be the richer for having you work for us.'

She could feel her cheeks colouring again.

'The pay's good, too,' he continued. 'Much better than a cleaning job and it'd help you to be more independent.'

Horror landed in Sarah's gut. Suddenly, she knew that she wanted this job and she also knew, with equal certainty, that she could not have it – not if she wanted to keep her home. She and the children lived on Dom's generosity because he had gone beyond the divorce settlement to keep them living in the family home. Even her bank account was due to his benevolence and if he didn't approve of this job, she couldn't even apply for it!

Neil said, 'Is something the matter?'

Sarah closed her eyes, 'I'm sorry, Neil. I'm really sorry; you've been nothing but kind to think of me, but I don't think I can consider this job.'

Neil said, 'Oh; what a shame. I really hoped that you would come and work for us. May I ask why?'

Sarah considered what to say, but the disappointment sitting in her stomach made it hard to think. She held onto her tears and said quietly, 'Because I don't know how it would affect my finances; my divorce settlement…'

Neil pulled some other papers out of the file. 'That's another thing I need to talk to you about. When I called in, a couple of weeks ago, when you were wallpapering, I was going to let you know that my solicitor was making progress. In the end it didn't seem like the right occasion to discuss your finances and then other things took my attention. Anyway, my solicitor has got to the bottom of the settlement. Here you go.'

He handed her the sheaf of papers and she stared at them blankly.

Neil said, 'Sorry. The settlement's a bit of a legal block-buster. Would you like me to take you through it?'

Sarah nodded. The conversation was taking on a dreamlike quality so it was probably best to leave the talking to Neil.

He settled himself in his chair. 'Okay; let me just check; you didn't have a solicitor, is that right?'

Sarah shook her head, 'Dom sorted everything out; making it easy for me was his way of saying sorry for leaving.'

Neil pursed his lips. 'And your ex-husband went beyond the legal settlement so that you and the children could stay in your house?'

Sarah nodded. 'He didn't want us to have to sell up and split it. He didn't want to hurt the children.'

Neil's face became unreadable, 'And you mentioned that you still have a joint bank account?'

Sarah stopped nodding; there was something in his tone that made her uncertain. 'Yes, that's right. It means that the children and I have everything we need. Have you got a problem with that?'

Neil held up his hands. 'Look; I'm just the messenger. You really ought to read those papers.'

Sarah tried to concentrate on the first page but the words swam around, 'Why; what do they say?'

'It's not really for me to tell you,' he suggested.

Sarah stared at him, 'I think it damn well is!' She hefted the papers. 'Why else did you give me these when you know what's in them?'

Neil held up his hands again and smiled, 'You know, Sarah, I really, really hope that you change your mind and come and work for Calvi!'

She stared at him, unsure of what to say.

He let his hands drop. 'Okay; here's the bottom line. Once you get below the layers of obfuscation your divorce settlement is very clear. The court awarded you custody of the children and defined your ex-husband's access rights.'

Sarah said, 'I know that. They visit him once a fortnight and he phones a couple of times a week.'

Neil nodded and continued. 'The court also examined the financial settlement very carefully. They took into account the early years, when you and your ex-husband were courting, while he was still scraping a living and you were contributing to his costs.'

Sarah frowned, she had forgotten about that.

Neil said, 'They also considered your married years together, your role as main carer of the children, your ex-husband's current and projected income, his investments and the new property he acquired some months before the marriage broke up.'

Sarah said, 'What property?'

Neil answered, 'The flat he now lives in.'

Sarah protested, 'That must be wrong! Dom and Alex bought their flat *after* Dom had left, not *before!*'

Neil sighed. 'No; they didn't. Your husband bought it some months before he left and, in short, the court awarded you the family home and a substantial income from your ex-husband's earnings until your youngest child reaches the age of eighteen and begins work or until your youngest child finishes further education. At that point, your income reduces but the family home remains yours.'

Sarah's brain was back to being a blob. 'But we have a joint account!'

Neil sighed again, 'I have no idea why. Your ex-husband has no business interfering with your affairs. None at all. In fact, if you wanted to, you could probably report him to the courts and he might well have his access to the children revoked – not to mention the impact on his legal career.'

Sarah shook her head to clear it. 'Are you saying that the house is mine?'

Neil gestured towards the papers in her lap. 'It's all in there.'

She stared at the papers stupidly. 'And that he should pay me alimony every month?'

Neil nodded, 'Into your own bank account.'

Sarah ruffled the papers uselessly. 'How much?'

He said again, 'It's all in there – but let's just say that you don't need a job if you don't want one.'

Her eyes tracked across the papers, down her legs, across the carpet, up his legs, up his body and found his eyes. 'Are you telling me that the house and the money are mine anyway?'

He nodded, 'I'm also telling you that you can apply for the job at Calvi if you want to. Your ex-husband has no say in the matter and it won't affect your finances at all.'

Rage swirled up inside her and she searched desperately for her forest glade. If she couldn't find it – what was she going to do? What was she going to do? What was she going to do?

Neil said softly, 'You're bound to be angry.'

Was she?

He continued, 'And you'll need some time to get your head round all of this; that's just normal.'

Understanding burst like daylight in her brain. Anger; confusion; disappointment; fear; excitement; love; hate... they were all normal! No wonder her forest glade had gone; she didn't need it; not any more! She knew exactly how she felt and exactly what she would do – and that; made her; normal!

She gathered the papers together and stood up. 'Thank you Neil. Thank you very much.'

He stood up uncertainly, 'You're welcome.'

She waved the papers in her hand. 'You know what this means, don't you?'

He raised his eyebrows questioningly.

She let the papers drop to her side. 'It means I'll fill in the job application and let you have it by the end of today.'

'Good,' he said.

She took a step towards the dining room door, stopped and waved the papers again. 'You know what else this means, don't you?'

He raised his eyebrows again but his face became guarded.

She said, 'It means that my ex-husband is a complete bastard, doesn't it?'

She marched out of Neil's house and into her own, dumped the papers on her study desk and pulled out her phone. She pressed the *call* button and held it to her ear.

After only three beeps a voice said, 'Hello?'

Sarah said, 'Henry?'

'Oh; hello Sarah; how are you?'

'I'm fine,' she replied. 'But I was wondering if you could do me a favour?'

'You only have to ask,' he said.

CHAPTER FORTY ONE

Henry drained his beer glass and put it down on a soggy beer mat.

Sarah said, 'What?'

He grimaced and glanced around the pub.

Sarah followed his gaze from the elderly one-armed bandit to the desultory lights over the bar, probably left over from last Christmas, to the appalling, multi-coloured carpet and back to his empty beer glass.

'What?' she said again.

He glanced at her. 'I don't know that I should say…'

'Go on,' she goaded.

He sighed heavily. 'All right. If what you've told me is true, why don't you just get yourself a solicitor and send him a letter? Why go yourself?'

Sarah said, 'Because I want it sorted straight away.'

He glanced at her sideways, 'And?'

She chuckled. 'Okay, it's a fair cop!'

He made a face.

She said, 'Sorry – do people say that to you all the time?'

'You have no idea; absolutely no idea; but don't change the subject. Why not just go through a solicitor?'

Sarah made a decision, 'Because I want to see his face when I tell him.'

Henry wobbled his head, 'So tell him; but why do you want me around?'

Sarah smiled slyly; 'Because I may need you to put the fear of God in him.'

'Ah,' Henry said. 'Now that, Sarah Price, I can do!'

She grinned.

He leaned forward across the table, looked carefully around the virtually empty pub and lowered his voice, 'And do you want him beaten to a pulp?'

Sarah lifted her hands in horror as an image of Gerald Bailey lying in a pool of his own blood rose suddenly in her mind. 'Of course not! He's the father of my children!'

Henry sat back and regarded her mischievously.

She laughed with relief. 'That's not funny!'

His expression was suddenly serious again. 'I know some guys…'

Sarah blinked several times.

He sat back and chuckled. 'You should see your face!'

She joined his laughter uncertainly – he *had* been joking, hadn't he? When he wasn't with her she tended to forget just how dangerous he could be; but when they were together…

Like a blind closing, his laughter disappeared and he was scary Henry again. 'And this is how you want me to be with him? Like this?'

Sarah swallowed but nodded. 'If necessary. Hopefully, you can wait in the car while we have a civilised conversation.'

Henry asked gently, 'And if it's not civilised?'

Sarah sighed. 'Then come and rescue me. Just don't overdo it, that's all…'

Henry nodded, smiled warmly and stood up. 'Let's go.'

'It's not very convenient,' Dom said. He was leaning against the frame of the front door to his building to keep her out.

'It is for me,' Sarah asserted.

'Oh. That's all right then!'

'Really?' Sarah said in surprise.

'No,' Dom answered. 'As I said, it's not convenient. So why don't you toddle off and I'll give you a ring sometime.'

Sarah stroked her temper. She didn't want to lose it but she didn't want to ignore it, either. She imagined it as a big, black, panther and she held its leash tightly. She studied Dom's face and his beautifully tailored suit; he couldn't have changed so much could he? When had he become this arrogant, selfish narcissist?

'Is there a problem?' asked a voice behind her.

'What's it got to do with you?' Dom asked haughtily.

Sarah glanced around; it was Henry.

He flipped his wallet open and showed them both his warrant card. 'Sorry to intrude but we received a report from one of your neighbours?' He pulled out a notebook and flipped over a few pages. 'Here we are…'

He climbed the steps so that he was facing Dom. 'A few weeks ago a gentleman fitting your description was observed manhandling a lady similar in description to you madam…' He glanced at Sarah and nodded formally.

She glanced at his notebook; it was blank.

Dom said smoothly, 'Nothing to do with us, officer.'

Henry's face became very still and he lowered his voice slightly. 'I'm sure that you're right, Sir, but, in the circumstances, best take this inside…'

Dom opened his mouth but Henry pushed his face fractionally closer to Dom and continued, 'I'm sure you understand.'

Sarah wasn't exactly sure what happened next, but Dom backed inside, she followed him and Henry closed the door behind them.

Dom said sourly, 'Well; now that you're here, you may as well come up.'

She followed him up a gracious staircase to the first floor. The mahogany banisters were beautifully polished and a couple of pleasant oil paintings hung on the walls. He led her through a door into a richly appointed apartment. The living room had a high ceiling and a glorious view from the large bay window and every piece of furniture looked antique.

Alex was reclining languidly on a chaise-lounge.

Dom went to him and everything about him softened. He laid his hand on the back of the chaise-lounge and said, 'Could you give us a minute?'

Alex pouted and stayed where he was.

Dom's voice became lilting. 'Please?'

Their eyes met and Alex sighed, poured himself off the chaise-lounge, across the room and through a door.

Sarah held her tears in invisible, cupped hands. In all the years she and Dom had been together he had never once looked at her, or spoken to her, like that…

Dom's demeanour changed and the familiar hardness was back. 'So; what's this about?'

Sarah stood where she was, in the middle of the room. She pulled the bundle of papers that Neil had given her out of her bag and held them up. 'Do you know what these are?'

Dom said disinterestedly, 'No idea.'

Sarah closed her eyes. She'd thought that she would enjoy this, but she was wrong. Now that she was here, she just wanted to get it over with and get out.

She let the papers drop to her side. 'You really have *no* idea?'

Dom studied her as if she was a lab specimen. 'No. And I have no idea what you are playing at, either.'

Sarah sighed wearily. Her marriage was over; she accepted that. Now that she had seen Dom and Alex together she realised that it had never, really, begun; she accepted that too. 'I'm not playing, Dom. Not anymore.'

His voice was packed with disdain, 'Then why are you here?'

She held up the papers again. 'These are the terms of our divorce settlement, Dom.'

His eyes flicked to the papers.

She said, 'I know what they say and I know what you did.'

He leaned away from the papers as if they might jump at him and bite him.

Sarah continued dully, 'The house is mine and I should have my own bank account. You've been lying about the settlement to me, to the children, to your parents and, presumably, to everyone else.'

Dom went pale and sat down on the edge of the chaise-lounge.

Sarah battled with her feelings. She felt only deep sorrow for him, and for herself, and for the wasted years they had been together. She hoped that he would be happy with his new life.

'What do you want?' he asked softly.

Sarah put the papers back in her bag. It took a lot of effort; they felt very heavy. 'I want a copy of every bank statement from our joint account since the Decree Absolute. I'll compare what's gone out of the account against the alimony you should have paid me. If I owe you money, I'll draw up a schedule and pay you back. If you owe me money, you can send me a cheque for the full amount.'

He looked at her with loathing and the colour began to return to his face. He said sarcastically, 'Anything else?'

Sarah nodded and placed a card on a fragile spindle-table. 'That's the sort code and number of my new bank account; from now on, make sure that you pay in what the court says you should.'

'Or what?' Dom said with a half-smile.

Sarah sighed. 'Or I hand everything over to a solicitor and let them drag you into court. That's what.'

Dom's face changed and he spread his hands wide, 'We don't need to do things this way, Sarah. Don't you trust me?'

Sarah held tightly to the invisible leash that held her temper, as it bared its teeth and strained to attack. 'No, Dom, I don't; and now that I've found out about the money, are you surprised?'

He stood up, folded his arms and looked down his nose at her. 'I never thought of you as a greedy person.'

She let go of the leash and her temper leapt forward. She took two quick paces and slapped his face.

He clasped his cheek and spluttered, 'That's assault!' He took a step forward; 'I'll report you!'

Sarah stepped away from him feeling nothing but regret. For all its straining power, in the end, her temper had been just a pussy-cat slap in the face. She said wearily, 'You go ahead. Report me. I'll send a letter to your Head of Chambers explaining your version of the divorce settlement – then everything will be out in the open, won't it?'

He fell silent.

Sarah walked towards the door; it seemed a very long way. She reached for the door knob and paused.

'Something else?' he sneered.

Sarah sighed, turned and said. 'Send me the bank statements and the monthly alimony. When you've done that, there's only one thing left for you to do.'

'And what's that?' he said truculently.

'I'll tell the children about the settlement, but what about your parents? Do you want to tell them or should I?'

All of the blood drained from his face and he looked as if he was about to burst into tears. He stared at her and she realised that she had been wrong, earlier, when she had wondered why he had changed. He hadn't changed at all; he had always been an arrogant, selfish narcissist. The change was in her and now she saw him as he truly was; as he always had been.

Sarah said, 'You can tell them, then.' It would do him good.

She hesitated and then said, 'Actually, Dom, there *is* one more thing,'

He refused to meet her gaze.

'I loved you,' she said sadly. 'When we first went out together, I loved you. When we married, I loved you. When we had our problems, I loved you. Even when you left I tried to love you.'

He said nothing; he just kept staring at the floor.

Sarah closed her eyes and turned away. It was right to tell him the truth but there was no need to tell him everything. There was no need to tell him that she didn't love him any more.

Sarah shook her hair in the stiff sea breeze. She and Henry were leaning against the sea wall, watching a fishing trawler battle through the waves towards the harbour. She wished that the salty wind would blow through her; she felt dirty inside.

'Wasn't it how you imagined it would be?' Henry asked gently.

Sarah shook her head. 'He's just a lost little boy, really. I never should have asked you to come.'

Henry said lightly, 'I didn't do much and, actually, I quite enjoyed it.'

She searched his face. 'Really?'

He grimaced, 'No; not really. I do the "heavy act" when it's necessary but only a freak or a psycho would enjoy it!'

She patted the back of his hand and left hers on top of his. 'You're a good man.'

He grunted, 'I have my moments.'

She shook her hair in the wind again. The trawler seemed to be coming into the harbour sideways but it turned suddenly and slipped into the calm, sheltered water.

'Thank you for being there, anyway,' she said again.

He turned his hand over and held hers. 'Like I said; no problem.'

The dirty feeling inside her turned into sadness and then into desperate sorrow.

Henry gathered her to his chest; she had never felt more safe and she sobbed her heart out.

Sarah sat in the car with Henry outside her home.

He twisted around in his seat. 'Well; I can't say it hasn't been interesting!'

She made a face.

He grinned and said, 'In fact, I have to confess, I've had worse dates!'

Sarah sat bolt upright. 'It wasn't a date!'

His grin widened, 'I know! I'm just saying that, being with you this afternoon has been more fun than some dates I've had. That's all!'

She eyed him suspiciously. 'You must have a very tangled personal life, then.'

He raised one eyebrow. 'You have no idea; absolutely no idea!'

Sarah laughed. 'Well; thank you anyway.'

He slapped her thigh lightly. 'For the last time; stop

apologising. You asked me for help and I was happy to help. It didn't work out as you'd planned – but hey; that's life! Like they say: "life is just a series of adjustments".'

'Do they?' Sarah asked in surprise. That sounded like something Di would say.

Henry shrugged, 'Probably. When they're being boring and not going to the pub, that is.'

Sarah laughed.

Henry glanced at her, 'So what about you and me going to the pub? One evening?'

Sarah closed her eyes. There was no way she would ever be able to cope with Henry, and now he was asking her out. Minnie was right; he *did* like her but how could she tell him that he wasn't her type; that he was scary? Was there anything she could say that wouldn't hurt him?

Henry sighed heavily. 'Story of my life. Meet beautiful woman; beautiful woman not interested. Never mind; no hard feelings?'

Sarah's eyes prickled; beautiful woman! He was making fun of her! She glared at him, but there was no humour in his face. In fact, in spite of his size, he looked very vulnerable, 'Oh, Henry…'

He held up a massive hand as if stopping traffic. 'Oh God; not pity! Anything but pity! Passion I can cope with; love or hate is fine; but pity? There's nothing worse than pity – except indifference, I suppose. Yes, indifference is definitely worse than pity–'

'Shut up, Henry,' she interrupted. She pushed his hand aside, leaned across and kissed him briefly on the lips.

She pulled away but his hand slipped behind her head and stopped her from retreating any further. He leaned slowly towards her and kissed her back. It was like melting into a wonderful, warm, bottomless pool.

Her eyes flicked open. What was she doing? This was Henry; Henry Driffield; the man who exuded danger! He was astonishingly strong but she pulled away easily and searched his eyes.

He leaned back, away from her, and let his hand drop gently

onto her shoulder. 'Was that a yes?'

She stared stupidly while her heart fluttered all around her body.

'To going to the pub? Was that a yes?'

She held onto the door handle for support. 'I suppose it must have been…'

He beamed at her, 'I'll call you then.'

She opened the car door, got out, changed her mind, squatted down, peered into the car and searched his eyes again.

His smile dissolved into a frown. 'Oh God. Not changed your mind already, I hope?'

She shook her head slowly. 'I don't think so.'

He shifted uncomfortably under her scrutiny. 'What, then?'

'I'll tell you what,' she said softly.

He raised one eyebrow and said, 'What?'

'You, Henry Driffield, are a very dangerous man.'

He threw back his head, roared with laughter and then looked at her, his eyes twinkling; 'I certainly hope so! I most certainly hope so!'

CHAPTER FORTY TWO

Di made some more notes in her notebook. 'That's very interesting. Very interesting indeed.'

What was Sarah supposed to say? Oh good? Hurrah? She looked around the small attic room; it seemed to have grown even dingier since their last session.

Di tapped the end of her pen against her leg. 'And you say that the compartment you created is gone? Completely gone?'

Sarah nodded. Her forest glade was a thing of the past.

Di said, 'And you don't miss it?'

Sarah shook her head impatiently; they had already talked about this. 'No; at first I was frightened, but then I realised that I didn't need it – not now that my compartments are all running together.'

Di looked unconvinced. 'I'm not sure that's exactly what's happened.'

Sarah stopped fidgeting, 'Oh?'

Di tapped her notebook. 'As we know, in many ways, being able to compartmentalise your life has been a good thing. It's enabled you to get through some very tough situations.'

'But I understand how I feel now,' Sarah objected.

Di smiled, 'If you don't mind me saying – that's a very *Sarah* thing to say!'

Sarah frowned, 'What is?'

'That you *understand* how you feel?'

'Oh.'

Di tapped her pen thoughtfully. 'Think of it like this. You, as we know, tend to live a compartmentalised life but your problem was never the compartments per se. The problem was that, for reasons we are well aware of, you had lost touch with your emotions. Your feelings were, kind of, leaking between the compartments – which meant that you couldn't access them. Yes?'

Sarah shrugged; that sounded about right.

Di continued, 'So we created a new "feelings" compartment that you could deliberately access?'

Sarah nodded; that was her forest glade; and her *Sarah* compartment for a while.

Di said, 'The thing is: as we've said before, there aren't, really, any compartments inside you at all. It's just a way of thinking. It's not like, if we cut you open, there would be something like an ice-cube tray in your head or anywhere else. The compartment thing is just an image.'

'To help me to understand myself?' Sarah offered.

'Exactly,' Di agreed. 'I think that what's happened is this: now that you've got used to thinking about how you feel you are increasingly choosing to listen to your emotions or ignore them. Now that you're aware of what's happening, though, even when you choose to ignore your feelings, you are learning to deal with them later. Is that fair?'

'I suppose so…'

'So the new *compartment* has become unnecessary. You are including your feelings in *every* compartment so you don't need a special one any more.'

Sarah frowned, 'So you're saying I still have compartments?'

Di said, 'You tell me – but your description of your row with Josh sounds pretty compartmentalised to me. You were in control; you left your emotions on one side to explain what was happening, and then you picked them up again. You did the same kind of thing with your parents and with your ex-husband. And remember, this is not a criticism; it's just a description of how you are dealing with life.'

Sarah closed her eyes in despair, 'So I'm no better than I was before!'

Di laughed. 'That's not what I said. Some people charge through life emotions first; some, like you, don't. But let me ask you a question: how do you feel right now?'

Sarah opened her eyes. 'Honestly? Like giving up.'

Di made her fly-catching gesture and hissed, 'Yes!'

Sarah blinked.

Di smiled warmly, 'Don't you see? You know how you feel!'

'But I still have compartments!' Sarah objected.

Di almost hooted, 'So what? It works. Who cares? Counselling won't make you a different person and neither will anything else. If you understand yourself and have a great life, what more do you want?'

Sarah sat back in her chair. It was as if something important, just out of reach, was dangling a hairsbreadth beyond her comprehension.

Di sat forward, 'If you want to continue to think in terms of compartments; that's fine. It may be, that at some point in the future, you lose track of how you feel again. At that point, you should probably create another new "compartment" and use it to help you to access your emotions until it disappears just like this other one has.'

Sarah nodded; that sounded like a good idea…

Di continued, 'But remember: the *compartment* thing is just an image, that's all. Maybe you should start thinking of your compartments as different aspects of your life or as different personality facets – all of them part of the whole person who is called Sarah?'

'Which is where I went wrong with the "Sarah compartment" thing?'

Di nodded; '*Sarah* is always all of you – not just a part of you.'

Sarah said slowly, 'Okay; but that might take a bit of getting used to…'

Di sucked her pen and then said, 'Okay – let's think about the little girl, the inner child you've talked about, the persona, or facet, or aspect of you, that wanted you to back down from your parents.'

Sarah folded her hands in her lap.

Di asked, 'Which "compartment" was she in?'

Sarah frowned, 'I don't know. She just sort of appeared when my parents were being overbearing.'

Di said, 'And paralysed you with fear?'

Sarah nodded; that was as good a description as any.

Di said, 'Try thinking of that little girl as an emotional response; an aspect or a facet of your personality, shaped over the years by the way your parents treated you.'

Sarah nodded again; that made sense too.

Di said, 'And the moment you stood up to your parents, she disappeared, didn't she?'

Sarah nodded again; the important thing, just out of reach, was even closer. 'Which is why you said I should have argued with my parents when I was a teenager?'

Di nodded enthusiastically. 'As part of growing up. In the past, they called it: "Cutting the apron strings".'

It was the nearest thing to a revelation that Sarah had ever experienced. It was like a burst of light in her head and she suddenly understood why she had initiated so many arguments. She had been cutting apron strings right, left and centre! The childhood fears that tied her to her parents: snip. The desire to be good enough for Dom in the eyes of her ex-parents-in-law: snip. The fear of being alone that tied her to Dom: snip. The family secret that made honest discussion forbidden: snip. All the tiny strings that had kept her dependent: snip! And the scissors that cut through the apron strings had two blades: her acceptance of her feelings and her readiness to say what she wanted!

Di asked, 'What do you think?'

Sarah answered, 'Give me a minute...'

How had she not seen this? How had she managed to miss what was really going on in these sessions? Another revelation burst in her head – of course! Her compartmentalisation had stopped her from noticing anything that didn't fit neatly into a compartment! But Di was right; her inner compartments were only in her imagination; they weren't real and she mustn't define herself by them. She could just as easily think in terms of facets or aspects – and those, too, were only images!

Another revelation exploded in her head. Di was right; being multi-faceted, or whatever she was, was a good thing. It enabled her to cope with her knowledge of the past and yet still continue a relationship with her parents and with Roy and Sandy. It enabled her to cope with the knowledge that Dom had never loved her. It enabled her to deal with Neil's rejection of her and still apply for a job in his company. It enabled her to tell Ewan that she wasn't interested in him and face the future as a single parent.

No: having compartments, or facets, or aspects was a good thing. It meant that she made mistakes – but who didn't? When push came to shove, in that regard, she was just the same as everyone else! Different; unique; but the same; as everyone else! Normal!

Di said again, 'What do you think?'

Sarah struggled up in her chair. It was amazing that Di couldn't see the light-show going off in her head, but it was important to now put it into words. 'I *think* I think three things.'

Di held her pen poised over her notebook.

Sarah said, 'The first thing is this: these sessions. I understand, now, that these last few months haven't actually been about me learning to cope. They've been about me growing up.'

Di made a note. 'Go on.'

Sarah said, 'I thought, when I first came here, that being an adult was about coping.'

Di looked up, 'And it isn't?'

Sarah shook her head, 'No; I now think it's about knowing when you're not coping.'

'And?' Di prompted.

Sarah smiled, 'And about asking for help.'

Di smiled back.

Sarah wrestled to put her thoughts in order, 'The second thing is this: I don't, actually, believe that anyone copes; not any more.'

Di laid down her pen. 'Really?'

Sarah nodded, 'I don't think life is about coping any more; I think it's about doing your best. Sometimes that will be good enough and sometimes it won't. When it's good enough, other people will thank you for it; when it isn't, well, you just have to say sorry for letting everyone down. The important thing, though, is to recognise how important those other people are – and to offer them help when they need it and accept their help when you do.'

Di brushed at her eyes and said gently, 'And what's the third thing, Sarah?'

Sarah could feel tears trickling from her eyes. 'The third thing is: thank you.'

Di smiled, sighed and closed her eyes.

Sarah grabbed a tissue and dried her tears. 'Thank you *Counsellor* Di. Thank you for helping me; thank you for these sessions and you were right. What you said at the end of the last session was right. I don't need to come here any more – so this is goodbye, and thank you…'

Di opened her eyes and they glistened with both joy and sadness. 'I agree. We'll book a final, catch-up session in, say, three months time; but you're right; it's time for these sessions to stop.' She nodded almost to herself and closed her notebook.

CHAPTER FORTY THREE

'Mrs Price? I'm Emma Wentworth.'

Sarah stood up and shook the young woman's hand. She was in her late twenties, she had dark hair and she wore smart, business clothes. Sarah smoothed her tailored trousers and adjusted her black vee-necked sweater; she was dressed appropriately for the occasion, so that was one less thing to worry about. She silently thanked Ruth for her dress sense.

'Would you follow me?' Emma said.

Sarah fell in step beside her and was ushered into a large room where individual workstations were separated by low screens. Emma led her to a workstation by a window and indicated that she should sit down. Sarah did as she was bidden and regarded the younger woman across a tidy desk. Now that she was here, it was difficult to know how she felt. It was probably best just to be objective; that had to be preferable to being a gibbering idiot…

Emma finished perusing the notes in front of her, looked up and smiled. 'So; this will be a new chapter in your life then?'

Sarah chuckled; maybe Di had been right; maybe she should think in terms of 'chapters' rather than 'compartments' after all?

Emma raised a quizzical eyebrow.

Sarah smiled, 'Sorry – private joke. Yes, you're right; this *will* be a new chapter for me.'

Emma held her gaze; 'And you were about to say something else?'

Sarah leaned forward and said confidentially. 'Actually, I almost said: "And it will be a new chapter for Calvi too." Happily I stopped myself – bit too "rah-rah" don't you think?'

Emma put her notes to one side and laughed. 'Indeed! Now, as you probably know, this is an informal interview.'

Sarah became very still; was it? When was the formal interview, then?

Emma continued easily, 'When people take a career break, Calvi feels that it is unfair to launch them straight into a competitive interview where the other candidates are moving from one job to another.'

Sarah nodded as if she knew all about this.

Emma said, 'So what we'd like to do is to put you on a three month assessment. You'll work here, in our Yelmouth office, receive pay appropriate to your experience and get back into work.'

Sarah nodded again; and during that three months, presumably, the company would form an opinion about her. Was that sneaky, or wise?

Emma continued. 'There are a number of other people working on the same basis at the moment.'

Sarah glanced around the office.

Emma laughed, 'Not here – they're in other departments and locations. Anyway, at the end of your three month assessment you will have the opportunity to apply for one or more posts within the company. At that point your application will be considered alongside other applications from within the company and from external applicants. If your application is successful, you'll be invited to attend a formal interview at that point.'

Sarah nodded slowly. Actually, it was a good opportunity. She would be employed for three months; she would be brought up to speed with the IT skills she needed and she would then be in a good position to apply for a job with Calvi, or with another company if she chose to. She said, 'It's a good opportunity, thank you.'

Emma smiled back, 'Actually, it's a good opportunity for Calvi.'

Sarah laughed, 'So I should have said what I almost said about chapters, should I?'

Emma wrinkled her nose humorously. 'No; you were definitely right not to! Now, let me show you around.'

Sarah stood up with her. 'When will I start?'

Emma smiled. 'How about Monday?'

Sarah blinked; the idea of working again had, up to this point, been just an idea. Now, it was very real.

'Is that convenient?' Emma asked.

Sarah took a deep breath. 'Yes. Thank you.'

Emma smiled again. 'Good; we'll sign the temporary contract when you've had a look around.'

Sarah followed the younger woman and listened carefully to everything she said. It was very strange, though. It was the first time she could remember making an important decision like this without reference to anyone in her family; and now that her counselling sessions had finished, she couldn't even talk it over with Di.

Sarah smiled to herself; she had even cut the apron strings that connected her to Di! She really was growing up; a bit late, maybe, but really growing up.

Emma led her back to her tidy desk by the window. 'Is that all clear?'

Sarah nodded and then signed the contract Emma slid across the desk.

Emma held out her hand; 'Welcome to Calvi.'

Sarah clasped and shook her hand; 'Thank you.'

The doorbell rang and Sarah slid her feet into her slippers, turned the radio down, and danced her way to the front door. Life was good and even a trip down the hallway deserved a bit of a boogie.

She adjusted her hair, composed herself, and opened the door.

'We need to talk,' Dom declared. He was wearing his favourite suit and his hair was immaculate.

Sarah's insides froze, melted and drained away.

'Can I come in?' Dom demanded.

She was on the point of backing away, allowing him to step inside when she realised that she did not want that to happen. She said, 'I'll be with you in a moment,' and shut the door.

She leaned against the wall. Her heart was hammering in her chest and she felt like sliding to the floor. Could she do that — could she just leave Dom standing on the doorstep?

The doorbell rang again.

She went into the kitchen and bullied her brain into action. She did not want Dom in her house. Yes, it had been *their* house but now it was *her* house and she didn't want Dom inside it. It felt like an intrusion and what if he sat down and refused to leave?

The doorbell rang again.

Sarah considered hiding under the kitchen table. She took a step towards it and then stopped and said aloud, 'No. Wait. This is *my* house. He has no right to be here. If I want to talk to him, I'll talk to him; if I don't I won't – in spite of how him being here makes me feel!'

A wave of anger surged through her. How dare he invade her privacy like this? She grinned: that was better! If she could add some indignation to her anger she'd be ready to face him!

The doorbell rang again.

She stormed to the door, lugged it open and shouted, 'I told you I'd be with you in a minute! Stop ringing the bell!' She slammed the door and set off to find her shoes and coat.

When she was ready, she opened the door and stepped outside.

Dom gazed past her at the closed door. 'Aren't we going inside?'

Sarah answered, 'No. Let's go for a walk.'

Dom looked genuinely perplexed; 'Where?'

Sarah gesture to her left, 'Up the road.'

His perplexity deepened; 'Why?'

Because she didn't want him in her house. 'Because you always liked Twisle Drift; so let's go and look at it.'

Dom seemed to surface from some inner conundrum. 'Do you really want to walk up the road?'

Sarah allowed her feelings to connect with her mouth; 'No, I don't. But I don't want you turning up on my doorstep without warning and I certainly don't want you in my house. So if you want to talk, let's walk.' She stepped around him and began to walk down her short drive. She smiled at her new car as she passed it – the insurance company had finally sent her a cheque and the garage had given her a good deal; her new car was even the same colour as her old one! She reached the pavement and glanced back. It was up to Dom: he could stay where he was or come with her.

He caught her up. 'You're being very childish.'

Sarah began to skip and enjoy herself. 'How about now?'

'Stop it!' he hissed.

'Why?' she asked, still skipping.

'You're embarrassing yourself!'

Sarah smiled sweetly and skipped higher. 'I don't mind.'

Dom stopped walking and declared, 'Well I do!'

Sarah shrugged and said, 'Not my problem.' She stopped skipping, though; it was exhausting.

Dom looked at her. For the first time she could remember, he actually looked at her. 'You've changed…'

Sarah checked her watch. 'Is that what you wanted to talk about?'

Dom shook his head as if remembering himself. 'No.'

Sarah began to walk again. 'Coming?'

He caught her up and said, 'I'm up for Head of Chambers.'

'Well done you,' she replied. 'I'm genuinely happy for you. It'll help us too.'

Dom glanced sourly at her; 'What do you mean: it'll "help" you too?'

Sarah smiled her sweetest smile; 'Well, you'll be paid more won't you? So we'll get more alimony, won't we?'

Dom looked as if he had swallowed something nasty.

Sarah stopped walking, and waited.

Dom said nothing.

She smiled her sweet smile again: she was really getting the hang of this; 'Well; thank you coming all this way to tell me. I hope you enjoy being Head of Chambers.'

She turned back towards her house but Dom held her arm.

She stopped and stared at his hand and he removed it. In her head, Sarah punched the air.

She had taken two steps away from him when he said, 'The thing is–'

Sarah stopped and turned; Dom showed no sign of moving and the distance between them seemed appropriate.

'The thing is,' he repeated, 'is that the appointment is not just based on work achievements.'

Sarah said guardedly, 'Oh yes?'

He nodded, 'Everyone in chambers needs to be confident in the person who leads them.'

Sarah nodded in return. That made sense.

He stared at the ground; 'So they need to know that I don't have any skeletons in my closet.'

Sarah took a deep breath and allowed the air to flow slowly from her body. For all his bluster and bullying, she had the upper hand and he knew it. 'So you need me to keep quiet? About your version of the divorce settlement?'

His cheeks reddened. 'Actually, I need you to write a testimonial to say that I treated you fairly in the divorce settlement.'

Sarah felt as if someone had hit her in the back of her knees. He couldn't be serious; surely?

Dom stared at her feet, 'Will you do that? You can write it now, if you like, and I can take it away.'

Sarah blew out her cheeks. If she'd been carrying a chain saw, she'd have felled him.

'I'll even wait in my car while you do it,' Dom said magnanimously.

Sarah turned and walked quickly back home. She did not want him to see her face but she could hear his footfalls following her. She had to do something – but what?

When she reached her door, she opened it, stepped inside and turned around. She knew exactly what to do. 'I'll think about it, Dom. I'll think about it.'

He took two steps towards her; 'That's not good enough!'

Sarah stared at him and closed the door a fraction.

He stood still.

She asked, 'Have you told your parents yet?'

Dom glanced away and glared at Neil's house, 'About what?'

Sarah sighed aloud, 'About the real divorce settlement. About what actually happened and about what you did.'

He stared at the ground again.

Sarah said, 'I'll tell you what. You tell Sandy and Roy about the divorce settlement and about what you did and I'll write your testimonial for you. How's that?'

He opened his mouth but she shut the door, leaned against the wall and slid down onto the floor. She had cut another string to the past! She was free of Dom and free to pursue the rest of her life.

CHAPTER FORTY FOUR

Henry finished his pint and said, 'Fancy another?'

Sarah smiled, 'Go on, then!'

He headed for the crowded bar but, contrary to her expectations, had no problem being served. Sarah's smile broadened. He made the world seem a different place and she had discovered that he wasn't just a dangerous man, he was an interesting man. Did that make him interestingly dangerous or dangerously interesting?

She had managed to reduce her smile to normal proportions by the time he returned with the drinks. She said, 'Well done you.'

He sat down, looking baffled.

She gesticulated towards the crowd of people besieging the barman. 'On getting through the crush!'

He peered over his shoulder as if noticing the other customers for the first time. He turned his attention to his new pint of beer and then said, 'So how's the job going?'

Sarah laughed, 'I've only been there three days!'

He shrugged. 'Even so?'

She laughed again, 'I'm enjoying it very much.'

He took another pull on his pint, 'But?'

Sarah said, 'No; actually; there are no "buts" at all. I'm really enjoying it. I'm already planning to apply for a full-time job once my initial contract is finished.'

He nodded. 'Good. I'm glad it's working out.'

She nodded back. 'It is. I've even told Minnie and Josh about it.'

He frowned, 'Why wouldn't you?'

Sarah sighed. 'It's complicated. I'll tell you all about it sometime.'

Henry grinned.

Sarah said, 'What? What have I said?'

His grin broadened, 'That you'll tell me about it another time!'

Sarah frowned, 'So?'

He leaned forwards across the table and held her hand. 'So you already know that you'll see me again.'

Sarah laughed. 'I'm not sure that going out with a detective is such a good idea!'

He glanced seriously at her; 'I might be able to solve that.'

She sipped her gin and tonic. 'How do you mean?'

'I've been thinking about, maybe, doing something different?'

'To the police?'

He nodded. 'If I want a full pension I have to serve for thirty years but I'm not sure if I want to keep going for another eight years. I don't want promotion – that would mean sitting behind a desk – and the job's changed out of all recognition. I'm seriously thinking of getting out soon.'

'But what will you do?'

He put the back of his hand on his forehead and stared soulfully into the middle-distance. 'I shall become an artist.'

'Really?' Sarah blurted out.

· He roared with laughter. 'No! Of course not! I've got a couple of ideas, though.'

She took another sip of her drink, 'Oh yes?'

His eyes twinkled and he said, 'But it's complicated. I'll tell you about it another time.'

Sarah snorted with laughter but a sudden ribald chorus from a group of men at the bar briefly drowned out all other conversation.

When the noise subsided, Henry leaned forwards and his expression became unreadable. He said, obliquely, 'Have you thought any more about your family history?'

Sarah glanced quickly at him. Had he investigated further? Did he know that her dad and Roy had been instrumental in Gerald Bailey's murder? And, if he didn't, should she tell him?

Henry said, 'Have you asked any of your parents' generation about it?'

Sarah sighed with relief: he didn't know; so it was up to her. She shook her head, 'They're as tight as clams. I talked to my grandfather though.'

Henry's expression softened, 'What's the matter?'

Sarah dashed away her sudden tears. 'He died; at the weekend. He struggled on for ages, but he died…'

Her vision became blurred but she was aware of Henry moving and then she felt his presence next to her and his arm around her. She turned and wept silently into his chest while he gently stroked her hair and muttered kind words.

Sarah pulled herself together, pulled away from him and dried her eyes.

His arm slid from around her until his hand rested on the seat next to her. 'Were you very close?'

Sarah nodded. 'In some ways I was closer to him than to my dad.'

Henry made a sympathetic face; 'It must be very hard.'

Sarah nodded again; 'The funeral's on Friday and I don't know how I'm going to get through it.' How could she be there for Josh and Minnie, and grieve herself, while trying to negotiate the relationship with her parents without causing an argument?

Henry said, 'Would you like me to come?'

Sarah stared at him.

'To the funeral,' he said. 'Would you like me to come with you?'

Relief and gratitude washed through her; if Henry came, she wouldn't be on her own. 'Would you? Would you really?'

He put his hand on hers and squeezed, 'Of course. If you need some moral support I'd be glad to help.'

Sarah dabbed new tears from her eyes. 'Thank you! Thank you so much!'

Henry smiled and took a drink from his pint glass. 'Do you want to talk about what your grandfather told you? About your family history?'

Sarah shook her head slowly. The thought of revealing the secret to Henry made everything, suddenly, very clear. 'No. I've decided to leave the past in the past. It's better that way.' It was —

especially as her secret knowledge enabled her to stand up to her parents and ex-parents-in-law.

Henry nodded, 'Very wise. It's clearly, as you first thought, a cold case, but sometimes letting things that are cold stay cold is the best thing to do?' He finished his drink and said, 'Come on, drink up. It's a lovely evening, why don't we have a wander round the harbour?'

Sarah finished her drink, expecting to elbow her way through the noisy throng. Instead, Henry set off and the crowd parted; she simply tucked herself in behind him. When they were outside, he offered her his arm.

They sauntered down Yelmouth High Street. It was brightly lit from street lamps and shop windows but above, the stars were sharp in the cold night sky. Henry said, 'I'm really glad you agreed to come out with me.'

Sarah said, 'Me too.' She stopped by one of Bertram and Sons window displays. 'Will you look at that?' The window had been turned into a snow scene with various clothes and winter sports equipment on display. What had caught Sarah's attention, however, was one of the manikins. It was leaning forwards, standing on one leg with its arms held out on either side.

Henry nodded sagely and said, 'Picky-Pooty.'

Sarah stared at him. 'How do you know about Picky-Pooty?'

He shrugged; 'Some of our new constables are very young.'

Sarah dug him in the ribs; 'I don't believe *that* for a moment.'

'They are!' he protested. 'Some of them are really, really young!'

'I'm sure they are,' she chuckled. 'But I do not, for one minute, believe that police officers, even young ones, play Picky-Pooty!'

He grinned and kissed her.

Just like that: no warning; no slow approach; no drifting together; he just kissed her.

The kiss ended and Sarah felt as if her eyes were uncrossing. She also had a first, nagging doubt about Henry escorting her to Poppa Jack's funeral. How would his presence be interpreted?

Would her parents take it as a sign that she and Henry were in a serious relationship rather than just friends? And yet, on the strength of Henry's kiss, *were* they just friends?

She tried to read his thoughts from his expression, but Henry just smiled and said nothing. He continued sauntering towards the harbour and Sarah sauntered beside him, her arm linked with his.

They had reached the harbour wall before she realised that their arms were no longer linked. His arm was now around her waist and she was leaning against him. She liked the feel of him, though; so strong and confident; and she definitely liked him and he liked her. It was just that he was *so* strong; and confident; and dangerous; and unpredictable...

Should she say something? Should she give voice to her doubts? What should she do?

What would Counsellor Di say? That she should acknowledge how she felt; that's what Di would say – so how *did* she feel? Comfortable; safe; excited; nervous; uncertain – but, most of all, just happy to be with Henry. Sarah closed her eyes; that was her answer. Whether he was interestingly dangerous or dangerously interesting, right here, right now, she wanted to be with him; and if that's how she felt, then her family needed to meet him.

Sarah opened her eyes. The sheltered water of the harbour twinkled with reflected light and the moored boats bobbed slowly up and down. Beyond the harbour, a crescent moon reflected on the dark water of the sea.

'I love it here,' Henry said wistfully.

Sarah leaned on the wall. 'I bet you bring women here all the time!'

He protested, 'I don't!'

She grinned at him with mock suspicion; 'Do you mean you don't bring women here or that you don't bring them here all the time?'

Henry looked uncomfortable, 'Well I–'

Sarah allowed herself to look disconsolate and sighed theatrically, 'We poor, abandoned, creatures...'

Henry laughed and stood close to her. 'If you must know, I did bring someone here, a couple of years ago, but she wasn't interested in me.'

Sarah nodded and leaned on the wall again. He was honest too: that was another thing to like.

She could see Ewan's moored boat slowly bobbing on the swell. Should she tell Henry any more about Ewan? No; probably not; any more than she really wanted Henry to tell her about any of his past girlfriends. In fact, Henry seemed to be very discreet and that was yet another thing to like about him. She grinned; he was honest and discreet; she could *cope* with that! And at least Henry, unlike Ewan, didn't want to discuss other women with her.

'Seen any good TV lately?' she asked.

Henry shook his head. 'Just sport. I don't have much time for anything else.'

'What, not even the art programs?' Sarah teased.

Henry chuckled.

Sarah relaxed against him; that was another mark in his favour. Unlike Ewan, he didn't want to spend his evenings slobbering over Josie bloody Tasker…

This time they drifted together and kissed. It felt very exciting but very safe.

A hubbub of voices intruded on their privacy.

Henry broke away from her and she leaned gratefully against the harbour wall; she didn't, quite, trust her legs to hold her up.

A group of young men dressed in hooded tops and low-slung jeans had stopped to jeer at them.

Henry straightened up and said in a friendly tone, 'Evening lads.'

The youths jeered some more.

Henry stood in front of Sarah as the youths drew nearer. He said calmly, 'Now then, lads. You've had a drink and a bit of fun; on your way.'

The jeering took on a hard edge and the youths kept coming.

Henry said loudly; 'Last warning. On your way.'

No one stopped.

Henry took two paces forwards and grabbed the largest youth. Before Sarah could see what was happening, the boy was lying in a heap, groaning on the pavement. Henry grabbed another and he fell, panting heavily on top of his companion. The rest of them stopped in silence.

Henry stepped back and said clearly; 'There you go. You've had a drink and some fun and now you've had a fight. Pick up your mates – and go on your way!'

The remaining youths scuttled forwards, helped their friends to stand and then walked quickly away, half supporting them.

Henry turned back towards Sarah and her grateful smile crumbled; the look in his eyes made her heart quail. He said, 'Sorry about that. Shall we stay here for a while or move on somewhere else?'

Sarah swallowed hard as a searing, unfamiliar emotion demanded her attention. 'Henry, I'm frightened.'

He gathered her into his arms. 'No need to be. They were just being stupid. There's no need to be frightened of them.'

Sarah allowed his strength to surround her but she began to weep. How could she tell him that it was not the youths that frightened her – but him? He was the most interesting, exciting man she had ever met but he was dangerous too; really, really dangerous. How was she supposed to cope?

Di had talked a lot about conflict with other people, but what was she supposed to do when the conflict was within herself?

CHAPTER FORTY FIVE

A thin mist of rain settled on Sarah's face as she guided Minnie and Josh up Binderfield Church path. Old, weathered headstones reared up on either side and, over on the right, an imposing yew tree cast a long shadow. The church, ahead, was built of flint and brick and, at one end, a squat, square tower sat solidly amongst the tomb stones while, at the other, a large oak door had been opened beneath an arch to reveal an inner porch beyond which double glass doors opened into the body of the church itself.

Sarah was wearing her black, business outfit, a new black raincoat and new shoes which she regretted. She would have been just as smart and much more comfortable in her old ones. The children were both wearing dark colours and Henry's suit was the darkest of charcoal greys.

Josh, she noticed, was holding Henry's hand.

Just ahead of them, her parents were waiting under umbrellas at the bottom of the short flight of steps that led to the church door. They were standing with Nanna Gwen, who had insisted that the funeral should be 'as fuss-free as possible'. 'After all,' she had declared, 'it's not as if I don't know where he's going or that I won't ever see him again!'

Sarah glanced around the sea of mourners who stood at a respectful distance from Nanna Gwen, and then back down the church path towards the road where a Naval officer was barking commands at uniformed Ratings. Nanna Gwen had accepted what she called 'the inevitable razzmatazz', but she had insisted that the family should not be caught up in it; declaring that it didn't matter to her whether the Navy or the funeral directors carried Poppa Jack's coffin. As long as it got into, and out of, the church, she didn't mind.

Margaret looked sourly at Henry. 'And is this your boyfriend?'

Minnie looked expectantly at Sarah.

Sarah nodded; 'Yes. Mum, Dad, Nanna Gwen; this is Henry.'

Henry shook everyone's hands; 'It's very nice to meet you; I'm just sorry that it's under these circumstances.'

Margaret snorted and looked away and Terry rubbed his hand on his trouser leg.

Nanna Gwen said, 'And I'm pleased to meet you too. Bugger the circumstances!'

Josh made a sound like a sneeze and then whispered loudly to Minnie behind Henry's back, 'Min. Min. Nanna said "bugger"!'

At the church gate, the officer snapped an order, a boatswain's pipe whistled and Poppa Jack's coffin, shrouded in a white ensign, slid out of the hearse.

Henry whispered, 'Is that usual? The whistle?'

Sarah whispered back, 'I'm not sure, but he requested it.'

The ratings stepped away from the hearse and three mourners squeezed between the coffin and the church gate. Roy, Sandy and Dom began to walk up the path.

'What are *they* doing here?' hissed Margaret.

Nanna Gwen grunted, 'Paying their respects; so behave yourself.'

Margaret subsided behind Terry and Sarah risked a glance at Josh; he was trying to attract Minnie's attention.

'Good morning, Gwen,' said a new voice.

Sarah turned to find Nanna Gwen clasping the vicar's hand. He was a tall, slim, middle-aged man with curly brown hair and a beard. He was wearing a purple stole around his neck and the gentle breeze moved it to and fro across his spotlessly white robe. He looked vaguely as if he had escaped from an advertisement for monk's washing powder.

Nanna Gwen said, 'Morning, Paul. Let me introduce you to my family. This is my daughter, Margaret, and her husband, Terrence. This is my granddaughter Sarah and this is her friend, Henry. And these are my wonderful great-grandchildren, Minnie and Josh.'

The vicar greeted everyone, expressed his commiserations and suggested, 'If you just wait to one side, and then, when the cortege comes past, fall in behind them?'

There was a general murmur of agreement and everyone moved towards the side of the path. The vicar spoke a few quiet words to Nanna Gwen and then took up his position in front of the church door through which gentle organ music was audible.

There was another barked order and a different whistle from the gate and the Navy men began to slow march up the church path.

Sarah glanced at the assembled crowd and then back towards the formal cortege; it was appropriate. For Poppa Jack, it was appropriate. In recent years he had become frail and old, but before illness and the passing years had drained him, he had lived a large life. It was appropriate that his passing should be marked in a large way.

The cortege reached the church steps. The officer barked another order and the whistle responded, the notes drifting poignantly through the damp air.

The cortege mounted the steps and Sarah followed her parents and Nanna Gwen into the church. The organ music swelled and Sarah glanced towards the front of the church. The organist, from his console in the chancel, nodded to her and she surreptitiously waved back.

Henry leaned towards her and whispered, 'Who's your friend?'

She whispered back, 'He's my neighbour.'

Margaret glanced sourly over her shoulder.

The vicar began reciting sentences from scripture and, with a final soft command, Poppa Jack's coffin was respectfully lowered onto two wooden stools at the front of the church.

Sarah was directed where to sit by the funeral director and, once the Navy men had marched to the back of the church, the service began.

Sarah closed her eyes and hoped that the vicar would help her to say goodbye to a man who had been so special to her.

CHAPTER FORTY SIX

Nanna Gwen surveyed the function room of Binderfield's biggest pub. It was crowded with people Sarah didn't recognise. They were all dressed in their funeral clothes so the gathering looked sombre, but the roar of conversation was happy and relieved. It was clear that these people all thought very highly of Poppa Jack; it was equally clear that they were glad that the funeral was over and, the more they drank, the louder their conversation became. Glasses chinked and sporadic laughter erupted in random patterns around the room. In one corner, Sarah's parents had withdrawn into an inaccessible nook and, in another corner, the Prices were keeping themselves to themselves. Only Nanna Gwen made herself available to anyone who wanted to talk to her.

'It was a good service,' Nanna Gwen declared.

'It was,' Sarah agreed – and she meant it. In the quiet of Binderfield church she had been reminded of her grandfather's life and grieved for his passing, but outside, at the grave side, she had said farewell. Now that everything that needed to be said had been said, everyone could relax, eat, drink and enjoy one another's company.

Nanna Gwen continued, 'And Paul's a wonderful vicar!'

Sarah smiled and prepared to resist her grandmother's well-meaning encouragement to take the children to Binderfield Church.

'He preaches really well, too. You should come along with me, you know, on a Sunday.'

Sarah smiled again.

Nanna Gwen chuckled, 'But you probably won't.'

Sarah chuckled in return.

Nanna Gwen held her hand, 'I only want the best for you; you know that, don't you?'

Sarah kissed her grandmother's cheek; 'I know; and I love you too.'

Nanna Gwen held Sarah where she was and whispered in her ear, 'And you know that what we haven't told you is for your own good too, don't you?'

Sarah pulled away and searched her grandmother's eyes; her oblique probing about the past had clearly not been as subtle as she had imagined. Nanna Gwen was right though, so she sighed and nodded. There was no need to say anything more and there was no need for Nanna Gwen to know that she knew about Terry and Roy.

Nanna Gwen gestured with her glass of rum to indicate all the people who filled the function room; 'They seem to be having a good time; I'm glad they all came.'

Sarah said, 'Well you did ask the vicar to announce that everyone was welcome!'

Nanna Gwen said, 'And it was kind of them to turn out for the service.'

Sarah squeezed her grandmother's hand. 'He was much loved.'

Nanna Gwen's eyes filmed with tears, 'But he was a poor old soul; at the end; he was a poor old soul!'

Sarah nodded, 'He was; but that's not what these people will remember; they'll remember him when he was The Captain.'

Nanna Gwen blinked her tears away and squeezed Sarah's hand in return, 'You're right, and there's no need for them to know what he became, is there? No need to know.'

Sarah nodded. She understood perfectly what her grandmother was telling her. 'No need to know.'

Nanna Gwen waved her glass towards Minnie who was leaning against a table, talking to a spotty teenage youth; 'She's growing up, isn't she?'

Sarah laughed, 'Isn't she just!'

Nanna Gwen waved her glass in the opposite direction, 'And Josh seems to like your Henry.'

Sarah waited.

Nanna Gwen smiled, 'I like him too. Got a bit of pep about him!'

Sarah muttered, 'You don't know the half of it!'

Nanna Gwen patted her hand, 'Now you listen to me. They say that "faint heart never won fair maid" – well, that's a load of old codswallop! Faint-hearted men end up winning fair maidens all the time and, let me tell you, those fair maidens are bored rigid! They *should* say: "faint heart never won fascinating man." That'd be more realistic. You shy away from your Henry and you'll regret it! You mark my words!'

Sarah sipped her drink to avoid saying anything.

Nanna Gwen persisted, 'He makes you nervous, doesn't he? Your Henry?'

Sarah put her drink down and nodded. 'Sometimes he scares me rigid.'

'Splendid,' Nanna Gwen crowed. 'Have you asked yourself why?'

Sarah was about to answer and to tell her grandmother just how dangerous Henry could be when Nanna Gwen said, 'Where's Roy?

Sarah looked across to where Roy had been drinking steadily. Sandy was talking to a group of women, but Roy had gone. She said, 'Maybe he's gone to the bathroom?'

Nanna Gwen had swivelled around to look at the other end of the room, 'No sign of Terrence, either.'

Sarah followed her gaze; she was right.

Nanna Gwen began to stand up but shouting erupted from the corridor beyond the main doors.

Everyone, apart from Henry, froze, turned, and stared at the doors. In the sudden embarrassed, inquisitive quiet, he said something to Josh and then strode through the crowd and disappeared into the corridor.

There was some more shouting and then silence.

Sarah was on her feet. 'I'll go and see what's going on.' She weaved quickly through the crowd, which was starting to buzz with speculative conversation, and slipped out of the room.

Henry was standing outside the Gents lavatory as if crucified, except that, in one hand, he held her father's shirt front and, in the other, her ex-father-in-law's lapels. As he held the two wriggling men apart he wore an expression of resignation and, when he saw Sarah, he rolled his eyes and said, 'They're both very drunk.'

Sarah strode towards them and, adopting the tone of an infant school teacher, snapped, 'Stop it; both of you. Just stop it!'

Her father subsided into feeble excuses.

'Shut up!' she commanded. 'Now behave yourself and go back to Mum!'

Henry experimentally let go of Terry's shirt front.

Terry wobbled on his feet, attempted to tuck his shirt in, gave up, and shambled back into the function room.

'How about him?' Henry asked, indicating Roy.

Sarah made a decision, 'He needs to go home. I'll go and get Sandy.' She went back through the function-room doors; every face turned expectantly, and then turned away. The hubbub of conversation went back to its original level.

Sarah found Sandy and half-shouted, 'Roy's had a skin-full; he needs to be taken home.'

Sandy answered disdainfully, 'Well call him a taxi. Dom's disappeared and I'm not going anywhere.' She deliberately turned away and initiated a conversation with a woman in a fake-fur coat.

Sarah hesitated and then decided that this was Poppa Jack's day – so not the occasion for yet another row with her ex-mother-in-law. She turned on her heel and stalked back into the corridor.

Henry raised one eyebrow.

'Sandy says to call him a cab,' she said evenly.

Roy mumbled something and began to weep.

Henry said, 'No need. Give me his address; I'll take him home.'

Sarah said, 'Oh, no, I couldn't ask you to do that!'

Henry grinned, 'Look at him! He probably doesn't even know where he lives! Check his pockets and see if he's got his house keys. I'll take him; don't worry. You smooth over the troubled waters here and I'll be back before you know it.'

Sarah nodded and checked Roy's pockets; his keys were there.

She told Henry the address and he half-carried Roy out of the building.

Sarah returned to the function room and went back to sit with Nanna Gwen.

'Well?' the old lady demanded.

'Goodness knows,' Sarah replied. She took a large swallow of her drink. 'Roy and Dad being infantile.'

Nanna Gwen chuckled and said, 'Nothing new there, then!' She glanced sideways at Sarah, 'Did they say anything?'

Sarah shook her head, 'Just gurgled a bit; Henry had them, er, separated.'

Nanna Gwen nodded thoughtfully, 'And where are they now?'

Sarah sighed, 'Dad's over there being told off by Mum and Henry has taken Roy home.'

Nanna Gwen smiled and patted her hand, 'I told you; that Henry of yours – he's a keeper; or whatever it is you call them these days!'

Sarah grinned sourly. She was mostly pleased that Henry had come, but embarrassed that he had been forced to separate two old men who should know better. It was a relief that he had taken charge of the situation but it was also a very intimate introduction to her family and she wasn't sure that she was ready for that.

Why couldn't it just be Henry and her? Why did there have to be youths with attitude problems or her ridiculous relatives to interrupt? Why couldn't it just be the two of them?

Nanna Gwen patted her hand again, 'It's not like being a teenager, is it?'

Sarah hauled her attention back to her grandmother, 'Sorry?'

Nanna Gwen waved her glass at the spotty teenager. Minnie was now sitting on the table and using her hands to describe something. 'Look at her; she's practicing now, but in a couple of years, all she'll need to worry about is whether she likes him and he likes her.'

Nanna Gwen looked Sarah in the eye, 'But for you, it's not just about you and Henry, is it? It's about how he and the children get on too; and about whether he fits in with your family and whether you fit in with his. That's the difference.'

Sarah stared at her grandmother and asked a question she had been meaning to ask for years, 'Nanna; are you psychic?'

Nanna Gwen cackled and said, 'Not a psychic bone in my body – and even if there was, I wouldn't get mixed up in anything like that anyway! No, my dear, I just watch and listen; that's all. I just watch and listen.'

Sarah blinked, 'And when you see me with Henry, what do you see?'

Nanna Gwen smiled inscrutably. 'Have you thought about my question yet?'

Sarah frowned; which question would that be?

Nanna Gwen said, 'About why you find your Henry so scary?'

Sarah shook her head.

Nanna Gwen patted her hand; 'Well; you answer my question and I'll answer yours. How's that?'

Sarah answered seriously, 'You're on! And I'll tell you what; I could do with a breath of fresh air, so I'll think about it right now!' She got up and went back through the function-room doors and outside. The moon had just risen over the horizon and, out here, with the noise behind her, it was quiet. She could wait for Henry to return and think about her grandmother's question: why was Henry so scary?

Sarah grimaced; that wasn't, actually, her grandmother's question at all. She hadn't asked why Henry was scary; she had asked why Sarah found him scary! So: why did she find him so scary?

The gathering gloom seemed to sizzle with the light of her understanding: it wasn't about Henry at all, was it? It was about her and, now that she recognised it, the answer was obvious!

She went back inside and sat back down next to her grandmother again.

Nanna Gwen said, 'That was quick!'

Sarah ducked her head. 'I think I must have been thinking about it, unconsciously, for a while.'

Nanna Gwen leaned closer, 'So what's the answer?'

Sarah smiled, 'I find him scary because I can't cope with him.'

Nanna Gwen nodded wisely, 'And why's that?'

Sarah said softly, 'Because I'm frightened that I might fall in love with him and, if I do, it won't be about coping but about sharing and trusting when there's no guarantee that he'll love me back or be trustworthy...'

Nanna Gwen crowed with delight and patted her hand again. 'Good for you. That's as good a description of love as I've ever heard!'

Sarah nodded ruefully; and it would be utterly different to her relationship with Dom – which was a prospect which was, at the same time, both exquisitely exciting and utterly terrifying!

Nanna Gwen leant even closer, 'And, to answer your question, when I look at you and Henry, I see potential. Lots and lots of potential!'

Sarah blinked hard, 'Then what should I do, Nanna? What should I do?'

Nanna Gwen pulled her close and smoothed her hair, 'You want me to give you advice? You want me to tell you what to do?'

Sarah nodded.

Nanna Gwen smiled kindly and asked slowly, 'You really, really want me to tell you what to do?'

Sarah nodded again.

Nanna Gwen pulled her even closer. 'All right then; just this once.'

Sarah waited and her grandmother pulled her closer still until she whispered in her ear, 'Do exactly what you want.'

CHAPTER FORTY SEVEN

'Are they both in bed?' Henry asked. He had slouched down on the sofa with his legs stretched out and his feet looked as if they were half way across the floor.

Sarah flopped down on the sofa next to him and nodded. 'Whether they'll sleep is another matter.'

Henry grinned but his eyes looked solemn, 'It's been a tough day for all of you.'

Sarah nodded again; it had. The funeral seemed to be located somewhere in the past, years ago, and the gathering afterwards seemed to occupy a completely different dimension. It was hard to believe that it was all over and that she would never see Poppa Jack again. She said, 'Thank you for driving us around, and for being there, and thank you for bringing us home.'

Henry slid his arm around her shoulder; 'It was a privilege; I think Minnie and Josh did very well; they must be exhausted.'

Sarah nodded in agreement and then stiffened.

'What?' Henry asked.

Sarah considered her reply – but if she and Henry had a future she needed to risk being honest. That's what Di would say, wasn't it? She said, 'It's about Josh.'

'Oh yes?' Henry rumbled encouragingly.

Sarah sat forward and spoke to the coffee table and Henry's hand slid down her back and rested on her hip. She said, 'Ever since Dom left he's been howling before bed every night.'

'Oh? I didn't notice.'

She turned her head and smiled at him, 'Exactly. Tonight is the first time he's just got ready for bed and settled down.'

Henry smiled uncertainly; 'Well that's good, isn't it?'

Sarah nodded happily, slouched against him and snuggled into his side. His hand, she noticed, stayed on her hip. Should she tell him that all that Josh had talked about, as he was getting ready for bed, was Henry?

Tears welled up in her and she began to cry. It just felt so *right* for Henry to be with them today; it felt like being a family and, evidently, for Josh, today had been about much more than the funeral.

Henry's hand slid up to her waist and he pulled her even closer as he whispered, 'I know; you loved him very much, didn't you?'

Sarah nodded and allowed her tears free reign. If Henry wanted to think that she was weeping for Poppa Jack, that was fine, but the truth was that, today, Josh had formally answered Dom's questions but he had horsed around with Henry and, even though it wasn't exactly an appropriate occasion, he had had a wonderful time.

Henry handed her a clean handkerchief and she dried her eyes.

He stroked her hair and said hesitantly, 'This probably isn't a good time but I don't know if there'll ever *be* a good time, and there's something I think I ought to tell you.'

A cold icicle formed in Sarah's gut. What was he going to say? That he had some illness? That he'd broken the law and was about to go to prison? What?

He continued, 'When I took Roy home, he was very, very drunk.'

Sarah blew her nose and frowned; she knew that.

Henry rumbled quietly, 'And he burbled on and on.'

Sarah leaned away from him and scrutinised his face. 'What about?'

His hand dropped from her waist and he shrugged, 'All sorts of things; maudlin ramblings mostly.'

She became very still, 'But?'

Henry smiled a small, tight smile, 'He also talked about Sandy.'

Sarah waited, forcing herself to breathe normally.

Henry's forehead creased as he continued, 'Apparently, she had a career on the stage for a while; when she was young; before she married and settled down?'

Sarah nodded, 'I read something that suggested she was a dancer but when I asked her about it she just denied it.'

Henry's expression became bland, 'I'm not surprised. From what Roy said, she was what, in the sixties, they would have called an *exotic* dancer.'

Sarah stared at him; 'A *stripper?* Sandy was a *stripper?*'

Henry wobbled his head, 'It was probably pretty tame by today's standards.'

Sarah's eyes widened, 'But even so! A stripper?'

Henry ducked his head, 'Apparently so.'

Sarah breathed out, hard; 'Well; blow me down!'

Henry smiled briefly, 'There you go. If that's *your* reaction, are you surprised she's never admitted to it?'

She nodded thoughtfully.

Henry became serious again; 'And there was more.'

Sarah raised her eyebrows; what was coming next?

He cleared his throat; 'According to Roy, your dad had a thing with Sandy too; before she and Roy got together.'

So she was right – Terry and Roy *had* both fallen for Sandy and not for Margaret!

Henry continued, 'He also talked about Gerald Bailey.'

Sarah's heart began beating wildly. She asked, 'What did he say?'

Henry clasped his enormous hands together in his lap. 'I know you said that you'd decided to leave the past in the past...'

Sarah nodded.

He continued, 'But you probably ought to know...'

Sarah waited, finding it hard to breathe. Had Roy admitted to the murder? To a policeman?

Henry studied her face, 'Amongst the drunken rubbish, he said, quite clearly, that Gerald never touched Sandy; never went near her for the whole of their marriage and that was why he had to know about Dom. Does that make any sense to you?'

Sarah closed her eyes with relief: even at his drunkest, Roy had said nothing about the murder; and yet, was it a relief or a disappointment? She had no idea; she would have to sort out how she felt about that later.

She opened her eyes again; she could answer Henry's question, though. Did it make sense? Yes; it did. If Sandy's marriage to Gerald had not been consummated, then Dom could not be Gerald's son; he must be Roy's. And, if Roy knew that Gerald had never made love with Sandy, it explained why he had been so obnoxious in his opinion that Minnie and Josh could not be Dom's children.

She asked, 'Is that possible? For a couple to be married and never make love?'

Henry seemed to gauge her before he said, 'In the sixties? Definitely. I've read about it as part of a course on Family Law. It wasn't as common as in previous generations but it happened more often than you might think.'

Her cheeks and neck began to burn.

'What?' Henry asked.

She closed her eyes again; this was another opportunity for honesty and she couldn't look at him; 'I shouldn't criticise Sandy and Gerald; it's not like Dom and I broke any records in the bedroom...'

He patted her knee gently.

She opened her eyes and glared at the carpet. She felt utterly exposed. Why had she told him such an intimate detail?

She risked a glance in his direction; he was waiting quietly.

Rage erupted within her; 'And before you get any ideas about me being an ice queen – it was Dom who wasn't interested, not me!'

He leered theatrically.

Her rage evaporated and she laughed and slapped his hand.

He squeezed her knee and smiled.

'Thank you,' she said.

'What for?'

'For being you.'

Silence descended and Sarah considered what Henry had told her. She blew out her cheeks and nodded thoughtfully; this confirmed that Roy and Sandy had conceived Dom while she was still married to Gerald.

A new thought hit her with such force that she almost slid off the sofa: did that mean that the murder was more than a random beating? Had Roy murdered Gerald to make sure that his affair with Sandy was never discovered? Or maybe, even, to get Gerald out of the way so that he and Sandy could be together?

Had her dad unwittingly helped him? Had he then discovered what Roy had done? That would cause a rift in their friendship, and it would also mean a life sentence for both of them if the case were ever reinvestigated.

Should she tell Henry what she knew? Should the cold case of Gerald Bailey's murder be reopened? Could she live with herself if she said nothing?

Sarah smiled a small, tight, personal smile: she probably could. That was one of the advantages of being a compartmentalised person; if she wanted to, she could keep everything she knew, and everything she felt, locked up in a secret compartment inside and it would never affect any other aspect of her life.

Sarah considered her options.

What should she do?

Tell Henry everything or keep quiet?

If there was an investigation and a court case, whatever the outcome, the process itself would rip apart what remained of her family. Did they deserve that? As far as Terry and Roy were concerned: probably – although they had both constructed, and lived in, very particular prisons since the evening of the murder. It was hard to see what real bars could achieve that the lives they had inflicted on themselves had not already accomplished. Terry had been imprisoned by Margaret for forty years and Roy showed every sign that he believed that some malicious judgment had fallen upon him: that his own son had turned out to be more similar to the man he had killed than to his own father.

What about Sandy and Margaret? Did they deserve to be roasted by the gutter press? Probably.

What about Nanna Gwen? Did she deserve to have her last years filled with vilification? No; even though she probably knew what had happened and had chosen to remain silent; no.

What about Dom? What about her? What about Gerald Bailey's family; whoever they were and wherever they lived? Did any of them deserve unexpected and unlooked for grief? No; absolutely not.

A new thought hit her: what about Minnie and Josh? Did they deserve to have their world shredded once again, just as some semblance of normality was returning? Definitely not.

In the end it wasn't just about doing what was right; it was about what was right for her children and, in the future, for *their* children. Should Mini and Josh be forced to carry the burden of what their grandfathers had done? Was every generation obliged to know? Or should the past be left where it was?

Henry held her hand. 'Are you okay?'

Sarah sighed. 'Not really; but I've made up my mind. Do you know, Henry, I'm going to leave all of this stuff in the past. I don't suppose I'll ever know what really happened and I'm not sure that I want to any more. Thank you for telling me, but I'm just going to forget about it now.'

She imagined a new inner compartment that looked like a bank vault. She herded her parents, her ex-parents-in-law and Gerald Bailey inside, shut the door and turned the key.

Henry slid his arm around her and drew her into his embrace.

She snuggled against him.

He muttered, 'Now; tell me some more about your sex life; oof!'

Sarah removed her elbow from his stomach.

Henry chuckled and held her close.

Sarah held him tight; glad that he was unable to see her face and her wicked grin.

CHAPTER FORTY EIGHT

Sarah tipped cake-mix into a cake tin and scraped the mixing bowl with a spatula.

Minnie asked, 'So Henry *is* your boyfriend?'

Sarah cleaned some remaining cake-mix off her fingers and nodded. 'Yes, he is – now. Is that all right?'

Minnie licked the spatula thoughtfully, 'Yes. I like him.'

Josh broke off from retrieving his racing car from under the kitchen table and declared, 'So do I.'

Minnie asked, 'Will you have sex with him?'

Sarah choked and then answered, 'Would it be okay if I did?'

Minnie considered this; 'As long as you didn't make a lot of noise.'

Josh's face appeared from under the table, 'What sort of noise?'

Sarah said, 'Do we have to talk about this?'

Josh glanced hopefully at the freezer, 'We could have a row instead, if you like?'

Sarah laughed.

Josh frowned at his racing car. 'Did you and Daddy have sex?'

Minnie snorted derisively, 'Of course they did! How do you think we got here?'

'I meant after that,' Josh responded hotly. 'Cos if they did, *I* never heard them!'

Sarah pushed a stray strand of hair away from her face, 'Well, if you must know, yes, we did have sex. Married couples do.' At least Josh had not asked if she and Dom had made love; that would be a very difficult question to answer. They had certainly had sex – but had it ever, really, been love making?

Josh thought this over. 'Does that mean that you and Henry are going to get married?'

Sarah said, 'No; I don't know; it's too early to say.'

Josh's frown deepened, 'But if married people have sex why would you have sex with Henry if you're not married?'

'That,' Sarah said, 'is a very good question and one I'm going to think about.' She glanced at Minnie who was avoiding her eye.

Minnie collected the empty mixing bowl and took it over to the sink.

Sarah made up her mind that she and Minnie were going to have another mother-daughter chat very soon.

Josh picked up the cake tin and Sarah opened the oven door for him to slide it inside. She shut the door and set the timer. 'There. Let's go and see what's on TV while that's cooking.'

Josh bounced to the table, picked up his racing car and ran through to the living room.

Sarah said, 'Coming Min?'

Minnie put the washed-up mixing bowl upside down on the draining rack and dried her hands.

Sarah waited.

Minnie said, 'Mum, I do understand about boyfriends and girlfriends even if Josh doesn't.'

Sarah nodded, 'I know. But Josh is right. Sex is a big thing. Boys will try to persuade you that it isn't but it is; and I kind of actually think he's right about sex and marriage.'

Minnie glanced at her, 'So you're not going to have sex with Henry?'

Sarah smiled, 'Honestly?'

Minnie nodded.

Sarah said, 'I don't know; but if I do it'll be because I love him and he loves me.'

Minnie asked, 'And do you?'

Sarah opened her arms, 'I have no idea – but I'm going to find out.'

Minnie walked into her open arms and hugged her. 'I love you Mum.'

Sarah hugged her back, 'And I love you too. Now, let's go and watch TV shall we?'

They walked through to the living room, settled down to watch a mindless program together and Sarah enjoyed the happy feeling that hugged her from the inside out. Finally, her life was as it should be.

She had a nice home and the prospects of a good job; her children were a joy and she had a fascinating, if dangerous, man interested in her. Her future was secure, thanks to Nanna Gwen's generosity and the inheritance that would come to her, and she had finally, after forty years of failure, learned how to survive a relationship with her parents. She was starting to make friends in her own right, she had benefited from a course of counselling and she even had a working, if distant, relationship with her ex-husband and ex-parents-in-law.

She sighed contentedly. Her life was, finally, exactly as it should be!

A contestant on the TV show fell into a swimming pool and Josh hooted with laughter.

Sarah chuckled with him and Minnie joined in.

Sarah smiled and hugged her children as they sat, one on either side of her. There was no doubt about it; her life was finally on track and she had no intention of falling back into her old ways. Now that she was able to access her feelings, she was going to make sure that her decisions, from now on, would not only *be* right, but *feel* right.

Another contestant on the TV show fell into the swimming pool and she laughed along with the children.

What about her parents? She loved them as her mum and dad, but disliked them as people. So, she would love them as a daughter but probably always dislike their attitudes and would, no doubt, fall out with them again and again. Sarah smiled; that was pretty much how Di described normal life, wasn't it? In the right sense, Sarah could now *cope* with her parents!

What about Sandy and Roy? She felt no love for them but she would keep the relationship going out of love for the children. She no longer expected to agree with anything they said, though, and she would never again be bullied by them into anything she didn't want to do. Sarah grinned; that meant that she could cope with them too and, if she could learn to enjoy arguments and the kind of mischief-making Nanna Gwen recommended, it might, actually, be quite fun!

What about Dom? Now that she saw him for the arrogant bully he really was she felt almost motherly towards him. Perhaps she could help him to grow up, or, at the very least, help him to be a decent father? Was that coping or resigning herself to the inevitable? In fact, in Dom's case, were those two things actually the same?

And Henry; what about Henry? If love was the one thing no one could cope with then she would never cope with him but she was starting to think that, actually, she might quite like that...

Yet another contestant on the TV show fell into the swimming pool and Sarah laughed happily with Minnie and Josh. She loved them without question and beyond reason and, as long as they were together, the rest of life would just have to fall into place around them.

Sarah sighed contentedly. Yes; her life was, finally, exactly as it should be.

CHAPTER FORTY NINE

'I'm not going to argue with you,' Dom said imperiously. He was, once again, standing on her doorstep.

'Good,' Sarah said with an air of finality. 'Then we don't need to continue with this conversation, do we?'

'That's not what I meant,' he snapped. 'What I meant was that I don't want us to argue about everything.'

Sarah nodded, 'Fair enough.'

Dom smiled and said in an irritatingly reasonable tone, 'So we are agreed?'

Sarah shook her head, 'No.'

Dom spluttered with exasperation, 'But you just said that you didn't want to argue!'

'I don't; but I also don't agree with what you're proposing. So if you stop proposing it we don't have to argue, do we?'

Sudden rage coloured his cheeks, 'But it's a great opportunity for Josh! Why would you stand in his way?'

Sarah folded her arms, 'Because I've asked him what he wants and he doesn't want to go.'

Dom gulped some air, calmed himself, and resumed his reasonable tone; 'But he's too young to understand. We're his parents; that's why we make the decision for him.'

Sarah shook her head, 'No. Sorry Dom, but that's wrong. It's not for his *parents* to make this decision; it's for *me* to make it. I'm his mother and the court gave me the final say, and I say that he doesn't want to go and that I don't think it's the best thing for him either.'

Dom hurled a brochure at her feet, 'But it's a first-rate school! Think of the advantages we'd be giving him!'

Sarah didn't bother to even glance at the brochure. 'I know it's a good school, but it's a boarding school and Josh wants to live here, with me and Min. He hates the idea of going away and I've told him that he doesn't have to.'

Dom made an inarticulate noise in the back of his throat.

Sarah continued, 'You should also know that Minnie asked if you were thinking about her going away to a boarding school too?'

Dom frowned in surprise, 'Why would I?'

Sarah said, 'For a good education? For the advantages it would give her?'

He dismissed this idea with a wave of his hand, 'She's doing fine at the school she's at.'

Sarah regarded him levelly, 'So is Josh.'

Dom said, 'But–'

Sarah interrupted him, 'And Minnie was also wondering if your idea of leaving her in the school she's already attending but sending Josh away to this expensive private school had anything to do with her being a girl and him being a boy?'

Dom hesitated and then said, 'Of course not! It's just a good opportunity, that's all!'

Sarah nodded; his hesitation had told her everything she needed to know. 'So the answer is no.' She stooped down, picked up the brochure and offered it to him. 'You may as well take this with you. We won't need it.'

Dom ignored the proffered brochure, turned on his heel and stalked away.

Sarah watched him go, shut the door, wandered through to the kitchen and dumped the brochure in the recycling box. She made herself a cup of tea and sat down at the kitchen table.

How did she feel? Tired, but fine. Arguments with Dom were always tiring but they were much less tiring than they used to be. That had to be a good thing, didn't it? And she felt fine, too, and that was important. Not so long ago Dom would have reduced her to a wibbly little heap; but not now; now she was fine.

She sipped some tea. She would probably have to argue with Dom for the rest of her life; she had already accepted that and, while it wasn't a situation to relish, it could be a lot worse. At least she was learning to follow Nanna Gwen's advice; there was a lot to be said for doing exactly what you wanted!

She sipped some more tea and sighed. She didn't want to be difficult and she didn't, particularly, want to argue with Dom, but when he came up with such idiotic ideas, she had no choice.

She sighed again. Until Dom learned to ask other people what *they* wanted before he decided what they should do, confrontation was inevitable.

She toasted an invisible companion; 'Hey ho; here's to confrontation, then.'

The doorbell rang and Sarah took a deep breath. Dom must have thought of what he imagined to be a winning argument.

She went to the front door and opened it.

'Hello,' Henry said. 'Is this a good time?'

She hugged him and pulled him down the hall and into the kitchen. They bundled together into the middle of the floor and kissed. How about if she pulled him up the stairs and bundled him into bed?

She giggled and pushed away from him. 'Tea?'

Henry grinned and sat down. 'Sorry it's been a few days – it's been stupidly busy at work.'

She fetched a mug she had found in a Yelmouth shop. It looked like a small bucket. She drained the tea pot into it and handed it to him.

He accepted it with exaggerated gratitude and, for a moment, looked quite tearful.

Sarah laughed and sat down.

'How are you doing?' he asked. 'That was quite a funeral.'

Sarah smiled, 'I thought it was just right; for Poppa Jack.'

Henry nodded, 'He was a great man.'

'He was. He had his faults but, you're right, he was a great man.'

'It was good to meet your family, too.'

Sarah made a face, 'You didn't exactly see them at their best.'

'Oh, I don't know. Your grandma was on pretty good form.'

That was true, and maybe seeing her parents, warts and all, was a good thing?

Henry took a gulp of tea. 'So; I'm off this weekend; are you busy?'

She answered, 'You know I'm not. You know Josh and Minnie are spending this weekend with Dom and Alex.'

Henry nodded; 'Just checking. Well, how about we go to Leicestershire? You can meet my parents and my brother.'

Sarah felt suddenly cold and the idea of pulling him upstairs lost its appeal. 'Well, I don't know, I was thinking of...'

'Of what?' he asked over his bucket of tea.

It was a good question and one she did not have a ready answer for.

'Come on,' he said. 'It'll be fun. I've met your lot, now you can meet mine!'

Sarah could feel her neck starting to glow.

He put down his tea with careful precision. 'Why not?'

Sarah made a decision, 'I don't want to.'

He gawped and then said again, 'Why not?'

Sarah stared resolutely at her mug. 'Because it feels too soon. If we go and meet your parents it feels like a big step and we've only just started seeing each other – so I don't want to go.'

'But I've met your lot,' he said reasonably.

She nodded, still staring at her cup. 'I know, but that was just a sort of by-product of coming with me to the funeral.'

'Oh I see,' he said with a hard edge to his reasonable tone. 'So it's okay for me to help you out but not for me to meet your family?'

'No. Yes. I don't know!'

'Well that's not fair, is it? Not fair at all!'

Sarah looked up, 'I don't care if it's fair or not. It's the way it is!'

His cheeks coloured, 'No it isn't! It's the way you're making it!'

Sarah could feel her own cheeks starting to glow. 'Don't you go blaming all this on me!'

Henry raised his voice, 'Well who *else* am I going to blame? Myself?'

'Why not?' she countered.

He shouted, 'Because I think I might be falling in love with you and I want you to meet my family, that's why!'

Sarah stared at him and he began to laugh.

She laughed with him and he reached around the table, pulled her off her chair, sat her on his knee and kissed her, hard.

Sarah surfaced for air and nestled against him.

'We don't have to go,' he murmured, stroking her hair. 'You know that, don't you?'

Sarah frowned, glad that he couldn't see her face, 'Why did you argue about it, then?'

He paused and then asked, 'Are you serious?'

She said nothing.

He sighed and said, 'Because it's what I want; but if it's not what you want, we'll do something else.'

Sarah began to cry.

Henry asked gently, 'What's wrong?'

'It's complicated...' she managed. How could she tell him how very different he was to Dom without explaining how she felt – when she wasn't, yet, sure?

'But you'll tell me another time?' he asked.

She nodded and sniffled.

Henry said very gently, 'Hey,' and kissed her again.

'I'm sorry,' she said eventually.

'Me too,' he said. 'It was a decent enough argument though – quite exciting, really, and making up was exciting in a different way.'

Sarah smiled into his chest and shifted her weight on his lap, 'I can tell.'

Henry chuckled, 'Oh, and just so you know, I don't go looking for arguments just so I can make up afterwards; I'm not weird. I just think they're healthy in a good relationship, that's all.'

Sarah nodded slowly. He was right – arguing with Dom was like trying to divert a river; but arguing with Henry felt like splashing around in the same pool, looking for some mutual solid ground.

She pulled away from his chest and looked into his face. 'Is it really all right if we don't go?'

He smiled, 'Yes. Of course. We'll do something else, but I'd like you to meet them sometime; when you're ready.'

Sarah nodded; when she knew whether she was falling in love with Henry or not. She smiled and nestled against him, grateful to hide her face. How amazing! He was falling in love with her! In fact: how amazingly wonderful! And if she *did* fall in love with him, what a future that would be! And, if she didn't, well, maybe she would meet another man and that future would be just as wonderful too!

Henry smiled and said softly; 'So – what would you like to do this weekend?'

Sarah felt an astonishing rush of the warm emotion she had felt for Henry before, but she stopped herself from saying anything just in time. It was just one of many emotions she had yet to define so it was probably unwise for her to suggest that she would like to find out whether making love really *was* different to having sex...

CHAPTER FIFTY

A gentle breeze wafted in from the sea and a gull wheeled and cried overhead. Behind the broad, paved esplanade, the steep Yelmouth cliffs, covered in sea grass and brambles, angled steeply up towards The Headland while, in front, the low tide had retreated from the pebble beach to reveal a jumble of rock pools. Josh, Minnie and Henry were hunched over and Josh was pointing at something.

Sarah leaned on the cool, damp, esplanade railing which was sticky with salt and appreciated the scents of the sea.

Nanna Gwen moved and her wheelchair creaked, 'They're having a great time!'

Sarah nodded; they were. She risked a glance at her grandmother; she was very brave to accept the wheelchair, but as she had pragmatically declared: if getting out of the house meant sitting in the infernal thing, she'd rather sit in a wheelchair outside with her family than sit in an ordinary chair alone at home!

Down by the rock pool, Josh picked up a strand of seaweed, straightened up and threw it at Minnie.

Minnie shrieked, gathered a large handful of weed, considered Josh briefly and then flung it at Henry. He was still stooped over, peering into the rock pool, and it hit him on the side of his head.

Minnie's face was a picture of excitement and horror and Josh's hand flew to his mouth.

Henry turned slowly, still stooped over. He reached slowly for the seaweed, pulled it across the top of his head, straightened up to his full height, raised his hands like claws, bared his teeth and roared.

Minnie shrieked in earnest and set off at a run across the pebble beach.

Henry pursued her, roaring, his weed-wig flapping behind him.

Josh brought up the rear, trying to hit Henry's broad back with even more weed.

Minnie was gasping with laughter when Henry caught her, snatched her up and tucked her under his arm. He stopped dead, turned, picked up a squealing Josh and tucked him under the other arm. He then pounded back towards the sea, still roaring, the children's legs kicking out behind them until he reached the water and pretended to throw them in.

Nanna Gwen chuckled; 'They love him, you know.'

Sarah made an indeterminate noise.

Nanna Gwen peered up at her; 'Children make up their minds very quickly.' She peered back down the beach.

The children were back on their feet, howling with pleasure and telling one another their own versions of what had just happened.

Nanna Gwen continued thoughtfully, 'He loves them too; you can see that.'

Sarah said nothing.

Nanna Gwen reached up and found her hand. 'He'd make a wonderful father.'

Sarah nodded; he would.

'And a good husband.'

Sarah nodded again; he would.

Nanna Gwen let go of her hand. 'And he's never been married?'

Sarah said, 'No.'

'It's hard to believe,' Nanna Gwen continued. 'And he's not a secret axe murder or anything?'

Sarah squinted quizzically at her grandmother. Was this about Henry or about Terry and Roy?

Nanna Gwen snorted derisively; 'All right; all right; I know – if he *was* a secret axe murderer, you wouldn't know because it would be a *secret!*'

Sarah chuckled appreciatively. Her grandmother might be in a wheelchair but her faculties were still, as she would say, shipshape and Bristol fashion.

Nanna Gwen peered down the beach; 'It's hard to understand why he wasn't snapped up years ago.'

Sarah shifted her weight and said, 'It's the job; being a policeman. He says that all the irregular hours grind relationships to dust. Lots of his colleagues' personal lives are in tatters and he says his never really got started.'

Nanna Gwen grunted.

Sarah sighed, 'I know; you and Poppa Jack made it work.'

Nanna Gwen sighed in return, 'Different days; different ways...'

Sarah felt a rush of love for her grandmother: she could have said *better days* but she chose to say *different*.

Nanna Gwen muttered, 'He won't stick around for ever, though. You'll have to make up your mind about him before long or you'll let him get away.'

Sarah smiled a tight smile; her grandmother was right – but making up her mind meant facing her feelings and she was frightened to find out how she felt. If she didn't love him it would break her heart to tell him, but if she did love him, her whole life would change; again; and that was a terrifying prospect. Right now, it was easier to just not know.

Nanna Gwen squeezed her hand. 'Dominic will always be their daddy but they'd soon get used to having a father too.'

Sarah glanced quickly at her grandmother and then thoughtfully across the beach to where Henry and the children were using each other as support as they pulled off their shoes and socks; they had evidently found a sandy patch between the rock pools and decided to go for a paddle.

Nanna Gwen's words sank into her: they could have a daddy and a father. It would be the equivalent of Sarah having another father as well as Terry; maybe someone very different; someone approachable; someone she could talk to; someone who accepted her as she was; someone with less baggage.

Could she imagine that? Yes – and not only could she imagine it, now that she thought about it, she felt a pang of loss that no such man existed in her life. If he did, the last twenty years would have been much more straightforward!

Sarah nodded; yes; she could see what a good thing a step-father could be for the children. As long as it was the right step-father...

She shook her head to clear it; she was rationalising. She mustn't marry Henry, or anyone else, just for the sake of the children. She had trodden one road of logic into her first marriage; she certainly didn't want to tread a different road of logic into a second marriage!

No; she could reason out the process, but not the decision, and the decision was simple to say but difficult to fathom because it hinged on the answer to one, loaded, question: did she love Henry?

Sarah smiled wryly; actually, there was a question even before the "did she love him" question. It was: did she want to know? However much he loved the children and however much they loved him, it didn't help her to ask, or answer, the question herself.

Nanna Gwen pulled her hand back below the tartan blanket that covered her legs. 'Can I ask you something?'

Sarah turned, leaned against the esplanade railings and smiled. 'Of course you can.'

Nanna Gwen studied the pebbles, four feet below them on the beach, as if counting them. 'It sometimes helps to talk about your feelings with someone else.'

Sarah nodded.

Nanna Gwen continued, 'Someone who will listen and not interrupt.'

Sarah nodded again.

Nanna Gwen shifted slightly in her wheelchair. 'What they say isn't really relevant – in fact it's often important that they say nothing at all. The important thing is to talk about how you feel out loud. That way, you get to hear what you think and that seems to help you sort out how you feel.'

Sarah smiled, 'I think you and I are very much alike, Nanna. I know just what you mean.'

Nanna Gwen looked up and smiled back, 'You do?'

Sarah nodded.

Nanna Gwen leaned forward a little and her wheelchair creaked. 'And do you have someone you can talk to? Someone you can tell anything to? Someone who will listen without interrupting and give you the space to sort out just how you feel?'

Sarah crouched down and hugged her grandmother. 'Yes I do, Nanna; especially since the funeral.'

Nanna Gwen hugged her and rubbed her back. 'And will you talk to them soon?'

Sarah kissed her cheek; 'I will; in this next day or two. It's a few days since I talked things over with them and you're right; I need to sort out how I feel about Henry.'

'Promise?'

'Promise.'

Shrieks and hoots drifted up the beach from the sea. Evidently the water was colder than it looked and Minnie and Josh were hopping around clutching their feet while Henry tried to find somewhere to stand that was both dry and reasonably flat. The three of them, socks tucked into shoes, hobbled back through the rock pools and up the pebble beach.

They reached the esplanade in a chorus of anecdotes and Henry lifted the children, in turn, up and through the railing before climbing through himself. Their faces were red and their feet were blue.

Nanna Gwen offered her lap to the children so that they could sit and wrestle their socks and shoes back onto their still damp feet and Henry half sat and half leaned on the esplanade railing as he sorted out his own footwear.

Josh shuffled around in a circle, forcing his feet into his shoes. He declared brightly, 'Henry says we can have a parrot's teeth!'

Minnie rolled her eyes, 'He said: *an aperitif!*'

'Or an ice cream?' Henry suggested.

'In this weather?' Sarah asked.

The children expressed their derision at her faintheartedness and Nanna Gwen said, 'Good idea; my treat.'

Josh and Minnie set off at a run back along the esplanade towards a confectionary stand and Henry grasped the handles of Nanna Gwen's wheelchair and began to push.

Sarah walked beside her Grandmother.

Nanna Gwen took her hand and said, 'You won't forget? What we talked about. You won't forget?'

Sarah smiled and shook her head.

Henry raised a quizzical eyebrow.

Sarah smiled at him; the warm feeling that seemed to arrive when he was around was back. Sometime soon she must figure out what it was.

She said to her grandmother, 'I won't forget.'

'Promise?'

'Promise.'

CHAPTER FIFTY ONE

Sarah raised her face and enjoyed the faint warmth of the low sun. Around her, the autumn trees were displaying their golden colours and the churchyard felt very peaceful. At her feet, the turfed mound of earth over Poppa Jack's grave was beginning to settle and the fresh flowers she had brought with her shouted a burst of colour amongst the subtle, muted gravestones.

Nanna Gwen was right; the important thing was talking; not whether the person you talked to talked back!

'So you see, Poppa, I'm very happy,' she murmured. 'My job is great and I've applied for a permanent post; the interviews are next week. Emma Wentworth thinks that I stand a good chance and she's given me some interview coaching. I just have to remember to show my feelings a bit more. Apparently, these days, candidates are expected to be enthusiastic and show it. I've been practising on Josh and Min but they think I'm nuts. As Min said yesterday: "How can you be so up-beat about a tin of beans?" I explained that if I can be enthusiastic about a tin of beans I can be enthusiastic about me and that it's all about selling myself. She didn't find that argument very convincing and later on I caught Josh trying to sell her the bathroom sponge for five pounds. I'm not sure that he really understands, either.'

Sarah chuckled. 'And then there's Henry. I'm sad that you never met him, Poppa. I like him very much and he seems to like me too. Oh, and he's handed in his resignation. He and an ex-copper friend of his are setting up their own company; offering leadership training to business executives. It sounds awful, but their website is already up and running and they have bookings for the next three months, so what do I know?'

Sarah smiled. She enjoyed her talks with Poppa Jack; he was the one person she could talk to who never interrupted or contradicted her. She liked to make sure that his grave was tidy too, and had fresh flowers.

Sarah cried softly. She hoped that Poppa Jack had known how much she had loved him.

'Look at me,' she muttered, drying her eyes. 'Now, where had I got to? Oh yes. I'm also discovering that Nanna Gwen's advice, about doing what I want, is a lot more complicated that I thought it was. Doing what I want often ends up with me doing the opposite! I want the very best for Minnie and Josh, so, most of the time, I end up doing things I wouldn't choose to do, just to make sure that everything is all right for them! Like arguing with Dom. I don't want to do it but, because I want the best for the kids, that's what I end up doing.

'In a different way, it's the same with Henry. I want the best for him so I do stuff to make him happy even when I don't really want to do it. I did that for Dom, of course, but with Henry it's different because he does things for *me* too, even though he doesn't want to do them, so I end up with what I want, not because I've done it, but because he's done it for me!

'That's what you and Nanna Gwen did, isn't it? She's a really wise lady, isn't she? I wonder what she would say if she knew that *you* were the person I was talking to?'

Sarah sighed; she was no further forward in understanding her feelings for Henry and she was starting to ramble. It was probably time for her to go home. It was a lovely afternoon, though, and the low sun would soon be dipping below the distant hills of Liggway Heath. She loved to see the sun set over the churchyard and so she moved back, through the headstones, to a bench under the majestic yew tree.

She sat quietly and watched the pale sun slide towards the hills. She enjoyed coming here at this time of day because there was hardly ever anyone else around and it gave her time and space to think things over. It had been a difficult few weeks, but now that she had given up her pursuit of the past, she understood that Counsellor Di had been right. Whatever the sins of her parents;

they were in the past. Now that she had accepted that, it freed her to experience the present, and she recognised that her life was on track and she was very content.

Low voices to her left interrupted her reverie and she glanced in that direction.

Between the headstones she caught a glimpse of a couple walking down the church path. Never mind, she would just sit quietly where she was and the other people would probably never even notice her.

The couple appeared briefly through another gap in the row of headstones and then again with the woman in profile. It was Sandy.

Sarah's brain bulged briefly. Was this some kind of waking dream brought on by her contemplations?

The woman appeared in a larger gap in the row of headstones. There was no doubt about it; it was Sandy. What on earth was she doing here?

Sarah toyed, briefly, with the idea of greeting her, but then slid silently off the bench and slipped behind the yew tree. It was a childish solution, she recognised that, but right here, right now, she didn't want to talk to Sandy and there was no reason why she should.

The sound of low voices reached her again and she peeped around the tree. She could see the back of Sandy's head and the back of the head of the man with her; they were both buttoned up in hats and coats. So; Sandy and Roy had come to visit Binderfield Churchyard. Why?

They stopped by a grave and stood, holding hands, looking down. Sandy leaned against Roy and he slipped his arm around her waist.

Sarah made a face. She had never seen them express affection so physically before; perhaps they had made a new start in their relationship or maybe it was just the peaceful effect of the churchyard?

They kissed briefly but passionately and then Roy left Sandy where she was and drifted onwards. He stopped beside Poppa Jack's grave and took off his woolly hat.

The sun dipped below the hills. Light flashed across the churchyard and then it was gone.

Sarah peered into the gloom; something was not right. That flash of light had illuminated the man just as he had removed his woolly hat, and he was not bald; he had white hair and plenty of it. Whoever he was, he wasn't Roy.

Sarah pulled back behind the tree and breathed hard. Was Sandy having an affair? Was she about to leave Roy and set up home with another man? She laughed quietly to herself – maybe Sandy the stripper had been a bad girl throughout her life? And after all her righteous indignation at Sarah's supposed immoral behaviour too!

'This I have to see!' she whispered to herself, and peeped out again from behind the tree.

At first she thought that Sandy and her mystery man had gone, but then she found their shadowy shapes; they were standing together on the path between the two graves and they were again kissing passionately in the dusk.

Sarah measured the distance and realised that she could not go any closer to them without giving herself away. Well, maybe that was what she should do? March down through the headstones and greet Sandy with a hearty, 'Hello! Who's this then?'

Sarah made a face. No, she didn't want to do that. She wasn't sure why, but something was nagging at her. She'd figure it out later, but her feelings were screaming at her, telling her that she shouldn't make a scene.

She looked to her left. That was where the church path lay and, in all likelihood, Sandy and her man-friend would walk back the way they had come. Between Sarah and the path there was a holly tree and, closer still to the path, a large rhododendron bush.

Sarah glanced back at Sandy; she was still locked in a passionate embrace.

Bending low and keeping her eyes on the elderly couple, Sarah scooted quietly sideways until she was behind the holly tree. It wasn't a perfect hiding place but, in the gloom, it would do.

She peered out again and crept on towards the safety of the rhododendron bush.

Low voices drifted towards her from further down the path and she stopped, dead. She could see nothing except headstones, though, so she ducked down low and continued until she was behind the bush.

The voices drew closer and she found a spot where she had a clear view of the path.

Suddenly, there was Sandy, not ten feet away from her, walking slowly and staring fixedly ahead and, next to her, with his arm around her, walked Terry.

Sarah's eyes bulged and she stopped breathing as she watched them retreat into the gloom and disappear up the church path towards the road. No wonder she had been reluctant to confront Sandy! Somewhere, deep inside, she must have recognised her father when he had removed his hat!

Her breath returned with a rush but the churchyard seemed to tremble and she held onto the bush for support. What had she seen? Was Sandy leaving Roy? Was her dad leaving her mum? Were the two of them, in their dotage, about to swap partners?

She drifted down the churchyard path on wobbly legs and found the grave where they had first stopped. It was the grave of George and Celia Grant, beloved father and mother and so forth.

Sarah nodded; that made sense; this must be the grave of Sandy's parents. Before she married Roy, she was Alexandra Grant. A random thought reminded her that this must be why Dom had never met his grandparents...

The lightness in her legs echoed in a lightness in her head and she drifted on towards Poppa Jack's grave. Of course! That's why her dad had paid his respects here. That all made sense; what didn't make sense was why Sandy and Terry had come together.

Something invisible hit Sarah in the stomach.

They had come together...

Come together...

What if what she had witnessed was not a reacquaintance but the continuation of a very old relationship? Roy had told Henry that Terry and Sandy had been together before she got together with Roy – what if, unknown to Roy, that relationship had continued even after Terry had married Margaret? Sandy and Terry had looked very settled together so what if their relationship was very, very long standing?

Another thought hit her and her already weak legs began to shake: what if it was Terry who had initiated the attack on Gerald and what if it was her dad who had kicked the stricken man in the head?

The enormity of what might have happened threatened to crush her and then, one more, final, possibility exploded in her brain and she sank to her knees at the foot of her grandfather's grave.

What if Dom's father was neither Gerald *or* Roy; what if his father was Terry?

The darkness rushed in from every side and, after a brief sense of falling, she flopped forward and lay still.

CHAPTER FIFTY TWO

Counsellor Di consulted her notes and said, 'It's a bit unusual; having this final catch-up session so soon.'

Sarah studied her nails. She had told Di about her grandfather's death, her job and even about her friendship with Henry; sometime soon she would have to explain why she had insisted on this meeting. She let her eyes drift around the familiar, dingy, attic room but nothing offered itself as a stepping stone into the conversation she needed to have.

Di smiled, 'It's clear that you've learned to listen to your feelings.'

Sarah nodded; she had.

Di said, 'And you're also choosing to have conversations with people instead of just working through the possible scenarios silently in your head.'

Sarah avoided her counsellor's eye.

Di smiled, 'Well; mostly! Anyway, by the sound of it, your prospects are positive.'

That was what she needed to talk about; her prospects.

Di continued, 'It's obvious that you feel differently about yourself.'

Sarah winced; that was exactly what she needed to talk about; but not in the sense that Di meant.

Di pushed the papers into a pocket file, put it on the coffee table and sat back in her chair. 'Sarah; why are you here?'

Sarah cudgelled her brain but there was still no obvious place to begin. She had answered Di's questions but tiptoed around the purpose of her visit and the pain inside threatened to consume her. She stared out of the skylight window where dark clouds were gathering; she would have to begin soon or give up.

Di raised her eyebrows.

Sarah tried to accept and ignore the pain at the same time. If she was going to do this, she would have to do it objectively.

Di's eyebrows moved slowly into a frown.

Sarah stared at the file on the coffee table. How ironic! When she had first sat in this room she had been utterly objective and struggled to find her feelings, but now she was so swamped with her feelings that it was almost impossible to be objective!

Di tapped the arm of her chair and said, 'Don't change the subject, Sarah; even in your head. Why are you here?'

Sarah blinked hard, screwed up her mouth, took a deep breath and said, 'It's hard to know where to start...'

Di smiled thinly and suggested, 'At the beginning?'

Sarah shut her eyes; maybe that would make things easier. She muttered, 'It's about Dom.'

Di said, 'I thought, now that you are telling him what you want, that your relationship with him was better?'

Sarah winced.

Di leaned forward, 'Is that why you're here? Because of your relationship with Dom?'

Sarah winced again. How could she say anything without saying everything?

Di sat back and waited.

Sarah tore her gaze away from the coffee table and managed, 'It's complicated.'

Di laughed, 'That's hardly surprising! This is *you* we're talking about!'

Sarah's cheeks and neck flared with heat and she spat, 'It's not funny!'

Di was suddenly serious. 'Sarah; what is it?'

She shut her eyes again; this was it; she had to speak; she took a ragged breath and whispered, 'It's about my parents and what happened between our families.'

Di said softly, 'Oh Sarah; I thought you realised how unhelpful that could be! I thought you'd given up delving into the past?'

Sarah glanced at her counsellor and then away. 'It's not what you think. It *is* about the past – but it's not what you think and I have to talk to someone.' Pain seared her throat like acid and she wept into her hands.

Di slid a box of tissues across the coffee table and said, 'Well; in your own time, then.'

Sarah wadded a handful of tissues against her closed eyes and began, her voice shaking: 'I know what happened. I know why there's a rift between my family and Dom's family and I know why my dad and his mum were so against our marriage.'

Di said resignedly, 'All right; I can see that this is important to you.'

Sarah moved her tongue around her mouth and swallowed hard; if only she could get rid of the acrid taste.

Di said nothing.

Sarah cleared her throat and spat into the wad of tissues. She had two choices; walk out or talk; she *had* to be objective! She took another ragged breath and began, her voice strengthening with every phrase; 'This is what happened. My dad, Terry, had a love affair with Sandy. She then met, and secretly married, Gerald Bailey, but he was gay and their marriage was completely platonic. Terry married my mum, Margaret, but he continued his affair with Sandy and, at some point, she began an affair with his best friend, Roy, too. Even though it was the "swinging sixties" I don't think either Terry or Roy knew what was going on but I think Margaret may have discovered the affair.'

She dried her eyes and the spittle on her lips with the tissues. Now that she had started, it was increasingly easy to tell the story objectively. 'At some point, Terry, or Roy, decided to go "queer-bashing", as they called it then. And, maybe by chance, they found Gerald and attacked him. Or, under the pretext of queer-bashing they deliberately sought Gerald out. Either way, they beat him up, and one of them, I don't know which one, kicked him in the head and killed him. A few months later, Roy married Sandy in a public ceremony, but she was already pregnant with Dom so they moved to London where no one would ask any questions. Roy knew that Gerald had never been a proper husband to Sandy and believed the baby to be his. A few months later, I don't know when, they came back to Yelmouth with the baby and, presumably, fudged the dates so that no one asked any questions. I know that my grandfather knew about the murder and I think my grandmother might have known too. It was a different time, though, and, for their own reasons, none of them said anything.'

Di's eyes narrowed; 'How do you know that your grandfather knew?'

Sarah laughed mirthlessly; 'He told me; before he died. He told me that Terry and Roy were bad boys; that they went looking for gay men; that they went looking for Gerald.'

Di's expression remained unreadable. 'And why do you think your grandmother knew?'

Sarah dropped her gaze; 'She told me that they didn't tell me things because they loved me.'

Di nodded thoughtfully, 'And why do you think that your mother knew about the affair?'

Sarah looked up, 'Because it explains how she kept my dad on such a short leash. He was terrified that she might find out more and then the police would find out; so he just did what she said.'

Di asked quietly, 'And how did *you* find all this out?'

Sarah sat up in her chair; 'I investigated the newspaper reports from the nineteen-sixties. Then the things that my family said fell into place.'

Di paused and then asked, 'And?'

Sarah smiled shyly, 'And now that I've learned to listen to my feelings, what my family *didn't* say was equally important!'

Di nodded thoughtfully, 'So you think that this murder caused the rift between your families?'

Sarah whispered, 'Yes.'

Di asked quietly, 'Are you sure?'

Sarah considered the question. She believed what Poppa Jack had told her and she believed the evidence of her own ears and eyes. She also believed her feelings!

Di crossed her legs; 'Is there any more?'

Sarah nodded slowly, 'It's about Dom.'

Di said, 'Go on.'

Sarah studied her hands, 'It's about Dom's father.'

Di remained impassive.

Sarah said quietly, 'I know that Gerald, Sandy's first husband, wasn't Dom's father.'

Di paused, as if replaying the recent conversation in her head, and said, 'How?'

Sarah continued, 'Because Roy got very drunk and told Henry. I don't think Roy is his father either, even though he thinks he is.'

Di frowned.

Sarah relaxed; she had nearly finished; 'I don't think that the affair between Sandy and my dad, Terry, ever finished.'

Di's frown deepened; 'Why?'

Sarah sighed; she was almost there! 'Because I saw them together, the other day, kissing. And it means that my dad is Dom's father too!'

Di stared at her, 'Because you saw them together?'

Sarah sat back in her chair with relief and nodded.

Di sat forwards, 'Have you reported any of this to the police?'

Sarah shook her head; she had said nothing to Henry.

Di sat back in her chair again; 'Well; that's a relief.'

Sarah blinked. What had she missed?

Di stared at her. 'Sarah, let's go through this one piece at a time. You say that your father and Sandy had a relationship? Presumably when they were young?'

Sarah nodded, 'That's what Roy said.'

Di continued, 'And that Sandy married this man called Gerald who was gay?'

Sarah nodded again, 'I found their marriage certificate and I know from the police records that he was gay and Roy said that their marriage was never consummated.'

Di said, 'And you know that he was murdered? Because he was gay?'

She nodded again. 'It was in the police report.'

Di blew out her cheeks, 'That's quite a story; the kind of story most families wouldn't want to talk about.'

Sarah frowned; she had expected Di to be shocked but there was something else in her counsellor's tone; something that wasn't shock.

Di said, 'And because your grandfather told you that Terry and Roy went looking for Gerald you've assumed that they killed him?'

Sarah frowned; 'No; I haven't assumed it; that's what happened!'

Di sighed, 'But how can you be sure?'

'Because it explains everything! What other explanation can there be?'

Di sighed again, 'Maybe they went looking for Gerald to talk to him? Maybe Sandy wanted a divorce and asked her old friends to reason with him? Maybe they found him after he was attacked? Maybe they were the ones who called the police? There are a huge number of possibilities!'

Sarah objected, 'But my grandmother knew! That's why she said there were things they had never told me!'

Di sighed again, 'But when she said that, were you talking about this murder?'

Sarah shook her head, 'No; but I knew what she meant!'

Di's expression became unreadable; 'You didn't; I'm sorry, but you didn't. She might have been talking about why she and your grandfather never interfered with your upbringing. She might have been talking about your grandfather – something that he did that they never told you about. She might have been talking about your father being unfaithful to your mother or your mother being unfaithful to your father. Sarah, she might have been talking about anything!'

Sarah held tightly to the arms of her chair; 'But I saw my dad and Sandy together!'

Di nodded, 'You did, but maybe that's a new thing? Maybe they've recently rekindled an old flame or maybe they were just revisiting the past. Who knows? Without asking them, how can you know?'

The room seemed to tilt as Sarah choked out, 'But it feels right! All of it! It feels right!'

Di sighed, 'Take a few deep breaths; that's right. Better?'

Sarah let go of the arms of her chair.

Di smiled wryly, 'I think I understand what's happened.'

Sarah grabbed another handful of tissues; the searing pain in her throat was back.

Di said, 'Before we go on, can I just ask: why didn't you tell me about your suspicions during our counselling sessions?'

Sarah mopped the bile from her lips, 'Because you said that I shouldn't tell you about my family history.'

Di made a face, 'In that case, I apologise. I hadn't realised that all this was going on in the background.'

Sarah said nothing.

Di continued, 'Which is, sort of, the point. None of us is psychic so we have to rely on what people tell us.'

Sarah nodded; that's what she'd been doing. That's why she now knew her family secret.

Di said, 'And we look to our feelings to confirm what we are hearing.'

Sarah nodded again; exactly.

Di smiled, 'As you know; if we ignore our feelings, we can become too objective and our thought-processes can then lead us astray.'

Sarah nodded more vigorously, 'Like when I first came here?'

Di smiled again, 'Like when you first came here. But, the thing is, if we rely on our feelings too much and ignore our thought-processes, we can become too subjective and that, too, can lead us astray.'

The room seemed to tip again and Sarah grabbed her chair for support, 'But I haven't been led astray! I've been led to the truth!'

Di dipped her head, 'And how do you know?'

Sarah spat, 'Because it feels right!'

Di sat back in her chair, tipped her head on one side and raised her eyebrows.

Sarah stared at the wad of tissues in her hand. What had she just said? That she had ignored logic and followed her feelings? But she hadn't! The facts all fitted together logically! She must be right!

Di asked, 'What, exactly, did your grandfather say to you?'

Sarah answered confidently, 'That Terry and Roy were bad boys. That they went looking for gay men. That they went looking for Gerald.' She nodded to herself; she was right about what had happened; she knew it!

Di paused and then said, 'Okay, you've interpreted that to mean that they attacked gay men and that they attacked Gerald; but what if your grandfather meant something else? Is it possible that Terry and Roy "went looking" for gay men for another reason? Is it possible that they went looking for gay men because they were exploring their sexuality? After all, a man of your grandfather's generation would probably think of that as "bad", wouldn't he? Is it possible that they went looking for Gerald because they discovered that he was a kindred spirit? You've also assumed that they went looking for him on the night when he was murdered; but isn't it more likely that they went to see him on another occasion and for another purpose?'

Sarah felt as if she had been kicked in the chest. What if Di was right? What if Terry and Roy had gone looking for gay men for the most obvious of reasons? She had been so quick to leap to the conclusion that they were the perpetrators of violence that it had never even occurred to her that they, themselves, might have been the victims of it! Was that what Marsha Hopkins had hinted at?

Another blow to her chest left her breathless. Could it be true? Could both Terry and Roy have had sexual relationships with men? It explained Roy's need to find out if Minnie and Josh were definitely Dom's children and it also explained the short leash Margaret kept Terry on!

Yet another blow exploded in her chest. What if, before they married, Terry and Roy were more than just friends? What if they had a sexual relationship with each other? Was their relationship the source of the rift between their families? And was it possible that both of them, in a more enlightened age, would have chosen very different partners to Margaret and Sandy? Did all of them understand, only too well, Dom's choices and despise him for, first of all marrying her, and then for not sticking by her?

A sick feeling arrived in Sarah's stomach. She had based her understanding of the past on facts; but what facts? Terry and Sandy's past relationship; Sandy's marriage to Gerald and Gerald's murder; Terry and Roy's shady past; random things that Roy, Poppa Jack and Nanna Gwen had said; those were the only 'facts'. Everything else was what Dom, with his barrister's wig on, would call 'hearsay' and 'circumstantial evidence'. And, when it came right down to it, Di's interpretations of the past were as likely to be as true as her own, and, in many ways, they were even more persuasive...

She could feel her cheeks and neck beginning to glow; 'I've made a fool of myself, haven't I?'

Di dipped her head sympathetically, 'Not really. You've just allowed the conversations in your head to take over and you just need to bear in mind that your feelings can be wrong; in the same way that your logic can be wrong. It would probably also be good for you to reflect on what happens when your logic and feelings join forces and lead you in completely the wrong direction.'

Sarah held up her hands resignedly, 'I was wrong, wasn't I? Completely wrong!'

Di shrugged noncommittally and said, 'As they say, the past is another country.'

Sarah closed her eyes. She was wrong; but how could she ever know? Unless she had actual, out loud conversations and someone told her, how could she know? And, even if someone told her, how could she be sure that they were telling the truth?

She made a decision. She let go of her theory – because that's what it was; a theory. She saw that now. It wasn't fact; it was just a theory.

Di cleared her throat, 'On the other hand, while most of what happened will probably remain a mystery, there's one thing you can check out if you really want to.'

Sarah hauled her attention away from her own stupidity and back to what Di was saying.

'If you really want to, you can organise a DNA test.'

Sarah experienced the now almost familiar sensation of being kicked in the chest.

'Then you'd know; for sure.'

Sarah struggled to order her thoughts, 'Of the children? A DNA test of the children?'

Di dipped her head again, 'Ideally, it would be your father and you and Dom and his mother.'

Sarah forced herself to breathe. Could she get samples for testing without their knowledge?

Di said, 'Everyone would need to give a swab from the inside of their cheek and, of course, everyone would have to give their consent.'

Sarah's eyes bulged, 'Couldn't I just send off hair samples or something?'

Di shook her head. 'No. The police can get those kind of samples tested but members of the public have to send in cheek swabs and consent forms. It's illegal for laboratories to test any other kind of sample.'

Sarah said hoarsely, 'It sounds like you know a bit about it?'

Di said, 'It happens. From time to time; it happens. But don't change the subject.'

Sarah closed her eyes. How could she even broach the subject with her dad, or with Sandy? It would be tantamount to accusing them! Come to that, how could she approach Dom?

Di said, 'What do you think?'

Sarah forced her eyes to open, 'I think it's impossible.'

Di gestured for her to continue.

Sarah began to think out loud and as she did so, the full ludicrousness of her assumptions clicked into focus; 'Because I'm probably wrong and if I asked for everyone to be tested, they'd ask why, and I'd have to tell them, and it'd destroy even the tenuous relationships we have. Dom might even use it as a way of showing that I'm an unfit mother. Now that I've got to know him all over again I wouldn't put *anything* past him.'

Di nodded slowly, 'And what if you're right? Can you live with the possibility? Even if it's very remote?'

Sarah considered the question. Logically, the answer had to be 'Yes'. But could she live with not knowing? Could she live with the low-grade uncertain feeling that still grumbled in her gut?

Di said softly, 'Can you?'

Sarah nodded, 'Yes. Yes I think I can.'

Di smiled, 'As I've often said; you are a remarkable woman. A truly remarkable woman!'

Sarah pursed her lips; 'Especially when I remember to have conversations out loud?'

Di grinned and nodded.

'*And* remember to access my feelings?'

Di laughed, 'And don't let them lead you by the nose!'

Sarah smiled. She felt idiotic but she had been right to come here and to talk everything over with Di. She had her answer and, although it wasn't the answer she had expected, everything was now back in perspective. She must make sure that, in future, her thoughts and her feelings checked and balanced real conversations.

Di said, 'So where does that leave us?'

Sarah smiled again, 'With me needing to talk to people more and guess what they mean less?'

Di chuckled, 'You're probably right. Look — why don't we think of today as an interim session rather than as the final, catch-up session? Why don't we book up a final session for a couple of month's time?'

Sarah said wryly, 'To make sure that I haven't gone off the rails again?'

Di smiled lopsidedly, 'So that we can formally conclude these counselling sessions. And, between now and then you can work on how you allow your feelings to inform your choices without allowing them to make them?'

Sarah nodded ruefully, 'Sounds like a plan.'

A familiar silence sat between them.

Di leaned forward, picked up her file, and said, 'Before we finish for today, can I ask one last question?'

Sarah smiled cautiously, 'Of course.'

Di regarded her and said, 'When you thought that your father might be Dom's father too, how did you feel?'

Sarah grinned with sudden embarrassment, 'I fainted.'

Di nodded thoughtfully, 'That's quite appropriate, really.'

Sarah frowned. 'Why?'

Di continued, 'It was the reason why you first came here, wasn't it? Fainting in that supermarket? Thinking you could cope when you couldn't?'

Sarah nodded; so it was.

Di said, 'And now you faint when you know you *can't* cope.'

Sarah's frown deepened; did that mean that she was back at square one?

Di laughed lightly, 'Which is about as normal as you can get! You may have let your emotions run away with you but don't forget how far you've come. Never forget that!'

The counsellor stood up and turned towards the door of the dingy room.

Sarah followed her and, together, they descended the stairs to the reception area. When they reached the front door Di shook Sarah's hand and said, 'It's always a privilege. You really are a truly, remarkable person.'

Sarah shook her counsellor's hand warmly, 'Thank you Di. You'll never know how much you've helped me.'

Di extricated her hand and opened the door.

Sarah stepped through onto the pavement outside and said, 'Goodbye.'

Di smiled and half lifted her hand, 'Goodbye, Sarah. See you soon.'

Sarah smiled, turned and walked away.

CHAPTER FIFTY THREE

Sarah set off deliberately early and drove to Liggway Heath. Farms and houses dropped behind her and she made her way increasingly carefully along the narrowing road as random sheep wandered across it. Before long she caught sight of Spraggle Copse, an ancient stand of trees on the highest point of the heath. She headed towards it, pulled into a rough pot-holed car park, parked her car and got out. There were two cars on the other side of the car park, no doubt belonging to walkers or dog owners.

She zipped up her walking jacket, adjusted her woolly hat and strolled across the car park and across a wide verge of rough turf before she entered the copse. As she walked, an earthy smell drifted up around her and it was wonderfully quiet in amongst the trees. She needed time to think before Henry arrived.

When she had spoken to Di she had thought that she would be able to live with the uncertainties of the past but now she was not so sure. Strange dreams had been waking her at night and, during the day, she had sometimes felt as if she was on auto-pilot. Was she fooling herself that she could contain not only the uncertainties but her emotions too?

She reached the middle of the copse and stopped. If only life could be like the inside of this ancient place; so peaceful; so quiet.

Sarah sighed and walked on. The copse was all that was left of an ancient forest that had rolled away for miles in every direction. That forest was now gone; replaced by farms, villages, towns and cities, and only the copse remained. Of course it was quiet and peaceful here – there were no people!

She emerged from the far side of the copse and the peace was immediately disturbed by a young couple who were walking down the footpath from Binderfield to Upper Fleaking. They both cried a cheerful, 'Good morning!' as they walked past.

'Morning,' Sarah replied resignedly. She crossed the footpath and made her way to a cairn of stones that marked something or other – no one knew what, exactly, although there were many theories ranging from it being a prehistoric burial site to a Victorian folly.

She reached the cairn, sat down and enjoyed the view. To her right she could just make out the spire of Upper Fleaking Church poking above the trees, to her left she could see the glint of the sun on car windscreens as they drove out of Binderfield and, straight ahead, she could see the dark sprawl of Yelmouth which, by a trick of perspective, seemed to sit below the grey-blue ribbon of the sea.

She breathed the fresh air deeply into her lungs and then sighed it out again. Yes, the only way to find true peace was to avoid other people, but who wanted that? It wasn't a solution; it was running away. The copse, the cairn, and the heath, were places of peace because they were places of retreat but when she climbed back into her car and drove home she would be surrounded by people again – and problems.

Sarah took another deep breath of the clean air. She didn't want to live her life alone. In a way, she had done that until she had collapsed in that supermarket. It seemed like an age ago now and she would never return to her former life; living amongst others but in isolated silence. No; she would never go back to living like that again; ever.

She flicked a pebble into the rough grass that surrounded the cairn. On the other hand, when she had been isolated and alone she would have been able to contain secrets and uncertainties without a second thought; but now? Could she? Could she really do what she had so confidently told Di she could do? It wasn't easy. Not now; not when she was acknowledging her feelings and connecting with other people – and risking.

Sarah shook her head; no; it wasn't easy, but could she do it?

She tried a different train of thought: *should* she do it? *Should* she just forget everything she had discovered and ask no more questions?

She had no real idea about what had happened all those years ago, except that her parents' generation had been bound by laws and social restrictions that were unthinkable today. Did Sandy and Roy love each other? Did Terry and Margaret? Did Terry and Roy? Who could say? Their lives and attitudes had been shaped by a different time and they had acted accordingly; how could she criticise them, let alone judge them, for that? If anything, they deserved her compassion.

And what of her own generation; had she and Dom done any better? When he had left her she had focussed totally on his homosexuality. Now that she was listening to her feelings, though, she found that his sexual orientation was, strangely, of little interest to her. What mattered was that she had come to know him in a new way and discovered that she didn't even like him. She was actually quite grateful to him for leaving! She *had* loved him, but now she didn't – and the thought of spending her whole life with him appalled her. He was, however, as much a victim of circumstance as she was, or their parents had been, and he didn't deserve for any questions about the past to destroy his future.

The key question, though, was about the next generation. What about Minnie and Josh? She wanted them to grow up to have happy lives – without any shadows hanging over them. If she could live with the uncertainties then as they, in their turn, became parents and grandparents those secret uncertainties would fade away and be lost. That was what she wanted for them, wasn't it?

She drank in the panorama spread out below her and noticed a hawk, hovering above a patch of gorse. It stooped and plummeted to the ground, behind a bush, beyond her view. The bird remained out of sight so, just beyond the bush, a life and death struggle might be taking place even now.

Sarah nodded to herself; she would never be certain about what was taking place behind that gorse bush. It might be that the final seconds of a terrified animal's life were ticking away. It might be that the hawk had missed its prey and sustained an injury.

It might be that the hawk had simply missed and was currently resting. There were so many possibilities and, if she had never seen the hawk stoop, she would have been oblivious of all of them.

And that's what she wanted for Minnie and Josh, wasn't it? For them to be oblivious of the possibilities...

She made up her mind. Asking questions wouldn't change anything that had happened in her parents' generation but, in her own generation, she could learn from their silence. She couldn't hold the uncertainties within a secret, hidden compartment in her heart because no such compartment existed. Compartments were only in her imagination. She could, however, live with the uncertainty and her love for Minnie and Josh would be the key. If her feelings overwhelmed her, then she would let them; it was better for her to have bad dreams and to find everyday life a struggle than for her to pass on her uncertainties to the next generation. She would keep silent because she chose to. Not because it was easy but because it was hard. She did not want her children to be tainted by that hardship and she could make sure that they were free to make the choices that made them happy.

She checked her watch and slid off the cairn. Henry would be arriving soon. She made her way back to the copse and entered the trees. The quietness enveloped her once more and a new thought struck her: whatever had happened in the past, it had empowered her! Never again would her parents or her ex-parents-in-law rule her life. Never again would Dominic overawe her. Never again would she be pushed into doing anything she did not want to do!

She would give everything she could to Josh and to Minnie so that they could have good lives, and she would keep the past where it belonged; in the past. In the present, and in the future, she would give love and she would accept love.

She laughed aloud and grinned at the silent trees. 'And you know what? That's what life is about, isn't it? It's not about *coping* at all; it's about *loving!*'

She emerged from the copse feeling as light as the air.

'Not light,' she corrected herself; 'free.'

Henry pulled into the car park. He waved from inside his car and she stopped where she was, on the rough turf between the copse and the car park, and waved back.

That was the other thing she needed to think about; she now knew how she felt about Henry; she had identified and acknowledged the warm, wonderful feeling that arrived whenever he was around. She loved him; and the novelists had been right, because it was a love utterly unlike her love for her parents or her love for her children. It was warm, and wild, and dangerous, and thrilling, and consuming!

Love, however, was only half of the story; the other half was trust. She loved Henry, she knew that now, but did she trust him? And, could she trust herself to him?

He seemed to be pulling on a jacket inside his car; either that or he was punching the roof and the windows for no reason.

Sarah smiled and love flooded through her again.

Her smile faded; but should she trust him?

It would mean abandoning her hard-won control over her own life. It would mean abandoning herself to uncertainty. It would mean trusting how she felt and how he said he felt about her.

She fought with a brief but powerful impulse to run back into the copse. It wasn't just about love was it? It was about trust...

Henry climbed out of his car and waved again.

Sarah began to walk towards the car park; she had to make a decision but could she trust her feelings? And there was that word again: trust...

Henry came towards her, dressed for walking. His jeans were tucked into his socks and his walking boots looked well used. His jacket was padded and his hat added unnecessary inches to his height. He slid his arms into his backpack, adjusted the straps and called, 'Have you brought a bag?'

Sarah reached the edge of the car park and called back, 'It's in my car. I'll just get it.'

Henry stepped sideways, into her path, and opened his arms, 'Hug first?'

Sarah paused; this was a crossroads moment. If she walked past him she might as well keep going; if she was going to hug him, and allow him to hug her, where would it lead?

His arms dropped a fraction and his smile became more of an enquiry.

Understanding burst in Sarah's head. Life wasn't about certainties any more than it was about coping. It was about loving and trusting and about constant questions and answers and frequent adjustments. It was about *out loud* conversations and, right now, Henry was asking her a question: out loud!

What was her answer? She tested the warmth of her love; at least she knew how she felt! She ran into his arms, wanting to answer him, and their jackets, as they rubbed together, almost sparked with static electricity.

Henry rumbled, 'This is nice.'

Sarah nodded; it was, and her love for him was no longer warm. Now that she acknowledged it, and accepted it, the heat of it threatened to overwhelm her. She buried her face in his chest; close to tears. She held him tight, took a deep breath and said, 'I love you, Henry!'

He pushed her gently away so that he could see her face; 'What?'

Sarah smiled happily; now that she had said it once, she could say it again; 'I love you, Henry.'

He stared at her and smiled with his eyes, 'I love you too, Sarah.'

She smiled back; she was right to tell him. This wasn't in her head; this was out loud and it wasn't about certainty or coping; it was about loving and trusting.

Henry's face became a living question mark; 'What?'

Sarah paused; it was about loving *and* trusting...

She knew how she felt but should she trust him?

Could she trust him?

When there were no guarantees?

It was a choice she must make...

Henry said again, 'What?'

Sarah smiled; it was an out loud question and he needed an out loud answer.

She tested her love for him again; she knew how she felt.

She made a decision — not because it was easy; not because it was hard; not even because it was right; but because it was what she wanted.

She said, 'You know that Minnie and Josh are with Dom this weekend?'

Henry nodded; 'What would you like to do?'

Sarah trusted her love, trusted Henry and trusted herself to the future.

She said, 'Well, I was just wondering; do you think we might go to Leicestershire? To meet your family?'

AFTERWORD

This novel is not a true story; it is, however, inspired by many true stories and it may resonate with your own.

For Further Reflection:

~ What is Sarah's biggest problem? How does she solve it?

~ Do any parts of this story ring true on a personal level?

~ If problems shared are problems halved, where do you share?

Riach.

Personal reviews help other readers discover books they may like and are very encouraging to authors. If you enjoyed this book, please leave a review on Amazon. Even if it's just a sentence or two, it would make all the difference and would be very much appreciated. Thank you.

ABOUT THE AUTHOR

'Riach Wilson' is the pen name used by David Robertson for this genre of fiction. David is the son of an internationally known musician, and, after forty-two years of hectic life as a Parish Priest in the Church of England, he now enjoys retirement with his wife, Gill, in Cambridgeshire. He also writes fiction and non-fiction under his own name and under the name of JB Duncan.

RIACH WILSON NOVELS & NOVELLAS

The Boxed-In Series

Slings and Arrows

Outrageous Fortune

To the Third Generation

Soul to Soul

Turn Around Twice

COMIC FICTION

Written by David Robertson under the pen-name of
JB Duncan

The Holy-Rude Diaries

The Curate of Cockleigh

The Vicar of Westfeil

The Bishop of Banford

The St Jude's Shuffle

Not a Leg to Stand On

An Aptitude for Avarice

FICTION & NON-FICTION
Written by David Robertson under his own name

DYSTOPIAN FICTION
Christian Oblate Zombie Hunters
(Volume 1) Kaleb's Testimony
(Volume 2) Arren's Testimony
(Volume 3) Eve's Testimony

BIBLE INSIGHT STORIES
These stories retell parables and biblical incidents in an accessible way giving twenty-first century readers fresh insight into biblical culture and meaning.

Zack's Difficult Day
Shammai Shares His Supper
Deborah's Denarius
Manny's Missing Mutton
Bertie's Quest for the Perfect Pearl

CHRISTIAN NON-FICTION

Marriage, Restoring our Vision
The Concepts of Marriage & Divorce
in the Hebrew Tradition,

Risking Romance Again
Dating after divorce

Collaborative Ministry
What it is, how it works, & why

What Would Jesus Post
A biblical approach to online interaction

PARBAR PUBLISHING

Parbar books & ebooks include:

Adult fiction

Children's fiction

Poetry & Pictures

Christian non-fiction

Made in the USA
Monee, IL
08 July 2026

56553274R00214